MIRROR LAKE

Also by Andrée A. Michaud
(in translation)

Back Roads
Boundary (The Last Summer)
The River of Dead Trees

MIRROR LAKE

ANDRÉE A. MICHAUD

TRANSLATED BY J. C. SUTCLIFFE

ARACHNIDE

First published as *Mirror Lake* in 2006 by Éditions Québec Amérique
First published in English in Canada in 2021 and the USA in 2021 by
House of Anansi Press Inc.
www.houseofanansi.com

House of Anansi Press is committed to protecting our natural environment.
This book is made of material from well-managed FSC®-certified forests,
recycled materials, and other controlled sources.

House of Anansi Press is a Global Certified Accessible™ (GCA by Benetech)
publisher. The ebook version of this book meets stringent accessibility standards
and is available to students and readers with print disabilities.

25 24 23 22 21   1 2 3 4 5

Library and Archives Canada Cataloguing in Publication

Title: Mirror Lake / Andrée A. Michaud ; translated by J.C. Sutcliffe.
Other titles: Mirror Lake. English
Names: Michaud, Andrée A., 1957– author. | Sutcliffe, J.C., translator.
Description: Translation of: Mirror Lake.
Identifiers: Canadiana (print) 20200368761 | Canadiana (ebook) 2020036877X
| ISBN 9781487005832 (softcover) | ISBN 9781487005849 (EPUB)
| ISBN 9781487005856 (Kindle)
Classification: LCC PS8576.I217 M5713 2021 | DDC C843/.54—dc23

Book design: Alysia Shewchuk

*House of Anansi Press respectfully acknowledges that the land on which we operate is
the Traditional Territory of many Nations, including the Anishinabeg, the Wendat,
and the Haudenosaunee. It is also the Treaty Lands of the Mississaugas of the Credit.*

 Canada Council
for the Arts

 Conseil des Arts
du Canada

ONTARIO ARTS COUNCIL
CONSEIL DES ARTS DE L'ONTARIO
an Ontario government agency
un organisme du gouvernement de l'Ontario

*We acknowledge the financial support of the Government of Canada through the
National Translation Program for Book Publishing, an initiative of the* Action Plan
for Official Languages —2018–2023: Investing in Our Future, *for our translation
activities.*

Printed and bound in Canada

MIX
Paper from
responsible sources
FSC® C103567

For Pierre, who entrusted me with his lake.

While men believe in the infinite,
some ponds will be thought to be bottomless.
—Henry David Thoreau,
Walden; or, Life in the Woods

M irror Lake's opaque surface conceals hollows that some people say are bottomless, though I believe I have sounded its depths. The lake's name is derived from the smoothness and serenity of its waters and the way they reflect the surrounding mountain peaks. In certain silent moments, their motionless mass makes the blackness of the water cleaving beneath the hull almost frightening, shot through with iridescence that comes not from the colours of the sky but from the deepest of chasms into which the victims of Mirror Lake have fallen, innocent people whose boat capsized one day. Nobody knows why they never reappeared, nor into what fascinating landscapes their bodies sank. But these are not the true motives that compelled men to give this lake the only name that suited it, so long ago that their testimony is lost in the rumours of unwritten history. After walking its shores on a thousand occasions, I have learned Mirror Lake is so called because gazing into its treacherous waters forces you to look yourself straight in the eyes and ask who you are and who you could have been, even as the image blurs and you conclude there is no answer to these questions.

After spending many years in the mountains' shadow, I have stopped asking myself who was that weary man whose mirror image followed me, step for step, along the beach. I would have liked, though, when the voices of the past quieted down inside me, to get to know this reflected figure that looked like me, and to discover what fate drew me to Mirror Lake, to this place where, in the wake of all those innocent boaters, I would lose myself in the lake's darkness. No question, I would have tried to carve out a path to the light through the hot sand, had Mirror Lake not led me to understand that all attempts we make to thwart fate are as futile as the distraught buzzing of the fly that has fallen into a honey jar; if experience had not shown me how fate's determinations have no equal but death's velocity.

Before settling by Mirror Lake, I believed, naively, that fate could be summarized as the squeal of tires on the wet road, or the spurts of blood an engine malfunction might cause to spatter onto dirty walls as machines roared. I had filed it under the category of time's indiscriminate acts, the sort of catastrophe that renders men silent at the village bar as news of the inexplicable drama starts to make its way from table to table. I didn't believe it could be organized or have a precise plan. In truth, I never realized that fate might take control of the way a life unfolded and determine its path — not even when the accumulation of chance events was such that I needed to find another name for this mechanism that was producing order out of chaos. And I did not suspect that the forces of destiny had been set in motion the day I arrived at Mirror Lake.

Somewhere on the other side of the lake, a set of bells gently chimed its bittersweet melody, a loon began its lament, an oar sliced through the water's clear surface with a shushing sound that evoked the indifference of slowness, and *voilà*, the dice was thrown, a domino had been positioned, the first in a series that, due to a clumsy movement, would then topple over one by one. And yet, I existed in a cloud of unknowing and thought myself free. The hallucinatory chiming had already bewitched me, as those pieces of music I think of as mad always do, the endlessly repeated monotonous motifs of their melancholy refrains causing the wounds of some incurable and distant ennui to start vibrating in me. Samuel Barber's *Adagio for Strings*, Ry Cooder's *Paris, Texas*, or Erik Satie's *Gymnopédies*; just about any one of Thomas Newman's less immortal compositions, and that Arvo Pärt piece, *Für Alina*, which just that morning had slipped into the soft pealing of the chimes, a word I prefer to *bells* first of all because of its sonority and then for the mystery it harbours, its quasi-homonymity with the word *charms*, in which the evil powers of seduction are contained.

I'd discovered *Für Alina* not long before I made the move to Mirror Lake, in a Gus Van Sant movie that was just as hallucinatory as the music. Two men are walking in a desert and doing nothing else — just walking in Alina's exhausted sorrow. For days, I too had been walking in a desert, followed by the spare piano notes of Alina and the feeling that I would never again find the way out of the sand path warming my bare feet. And then a piece of

3

music from another movie broke the spell, permitting me a measure of respite from Alina's pain.

This is the way my life has always proceeded, drifting from images to melodies, as music does nothing for me without the scenes I end up believing belong to it. So all I know about music is what I've learned from dreams and movies, watching other people's stories in an attempt to forget my own before falling asleep, back when cathode rays were a part of my daily life. I would get undressed, sit with Jeff in the living room in the light of the television, a beer or a bourbon in hand, and let myself be told any story, whether about star wars or Vietnam, Bobby Kennedy's assassination, the erotic or pornographic adventures of some girl whose life is determined by her cup size — anything for me to be able to forget that what was happening outside my window simply reflected the boringness of my existence.

The day I heard the chimes evoking Arvo Pärt for me in the discombobulating tranquility of Mirror Lake, I believed, at last, that reality was taking on the reassuring colours of fiction and gave in to the music's madness. Something that couldn't have happened anywhere else, this beguiling could only have taken place in the lost little corner of Maine I'd chosen for its complete isolation. And when I say "lost," I don't just mean far away from everything, because that's true of many parts of this state. All you have to do is follow a path through the woods and you'll stumble on some descendant of Daniel Boone completely unaware the world is at least meant to have moved on since the invention of gunpowder and who doesn't care anyway, who still hunts martens and beavers even as he curses the dull-witted animals without ever wondering which of them is encroaching on the other's territory, or who is dumber, him or the animal. No, when I say "lost," I am thinking more along the lines of being a lost soul, someone in perdition. I see a boat run aground on a stormy cape.

That day I sat on the north shore listening to the music of the chimes as the twilight coloured the other side of the lake in heartbreaking hues of pink. That's if you still have a heart to be broken; if life hasn't erased your ability to marvel at the ephemeral despite the searing pain it engenders in you every time, the sorrow you feel in the face of life's tenderness passing so quickly, so fast that you cannot but be reminded of your own passing too, and that, all things considered, your heart isn't what it once was. I suppose one of my reasons for choosing to live on the north shore of the lake was for Jeff and me to be the only ones with a direct view of the sunset, which meant that I wouldn't be likely when, like an insomniac or a warmed-over corpse, I stepped out onto my porch come breakfast time with a sandpaper mouth, to be whipped right in the face by the cheerful "good mornings" of neighbours completely oblivious to my misanthropic matinal nausea. On this shore, I would only have myself to hate, and would only despair of humankind at moments when I saw my own reflection in the clear water lapping at the end of the dock.

So, driven by the utterly puerile fantasy that rest was something that might even be possible, and by the urge to get away from people—and the image of myself they reflected back at me—at all costs, I'd hit the road one morning in my old Volvo 2000, windows down and hair blowing in the wind and as free as the hero of a road movie from that golden age before cinema moved on from citizens of no country to psychopaths and lunatics. And, in order to soften the feeling of devastation gnawing at that part of my soul less and less affected by the beauty of a sunset, I needed to go where no one could follow me, where I myself would become a beast in total harmony with the cruelty of my hunger. But, unfortunately, Mirror Lake was not so remote. Rather than providing me with the serenity of soul and mind that in truth exists only in the innocence of hope, it decided instead to gradually reveal my stupidity to me, and though I still believe there are men capable of living in a place without destroying it, I'm not sure this can be said of paradise. Man is heaven's bastard; I have never felt that more strongly than at Mirror Lake, where all my attempts to turn its Eden into a habitable place and recover what I like to think of as "original purity" turned into catastrophe.

Today, all that remains to reconcile me with a certain vision of eternity are the stars, illusions among illusions. When thoughts of my own past grow too heavy, I turn toward that of the universe. I go sit on the porch or the dock and gaze at the light of dead stars, propelled from the abyss of an age compared to which we are nothing, no more than an echo on the shore, a tiny piece of chickadee or sparrow shit. That's when eternity starts spinning, catching me in its whirlpool and dragging me into a vertigo where everything becomes a spiral. The lake, the trees, time, even life, launch with suspect enthusiasm into death's gaping maw—where everything repeats, where everything becomes spiral. And then, depending on whether my day has been good or bad, this idea that eternity will only ever be a starting over of the same things calms me slightly, allowing me to put the price of life in perspective and stop my hands trembling. Alternately, it plunges me into dark thoughts banishing all possibility of redemption for the simple reason that when life finally manages to bite its own tail, it strangles itself with ferocious irony. When I'm having one of the bad days, I wonder why I came here when it would have been so easy to stay in Quebec on a snowy plot of land with enough clandestine corners to shelter a fleeing man, enough stars to pre-empt the very idea of escape.

I have no clear answer to that question. I suppose I needed to put the name of a country between me and my past and take refuge under the stars of a flag to which I owe no allegiance. And, given its geographical location, Maine was the ideal place: an elsewhere in which I wouldn't have to experience the confusion an exile typically feels. With its smugglers' routes, its diners popping up in the middle of nowhere, its roads bordered with shadows and ravines, Maine had always struck me as the very incarnation of mystery, circumscribed by a winding line of a border that follows that divide in the middle of the water where rivers flowing to the Atlantic turn their back on others depositing their rocks along the Saint Lawrence, and beyond which, in my perception of place clouded by spending too much time in movie theatres, everything differs, even the trees, even the forests. I had needed that—to set off along roads where the slightest of things indicated to me I'd arrived in a foreign territory, at a place where even the trees and forests speak a different language.

I found names like Bangor, Penobscot, and Chesuncook spiritually impenetrable, ones people like me could not inhabit, and even if time has diminished that impression, Maine still strikes me as a land filled with secrets. It is not so much an extension of Quebec as its dark side, on whose humid slopes the slightest misstep can prove fatal. And yet, for the broken man I was and still am, the spectre of an endless fall holds both a morbid appeal and a feeling of salvation, and I like to abandon myself to the prospect when reality renders my life too stable, as is the case this evening when the dead stars shine and Victor Morgan, Bob Winslow, Jack Picard, Tim Robbins, Anita Swanson, and John Doe, alias Doolittle, appear on the opaque surface of the lake.

We weren't so many when I first arrived. Jeff and the birds aside—just one man, one, whose cottage is opposite mine, sometimes churned up the lake's mirrored surface. The cottage remains, but not long ago the man who lived there left Mirror Lake, leaving me alone beneath the black sky, hands trembling from the sudden chill solitude brought on.

I.

NEW DEPARTURE

But what then pushes the present
To flow toward the future
(unless it's actually the future flowing toward us)?
—Étienne Klein,
Chronos: How Time Shapes Our Universe

I arrived at Mirror Lake in the middle of May, not long after the swallows and the lilacs, at that time of year when garden gnomes, peeing angels and half-naked teenagers reappear in the suburbs. All the usual horrors and temptations, the sight of which I'd no longer have to abide in the paradise awaiting me.

I'd driven a good two hundred and fifty miles, my windows rolled down. Eyes dazzled by the brightness of the still-young leaves, face screwed up against the freshness of the wind and the persistent smell of earth rising up through the damp undergrowth, I belted out my favourite music, from Lou Reed's "Walk on the Wild Side" to songs from Lucinda Williams's *Car Wheels on a Gravel Road* via the great Jacques Brel, Johnny Cash, and Robert Charlebois. I could not have chosen a better moment to begin this new stage of my existence, which I felt would be nothing less than a resurrection after the ordeal of the preceding few years spent among those I suppose I must call "people like me." I'd reached the point where I was so devastated by human company that I almost envied the fate of Gregor Samsa—that unfortunate whom Franz Kafka turned into a beetle, or was it some other repulsive insect, without bothering to ask how he felt about it. But at Mirror Lake I would have no need to metamorphose into a bug in order to feel alive again and I would finally be able to rest, far from the noise and agitation of a time when I felt as if I was permanently holding my breath.

As soon as I got out of the car, I was able to breathe again and knew I was finally home, a word that had until then denoted a dream I figured I'd never be able to attain, and now here was the dream taking shape at the edge of a lake that had been calmly waiting for me ever since streams had dug their furrows through the mountains in order to flow out here. "We're home, Jeff," I said, a murmur intended for the big yellow dog who understood right away that we'd arrived at our destination. That we'd found our place in this absurd world, he and I. Jeff was racing around in circles, excited by the luxurious new smells and the bitter perfume of the soaked earth, rushing first to lap water from the lake, then coming to thank me by knocking his big head against my thighs, before turning away and sticking his snout into a bush or a pile of rotting leaves.

I was finally home, and I was finally free, another word I'd never believed I'd hear without immediately thinking of it as a pure abstraction. *Free, free, free,* replied the mountains to the shout that spontaneously rose up from my stomach, before I started humming Bob Dylan's "Blowin' in the Wind," the tune coming to my lips reflexively, just like all real things: I'm cold, I'm hungry, I'm in pain. Singing along, I asked how many years people do exist before they're allowed to be free, reflecting on just how many years it had taken me to understand that real free-dom is the result of a man being true to who he is, and then I wondered if I'd live long enough to forgive myself for having been so stupid. Pal, the answer's in the wind, Dylan reminded me. At which point the wind grew stronger, making waves in the lake and clinking the chimes hanging on the porch of the cottage opposite. A loon launched into what sounded like a yodel, its lament followed by a long ululating cry — *tourloulou, tourloulou* is how I've read it transcribed — and then I closed my eyes and wiped away a tear that had managed to break through the barriers I'd long ago erected against the possibility of crying. The soft music of *Für Alina* travelled out over the lake, so beautiful it made me want to howl in turn, a declaration that my desert wanderings had ended.

If I hadn't been afraid of shattering Jeff's joy, I'd have melted. I'd have let Alina open up the floodgates and watched my tears drown in the lake after cutting a little channel through the sand, sufficiently sinuous to show they were serious. Not wanting to inflict upon Jeff the peculiar manifestation of my joy, I shrugged it off and cried, "Hurry up, Jeff!" But Jeff had no need of me telling him to get a move on and certainly wasn't interested in helping me unload the car. Dutifully, he cocked an ear in my direction but then went back to staring at a frog that had probably never seen a dog in his life and was no doubt wondering if he shouldn't maybe move to a swamp in South Carolina. I understood the frog's train of thought, but wasn't about to go back to town just to make him happy. To each his period of suffering. Discreetly, I advised him to push off: "You'd better scarper, frog," I said, and headed over to the car.

Since the cottage was furnished, I'd only brought essentials—a few boxes of books, clothes, food, a case of beer, and four bottles of bourbon to see me through the first month. The beer was part of my regular diet, the bourbon more about nostalgia. I'd been drinking it since my early twenties in memory of Ned Beaumont, one of the Dashiell Hammett heroes I'd discovered at the same time as I did the day-for-night technique in cinema. When I realized that a good half of Hammett's private eyes drowned their sorrows in bourbon, it became my own melancholic habit, as I'd have liked to be one of those characters brooding over the world's sorrows in dive bars in New York, Los Angeles, or Chicago, cities where day-for-night worlds had firmly established residence. I winked at Ned, who was never far away whenever the smell of alcohol hit my nostrils, and I carried the bag of bottles into the cottage with my battered old boiled-leather suitcase, belting out "Freedom" by Richie Havens so that the melancholy couldn't get a hold. Since I didn't know any of the words other than "*freedom, freedom, freedom*," that heady chant of Woodstock and the lost youth to which I belonged at the time, I quickly became tired and moved on to Dylan, given that several of his songs were engraved on my memory like prayers, albeit imbued with a hint of regret for that time when I used to have faith.

By the beginning of the evening, I'd almost finished settling in and went out onto the porch with a beer and a frozen pizza, traditional moving-day food, which Jeff had equal right to, as it was our party, the first day of our new life. On the other side of the lake, the chimes were still sounding, and the loon that had welcomed me was greeting the twilight accompanied by a robin warbling near the cottage. The sun was setting gently and the lake was taking on all the colours of the sunset: it was a perfect moment. I wanted to find the right words to describe its sweetness, to formulate some unforgettable phrase about the magnificence and glory of it all, but the only words that came to mind were incredibly simple. "Damn, it's beautiful," I murmured as I sank comfortably into my chair. I had nothing to add. Simple as that. It was beautiful, we were home. And then, along with the robin singing and the tinkling of the chimes, came the creaking sound of a rowboat being dragged along the sand, and I watched as my neighbour opposite climbed into it. A few seconds later, the ambient noise was compounded by the soothing sound of an oar slicing through the water as the little green rowboat moved slowly across the pink-dappled water. This idyllic image could have featured on a postcard, in a tourist guide, or in an old yellowing calendar, the kind you see pinned to the dirty wall of a gas station and which nobody has ever considered replacing even if it's been hanging there since the Second World War or the giddy years afterwards, because time has no vintage and I don't know what it is about immortal pictures but, like first loves, they never disappear. Moved by the purity of the tableau presenting itself to me, I repeated, "Damn, it's beautiful," as I took a slow glug of beer, letting the flavours soak into my palate, and then nearly choking on it when I realized that the tiny boat was heading straight toward us and that the man in it, wearing a cap the same shade of green as the boat, was raising his hand to us in greeting.

"*Baptême*," I muttered, catching my breath. That's a swear word I only use in grave situations of imminent catastrophe, like when neighbours turn up. If I'd been as brutal as the world in which we live I'd have fetched a Kalashnikov and sorted it out then and there, but apart from the fact that I don't own a gun, I don't like blood in any form—blood sausage, a drop of blood pearling on the skin after an injection or a vampire bite, a dried scab in the middle of a knee, a little rivulet cooling as it trickles down a forehead. I hate it. I thought sneakily of strangulation, but by the time I had my hands on a piece of rope the attacker would have invaded my land and planted his flag, which he was going to do anyway, though I didn't know that yet. "We're done for," I whispered in Jeff's ear as a new creaking echoed off the mountains, a sign that the enemy had just touched land. But since Jeff was not only a pacifist dog but a pacifist dog who gets a bit silly after drinking, he raced off to the beach wagging his tail to welcome our visitor with great joyous barks. "Good dog," said the idiot, manoeuvring out of his boat and panting like a dog. "Fuck," the man added as he put his massive boot in the water, and we were off. The barbarian invasion had begun.

A few moments later, the man who'd just soiled the

virginity I'd been a bit too quick to assign to Mirror Lake ascended onto my porch without an invitation, moving with the joviality of a simple man who fails to see the world is a place of suffering and that he is one of the principal elements fanning the flames of this hell.

"Hi, I'm your new neighbour," he said cheerfully. As if I didn't know. As if I hadn't lived long enough to recognize the multiple faces calamity can wear. Then he corrected himself, saying that in fact *he* wasn't the new neighbour, *I* was, which set him off on an endless narrative about anteriority and posteriority, and the chicken and the egg and the cock. The cock!—the piece of the anteriority–posteriority puzzle that is always forgotten—and then the jerk started rambling on about the importance of expressing oneself precisely, even quoting Nicolas Boileau-Despréaux and then spouting Wittgenstein's "Everything that can be said can be said clearly." All to point out that actually I was the one who was the new neighbour.

In one way he was right, except if you think too much about what newness itself is, about newness's essence, for he was just as new to me as I was to him. On the basis of that argument, you could deduce that there were two new neighbours around the lake, one who was there before and one who wasn't; one who seemed happy to be new and one who would have preferred not to be anything at all, would have preferred to return to a larval state or the innocence of a sperm; one who believes he has the right to, without warning, launch into a discourse about logic and one who, all of a sudden, has a headache.

He must have noticed that I didn't really feel like chatting, because, trying to be friendly, he finished up with "Never mind, you're here, I'm here," though his words had the ring of an eternal condemnation. "Bob Winslow," he added, holding out his hand.

"Robert Moreau," I replied reluctantly, putting my hand in his. If I'd had the requisite presence of mind, I'd have kept my hands in my pockets and told him my right hand had been amputated, that I had a contagious disease, or that I was Howard Hughes's grandson and had inherited his germaphobia. But by the time the idea occurred to me, it was too late: Bob Winslow's germs were frolicking all over my hand and even venturing up my forearm. Noticing my silence and the slight awkwardness that had settled over us, Bob Winslow followed up with a "hmm-hmm," a sniff, and then a "So, do you like this place?"

How can you answer such a question when the person asking it is none other than the sordid vandal, the profaner who has just destroyed your childish illusion that there are still a few havens of peace left on this overpopulated planet?

"I liked it," I replied somewhat dryly, and Winslow, who wasn't as stupid as he looked and knew how verb tenses worked, understood that I wasn't very sociable. Nonetheless, he offered the greeting "Welcome to Mirror Lake, stranger," and then an ingratiating, cheeky wink—I can't think of any other way to describe it—before walking back to the lake hollering, "See you soon, raccoon," the phrase confirming the death sentence he'd already pronounced. As he was getting back into his rowboat and Jeff was barking a joyful goodbye, the moron actually thought it would be a good idea to carry on the nursery rhyming by calling out, mockingly, "See you later, alligator."

See you later, alligator! That was all I needed to make a radiant smile stretch across my tense face and light up this glorious evening. Then I realized that it was getting dark and I'd missed the apogee of my first sunset over Mirror Lake's peaceful waters, which only made me hate Bob Winslow all the more. I remained outside admiring the stretch of dark, strangely luminescent blue sky still lingering behind the mountains that the night would rapidly consume. As Bob Winslow's rowboat, a small black speck in the middle of the shadow, proceeded calmly over the oily surface of Mirror Lake, an "In a while, crocodile" emanated from it just as the little speck was eaten by the penumbra. *Dile, dile, dile,* repeated the mountains' enchanting voice, echoing beneath my brilliant retort, "Don't count on it, you piece of shit," as well as various other spontaneous rhyming gems I'd have written down if I had a notebook. After which, what with Winslow having removed all possibility of my mood being anything other than murderous, I called Jeff back inside.

It was during that first night that, to my great consternation, Humpty Dumpty appeared on Mirror Lake. When I was a child I'd suffered from Humpty Dumpty syndrome, a hitherto unknown neurosis and species of paranoia that was the cause of my having developed an extreme aversion to this character who struck me as the absolute archetype of stupidity. Back then I was certain that the expression *bad egg* was related to the depressing tale of the bad-tempered, suicidal egg, about whom my mother told me stories to help me get to sleep, not knowing that I wasn't taking on the morals of Lewis Carroll's story, or his poetry, but the boundless complacency of this big yellow splotch reeling off whatever nonsense to Alice. Then my aversion became an obsession and I started having nightmares, with Humpty Dumpty in a starring role, any time some new frustration came along to remind me that life wasn't a beautiful meadow where beautiful girls kissed toads. The syndrome lasted for several years, and then Humpty Dumpty was shoved aside by Godzilla, Goldorak, and Frankenstein, whom I, just like everyone else, confused with his monster, after which my hauntings took on a more human form — in other words, moved closer to what we would think of as mere unhappiness.

That night, though, a breach opened up in the muddy recesses of my subconscious where the monster lay crouching, and Humpty Dumpty regained his rightful place in the tormented landscape of my dreamworld but wearing the features of Bob Winslow, whose ovoid body lent itself perfectly to such a part. In my dream, he was sitting on Humpty Dumpty's wall, beating his scrawny legs on it, pompously reciting the speech exactly as he'd delivered it to me that evening — but for a few variations regarding the order of appearance and the degree of truth of its constituent elements. "The proposition is the expression of agreement and disagreement with the possibilities of real-ness of the elementary clauses," he repeated as he scratched his stomach, so close to his forehead, as I, kneeling at the foot of the wall, prayed silently for Godzilla, foaming at the mouth, to appear behind him and squash the pompous scumbag with an irreversible swipe of his claws.

I woke up sweating in the small hours of the night, just as the first rays of sun were filtering through the trees, and saw in the mirror the pale face of a man whose nightmares had just killed his last childish dreams. "*Baptême*," I mur-mured, but the mountains didn't respond, the mountains only answer to shouts, just like people pretending to be deaf. Endeavouring to prove that the speed of sound is slower than the speed of light, my reflection, trying to fix its hair, mouthed the word silently before muttering "*Baptême*" after me, and then it exited stage left. I told myself that, at the end of the day, a man's freedom is only obtained at the cost of his total brainwashing. As for what was happening on the other side of the mirror, that I would find out later.

Over the next few days, Jeff managed to play in relative peace, but I couldn't, because Bob Winslow's *see you soon, raccoon,* still lingered in my mind, along with his *in a while, crocodile, dile, dile,* echoing sinisterly in the ink-black night that had left an indelible mark upon my arrival at Mirror Lake. Instead of enjoying the respite, I lived under the burden of imminent threat with my ears on high alert, monitoring Bob Winslow's comings and goings and reacting to the slightest sound that just might have been the creaking of a rowboat being pushed across the sand. In my increasing craziness, I was starting to imagine the enemy would opt for a stealth attack — one step forward, two steps back — wearing me down and forcing me to capitulate.

Three days passed, I relaxed my surveillance a little and decided to have a word with myself. "Sit down, I have to talk to you," I told myself with a degree of weariness. I chose to go sit below the porch on the rock that had, I guessed from a quick glance, been sleeping for three or four hundred million years — since long before there even was a porch, a gravel road, an old garbage can, and other traces of the irredeemable human presence — unless it had been deposited there during the last glaciation. Since the latter hypothesis wasn't getting me anywhere, and as a few thousand years are neither here nor there in geological terms, I decreed that it was four hundred million years old, doing my best not to think of the dizzying amount of memory recorded in the metamorphic or granitic matter of which it was composed. The rock looked like it would be comfortable, despite its appearance of hardness, which was perfect for what I needed to do. "Hi rock," I said in greeting, before sitting upon it and telling myself that I was an idiot, mentally ill, stupidly paranoid, that my fear of seeing Bob Winslow pop up again was unfounded and I was creating my own hell. If there were products for exterminating vermin, then one really ought to exist for destroying neighbours, and if it didn't exist, then I needed to invent it and get rich.

After twenty minutes of this therapeutic soliloquy, I felt somewhat better, but it didn't stop me from glancing across to the other side of the lake *just in case*. As everything seemed quiet, I let myself slide down the length of the rock, pressing against it and, closing my eyes, noticing the play of sunlight through my eyelids, other suns, comets, galaxies, and yet more comets appearing, these about to land on the concealed face of my ocular globe as they sent their tails spinning. Just as I was starting to lower my guard, telling myself how stupid I was for not enjoying my new retirement, I heard Jeff bolt off, barking and snorting. Then a voice like Humpty Dumpty's rose up from behind the four-hundred-million-year-old rock and whispered in my ear, "Getting a bit of shut-eye, stranger?"

This phrase, spoken in a mildly sarcastic tone, could not have been better chosen, because it confirmed that all paranoia has a reason; you just have to close your eyes for thirty seconds and the object haunting you will take advantage of it to surreptitiously insinuate itself into your ear. I decided not to move, to play dead, because surely this was a nightmare. It couldn't be anything else. It was a nightmare, a terrible nightmare starring Humpty Dumpty as himself, a segue into my dreaming that in fact turned out to be a waking nightmare on a loop, the sort of recurring reminiscence that can be attributed to the vague persistence of a phenomenon long after whatever might have caused it has disappeared. Still, I experienced a measure of doubt when Humpty Dumpty's voice said "Ahem," before sniffing and clearing its throat. Just to be sure, I cracked open an eyelid before immediately shutting it again. What had come in through the aperture was actually nightmarish, but also real. Not knowing what to do, I uttered the supposedly magic formula "Abracadabra," and prayed to the Saint of Lost Objects for him not to have to help me locate my absent serenity.

When I opened both eyes wide, nothing had changed; hovering over me were Bob Winslow's gigantic face, Jeff's big head, and the head of some stranger who, as Winslow would later inform me, was called Bill. Seen from without, it might have all looked a bit ridiculous, and me especially, so I stood up, dusted myself off, and asked Winslow what it was that he wanted, though not before first whistling for the Saint of Lost Objects, who would have some work to do after all.

"To introduce you to my new friend, stranger," he said jovially.

Whether or not I wanted to be acquainted with this moron's friends, new or not, anterior or posterior, two things about what he said disturbed me. First, there was the word *new*, which might embroil Winslow in another discussion concerning the meaning of newness; second, the word *stranger*, the offhandedness of which, like all offhandedness, had a quality I found irritating. The word made me think vaguely of a movie whose plot I couldn't recall, but that I knew to be key to figuring out which character, in which movie, was calling the other guy "stranger." And if there's one thing that irritates me, it's realizing that memory is flaky and full of holes, cliffs, abysses, and peaceful silences that make you look like an ignoramus. We were going to sort this out right away.

"My name is Robert, Bob, so you call me Robert, okay, not 'stranger.' Never 'stranger'!"

I'd opened the floodgates with this permission to use my first name, which I knew full well, but what else could I have done?

"Okay, Ro*bert*," he said, smiling as he emphasized the *bert*, which forced me to grate my teeth and smile, what with my face being arranged in such a way that when my teeth grate I smile, and vice versa. I'm not particularly sociable, as I said.

With this clarification settled, Winslow introduced me to Bill, his new friend, who was yellow. Not the yellow of jaundice, but more like Jeff, with whom he also shared the traits of four legs, a snout, pointy ears, a short tail that would grow longer over time, and so on. In fact, in a few weeks, Bill the puppy would be identical to Jeff the dog in every way. Jeff could have been his father if he'd known Bill's mother, and, to be honest, I found it pretty annoying. If this guy was not only going to deplete my joie de vivre, but also wanted us to shop for matching underwear together, then the new existence I'd thought awaited me on Mirror Lake's peaceful shores was going to be a long time coming, since time, in such situations, is linked to a kind of relativity that does no less damage for being relative.

At the sight of the tricolour elastic waistband of Winslow's underwear, a good three inches of which were visible over the top of his pants, a surge of slightly acidic nausea rose in me, fuelled by all those petty vexations that slowly eat away at your insides, and I thought, without explicitly formulating the words, that Bob Winslow was a dangerous man, a loser who'd been driven crazy by isolation, a degenerate fired up by the insalubrious desire to imitate his neighbour and thus prevent himself from losing his selfhood due to his own lack of personality. He was feeble-minded, a person who thought that getting a dog was enough to prove to me that the two of us were alike and that my relationship with Jeff was nothing special; that what made me different could be eliminated by a simple mirror trick.

Bob Winslow's strategy, or what I considered to be his strategy, was not remotely original. It was based on the exceedingly banal principle on which the society I'd tried to leave was also founded: the abolition of identity through the multiplication of the self and the creation of new multiples, with the aid of which identity will try in vain to reconstruct itself. I hated this slavish mentality and had the feeling, as I contemplated Bill's face, that I'd been catapulted into the pastel suburbs of *Edward Scissorhands* or *Pleasantville*, or any such nightmare where you only have to peep over the inevitable hedge to observe your charming wife, your elegant house, your gleaming car, your adorable children in your neighbour's yard—or worse still, to see yourself, all smiles, busy mowing the lawn or trimming the inevitable hedge. *The horror.* The idea, as I stood in front of the mirror, that one day I might come face to face with Winslow revived my nausea, which was immediately followed by shivers set off by the cold man inside me nibbling away at my resentments.

"Nice doggy, good puppy," I nevertheless babbled like an idiot, crouching down next to Bill, who was busy prancing around me under Jeff's jealous gaze. Jeff likes everyone except other dogs—or at least dogs trying to seduce me. To show Bill I was his owner—and who was master—Jeff gave a snarl that lifted his lip on the left side and revealed his yellow teeth, then growled a little. Bill seemed to understand what Jeff was telling him, because immediately he lay down at Jeff's feet and wagged his tail. Well, at least one of us knew how to get some respect, proof that in a half-empty glass there is always a little liquid, or that the dynamics of any duo is invariably determined by which is the one ready to bite and which is the one who'll let himself be torn to shreds — by the biter and the bitten.

As we waited, Winslow looked at Bill with the loving gaze of someone who's just discovered the meaning of life, which made me feel a certain respect for him. I've always thought any man who loves dogs can't be entirely bad or entirely stupid, but I wasn't going to give in to this brief surge of sympathy. Although I might feel a modicum of respect for men fond of dogs, I vastly prefer those who only like dogs and leave the rest of us in peace. This wasn't the case with Winslow, who took advantage of my moment of weakness to announce that he'd not only come to introduce me to his dog, but also to invite me over for dinner — to officially welcome me to Mirror Lake and celebrate Bill's arrival into our little community. Those were his exact words, "our little community." What a jerk.

It was now or never, were I to explain that I didn't like communities, small or large, new or old, anterior or posterior, and that the best way to welcome me was to ignore me, so I said as much, but he didn't get it. There are some people, and Winslow was one of them, who are so convinced that harmony among men — and particularly good neighbourly relations, complicity between spouses, the collusion of minds, and other such baloney — is going to save the world that they don't listen when you point out such concord isn't born of promiscuity or overpopulation. So Winslow turned a deaf ear. He'd sensed that, due to some perfectly ordinary embarrassment or awkwardness, I'd not accept his invitation, so he'd made us a little something to eat and brought it with him. Without even allowing me the chance to protest, or to claim I wasn't hungry — that I was anorexic, that I was on a strict fennel-based diet, that I had multiple allergies and was Howard Hughes's grandson — he ran over to the car he'd parked at the top of the driveway to my cottage (so that was how he'd got here, the schemer) and returned with a basket like Little Red Riding Hood's, two bottles of bubbly, and a box decorated with a tightly curled ribbon he must have unearthed from an old box of Christmas decorations.

"For you," he said, blushing, as he handed me the box.

The sneaky old bastard had thought of everything, right down to the most trivial, microscopic details, which was why it had taken him three days to turn up again. I had no choice but to invite him onto the porch, where I unwrapped the gift while he took a tablecloth out of the basket, laid it on an old wooden table that actually seemed to be waiting for it, and started serving dinner. The gift was a book, *The Maine Attraction*, a novel by one Victor Morgan, whom I didn't know from Adam; Winslow was enthusiastically recommending it to me partly because, he said, the characters were very realistic, though mostly because the story took place in a little village not far from Mirror Lake. I had no idea how he'd guessed I liked reading, so I asked him.

"Intuition," he said, adding that he was like a woman in that respect. It was the anima side of his personality, and his intuition never failed him. He then appraised me, with that disagreeable little smile on his face, and I noticed his eyes were the same blue as mine, either faded blue or periwinkle blue, depending on the light and what we'd consumed the night before.

But I didn't have time to dwell on the resemblance, because he'd handed me a glass of sparkling wine, raised his own, and said, "Live long and prosper, buddy," then clinked his against mine — which was full and spilled. To hide my irritation, I ground my teeth, and therefore smiled, and talked to him about my reading, which brought us to a place where men can get along. If I hadn't felt about Bob Winslow the way any normal person would about someone suffocating them, I might go so far as to say we had a pleasant evening, sitting on the porch and discussing Victor Morgan, David Goodis, and Stephen King, whose shadow hovered over the Maine forests. But when Winslow referenced Irish, William Irish he said, and Woolrich, Cornell Woolrich of course, I was at my wits' end and tried to come up with the right word to define the frankly unspeakable irritation flooding over me.

Winslow had just articulated the double name of an author holding a place in my own personal pantheon, with whom I had a singular relationship. Nobody I knew had ever read Irish, and here was this ape taking ownership of William and Cornell as if they'd been to bed together. The corollary of my annoyance was that the more we talked, the more I discovered how much this jerk and I had in common. If Winslow had detested the company of his peers, I'd have been fine with us being alike, especially as I would never have found out at all, except by chance, but apparently this was one of the few traits we did not share.

Winslow must have noticed, as I was compiling a list of our similarities, that I was doing my best to contain myself because, whether out of sympathy or simply to imitate me, he started grimacing, reflecting back a parody of myself and Kermit the Frog, curing my dyspepsia immediately. Not exactly delighted to learn that my face reminded others of Kermit, whom I didn't like, I turned away and sank inside myself — deep inside myself, far from the annoying surface of things — letting Winslow badmouth *Waltz into Darkness*, Irish's masterpiece, during which time Catherine Deneuve, who'd rendered the mermaid of the novel immortal for Truffaut's camera, appeared on the screen between Winslow and me, pursued by a crazy-in-love Jean-Paul Belmondo. When Deneuve disappeared — after a period of time hard to measure for a man enthralled by beauty — Winslow launched into a shot-by-shot analysis of *The Bride Wore Black*, and I let Jeanne Moreau and her black veils invade the screen. After the third or fourth victim's blood squirted me in the eye, I changed the channel and became, instead, interested in the moths burning their wings on the dusty bulb shining inside the lantern. Winslow must have turned it on as I was kissing Catherine Deneuve while Belmondo's back was turned, because it was now pitch-black out.

I like that expression, *pitch-black,* almost as much as *black as the devil's lair*, except that it's more realistic, because if we are to believe what we've been told, the devil's home is red with a touch of fiery yellow. A blast of heat came to my face as I thought about people who don't love their neighbours as themselves being good candidates for Lucifer's team, subsequently realizing that I risked spending eternity in a disco setting. What with this perspective frightening me as much as the prospect of waking up in the same bed as Winslow, I assuaged the fear with the first argument that came to mind: since I actually hated my neighbour as much as myself, I'd be able to plead my case when angels from heaven and hell grabbed me and started fighting over which side I would go to.

The matter settled, I looked at Jeff and Bill tussling over the moth corpses littering the porch. Bill was clumsy and didn't really know what to do, so he was watching Jeff and trying to copy him. A bit of hairy wing was stuck to the side of his jaw, making him look kind of stupid, but he didn't seem to care any more than he seemed to feel the slightest hint of compassion for the little creatures trying to shorten their already brief lives.

I wondered how dogs feel about death — not their own or their masters', but the deaths of butterflies, squirrels, field mice. Hard to say... With the two-part aim of satisfying my curiosity and silencing Winslow's voice, I focused on Jeff's large head, on his round eyes, tried to place myself there, behind those eyes staring at the moths. At first, I saw tiny, crazy, useless, meaningless things flapping about the light amid the crackling noises of the flame, whirling in the cool evening air, and then falling, insignificantly, at my feet. I watched a moth that had taken refuge under Winslow's chair, and since the sight made me feel neither hot nor cold, I concluded dogs feel nothing about the death of creatures not like them. This was perhaps also true for one or more of the pariahs of Morgan's *The Maine Attraction* — seven of them, all on death row, who a nice fictional licence permits us to see gathered around the table for what will be their final meal, or that's what Winslow was telling me right then, having finally decided to leave Irish in peace.

I listened to him distractedly, my consciousness still half inside Jeff's big head, but nevertheless the information filtered through the other half in my attempt to find out if the seven death-row inmates of Holburn prison were like dogs and Winslow's universe truly overlapped with mine, but I was too tired and hadn't actually learned anything interesting about the novel nor the select affinities that might bring Winslow and me together, except for the fact that Morgan, the novel's author, hadn't published anything afterwards and, in 1951, the year I was born, had vanished into thin air.

After his exegesis, I pulled myself out of my torpor and saw that Winslow was serious and thoughtful. Reading the book had clearly made a big impression on him, so much so that all traces of his easygoing smile had disappeared. It occurred to me that at least reading could do one good thing: it could sometimes make us seem less stupid. I also noted that Winslow was a difficult character to pin down, rough around the edges on the one hand, and fit for decent company on the other, like a big branch whittled and sanded on one side only. While I was trying to come up with a way to properly express Winslow's elusive side, Wittgenstein came to mind again and I remembered that he'd written something about the inexpressible. "If it can't be expressed, it can't be said," or something like that. So I allotted Winslow to the category of the inexpressible, and poured the last of the second bottle of sparkling wine into his glass, a gesture briefly enlivening his expression before it immediately reverted to that of an idiot.

And that's how the evening ended. Winslow put his glass down, picked up his Little Red Riding Hood basket, tablecloth, dirty dishes, and then got into his car with Bill, two shadows big and small that the night quickly swallowed up as they emitted a "See you soon, racoon." But the mountains didn't take up the call, as mountains only answer to shouts, and because Winslow, at the end of that night, was looking peaky. And, as everyone knows, folk with peaky complexions don't shout. They mumble, murmur, and talk only to themselves. Actually, I intuited the words *see you soon* more than I heard them, enough that I was not at all certain of the words that, as was the image of Winslow, were perhaps enigmatic and that the dark, like a ruminant, masticated and then gulped down.

The most basic courtesy demanded, after Bob Winslow kindly invited me to my place for dinner, that I do the same in return; that like Little Red Riding Hood, I gather together a few galettes, a small jar of butter, and other food in a basket, jump into my rowboat and hurl myself into the wolf's mouth. But courtesy was an alien concept to me. I'd come to Mirror Lake to be alone and not to have to worry about the propriety that burdens all men bereft of the liberty of isolating themselves deep in the woods and who, instead, must pretend to love their neighbours.

So I opted for silence and rudeness, sure that Bob Winslow, however tenacious his desire to erect a bridge between the two sides of Mirror Lake, would end up figuring me out. I ambled around in my supreme innocence for two days, until he rowed across the lake a second time in his old green rowboat, this time to invite me to share the harvest of his miraculous fishing trip. "Twenty trout in half an hour, Robert. Never saw that in this fucking lake," he couldn't stop repeating, making the word *fucking* ring out because Bob Winslow, along with most of his compatriots, peppered his speech with *fuck* and *fucking* almost like breathing, a punctuation that emphasized the intensity of his emotions, *fucking* life, *fucking* shit, *fucking* sun, which he followed by telling me I was the one who'd brought him luck, *fucking* luck, Robert, so that it was only fair I share the trout with him. I told him he was wrong, that a man like me brought *poisse*, a word his rudimentary French led him to interpret as fish, *fucking* fish, and it took me a while to get it into his head that misfortune dogged my heels.

"Ill fortune dogs my footsteps, Bob," I said, adding that if my presence at the lake were having any influence at all on the local habitat, it was to bring bad luck to the fish rather than good luck to Bob.

Then I tried to explain to him that I wanted — "like a rat, Bob" — to be alone with Jeff. And in his great perspicacity, having again anticipated my reaction, he produced a few trout fillets from the wicker basket lying in the bottom of his boat and advised me to roll them in flour before frying them. Then he set off again, slowly rowing toward the other bank with his head down, perhaps mulling over old, stubborn miseries as he did so. Bill, meanwhile, was sitting in the back of the boat and looking at Jeff with his round eyes, smiling the way dogs do, with that meek expression containing all the innocence of the world. Then I felt strangely uncomfortable at the sight of this man who seemed unaffected by the contingency of existence, and wondered if perhaps his innate good humour was simply a charade to prevent his collapse. But I let my discomfort ebb away, called Jeff, and went inside to fry Winslow's fucking fish.

At eight o'clock, wanting to enjoy the sunset, I went out onto the porch with Jeff and my plate of steaming trout, at the same time as Bill and Bob Winslow, the two of them silently sitting opposite us on the far side of the lake and watching us as they ate. At least, I felt as if they were watching us, though it's hard to see what someone's eyes are looking at from a distance. Still, I was almost certain Winslow had waited for me to go outside and then copied me. I had no idea what he was hoping to achieve by acting this way, or why he'd decided to start such a game with me, because it's similarly tricky to read a person's thoughts from that distance, but the fact that he'd hit his target killed my appetite. I spat the mouthful I was chewing off the porch and smack onto the four-hundred-million-year-old rock, which would have jumped had it been a pebble, but which remained stoic, as rocks comfortably are. The rock had nothing at all to do with the story, but subconsciously I blamed it for me having let my guard down with regard to Winslow and the deplorable situation that had resulted. Since the subconscious, which doesn't understand itself, is slower to forgive, mine decided that all this was the rock's fault. Now that I had someone to reproach for my unhappiness, I should have felt better, but didn't, so I gave the rest of my plate to Jeff and slammed the door as I went back inside, this to make the rock think a bit and so that Winslow would understand I hadn't fallen for his little trick.

I brooded all the next day and, on the stroke of six, loaded Jeff into my rowboat and set a course for the south bank and Bob Winslow, determined to let him know that I no longer wanted to see him, hear him, or breathe the same air as him: that he was giving me hives and made me want to retch; that I hated fish, Red Riding Hood, brotherly relations, Victor Morgan and his band of murderers, and that I had absolutely no desire to read his vapid plot twists. In short, I was determined — but I don't know what happened, I really don't. Before I'd even opened my mouth, Winslow bombarded me with an incoherent stream of words, going on about the miraculous fishing trip and fawningly giving me two or three pats on the back as if there was nothing wrong, as if he'd not seen me cursing as I spat his trout out on the rock that had become my scapegoat. And before I even had time to realize what was transpiring, I was sitting opposite Bob Winslow eating a trout stew made from the previous day's leftovers, his periwinkle gaze assessing me, it seemed, with a hint of the superciliousness that distinguishes winners. I hated him all the more, which was getting to be quite a lot, but nonetheless I ate my stew, washing it down with a local brew and listening to him pontificate about line fishing and the silent cries the fish make as the hook rips through them.

Actually, Winslow didn't explicitly mention their cries, I just imagined them while he went on about the flies he made out of feathers collected from the woods or at the lake's edge, and how a fish wriggled at the end of the line when you pulled it out of the cold water. I was listening half attentively when I saw a fish — just like the one swimming in my bowl in chunks — take shape at the perimeter of my vision, gills open in the suffocating air. Then I heard a cry, a plaintive muffled call for help, along with what sounded like a whistle emanating from its bulging eyes that the mountains, not knowing how to whistle, did not echo. To be frank, this death whistle shook me. I'd never been especially moved by the sight of a trout but deduced that my indifference arose out of the fact that fish make no sounds audible to our feeble ears. If fish were able to speak like other animals, the barbaric activity that is hook fishing would surely have put off a few of its disciples. But the silent suffering of fish, condemned to wiggle at the end of a line without audible protest, suits everyone, because a mind at peace associates the lack of a scream with an absence of pain, thus relieving what serves them as a conscience. After these ruminations I had trouble finishing my meal, which ended up in Jeff's belly once more, though I did have another beer, and then another, which made the boat pitch around when, finally, I managed to extricate myself from the swing on Winslow's porch, announcing that all good things must come to an end and it was time for me to go home.

That is actually pretty much what, like an idiot, I said to Bob Winslow and his sparkling eyes: "Every good thing must come to an end." Then I took to the lake and rowed to the cadence of my beery evening with a sad song on my lips. *They will live on love* and *no more sorrow*, the mountains echoed, because in drinking Bob Winslow's beer I had effectively sealed what is sometimes called a friendship. And I have to admit that once the wind got up, the conversation had taken a more intimate turn. As the chimes jangled softly from their corner of the porch, Winslow had talked to me about his childhood in the Adirondacks, insisting that he could never live far from the mountains. And then he told me what had brought him to Maine.

"I wanted to stop hurting," offered Winslow as his justification for buying a cottage on Mirror Lake. "I wanted to chase away the pain." He recalled the day he'd decided to leave his boondocks village and to do so without looking back. "It was spring, the end of April," he continued as the chimes tinkled, though nothing about his story suggested that season. Given the sky he was describing, you might have guessed October or November, just before the first snow. Outside, he recounted, still-leafless trees were bending under the force of a wind whipping up the embattled hair on Bob Winslow's forehead. He'd found himself on a deserted road, a few miles away from his home village, which formed a part of the collection of nostalgic snapshots he described for me as the sun set over Mirror Lake. He'd stopped his car at the bottom of a steep path that opened onto a wide, ill-defined piece of land—a garbage dump, actually—where dense smoke rose up from the ashy detritus. A man he'd always thought of as his brother was coming his way along a gravel road, alone and silent, and approaching a heap of filth on which a few crows were hopping about, indifferent to the violence of the wind, indifferent to the squawking birds and stinking odour that, fortunately, the cold of this peculiarly autumnal April tempered somewhat.

"In the depths of the fog," Bob Winslow muttered at this point in the tale, "I had perceived the lonesomeness of that man, my brother, as deep as the deep waters of Mirror Lake," his eyes misty as he pointed his crooked index finger toward Mirror Lake's abyssal centre and considered the notion of an unfathomable distance separating us from the beings we love. An image from the day before of Winslow moving further away on the lake, a big gloomy carcass pondering his sorrows, flashed furtively across my mind. I followed it for a few seconds before swiping it away with the back of my hand, because I had no intention of letting myself emote about something that might as easily have been a mirage, and returned to Winslow. His voice was caught up with the hallucinatory music of the chimes, as he recounted how he'd watched the smoke gradually obscure the shoulders and head of the lone man, how he'd seen the solitary figure slowly disappear at the end of the bleak road, before convincing himself that this was how people we love disappear: they take a path we can't follow. "They take a narrow path, too narrow for two men, so we stay helplessly at the trail head, forced to watched their silhouettes diminish and disappear as the distance and fog gnaw away at them. We know that anything we do or say is futile. And then we're made aware of our own isolation, of our own fucking solitude, Robert."

Which was when Bob Winslow swallowed noisily, his shoulders bowed under the weight of the fog. For the first time since I'd met him, I felt something for the man, by which I mean something positive, this despite my efforts not to be moved by the parasite, lowering my gaze so he wouldn't notice the emotion I attributed to the several bottles of Gritty McDuff's I'd knocked back—and so I couldn't see him either. Then his story stopped there, with the image of a man whose death he couldn't envision without also imagining the collapse of the world.

A brief silence followed, during which Winslow's lonely friend hovered over us, and I wondered yet again who Winslow was, this man who moved seamlessly from vulgarity to tenderness, from seriousness to truisms. "Your new neighbour," answered a gentle voice, one endeavouring to put me on guard against any undue sympathy. Something told me that this voice was wise, so I said goodbye to Bill and Bob Winslow and climbed back into my boat with Jeff, though not without reflecting on the fact that this evening I was the one appearing to be a person on the run, a blurry shape moving away in the night, my boat furrowing a path through the black water too narrow for two men, and then I started singing Raymond Lévesque's "Quand les hommes vivront d'amour," hoping the thought of men living on love would dispel the image from my mind and prevent Winslow from associating me with this man, his brother.

Once home I felt dirty, icky, coated with the viscous sentimentality Winslow's confidences had layered on my skin. I took a lengthy shower to try to clean off the glue clogging up my pores. Next, I opened Morgan's novel, but I wasn't in the right frame of mind for reading. I flipped through it distractedly and did what happens to me when that part of my brain dedicated to reading is looking at the page but my eyes are not following, so that I read the same page five, six, or even ten times over, as the rest of my brain abandons itself to a slumber penetrated now and again by a word, sentence, or picture conjured by the text.

Perhaps it was down to the Gritty McDuff's, but the novel's first lines made me feel pretty nauseous, so I returned to the bathroom to splash my face with cold water and told Jeff I was going to sleep, which made him feel relieved as he doesn't like seeing me in such a state. I lay down on my bed, he snuggled up to my side, I adjusted my side to the curve of his back, and then sank into an agitated sleep that hurtled me into the middle of a dream in which the real Humpty Dumpty, that bad egg, was out of sheer stupidity falling off his wall, appearing again, then tumbling off it again, a large crack running from his forehead to what could be described as his missing penis, all the while displaying the vapid smile that made me want to strangle him, to crush him by wrapping my arms around his big idiotic stomach. But my disgust at the idea of being bogged down in the sticky yellow substance that would spurt out of his stomach prevented me, which he knew, the imbecile, so he carried on his little game, staring at me with his idiotic eyes, and was not in the least affected by the string of curses I was hurling at him: *stupid fool, fucking bloody fool, bastard, moron, tête de noeud, twit, twit, maudit twit*! Then a fish suddenly went by in the cardboard sky sketched behind Humpty Dumpty's wall, emitting a silent cry, immediately followed, if you can put it like that, by a fish travelling in the other direction, unless it was actually the same fish which had decided to do a U-turn off camera—I would never know and didn't care. And then the dream abruptly stopped there, without a word of explanation.

When I heard birdsong, I wasn't at all unhappy that the sun was rising. I opened my eyes, got out of bed, albeit unenthusiastically and went to look out at Mirror Lake, which might have been the most beautiful place in the world after Capri and Niagara Falls but for the little green boat right in the middle of it, from which a man wearing a green cap was casting a line, oblivious to the distressing silence of the fish. I took the simple option and went back to bed.

For the next three or four weeks I cooked up all sorts of plans to get rid of Winslow. I thought again about strangulation, fell back on poisoning, and leaned toward asphyxiation once more. I even thought about making a hole in his boat, hoping he wouldn't know how to swim, or setting fire to his cottage, maybe employing a hired assassin, but didn't put any of these plans into action as I didn't want Bill to be orphaned. I ate Winslow's fish, spitting it back out onto the four-hundred-million-year-old rock any time a talking fish went by, prancing in front of the mountains, and let Winslow become embedded in the landscape as if I had a choice in the matter. Trying to make the most of Mirror Lake, I endeavoured, like any animal focused on survival, to establish a certain routine. After a while I even managed to smile again, which was enormously pleasing to Jeff, who was starting to worry. I was sure my life in Maine would unfold like this—between Winslow, Bill, and Jeff—but was forgetting that there are six billion of us on the planet, and just how real the risk is that one or other of these six billion degenerates might leave his house one morning, deciding on a path leading right to Mirror Lake and bringing with him everyone else who has it in their head that I deserve no peace or quiet.

I'd chosen Lolita because of Nabokov's novel and Juliette Lewis's performance in the remake of *Cape Fear*, where she plays one of the most authentic Lolitas created in cinema or literature since Nabokov's. I hardly expected Juliette Lewis to turn up, but was secretly hoping the girl would have the same full lips and, if I paid the asking price, that I'd be able to convince her to reproduce the actress's demonically sensual pout. Since bringing a girl out to the already overpopulated Mirror Lake was out of the question — the casting agent, so called, would no doubt have refused anyway — I came to an arrangement with the agency's impresario, as he styled himself, and set up a meeting with the girl in question at a motel in the nearest village.

From the moment of my arrival at Mirror Lake, I'd limited my forays out to a few quick stops at the state liquor store and the Mirror Food Market, but the fervid dreams that had for some time been waking me in the middle of the night, alternating with the nightmares in which Humpty Dumpty conspired to drive me crazy, were a fair indication to me that I'd not attained that degree of asceticism necessary for me to forget my needs. So I decided to act, particularly as I was terrified the two categories of dream might mix. If ever that happened, I could well find myself doing stupid things to Humpty Dumpty and subsequently be fit for the asylum. I should add, here, that contrary to what you might think, the temptations at Mirror Lake were numerous, particularly in my bedroom closet, where I had stumbled upon enough girls to destabilize even the most ordinarily constituted men.

Out of masochism, magnanimity, or plain stupidity, one of my predecessors had left an impressive collection of magazines ranging from *Real Smart* and *Paris Sex-Appeal* to *Playboy* and *Penthouse*, along with *Duke, Rex, Jem, Chicks and Chuckles, Girlie Gags*, and other monthlies in which the spread of scantily clad flesh constantly tested my determination to abstain from all contact with the opposite sex. For me, such contact had only led to tortured relationships in which, invariably, I would be admonished and at the same time it would be demanded of me to be a man, specimen of a species whose essence I'd never quite succeeded in capturing.

When I discovered the magazines, that part of me I wrongly or rightly associate with man's intrinsic nature experienced a sudden surge of vitality, and I spent several evenings leafing through the matte or glossy pages asking myself how the devil women were so beautiful. That's when the torrid dreams started, despite my quickly subscribing to a pact with my conscience that allowed me my solitary pleasures with the magazine, this doing no harm to either of the protagonists involved, what with their having consented to their respective positions freely, but that wasn't enough. The morning I woke up with a sore wrist I dismissed any scruples, grabbed the telephone, and came to an arrangement with the impresario, even though I have a horror of motels and would need to embark on an unanticipated journey into the world of men for the sake of a woman's touch.

I asked for room 11, that number having brought me luck in the past, and went there to wait for Lolita with a bottle of bourbon. Drink would help me forget that Lolita's real name could easily be Conchita or Marie-Chantal, or that I was about to pay for a woman's scorn in order for her to let me access a part of her body where dozens of others before me had cried out before getting dressed again. The notion of deriving pleasure from a body some lamentable destiny had dedicated to communal usage pushed me to drink more, all this as the reflection of a drunkard was distorted in the mirror of the plywood dresser.

From the evidence, Lolita had never read Nabokov and must have been persuaded to choose the name because of its slightly vulgar exoticism. When, finally, she arrived—a few minutes late, one drink too many in her, the figure she cut resembling Anita Ekberg's more than it did the delicate Juliette Lewis's—I was relieved, not only because she distracted me from my reflection, the alcohol metamorphosing it in the dusty mirror, but also as the image her body conveyed had none of the frailty my fantasies would have defiled. As she asked me to wash the part of my body that had led me to this motel, I secretly thanked her and then I downed another glass, this time to try to forget that I was hard despite or because of the shame—and, too, to forget that the room was already rank, even before I'd touched her, with the smell of cold cum.

It was quick, as it has to be. You don't linger in the dispassionate arms of a woman who wants nothing more than to be done with you. Nonetheless, after folding up my money and slipping it into a minuscule fake-leopard-skin purse matching her underwear, which was bigger than the purse, Lolita leaned toward me, offering me a view of that voluptuous valley of death into which men have been blindly hurling themselves for centuries, insensitive to the dangers archetypal memories should guard us against. Then she did what all women do when confronted with sad men: she kissed me on the forehead, slid a hand through my hair, and attempted what, in my distress, I really wanted to interpret as a smile. This tender gesture, which perhaps had no other purpose than to show me I wasn't as bad as all that, still managed to tarnish the image I had of myself, which was already in pretty bad shape. I'd left the world I came from so that I would no longer have to see what men did to beauty, how their vulgarity diminished it, and now the maternal instinct of a whore, even as it proved to me the inalterable gentleness of a woman's touch, had emphasized my own ugliness.

Had Lolita not made me feel so tender, I'd have high-tailed it out of there. Instead, I murmured that I'd like to see her again, feel her hand caress me again. Since I'd been fascinated by her curves from the start, these having the

49

same hypnotic power as Anita Ekberg's, I added without further ado that I would call her Anita from now on. She must have thought Anita the name of the woman who'd gotten me into such a state, because she accepted immediately, again with that hint of a smile striking me like a blade right in my chest, right where I thought myself invulnerable.

When I returned to Mirror Lake, Bob Winslow was waiting for me, Jeff was waiting for me, Bill was waiting for me. They were all wearing the same fearful, reproachful look that was on my mother's face when I came back from my first school dance. I was propelled forty years back in time, to a period of my life when the only thing I knew about the female sex was that they bled every month and that this bleeding could turn sin into drama. I must have started a good two weeks before, trying to convince my mother to let me go to the dance that night, promising to mow the lawn all the way through to December if necessary, to be in by ten o'clock every night, and to keep my hands where I was supposed to when I was dancing with young girls—which meant on their shoulders, whatever the dance and whatever mockery I risked in consequence—all this a lot to pay for the privilege of seeing Rosie, Rose Bolduc, outside of school hours and to be able to admire her in the wrinkled cotton dress revealing her knees, which I was sure would be as white and soft as boiled eggs. But it was a price I was willing to pay.

So I was present that evening and behaved as my mother wished, partly because I knew breaking my promises would weigh on my conscience, though mostly because Rose Bolduc, the only girl worth starting a life of lies for, had eyes exclusively for one Gilles Gauthier, an imbecile whose sole positive feature was his James Dean mane of hair, though the majority of the girls hadn't even heard of James Dean and to this day I still wonder what they all saw in Gilles. Basically, I was a model of good behaviour. I lightly brushed fat Ginette Rousseau's neck, accidentally, as we danced an imitation of a waltz to a Fernand Gignac song, though we'd all rather have let it all hang out to an Elvis or Beach Boys hit. The musical selection was the task of the school principal but we tried to get what we could out of the school snoozefests, as we would call the school dances from then on. Julien Lapierre had heard the word in some movie, I think: "What a snoozefest." Without Julien Lapierre and his movie, the dances would simply have been "boring school dances," an expression with way less character and no chance of being passed down through history.

So I had behaved myself, which did me no favours, because when I got home my mother was waiting for me in the kitchen with a look that decreed once and for all that I was a man, and that men desperately wanted flesh. I never forgot that look, nor Rosie Bolduc's knees, nor Ginette Rousseau's half-horrified, half-delighted stiffening when my fingers slipped involuntarily from her shoulders to her neck, nor the sheer boredom of the deathly dull evening. Most of all what I remembered was my mother's expression, traces of which I could now see in Bob, Bill, and Jeff's gloomy faces as they waited for me by the cottage with unjustified panic.

"Thank God," Winslow shouted, rushing over and putting his arms around me, using words and gestures I'd long hoped for from my mother, who was always quicker to reproach than to show tenderness. But Winslow's relief was not derived from my having escaped my demonic temptations, which wasn't the case anyway, but from the fact that I was alive, never mind the lapses I might be guilty of.

"There's been an accident on the lake, a total fucking drama," said an out-of-breath Bob, wiping away the sweat running down his face. A man, whom Winslow had naturally thought was me, had got into my boat and taken to the water—and then the boat capsized, the man sank, and there was nothing Winslow could do about it. "I thought you were dead, Bobby, I thought you were fucking drowned," he repeated, passing a crumpled handkerchief over tears I'd thought at first were sweat, and—confirming that I was alive, that I'd escaped death—the words kept swirling around in my head: *dead, drowned, a man in your boat, Bobby.* And then I realized Winslow was calling me Bobby, that bonds are forged in drama, and that fear, afterwards, brings people closer.

I was annoyed by this familiarity and, simultaneously, Winslow's agitation was irritating me, and yet the feeling that a man was worried about my fate, barely an hour after a woman had sought to relieve my pain, moved me more than I cared to admit. So I put a hand on Winslow's shoulder—his concern deserved appreciation—assured him I was as right as rain and then added, suddenly realizing the seriousness of the situation, that we should still go and get the cops. Winslow agreed but didn't budge, so I held out my car keys, pretending that I was suddenly feeling dizzy. This wasn't very fair of me, I could have asked Winslow to call, but apart from not wanting him to know I had a phone, I hated histrionic displays dragging on, drowning in tears, in snot, swamped in liquid words and ending up making emotion look ridiculous. So I dispatched Winslow before he suffocated me in a resurgence of joy.

As I waited for his return I sat down with Bill and Jeff by the lake with a man in it, or, more precisely, with the body of a man in it, dead in my stead, wondering if it would resurface or wash up on the bank before the divers arrived and mulling over the identity of the stranger who'd shown up at my place, taken my boat, and disappeared into Mirror Lake's abyssal depths.

As I kept an eye out for eddies in the lake heralding the improbable resurfacing of the drowned man — whom I would call at first John Doe, when the need to name him occurred, and then, when the desire came to shun the anonymity of Doe, John Doolittle, and then, when his anonymity became the thing that characterized him, John Doe again — I started to draw geometric patterns in the sand. I joined them together in an effort to make meaningful shapes: a stick man, a school or a skyscraper (depending on whether you were looking at it vertically or horizontally), a Big Bird costume, then a tin of peas, before erasing all of it and starting again with squares, triangles, rectangles, small circles inside big circles, diamonds inside hexagons. This activity not only allowed me to kill time, but also had the advantage of erasing the image of the man at the bottom of the lake, who wouldn't have bothered making his bed in the morning had he known he wouldn't be lying on it again that night. It's crazy what we would or wouldn't do if only we knew what was right around the corner. Just as well we don't.

To put John Doe and his misfortune out of mind, I abandoned myself to non-thinking, to that delicious feeling of veering close to the void without being driven crazy by it. Then the slam of a door, a salvo of barking, two more doors slamming, and voices talking in short sentences interrupted my meditating on a circle lifting me into nothingness. So I got up, brushed off my pants, and went to meet Winslow, who was flanked by the county sheriff and his deputy. Winslow introduced me to them as the survivor, the man who *didn't* die.

The sheriff, with his Ray-Bans and toothpick, could easily have been mistaken for Tim Robbins in the movie *Short Cuts*, which for me shows Robbins's unequalled talent, his ability to take on the appearance of guys who then start to look like him, and I immediately pegged the sheriff as a rotten cop, along with his acolyte, since rot spreads and makes more rot, and, statistically speaking, men rot fast.

After a quick look around the place, they interrogated me about my comings and goings, about which I lied, failing to mention Lolita's caress of my forehead, before they asked me if I'd been expecting anyone, if I had visitors often, if I had any ideas concerning the identity of the man who'd borrowed my boat, me answering "no" to every question as I observed my curved reflection in Tim Robbins's Ray-Bans, which made me look like Humpty Dumpty. Then they inspected my boat, which Winslow had brought back to shore by tying it to his own.

Which was when things got a little sticky, because there was a hole in the bottom of the boat through which water could have flowed, causing the shipwreck of John Doe, and from that moment I became a suspect, due to a breach that hadn't been there the night before, I swore, which didn't help my case. Then Winslow came to my rescue and said the boat must have smashed into a rock as he was hauling it in, which brought us back to the first question: What had made John Doe sink?

At this point in the interrogation my head was spinning and I would have been perfectly happy to have been absorbed by the nothingness of my circle but, given that the voices around me were occupying the space, I started to ramble. In my mind I'd re-baptized John Doe, who temporarily became Harry, because of the Hitchcock film where people ask who killed Harry, who Harry is, why Harry was wandering around the area, which weapon the fatal missile had come from and other questions pertinent to the discovery of an unidentified body. I asked myself the same questions, and then one thing led to another and I suggested the possibility of suicide: a guy's out for a walk, he's in despair, his life's hell, he sees a boat on a bottomless lake, hears a loon's heart-rending cry, wonders why he made his bed this morning, and puts his darkest thoughts into action. But Tim Robbins wasn't only corrupt, he was stupid. Not satisfied just to reject the theory outright, he also interpreted it—as I could see in the reflection of his Ray-Bans—as another way for me to conceal my guilt, no surprise as he was also xenophobic, just like three-quarters of the population of Maine, or of the planet for that matter.

What happened next is still confused in my mind. I became enraged, I think, and told Tim Robbins that I wasn't about to shoulder responsibility for the moronic John Doe's suicidal madness, this guy who'd not only shown up at my house to die but had also trashed my boat. Then I added that if I did want to kill someone, I wouldn't have chosen such an aleatory method—that's the word I used, "aleatory," because I didn't know how to translate the French word *aléatoire*. Not that Tim Robbins would have understood the word anyway. I'd said "aleatory" deliberately, remembering that I myself had considered using such a method not so long ago, planning to be rid of Winslow by making a hole in his boat, but then rejected the scheme for its being too *aleatory*, which wasn't the issue here. The issue was whether or not Winslow really had damaged my boat on a rock or whether someone— Winslow, for example—had freely elected to put into play the overture of a plan, if I can call it that, not intended for some John Doe randomly appearing at Mirror Lake, but for me, Robert Moreau. But the hypothesis wouldn't stand up, because why the devil would Winslow have wanted to kill me when *he* was the irritant and I was the one being irritated—i.e. I was the one with all the reasons for wanting to kill *him*. Anyway, if Winslow hoped to see me croak, he'd made a good start. He only needed to stay true to himself, a stance that enabled his committing the perfect crime.

Regardless, I was pretty shaken, this noticed by all three of the idiots looking at me as if I'd just tumbled down from the moon, the pale circle of which shone behind the mountains despite the sun being a long way from setting, and the sight of it reminded me of "Le soleil a rendez-vous avec la lune," that stupid Charles Trenet song about the sun meeting the moon. It had been a long time since I'd heard it, but I knew it would now be stuck in my head until the next day. Its banal lyrics would leave me fulminating against what some people like to call poetry, when any poem worthy of the name would have alluded to the disaster any meeting of the sun and the moon would cause, described the cataclysm brought about by such a meeting, or maybe related the phenomena to the refraction of light, the otherness of mirrors, what do I know. A poem like this would have talked about the blindness of the stars colliding with each other, or the influence of the tides on the madness that lacerates the stomachs of people whose chests and throats have already been cut. I must have hummed a few bars of the song in question, because Winslow said "Trainy," meaning Charles Trenet. I walked back from the edge of the lake in Tim Robbins's

Ray-Bans to where Humpty Dumpty—that is to say, a sadly misshapen reflection of myself—was opening his mouth to say "moon," which made me realize why, when they turned to look at me, they were all staring so beatific-ally. Not wanting to make things worse, I pulled myself together, apologized, and stared at my reinforced toecaps so that I'd no longer be looking at the moon, Humpty Dumpty, or Robbins's deputy's hand, ready to draw his weapon. I named the deputy Indiana Jones because the greenhorn obviously thought he was Harrison Ford and was just waiting for an outburst of evil in order to become one of those heroes America anoints with glory as fleet-ing as it is pitiful, a derisory pleasure I was not about to accord him.

I apologized and then murmured—in French, so they wouldn't understand—that I wasn't planning on giving this cowboy his tabloid moment. Besides which, he'd never get over it, because nobody can really withstand fame's ephemeral aspect. There's nothing sadder and more pathetic than a man repeating the same story for twenty years and thinking that is enough to earn his father's respect, impress a classmate, or make a woman love him. It would actually have been a good trick to play, but I wasn't about to take a bullet in my stomach just to poison the future of a cretin I would not even see grow old, given that I'd have died in the flower of his innocent youth.

At this point in my ruminations, the slamming of two more doors reverberated around the mountains, and Robbins went to greet a couple of guys pulling diving equipment out of a yellow truck. Then there was some sort of discussion in which I preferred not to involve myself. Winslow walked over and we sat down at the edge of the lake with Bill and Jeff at the spot where I'd been drawing circles and perfect equilateral triangles that Bill's small paws and Jeff's big ones had turned into fractals. Then the divers headed out to the middle of the lake in their yellow canoe, which made me think about yellow as the colour of madness, or that's what the books say. I don't know why. I've never seen a crazy person turn yellow.

Finally, as I was dwelling on the waxy hue of madness, the yellow stopped moving and the divers toppled backwards out of the boat, crouching like toads, though of course toads don't dive like that, and I remember thinking that the reason we call divers "frogmen" must be because of the flippers, not the diving. Then one memory led to another and the image of the girl who'd supplanted Rosie Bolduc in my most obscene thoughts came back to me with the divers' gentle plinks.

Leslie Bégin, she was—I hadn't forgotten her name. Her flippered feet made her feel ashamed, so that she never wore sandals, claiming she had a strange skin disease. The first time she showed me her feet, in the shadows of the hangar where we'd taken refuge, I thought of the monster that falls in love with Julie Adams in *Creature from the Black Lagoon*, and then of the creatures that emerged from the ocean millions of years before Leslie Bégin let out her first scream—of the batrachian, pseudo-batrachian, or archibatrachian line, I didn't really have a clue, that would lead in time to humans. Leslie seemed to me, then, to be nothing short of an evolutionary mistake, a monster that should not have survived. When she took advantage of my astonishment to stuff her tongue down my throat, I'd had the impression of being invaded by a salt tide and rescued myself before I suffocated. Afterwards, I started sexualizing Leslie's feet. Leslie became the centre of my fantasies and, when finally she allowed me to strip off her underwear, I traversed the memory of the time.

"The memory of the time," I murmured as Leslie Bégin faded away. Then I looked at the mountains, the lake, my own feet, Jeff barking a little for form's sake and then copied by Bill, who repeated everything Jeff said. But Winslow and I said nothing more than "The memory of the time." We watched the bubbles rising and disappearing around the canoe as we thought about the dead man. And then we waited by the now-still water for a head to reappear, for the silence of our waiting to be broken.

After a few minutes, Winslow declared they would never be able to fish him out, that the lake was too deep, and that if the man did reappear one day it would be because the lake wanted nothing more to do with him and had thrown him out. In the heat of the moment, it never occurred to me there might not be a dead man, that Winslow might have introduced this drowned character into the story in order for me not to see the hole in my boat and its irrefutable proof of his murderous plans for me. All I was thinking was that they had to recover the drowned man; I couldn't bear the thought of a dead person being at the centre of the lake, a person whose bluish body might rise at any moment and collide with my boat, his belly full of noxious gases rubbing against its hull. If the divers came up empty-handed, I'd be living in constant fear of seeing a face appear at the end of my dock, the face of the man who'd drowned in my place in my ruined boat.

Then, as the mountains obscured the first quarter of the setting sun, I began to confide in Winslow, something I never thought I'd be capable of. I don't know if it was the meeting with Lolita, or the atmosphere of tragedy hanging over Mirror Lake, but I suddenly felt as if my entire past was struggling to come back into my mind. I looked down at the ground and told Winslow nothing could be worse than not finding your dead, knowing they were out there somewhere in the world but not where this somewhere was — this essentially the defining feature of "somewhere," especially when you've not had confirmation of death. It was all a bit confusing, so I started to tell him about Alfie, a dog I'd had when I was a kid. I told him about the red car that had run him over and left him crazy, and then about the two men who'd taken him into the woods to put a bullet in his head, because that's what you do when animals are suffering. When I found out Alfie had gone mad, I told Winslow about the thousands upon thousands of lilac blossoms blooming — told him everything: about the madness of the lilacs, about my own madness, about the sun beating down on our heads, and the silence of the church bells that had scampered off to Rome to mourn Christ and wait for his resurrection. And then I spat the iron taste of my mouth out onto the sand, this happening to me any time I bite my cheeks and the skin breaks. That was the last time I saw Alfie, never saw his body, I said, finishing up with a curse, and with blood in my mouth, and then I squeezed Jeff's big head against my side, and started to curse again. "Winslow," I said, "I never saw his corpse, never saw the blood," and that's the worst thing, no cadaver to prove the death, no blood to show the pain had a cause.

So, if the corpse of John Doe doesn't float back up, we'll never know, we'll be asking for the rest of our days if this *foutu* John Doe (except I didn't say "*foutu*," I said "fucking"), if this *fucking* John Doe — because Winslow's obsession was bleeding sadly into me — if this fucking John Doe ever really existed. And that's when it hit me — just as the head of one of the divers emerged near the yellow canoe, the black rubber hood shining in the sun and his breathing tubes, like long external gills, making me think remorsefully of the silent cries of suffocating fish. That's when I first wondered if perhaps there was no John Doe. Maybe Winslow had made the whole thing up for reasons I didn't know and would never know unless Winslow admitted it or John Doe washed up on the beach. Without either John Doe or a confession, I had no way of knowing if the whole thing had been a lie, and I sank down into the sand, inch by inch, just as the other black rubber suit appeared amid the ripples of water and gentle atmosphere of the languid afternoon.

The divers hadn't found John Doe and never would

62

find him, because the lake was too deep, because Bob Winslow had lied, or because the fish of the deep had already taken John Doe's clothes, flesh, and organs and torn them to shreds, in celebration of the light they remembered haloing his body as it fell toward the hellish algae and zigzagged slowly down, like a leaf falling from a tree on a windless day.

"What colour were John Doe's clothes?" I asked Bob Winslow as I burrowed into the beach. But Winslow couldn't remember, hadn't been paying attention. Grey, maybe? Black? He didn't know. Why was I asking?

"No reason," I lied. "Just preparing myself for the dead man's return."

That evening I didn't eat with Bob Winslow or even at the same time as him. I stayed under cover of the trees looking out at the lake for John Doe, for John Doolittle, and wondering, "What, if he does exist, would make a man show up at a stranger's house, steal his boat, and go capsize in the middle of the lake, except distress, Jeff?" I caressed his big yellow head with its eyes shining out into the dark. "What, except fucking pain?" Then I went back inside and carried on surveying the lake from my window, Victor Morgan's novel on my knees. But nothing happened to disturb the peace of the starry night. John Doe was sleeping, and if called upon to haunt the lake he wouldn't do so in the shape of an ectoplasm, or a zombie with its flesh eaten away by maggots, but in the shape of nagging questions.

Despite John Doe not appearing as a ghost, I'd often see him prowling around the lake, whenever bad weather distorted the landscape and blurry penumbras that had been hiding in it for centuries revealed themselves. The first time I noticed John Doe, who'd in the meantime become John Doolittle, it was pouring with rain.

I'd been up since dawn, what with Humpty Dumpty deciding I'd slept enough, and went out to sit on the porch hoping the rain and westerly wind battering the cottage would dispel the images bogging me down. And this is, in fact, what the rain did, thus proving to me that our hopes don't always die like rats. The rain washed my face, soaked my sweatshirt, my ancient hole-ridden cotton pants covered in Jeff's golden hair — a bit gross now that the rain was plastering it to the fabric — and then the sandals in which my feet made a heavy squishing sound each time I flexed my toes. It was a reassuring sound, really, and brought me back to the reality of the day, opaque and grey, the pleasing cool of August dawns. Finally it soaked into me, a creature of little faith whose life in retirement was sinking into a daily torment of unexpected ennui, so far from the battle-field where men shoot each other at point-blank range.

I had barely reintegrated myself into the pain of daily life, which was not in the least bit preferable to the pain of the dream, if less abstract, when I saw a dark shape on the lake that seemed to be approaching the shore. If the John Doe incident had not happened, I'd have taken this dark shadow for what it no doubt was: a tree trunk ripped from the beach by the waves, except that the doubts I was entertaining concerning the truth about John Doe immediately put me on the alert and I leapt to my feet, only to notice that my legs were trembling and my heart was drumming out a jerky beat, maybe a rumba or a samba, as it had on one of the few nights in my twenties when I'd taken cocaine and tried to be part of the chic, fashionable world living life in the fast lane. I remembered nothing of this dead time, not even the one or two bits of flesh I'd savoured on a Garouste and Bonetti couch to the tribal rhythm of my atavistic impulses, though I did recall the whip-crack of the coke almost sending me to an early grave while the entire continent of Africa thrashed out a pulse beneath my sternum. I felt the same thing that morning by the lake, shaken as I was by the sudden rush of adrenaline that made me leap to my feet and able to see my heart's wild somersaults lifting the fabric of my soaked sweatshirt. Jeff was also on the alert and looking in the same direction as me, his ears pricked up and ready to race over to the intruder the second he detected a note of exasperation in my breathing. We stayed like that until the blurry shape disappeared, or was once more swallowed up by the lake's restless swells, and I rushed to the beach, legs shaking and

Jeff at my heels, begging Mirror Lake to release the dark shape and give it back up to the rainy light of this August dawn, but all that animated the lake now were a few white crests, in which I was naively convinced I'd spotted the hypothetical John Doe several times, his face foaming with drool that was quickly whisked away, along with his face, by the lake's uncharacteristic turbulence.

After conceding that the dark shape I'd mistaken for John Doolittle was nothing more than a figment of my imagination, I went back into the cottage telling myself that if not all hopes die like rats, certainly the majority of them do — that people are swimming in a sea of dead rats. This hardly improved the opinion I had of my fellow humans, the company of dead rats being all they deserve. Then I shut the door abruptly and intimated to Jeff that he should stay on the carpet. That's actually the verb that went through my mind, *intimated*, when I said, "Carpet, Jeff, stay there," in English to make it clear I wasn't joking, then I undressed next to him and, stark naked, went to stand by the window, observing the rats accumulating on the beach from there, as I pondered the supposed magnificence of my nudity. Only women can be said to possess such "magnificence," I decided, remembering Anita's opulent flesh that I'd not seen again, but had dreamed of enough for her to sense, even from miles away, the lewd waves incited in me by her body, which was soft enough to lose a hand in without its being swallowed up. Then I realized I was bored, which was not part of my retirement plan, and that the rain was simply reinforcing this boredom.

So I did what all bored people do who are lucky enough not to have a television so they can't fool themselves into thinking any old junk will help them escape the emptiness: I looked for someone to call, headed to the phone and called Anita's pimp, no doubt irritable because of the rain. That bandit sent me packing, saying that if I wanted to pay for a whore in this weather, I was going to have to go out. He didn't actually use the word *whore*, but that's the word I heard in the go-to-hell tone of the jerk's voice, which made me want to retort that Anita wasn't a whore, but I let it go, lacking any convincing arguments, and went back to the window and noticed that I couldn't even make out Bob Winslow's cottage on the far shore.

I was alone, like any one of the thousands of dead rats the tide was bringing up, and this wasn't quite the feeling of solitude I'd been hoping to experience in Mirror Lake's forest, far from the harrowing pressures of a more gregarious society. It was a kind of solitude that renders you bitterly conscious of the burden of existence and leads you to understand why men sometimes seek out the company of others. I would never have believed it possible, but I was actually starting to miss Bob Winslow, whom I hadn't seen since John Doe had arrived at Mirror Lake, though I suppose boredom can make you irrational. I even considered stashing a bottle or two of bourbon in my new boat, the other one having been turned into firewood, and paying Bob Winslow a surprise visit. But the voice of Anita's pimp, yelling at me that he wouldn't even make a dog go outside in weather like this, was still ringing in my ears. "It's raining cats and dogs," he'd berated me, though instead I heard *It's raining* tarts *and dogs*. So I got drunk all by myself. Well, no, with Jeff, even opening a beer for him—just this once wouldn't hurt, and besides, he doesn't care for bourbon. And then I tried to wait for the storm to blow itself out.

To kill time (which is just an expression, because if there's one thing you can't kill it's time—time is unkillable, absolutely immortal), I leafed through some of the magazines my generous predecessor had left behind. But I would have preferred Anita's hot, living presence, so my heart wasn't in it any more than the rest of my anatomy was. Nevertheless, I embarked on a little sociological analysis, and what surprised me most was that a good number of girls from the fifties looked like housewives, or like ordinary girls whose clothes had somehow evaporated just as they were getting ready to make a trip to the post office or put a chicken in to roast, and this depressed me, because I couldn't help thinking of my aunt Jeanne, whose Himalayan chest had always held such fascination for me. As I have more of a propensity for guilt than incest, the magazines suddenly seemed soiled to me, but I carried on flicking through the pages just for the sake of it. My ennui was depriving me of ideas, and then I came across Anita Ekberg—the real Anita, the one and only—tanning herself in a studio setting above a text box about Sophia Loren. Talk about *la dolce vita*! I may be a little paranoid but I'm not a masochist, so I set that particular magazine aside, and things went from bad to worse. It was as though all the stars of the fifties and sixties, from Jayne Mansfield to Kim Novak via Gina Lollobrigida and Jane Russell, were in league against me. When I came across Marilyn Monroe reclining across a double-page spread singing "Do-be-do, do-be-do!" I thought, *Whoa, that's enough*! and stuffed the whole lot into the closet and got dressed.

I'd not managed to kill time, but had given it a little shake. Outside, night was falling, the sky was still discharging its overflow onto the thirsty natural world below, but my boredom hadn't evolved in the least. Over on the other side of the lake, I could now make out the light of a lantern moving in the fog, a sign that Winslow was walking along the bank. This reminded me of John Doolittle, whom I'd put on the back burner under the wily influence of alcohol and Anita Ekberg. Maybe Bob Winslow had also noticed a dark shape appearing at the crest of a wave, and he was searching for the body that the storm had scraped up from the bottom of Mirror Lake? What else could he be doing out in the rain, swinging a lantern like that in the fog? Maybe it was a message, or a distress signal. I was absolutely clueless about signalling with a lantern, but Bob Winslow didn't know that, and maybe he was desperately trying to get in touch and translating the rudiments of Morse code into a language unknown to me.

This was the pretext I'd been waiting for since morning to dispel the atmosphere of gloom covering the landscape in opaque grey. I didn't hesitate for a moment, fetched Jeff, a flashlight, and two lifejackets and put them onto the boat, which was as ostentatiously new as Marilyn Monroe was showily beautiful. I did forget the bourbon, but that was no big deal, since I was already drunk and Winslow had a stock of De Kuyper and Gritty McDuff's in his cellar. And then I set off astride the waves, ready to brave the hostile swells.

I had a little trouble leaving the bank because the waves kept driving us back to the dock, which was banging into us in turn and pushing us the other way. We were stuck in one spot for long enough that I exhausted my supply of swear words, and as remaining stuck on the north shore wasn't an option, I jumped out of the boat and pushed it into the lake until I was chin-deep in the water, while Jeff navigated. Then I had to return to shore a little way in order to climb in myself, and promptly found myself face down on the bottom of my spanking-new boat, which I christened *Jane* as a tribute to Jane Russell and Jayne Mansfield, without even sparing a thought for my own aunt Jeanne, whom I'd relegated to the limbo of my childhood, and I swallowed a wave as Jeff, tossed from one side of the boat to the other, barked hard enough to destroy his vocal cords. When I chanced a look behind us, I noticed we'd been pushed back to the dock again. Another man would have abandoned the entire plan, but I was me and couldn't help myself. Knowing how useless it is to fight one's own nature, I picked up the oars, flexed my muscles, and used my biceps to give the boat a big shove, which propelled us a good three feet from the dock, then another shove, accompanied by a manly grunt.

And we were off, I just had to keep the rhythm going, and I maintained it by mangling "Po' Lazarus" as sung by James Carter & the Prisoners in the Coen brothers' *O Brother, Where Art Thou?*—by far the best movie I'd seen in the last few years. I'd have liked to identify with George Clooney, playing the movie's hero, even though he's not exactly sparklingly intelligent in it, but the waves pushed us ceaselessly to the side, so much so that I felt like a useless idiot and instead identified with John Turturro's character, who was, as we say in Quebec, as dumb as the moon. I started wondering about why we associate the moon with being not very smart, this bringing the stupid Trenet song about the sun meeting the moon back into my mind, his tune interfering with "Po' Lazarus," which I then massacred even more. I set my compass for Winslow's lantern, Turturro disappeared into the storm—just as he does in the movie, when a big wave of water comes out of nowhere and carries him off—and finally I slipped into George Clooney's skin, all smiles, teeth white enough to gleam through any fog.

When I set foot on dry land, which reeled a little until my centre of balance regained its bearings, Bob Winslow was completely beside himself. "What the hell are you doing on the lake in such a fucking goddamn storm, Robert? It's raining tarts and dogs." He didn't say "tarts," but that's what I heard, because I was happily experiencing an interruption to my boredom, despite Winslow's obvious anger. "And why the hell are you screaming like a pig? They could hear you in Alabama," he added, which was appropriate because the Coen brothers' movie is set in

71

Mississippi, the rotten state next to it. "Wasn't screaming, Bob, was singing," I said, but he wasn't listening to me, so I told him that I'd seen his lantern. "I saw your lantern, Bob," and I felt sorry that in English there's no distinction between *tu* and *vous*, because he would have felt the warmth of my using *tu*. Up to that point, I'd been calling him "*tu*" in my head, but scornfully — *go fuck yourself, Winslow, tu me fais chier* — though now there was a genuine congeniality to my use of the first-person possessive, as in, if it wasn't *ta* lantern, as in a lantern belonging to you, my friend, I'd have stayed put and been condemned to moping wearily at home.

"I saw your lantern," I started again, "and thought I saw a message in it." But since he didn't appear to understand, I told him about the dark shape, about John Doe's multiple shadows in the storm. That assuaged him somewhat, because Winslow also thought he'd seen the body of John Doe appear — which was the reason, if I wasn't mistaken, that he'd been surveying the bank with swings of his lantern and hoping to spot the stranger who'd disturbed the peace of Mirror Lake — its eyes bulging and catching the glow of the lantern light like the eyes of a wolf in a patch of pine trees. And that's when he admitted to me that he'd been keeping a lookout for the dead guy — hunting the deer, so to speak — since dawn on this grey day, speaking with a trembling voice in which I could make out not only the entirely normal fear of someone preparing to fish out a stiff, but also genuine anxiety quickly confirmed by his haggard eyes and slightly dilated pupils.

Winslow was effectively behaving as if he'd not at all expected the dead man to resurface, from which I deduced that, as I'd suspected, he'd been lying to me about the existence of John Doe, alias John Doolittle, whose existence was becoming more hypothetical by the minute. If Winslow was in fact so concerned, it meant he was afraid of ending up with the cadaver of a man who wasn't dead— or, more precisely, with one that had never existed in the first place. He was caught in his lie, and the piece of shit certainly hadn't expected a cloud of phantoms to head over to the south shore and make him pay for his deception.

My anger was giving way to boredom, and I was preparing to leave him marinating in his remorse, rain or no rain, drunk or not drunk, when suddenly he collapsed onto a stump, wailing that he couldn't remember the colour of John Doe's clothes and this was haunting him. "I'm haunted, Robert," the idiot snivelled. He claimed it was bothering him so much that he was wondering if he'd invented the whole thing, if he really had seen a man take my boat and my boat leave the dock and then a man disappear— that is, *drown* in Mirror Lake's unfathomable depths. So he'd needed a body, a corpse, just as I had once needed Alfie's cadaver to prove to me that love had meaning. At which point I said, "Stop, Bobby, *whoa*, hold on," because I didn't understand what was going on anymore. I was the one who had reason to be suspicious, and here he was stealing my role from me. Either Winslow was a born actor or I was the king of fools. As I couldn't decide one way or the other, I dragged Winslow into the cottage, where we proceeded to get drunker than anyone had ever done in the entire history of Mirror Lake, with him incessantly wailing that he couldn't remember what colour John Doe's clothes were— "Maybe it was because he was completely naked, Robert"—and me replying, "Completely naked," like Anita Ekberg, whom I'd undressed without her permission as I flicked through my magazines.

Then I noticed I was calling Winslow "Bobby." Alcohol, when mixed with worry, boredom, and loneliness, leads to the unexpected; mostly to fear, in my case, because once again here I was afraid of having fallen into the hands of a crazy man, or of going totally insane myself, which would have made no sense. So it didn't take much to persuade me when Winslow, after his De Kuyper, got out the crème de menthe, which I called *crème d'ectoplasme*, given the presence of John Doe's spectre in the waters and in homage to the Pink Flamingo Sperm cocktail invented by Boris Vian and Louis Barucq, a barman with a fantastic imagination, but we couldn't concoct this drink with our *crème d'ectoplasme* because we lacked the necessary ingredients.

We really tied one on, the kind of session that leaves you with a gap in memory as inconsolable as the headache in which the memories have drowned.

The next morning I'd made no progress. You might even say I'd moved backwards. I woke up around noon underneath Winslow's porch, off which I figured I'd tumbled, my left buttock hurting as much as my skull, and I wondered why daylight felt the need to be so cruel every morning after the night before. I decided it must be to punish us for being so stupid. When I tried to stand up, the world did a perfect flip-flop, ten out of ten, the lake immediately climbed to the ceiling, and vice versa, and I could no longer tell if it was the water being reflected in the firmament or the other way around. Suddenly I spotted an arm poking out from behind the pile of rocks Winslow had built close to the lake now occupying the space where the sky should be, and then it was my heart's turn to do a thunderous somersault — John Doolittle!

The storm really had ended up bringing us John Doolittle, who must have been curing by the rocks since the small hours of the morning. I wanted to yell to Winslow that Doolittle had surfaced and was wearing a grey sweater — he wasn't wrong, he wasn't crazy and neither was I — but the echoes of my first shout made a bit of my brain jump out, ripping off my uvula as it passed, so I settled with emitting a few curses *sotto voce*. Painfully, I swallowed the few drops of saliva I'd managed to extract from the little recess between my gums and the back of my tongue, and then, in an unequalled act of bravery, I managed to shout out. When I arrived at the point of sacrilegious moaning, I saw the grey arm moving through the blue sky and simply passed out, fainting being the only means I had of escaping: you do what you can with what you have.

I wasn't unconscious for long, because when I opened my eyes the arm had only moved a few inches, this enough to show me that it was attached to Winslow's shoulder, which was emerging, dishevelled, from behind the rocky outcrop. "*Baptême*, Winslow, what the fuck are you doing there?" I cursed, careful to speak softly, and entirely in French, because moaning in English was beyond my abilities at that moment, and then I fell back to sleep to the delightful image of Bob Winslow throwing up our *crème d'ectoplasme*.

On my third and final wake-up, the sun was setting behind the mountains, a light breeze was ruffling Jeff's golden fur, the dog was licking my face with bona fide love — eternal, doggy love — the lake had settled to its proper place, and I'd not moved one iota. As for Winslow, he was still stretched out near the rocks, wearing the grey sweater that had almost belonged to John Doe, giving off spectral vapours from the night before, and sporting an enormous bruise on his forehead that might have made me laugh had I not been afraid of the effect it would have on the extremely fragile, quarter-inch surface covering the entirety of my skull, which was saturated with deadly alcohol.

"Fuck," I heard him murmur, and that was the only word he uttered, except for "black" when I asked him how he wanted his coffee, and then I took to the lake with Jeff again, floating on top of the last of the pink clouds the calm water was absorbing, and all the while trying not to think of pink flamingoes or Boris Vian, with whom I was seriously annoyed, concentrating instead on the sweetness of the remaining cirrostratus disappearing beneath the boat.

Over the next three days Winslow and I kept to our-selves, this for the best, as otherwise we'd not have been able to avoid seeing the extent of our stupidity in the other one's puffy demeanour, the periwinkle blue of our eyes striated with red. I also needed to come to terms with Winslow's significant and disconcerting resemblance to me, looking as if he could be my brother, congenital flaws included, and that I'd never know who John Doolittle looked like.

I was still entertaining a glimmer of hope when Tim Robbins and Indiana Jones came back on the third day, bringing a couple of photos of a guy who'd disappeared into thin air the day John Doolittle drowned. They showed up shortly after lunch in a cloud of dust, tires squealing and the handbrake pulled with a crunch, stepping out of their 4×4 in perfect synchrony. As the dust settled, these two unblinking figures called to mind Arnold Schwarzenegger's impressive physique as he rises up out of the debris in *Terminator*. "I'll be back," I heard him say over the scene's gentle music, and then Robbins started walking over, gravel squeaking under his spurred boots. As he approached, he took some photographs out of his pocket and threw them on the steps, where I was sitting and not bothering to get up, in a gesture that was theatrical to say the least.

"Ever seen this man around here?" he asked as he chewed on a toothpick, and for a few seconds I could see Humphrey Bogart lurking behind his features, though he disappeared along with Schwarzenegger when I realized that the Ray-Bans were waiting for an answer.

The photographs showed a guy of around fifty, unsmiling and not wanting to smile — just like Robbins, apparently, in whom the ability to do so seemed to have atrophied when he was young. The man in the photograph had the ravaged face of a man who's lived hard and feels proud of it, which describes pretty much all the men I'd met in Maine, but his face was unfamiliar to me.

"No," I said to Robbins.

"Sure?" he barked, looking me up and down with the sort of disdain you would display for something contempt-ible or vaguely repulsive.

"I'm sure," I replied, letting it be understood that that would be my last word on the subject — and that I found the man repellent, too. He packed the photos away and told me that this shifty-looking character had disappeared the same day John Doe drowned in my boat, and he emphasised the "your" — *your* boat — so maybe he could be the drowned guy or, worse, there could be one guy who'd drowned and another who'd gone missing. That was all I needed on this beautiful sunny day — two John Does instead of one or, worse again, a real John Doe and a fake John Doe, since there was nothing to prove there even was a drowned man. And if that was the hypothesis we started with, then the cheerful fella staring at the photographer through the lens as if he wanted to slit his throat might still be running around the countryside on the loose. "Oh *great*," I muttered to myself, spitting on the four-hundred-million-year-old rock, which had done nothing to me and didn't deserve it, except that the whole point of scapegoats is to suck up other people's spontaneous angry gestures.

Before leaving, Robbins handed me a scrap of crumpled paper with the number where I could reach him should my memory come back. That's not what he said, but it's what he thought, so mentally I told him to take a hike, *va chier, Robbins*, though I smiled his way, because suddenly I had an irresistible desire to taunt him but also to see if the mimetic effect of my smile had the power to make him unlock his face muscles. But no, Robbins had something of the icon or statue about him — or more prosaically, a plastic doll that only closes its eyes when you tilt it. His sinister expression valiantly resisted my charm, so I didn't bother tiring myself out by smiling any more.

As he left with Indiana Jones, who'd been miraculously absent from the scene, I knew we'd see each other again. *I'll be back*, I heard again in the cloud of dust that also evoked John Wayne and the Wild West, the words a sinister warning that the mountains repeated as an echo at the very same moment that I rose from the steps and a bird, a single one, flew past and relieved itself in the immensity of the blue sky. "Shit!" I exclaimed, an interjection that seemed especially apt, before taking my clothes off and, pride to the wind, proceeding stark naked to the beach, where I slowly immersed myself in the cold water and washed off the minuscule chickadee or sparrow shit shining in the silver of my hair. I tried telling myself it was no big deal, that dust returns to dust just as bad luck follows the unlucky around, this and other ineluctable truths it's as pointless to try to avoid as it is to attempt to stop a bird from flying, a fish from swimming, a grasshopper from hopping, or a man, let's say, from running to his ruin. Which, incidentally, is precisely what I felt I'd been doing ever since I'd come to Mirror Lake. Heading slowly toward the precipice, I was helpless to put a halt to the movement because the machinery had been set in motion the day I'd hit the road believing I'd left everything behind me when in reality everything was clinging to me the way a duckling sticks close to its mother's butt.

Ever since John Doe's hypothetical drowning, I'd not ventured out on the lake much at all. I'd cut my swims down to quick dips, or made do with getting my bottom half wet at the edge of the beach, and now I'd had enough of that. But the lake would soon disgorge multiple John Does, so better to behave as if everything was normal and rub their heads in the mud should they bother me or hinder my movements. I inhaled a big gulp of air and dove into the clear water, eyes wide open and taking in the muddy rocks of all different sizes carpeting the bottom of the lake, and then the specks of quartz in the sand glinting in the sun in the places where the water was shallower. Finally, I was able to breathe, three feet below the surface, carried by some dark liquid mass that I had always thought of as the element between elements, liberating and purifying, that ensures both joy and redemption. Here I was free again, regardless of all the John Does in the world, in the cool amniotic spaces that give me back my life, washing me clean of the grime blocking my pores and the filth growing in my brain like mushrooms—not poisonous enough to kill me, but rotten enough to make me sick. In short, I was in waters ridding me of all the dirt corrupting my life.

I must have been swimming for a good half-hour, alternating between periods of breaststroke, diving underwater, floating on my back, and doing frogs and swans. I had to keep pushing Jeff off, because he was constantly trying to bring me back to shore and becoming hysterical anytime I disappeared for a few seconds, because he loved me unconditionally, this dog. I hadn't felt such lightness of being since the day of my confessing to all possible sins merely to have a few months' respite, and now I didn't want anything to impinge on my happiness—not even a dog's unconditional love, which exists to warn you of the world's innumerable threats. That's what love does, that's its job. Don't go on the rocks, don't run in the storm, don't cry in the dark, the kind of love that makes you suffer by tearing at your heart, like in the song "Avec le temps," when Léo Ferré sings, *"Don't stay out too late, don't catch cold."* Every time I hear the song my emotions are laid bare, which is why I absolutely did not want Jeff to start humming Ferré's lyrics about the pitiful that morning.

To unsettle Jeff, I hummed "Boo-Wah Boo-Wah," by Cab Calloway, and then went to slump on the sand, out of breath but content, purified, new. This was exactly what I'd come to Mirror Lake for, these moments of pure symbiosis with the self occurring at the heart of a silence in which thought is finally absent. After which I started reflecting on happiness, about how it comes from such ordinary things and we're too stupid to realize it, too stupid to bend down and gather them up, put them in our pockets, shut our big mouths. So I tackled Jeff head on and started wrestling with him, just as we did in the good old days, despite his being too old for it really. I couldn't even have said when the good old days had ended, or where I would trace the line marking the border between a life upright and an existence on the skids, but in this blessed moment I was propelled back to a time in my life when all I knew of bitterness was that which I read on the tense faces of people scraping the ground with their clipped wings.

Carried away by a nostalgia still tinged with innocence, I promised Jeff we'd swim some more even if he was afraid, even if I was afraid, because it was so good after the fear. Effectively, I was offering nothing less than a promise of paradise, because I also loved him unconditionally, the way men do when they have nothing else left but their dog, even if I knew full well a simple rain shower would wash away my promise in a sea of indifference and that I would have to wait until I was senile to start gambolling around in the green and aromatic meadows of the good old days.

Waiting on senility, which I wouldn't wish on anyone, I pretended to be young. But youth being too beautiful to last, the rain shower soon arrived in the form of the Robbins-Jones duo, their 4×4 throbbing on the other side of the lake. I lifted my head, what with my being in the position happy men adopt when they've been wrestling with their dog — shoulders to the ground, knees wide open, chest panting. And when, in a familiar gesture, Robbins hitched up his pants so you could see he had balls and where they were, a veil of anger stronger than I was briefly passed over me: the guy made me want to kill him.

This, I think, was the moment Jeff began to hate Tim Robbins as much as I detested him myself, when he realized the game was over and Robbins was the reason for my frivolity's unexpected demise. He started to groan; I joined in and started muttering, and together we watched the scene unfolding on the other side of the lake, same as the one we'd participated in an hour before, miming Robbins's responses, which were rather laconic responses, and Bill's, though he didn't have much to say, and Winslow's, whose lip movements didn't match the script, but admittedly it's difficult to lip-read at such a distance. What I mean is, I noticed Winslow was gesticulating much too much for him to be answering with words of one or two syllables. After Robbins's departure and the return of calm, which went hand in hand, even if Robbins always left a lingering stench of late-stage compost behind him, I had to resist the desire to jump in the boat and go see for myself if Winslow knew the guy in the photos, as this might have explained the length of his gesticulations, and so I stopped here, given that my visits to the far shore usually culminated in new irritations.

As I'd resolved to give in to salubrious euphoria, I rushed to the end of the dock hollering wildly and threw myself noisily into the lake, throwing up around me one of those cavalcades of water I call "atomic" because they're the same shape as a mushroom cloud, and then I swam, got out and dried off, and then swam again, wrestled with

Jeff again, going on like that until a sweet exhaustion took over our play. By the time we were back inside, a fine rain was drizzling on Mirror Lake. We ate in front of the little people starting to panic on the lake, all of them identical, thousands and thousands of minuscule John Does trying to shelter from the rain, not realizing that they themselves *were* the rain, before sinking one after another down to the depths that terrified them, not realizing they themselves were the depths, and that the darkness of Mirror Lake was nothing other than the accumulation of as many minuscule John Does and John Doolittles as a mirror without a bottom can contain.

When I went to bed that night, I was fairly certain the minuscule John Does would follow me into sleep, and I was right. After a first act I've pretty much forgotten, although it had something to do with flying fish, I found myself in the middle of the lake, where thousands upon thousands of John Does were unceremoniously jostling each other, like in a disaster movie when the panicking crowd flees the aggressor and tramples over children, old people with walking sticks, pregnant women, and the blind, who might also be old but don't carry two canes as a single white one already indicates they cannot see and their trembling demonstrates the other aspect.

To sum up, I was in the middle of the lake, just one John Doe among many, when I spotted Anita Ekberg, whose head was sinking under the water as a result of the stampede of Does. "Help!" she called out in Swedish every time she resurfaced. But her shouts were utterly pointless, what with the Does, who didn't know who she was and didn't care, continuing to trample spitefully on her skull. Listening only to my courage, and anticipating the passionate kiss to which I'd be entitled when we washed up half-naked on the beach, I launched toward her, realizing I knew how to walk on water like an amphibious Christ. (This was the dream's logistical side.) In anticipation of the kiss to come, I grasped her long curly mane, no longer curly because it was wet, and loose hair a foot long is always longer than a braid that would only measure twelve inches if it weren't in a braid any longer, towing her in to firm ground, where we fell into the same position as Burt Lancaster and Deborah Kerr did in that torrid, unforgettable scene in *From Here to Eternity*.

Just as the violins were getting louder and I was getting ready to enter eternity by putting my tongue in her mouth, Ekberg offering herself up to me with touching abandon, Humpty Dumpty was tossed up onto the beach by an unexpected wave, probably a wave of nausea, which threw me three or four feet away from Ekberg, and he took my place next to her and pressed his big round belly against the curve of hers. How could their lips even meet in such conditions! I have no idea, because at this point of the dream turned nightmare, I was back in the middle of the lake, where a horde of John Does, galvanized by fear, were riding in my direction.

"Marilyn Monroe," I whispered, and Anita headed my way from the fan on the bedroom floor that was making her skirt whirl up as in the famous photo of *the* Monroe, a radiant smile on her raspberry lips. And then she struck Marilyn's pose, coyly holding her skirt down over her knees and swinging her hips out. That's when I stopped her; when I said, "Stop, Anita, whoa, stop, change of character." Irritated by my abrupt tone, Anita switched off her smile, tucked her butt in, and then the fan made her skirt fly up again, revealing her fake-leopard underwear and completely breaking the spell my command had already discombobulated, because I couldn't imagine Marilyn Monroe wearing underwear like that, unless she was playing a girl in the jungle, a role to which, happily, she'd not been lowered.

"Sorry," I said. "Sorry, it's just your underwear." So, naturally, she wanted to know what was the problem with her panties, which led to an endless discussion in which I ended up conceding that her panties were perfect, even though I was lying, even though she knew I was lying, and eventually I agreed to start the Marilyn scene over to make her happy, but my heart wasn't really in it. I swore to myself that never again — even if the comment in question was measured, subtle, delicate, and nuanced — would I remark on any part of a woman's anatomy or any item of her dress.

It was one of the first things I'd learned when I started encountering the fragility of the opposite sex — to shut my mouth, to not point out to a girl impatiently waiting for your positive appreciation that a lock of hair is misbehaving, or that her new dress is maybe a little, oh, just a teensy bit revealing. But spending time with Jeff and Bob, who were less sensitive about their physique, had made me forget this golden rule. The modelling session fizzled out, Marilyn was swallowed up by Anita's leopard-print underwear, and I proposed other imitations to Anita but in vain; she had turned into a waxwork because she adored Marilyn, she idolized Marilyn, and she'd long been ready to act out the scene which she had, I have to admit, reproduced with a certain amount of talent. I even suggested the greats — Rita Hayworth in *The Lady from Shanghai*, Grace Kelly in *Dial M for Murder*, Gloria Swanson in *Sunset Boulevard* — but only managed to increase her resentment. I'd tarnished Anita's sense of her own sex appeal, and this, I took from her silence, was the worst thing you could do to a woman.

It was the fourth time Anita and I had met up, and we'd invented this game at our second meeting, when we discovered a shared love of cinema that had quickly transformed our client-whore relationship into something a little less ornery. Of course, she still expected remuneration, and of course I still always did what I was paying for. But we'd added a playful aspect to our relationship which had led to our becoming better play-mates, you might say. Anita was bored stiff in her own backwater, caught between a pimp who was as much of a bastard as a pimp can be, and a boyfriend, if you could call him that, who, fearing reprisals from the impresario's associates, had found a way of hitting her without leaving marks, the impresario himself unable to beat people up because of his arthritis, and who, in any case, only dirtied his hands beating his girls.

However, that day the game had lost something of its flavour and, when we left the steamy bedroom, the fan's blades must have blown a cool breeze across the sheets we'd not managed to wrinkle.

Out in the asphalted courtyard, I was still trying to cheer Anita up by monkeying around under the plastic palm that barely threw a shadow over the dirt-filled swimming pool, but she started to cry, her eyeliner running, and I wondered what I'd done to set off such a meltdown.

"You don't like monkeys?" I added carelessly, to make myself seem interesting and because I was helpless — utterly useless — in the face of these inexplicable tears that can only be provoked by a man's stupidity. Then, before she ripped my guts out, I apologized: "Sorry, Anita, I'm stupid, I monkey about your time," I said, my attempt at English drawing a feeble smile out of her — a smile, inci-dentally, that had the same effect as a load of TNT on a beaver dam, her hesitant rictus smile immediately giving way to another terrifying volley of tears. By that point I had absolutely no idea what to do, so I just gave up.

Ten minutes later I was sitting next to her on the edge of the pool, my arm around her, her head resting on my shoulder, our feet in the dirty water, asking myself how it was possible that I was mopping up the fallout from a lovers' quarrel, even though I was no more in love with Anita than I was with Winslow and, let's face it, she was no Juliette Lewis. As I waited for Anita's final snivels to fade away, I looked at the insect corpses drifting around in the water, pushed by the little wavelets Anita's feet were stirring up as she gently and rhythmically kicked the pool's slimy wall. When Anita finally said she had to go home, I peeled the remains of a moth off my left calf, examined it closely for a while thinking what disgusting little creepy-crawlies moths were, and we both headed our separate ways, me toward the lake and she toward her dump, her pimp, her boyfriend. As I watched her Ford Taurus disappear along the road, I thought that, of the two of us, I was the one in the more enviable position, which wasn't hard given the shitty life she led. But, regardless, the comparison would help me not to get too upset the next time Winslow paddled merrily "over the blue summer swells" and toward my cottage.

Back at my house, I went to sit by my window, a little stunned by a day in which, like some drone-bee excited by the promise of nectar underneath the inviting circle of Marilyn Monroe's skirts, I'd hoped to sample Anita's delectable pollen. In the state I was in, I could have done

89

with watching a movie, and preferably an action movie: one in which the women don't cry and the only part of your brain that needs to do any work is the damage-assessment part. But I hadn't brought any of the trappings of my former life with me — no TV, no video player, no DVD player, nothing at all — believing the majesty of the silence would be more than enough.

So I fell back on *The Maine Attraction*, which I'd abandoned on page 94, right in the middle of a passage in which Jack Picard, the brute Morgan cast as the hero, talks about the women who have passed through his life, starting with his mother, who thought she was Marilyn Monroe and whom he'd murdered one evening as she was walking the streets. Sordid stuff. I closed the book again, took Jeff outside, and picked up a piece of wood to throw for him, pretending to be happy, behaving as though I were free of human limitations. But it was a lousy day, as so many are over the course of a life, and my efforts to challenge the laws of nature were useless. When a day is lousy it's lousy, the process is irreversible, when something has fallen from the tree it can't be put back, when it's split it stays split, when it's boiled, *idem*, it can't return to being firm, it can only bend and sag, when something is born with a flaw, time can't help. Winslow's arrival only confirmed the day's lousiness. I hadn't seen him coming, busy as I was trying to add colour and light to a day ending in darkening cumuli.

If Tim Robbins's showing up was always like a disagreeable drizzle, I'd have put Winslow's more in the category of a *diabolus ex machina*, his sudden appearance always managing to worsen a situation that didn't need worsening. Here he was coming over to talk about the man in the two photos, someone I'd not forgotten but was forcing myself not to think about. Winslow was sure he knew the guy, but couldn't remember when and where he'd met him. I told him he should go ask Robbins, whom I called by his real name, Paquette, but Winslow didn't like the idea at all. But it seemed as though Paquette had decided not to approach Winslow either, preferring to sort things out without him.

And then Winslow casually asked me, point-blank, if I'd noticed that Paquette looked like the dirty cop Tim Robbins had played in a movie, the name of which he couldn't remember. "Did you notice that, Robert? They're like two peas in a pod."

"Yes, they're like two drops of water in a pond," I replied. "Two John Does in a pond of boredom." And then I said, "*Short Cuts*, the movie was called *Short Cuts*," and from my answer Winslow deduced that I too had noticed the resemblance.

"Amazing," he said, slapping his thigh, without specifying whether he thought it was amazing that Paquette looked like Robbins or that we'd both used the same reference to establish the similarity. Frankly I didn't care which, because Winslow was starting to seriously annoy me with his mania for doing everything like I did, including thinking.

"But where does that get us?" I continued.

"Nowhere, it's just funny," he said, though I couldn't see anything funny about it. It seemed more depressing than anything to me, and I would have gone in to bed if I hadn't noticed that Winslow was hovering near the four-hundred-million-year-old rock and waiting for me to show some manners. So I invited him onto the porch and went inside to get a couple of beers, pointing out that unfortunately they were my last ones, which was a lie, but I didn't want Winslow hanging around for too long. He hung around for too long anyway — so long that I looked like a complete fool when, after I'd shared a whole pot of coffee with this guy determined to stick around, I miraculously found two more beers, and then another two. "There's a god of drunkards!" the buffoon guffawed, or something like that. I forced a laugh and watched the yellow sky disappearing behind the mountains between two cumulonimbus clouds, a sign of bad weather the next day.

The evening dragged on interminably, but Winslow did tell me a couple of details about the man in the photo, who, he was convinced, was not the drowned man. He was so certain, I decided there must actually be two John Does, unless Winslow had lied about the first one, the drowned one, which was what made him so sure. Indeed, if Winslow hadn't seen anyone drowning, the man in the photo couldn't be the drowned man, logically speaking, unless he'd also drowned.

To put it clearly, there was either a drowned man and a disappeared man, two drowned men, one missing drowned man, or one missing man who hadn't drowned, at least not yet, none of this helping me in the slightest. But I did learn that the man in the photos was dangerous because Robbins—that's what, between ourselves, Winslow and I were calling him from then on, "Paquette" not suiting him at all—had told Winslow to be careful.

"Be careful, Bobby," Robbins had said as he was leaving Winslow, an enigmatic phrase Winslow would puzzle over, while for my part I noticed that Robbins hadn't warned me, this not surprising me, since it was obvious this great-great-grandson of a French Canadian was more racist than the founder of the Ku Klux Klan and had sworn to himself that he would make me pay for the misery my face and accent triggered in him. Never mind. As far as he was concerned, I was racist too, which was proof that you can hate even the residue of your own race. This strain of bigotry must have a name, I was thinking as Winslow pissed away his third beer behind a third oak and I had a bit of time to myself. "Everything has a name, if it exists it has a name," as Wittgenstein almost said, but still I couldn't come up with it.

Afterwards, we picked up the conversation where we'd left off, wondering what we should be careful of, but our narrative was not yet sufficiently illuminating, so we'd have to wait for Robbins's next visit to find out. Then, as a cool breeze started blowing, Winslow stood up, immediately followed by Bill, who had been sleeping at his feet, and Jeff and I were able to end the evening in peace, watching a few shooting stars fall behind the mountains.

The fact that the universe has neither beginning nor end is beyond my understanding, as it is beyond most people's, but the opposite seems just as inconceivable, so every time I look up at a starry sky I start hoping God exists for him to explain all this to me once I'm in heaven. At least, that's what I used to hope, when I could still claim a small chance of going to heaven. I know now that I'm screwed. If God does exist, he'll be sending me straight to hell, which can't be all that different from here. This is what makes me saddest, believing that hell is basically just a reproduction of the earth, with maybe a few more volcanoes, deserts, forest fires, and fire eaters, but above all a higher proportion of idiots. Some other company would be welcome. Anyway, after Winslow left that evening, I was certain I would be awarded a place in heaven alongside Gandhi, Malcolm X, Jeff, and Martin Luther King.

"Look," I said to Jeff, pointing randomly at a star, "that's where we'll be soon, you and me," and Jeff followed the tip of my finger as if it really was heaven up there. Dogs are like that, they understand the immensity of microcosms, the inexhaustible power of small groups of atoms, while the rest of us are trying to confront the universe, yet oblivious to the fact that we are the universe and we are nothing, like the thousands and billions of John Does of the rivers, oceans, mountains, and galaxies. Then, as the star I'd called John Doe A-01 disappeared behind the clouds — *A* for August, for the alpha, the beginning, and *01* to mark my first and likely last attempt to name Mirror Lake's skies — I petted Jeff's big head, which happened to be the centre of my universe and of all the universes orbiting in my saturated mind. Then I started to cry, I don't know why, probably because I wasn't happy — that's a good reason — a fact the sky's beauty made me realize, no doubt because I felt useless and it was too much, all this, the night, the stars, Jeff's big head, though probably, in the end, because I was not so stupid that I did not see my life was slipping away and that this changed nothing, absolutely nothing, in the order of the cosmos.

"What are we doing here, Jeff?" I whimpered, the lake blurring with the shimmering of my pain while a brook, a stream, a river of brackish water flooded the dozens of tiny craters emerging in the surface of my hot skin. "What the fuck are we doing here?" I asked, but Jeff didn't answer, he was happy simply being, which was the only valid answer to such a question. I took him in my arms, he didn't resist, and we said "I love you" to each other in the water of the doleful night and its abundant stars, Bob Winslow perhaps doing the same thing on his side while taking refuge in the invisible fog shy people conceal themselves in when the sky is really dark so that nobody is able to witness their distress.

I couldn't speak unreservedly to Winslow's suffering, but as apparently we did have some things in common, there was every chance that a man on the other side of the bottomless lake was sitting on the sand with his own dog in his arms and water in his eyes, wondering what human existence was all about.

Indeed, there was every chance — and here I told myself that, deep down, Winslow wasn't a bad guy — that maybe I could get used to his presence, not really having any choice in the matter. When I think back on it today, I realize the stars sealed the bond between me and Winslow, that and our relationship with a pair of dogs, the love we had for them and that they had for us, encouraging our shadows to mingle on the bank when time was slowing us down. It happened long ago, so long ago that a few stars must have died in the meantime, and others lit up, and yet more exploded in the gaze of depressed men believing in nothing but the love of dogs. As for the world, well, it hasn't changed. We're still obliged to kill each other invoking one of the names of God, who, given the circumstances, must be regretting that we ever invented him.

To make Pink Flamingo Sperm you need crème fraiche or Nestlé condensed milk, L'Héritier-Guyot Crème de Fraise, and cognac, Rémy Martin preferably. This was the present I'd decided to give Winslow to show my goodwill and provide a little boost to a relationship I'd only invested in due to a sense of urgency that wouldn't abate. After weeping beneath the stars, I'd slept like a baby, which is always what happens to me after a bawling session, and in the morning I felt unabashedly generous toward the man who'd been snivelling in silence along with me on the far side of the lake.

The sperm idea hit me during breakfast. In the sky, delicate pink and white clouds were converging due to the heat of the sun, and Anita Ekberg's wan image floated on the horizon. Soon after, Ekberg disappeared, but the clouds, as always happens when you're in a good mood, started making all kinds of animal shapes over the mountains — lions, sheep, giraffes. All the classics, basically. A flight of ducks had traversed the lake at the height of the pinks, and I hallucinated flamingos, a flight of flamingos from the east, off to drink the nectar of the gods. Ten minutes later I was singing "La vie en rose" in Julia

Migenes's accent as I drove along in my Volvo 2000, Jeff's ears pushed back by the wind streaming in through the passenger-side window, the two of us joyously making our way to the state liquor store and celebrating friendship.

The liquor store had no L'Héritier-Guyot Crème de Fraise, so I decided on a crème de cassis that looked kind of gross and was a bit too pink, but could be diluted with a couple of extra spoons of cream. To make up for this, I also bought some good champagne. And then I left, warbling "Summertime" in Louis Armstrong's hoarse voice and accompanying the warble with a few Gene Kelly dance steps — and hey presto, what a wonderful world! "Summertime, and the livin' is easy," I hummed to Jeff as we got back in the car. "Yes, the fish are jumping," he replied, careful not to make crooning fish appear in front of the windshield, but only little fish shivering with joy. The lyrics of "Summertime" were followed by those of "Lady Sings the Blues," and when turning a corner I spotted Anita on a park bench — the other Anita, the real one, not Ekberg — appearing beaten up and distressed, staring into space and smoking what looked like a joint.

I braked suddenly, double-parked, and ran over to her. I'd never seen Anita in such a state, and had I seen her like that before I'd never have wanted to see her again. She was wearing a pair of those hideous baggy sweatpants with a wide stripe on each side that I called, and still call, "hanged-man pants," because they sag so awfully that you need to be on the brink of being beyond repair to ever wear such a horror. She was also hidden behind a pair of no-less-hideous sunglasses shaped like a duck's tail, their large size failing to hide the green and mauve circle decorating her left eye. Evidently her boyfriend had forgotten how to hit without leaving a mark. If the bastard had been there with us, I'd have invented, just for him, a type of torture that would make all the torturers on the damn planet flinch, but bastards are never there when you want to kill them, and I was hoping only one thing: that he was at that very moment dying deep in some back alley, soaking in the last pint of blood left after the careful attentions of the sidekicks of Anita's impresario, who was at least good for something.

"That fucking bastard," I began, but Anita interrupted with a flailing gesture of her hand, adjusted her glasses to make sure she really did know the person she thought she recognized and then, convinced it was truly me, threw herself in my arms and started crying. History was repeating itself, and dourly, which isn't to say that all histories repeating themselves are dour, but that dourness is anchored in repetition, and as Anita dried her green and mauve eye on my striped summer shirt I thought to myself there was enough for a syllogism there and led her to the car, where a police officer was about to give me a ticket. I let him amble on and dodged discreetly behind a tree, because Anita still had her joint, which I crushed into some dog shit in which I'd already stepped.

My rare experiences with drugs were all a long time past, but I'd have happily smoked the joint myself. The first one I ever smoked was in identical circumstances, except

that it was winter, I was fifteen, and the person I was holding in my arms wasn't a woman but Gilles Gauthier, the
pretty boy who'd stolen Rosie Bolduc from me. She'd just
dumped him, throwing a dictionary in his face. Even had
he been about to breathe his last, I'd never have believed
myself generous enough to hold Gauthier in my arms but,
given the stunt Rosie had pulled, his hot breath rank with
the smell of beer provided me with a feeling so close to
enjoyment that I'd gripped him very tightly and given him
a few words of solace, explaining that sometimes books
make people less stupid, and getting a good whack in the
face from the Larousse wasn't going to do him any harm.
Then I took the joint he was trying to light and went to
lie down at the crest of the little hill behind the school,
and drew owls in the snow as, through the marijuana
smoke, I counted the stars that even back then already
fascinated me.

I can't remember how many stars I counted, though I
do remember how clear the sky was, how magnificent the
night, and the way the future, now that Gilles Gauthier was
no longer an obstacle to my desire, seemed to be opening
up for me. Everything was perfect. The snow wasn't cold
and, if we ignored the squeaking of the rusty chains of the
old swing half buried in in it, the silence of the schoolyard
was complete. That squeak, evoking so many happy memories, was like gentle music born of laughter and a carefree
time when we used to fly higher than the stars, higher than
the sun, short of breath but not of dreams. In my mind,
everything was mixing together in a sweet ballet that the

years would transform into melancholy, but right then it was as light as Rosie Bolduc's skirts, spinning through the stars like the kids we used to be. I even saw a shooting star, which burned itself out in the middle of the Great Bear, the only constellation I can confidently identify, and took it as a sign, doubling it up with a wish that one day Rosie Bolduc would become my wife, in the sight of other people and of God, who finally seemed to have adopted me. Then Rosie showed up dressed in veils, the veils flew back, stroking my face on their way past, and I fell into a dream as soft as what I was imagining under the veils.

Ginette Rousseau woke me up by putting her big chubby hand on my cheek. "Robert, you'll freeze to death," she whispered, as if it were a big secret.

In the languor of my dream I mistook her for Rosie and embraced her, which only added to the poor girl's confusion concerning my feelings for her, despite my pushing her sharply away as soon as I realized the lips gently descending from heaven and touching mine were not actually Rosie's.

"Robert Moreau, you are seriously high," she said a bit more loudly, brushing off the snow clinging to her wool coat. Words over which, in time and space, the ones Anita had spoken superimposed themselves. "You look completely stoned, Bob," she said, which was true, because for a few moments I'd been enjoying the quasi-magical power of reminiscence, though I'd just come back down to earth and right into the shit Anita pointed out to me. "And you have shit on your shoes."

"I know, I step in shit on purpose, I like it," I answered, wiping my Doc Martens on the green grass and then resuming our trip to the car.

"You got a ticket," she added, cocking her big sunglasses at the little scrap of paper tucked under the windshield wiper. "It's not your day."

It really wasn't. At least, it wasn't anymore, because it had been a few hours earlier, when I was drinking my coffee in the pink flamingo mist. I wanted to point out everything had been fine until she showed up, but stopped myself because it wouldn't have been kind, for one thing, and for another I didn't want to be the cause of fresh tears. I kept quiet and drove her home, where I waited for her to pack her bags so that I could take her to my cottage until we came up with a solution.

Anita lived in a one-bedroom place that could well have been attractive were it not for the innumerable fake-leopard-skin cushions strewn across the floor and the furniture, and I wondered what kind of cult made Anita so devoted to this animal rendered kitsch as soon as it is removed from its native savannah. Later — that is, the next day — I learned she'd been so since childhood, after a trip to the zoo with her father. Around the middle of their excursion, he went to buy her a cone of cotton candy and they both sat down on a bench in front of the leopard cage, where he told her incredible stories set in Africa, in which two baby leopards called Bambi and Bamboo had starring roles. Then her father foolishly promised her that one day they'd go see Bambi and Bamboo, who lived somewhere in Mozambique, and she'd believed him. And she believed him still, even though her father had moved on to new pastures and tossed her over his shoulder ages ago.

"It was the most beautiful day of my life, that brief hour in front of the leopards' stinky cage," she admitted before pursing her lips, biting them, and bursting into tears. Which made me really hate her father, along with all the other parents who put such ideas in children's heads, convincing them the world is beautiful, that carnivorous animals have names like Bambi, clowns are called Adolf, and sharks are called Snoopy. This sort of foolishness inevitably leads to Anitas living in fantasy worlds, waiting for a father who'll never come home again and burying themselves in cushions so they don't start screaming. Obviously I was wrong, Anita's case was special, and I shouldn't have resented her father for sparking her dreams in a zoo stinking of urine, but because he'd made her dream at all, for once in her fucking life, and because she idolized him.

Right then, as Anita was packing her bags, I was not yet cognizant of this story and thought the leopard print some kind of fetish, what with the matching underwear too, and I really didn't want to be involved. I simply asked if she could wear something else, take off her hanged-man pants and leave them on the bed, or, better still, pop them in the garbage chute. But I didn't say anything about the underwear, I'd already learned my lesson on that front, and this thing she had for spotted fabrics was obviously serious. I also asked if maybe she had some cream in the fridge for my Pink Flamingo Sperm, which I quickly described to her, and we set off again, closing the door on the dozens of Bambis and Bamboos sleeping in her bedroom and to whom I'd not had the honour of being introduced.

Ten minutes later, after a detour to the grocery store, we were driving to Mirror Lake but not whistling, Anita because she had no reason to be filled with joy, and me because I'd just opened up a corridor between the rest of the world and Mirror Lake, and because I was creating fresh ties with people I'd hoped to leave behind in my efforts not to have to endure the suffering caused merely by encountering another two-legged creature. Only Jeff was whistling, ears blowing in the wind as usual and his nose sniffing the mingling scents of the Maine forests—of hare urine, fox feces, and spruce tips, which were telling him stories whose meaning I, or any other man, would never understand. And it was better that way, not just for dogs but for all animals. Then, just as we were doing a U-turn, Anita said, "It's not John, it's Jack."

"What's not John?" I muttered distractedly.

"You think it's John but it's Jack," she went on, and since I knew no Johns other than the dead man, the drowned man, John Doe, naturally my thoughts turned to him and the possibility that Anita, contrary to all expectations, had caught wind of his identity.

"WHAT's not John?" I said again, less distractedly, emphasizing the interrogative nature of my words, and experiencing a mounting anxiety that nearly transformed my U-turn into a Greek omega: Ω.

"What the fuck are you doing?" she shouted, clutching the dashboard, "John or Jack, it doesn't matter, it's the same fucking end result."

"It's absolutely not the same," I yelled in turn, amazed to discover such nihilism in Anita, though I ought to have suspected it, given her profession. "The man is dead, Anita! The least he deserves is to be rescued from anonymity, even if we can't rescue him from the lake," I said, which made her not shout but scream, and I needed to stop the car because I'd already sent Jeff flying into the door twice and Anita was close to getting another black eye. I didn't care about me. All I wanted was for the truth to show its big pale face and for Anita not to throw up in my car, given that the truth always makes people want to vomit.

So I brought the car to a stop with a big squeal of tires that was a testament to my exasperation and, in a silence only broken by the chirping of grasshoppers, although you could have heard a fly if a fly had been passing, I repeated, "The man is dead, Anita."

She fiercely denied it, calling me a murderer, and then the whole thing devolved into a yelling match, which Jeff then waded into. I had to kick all of them out, the truth included, so that Anita would listen and understand I'd not killed anybody yet, neither John nor Jack. Then she threatened to start crying again, if only to make me listen in turn, so I would realize that she wasn't talking about the drowned man or even about the missing guy, but her boyfriend John, and Jack, her pimp. Basically, it was Jack who'd hit her, not John, did I understand?

I absorbed this piece of news with a long, very long, silence, because in my mind John Doe had just drowned again. Then I said, "The fucking bastard," an insult Anita thought was directed at Jack the pimp, and which she brushed away with another limp movement of her left hand. "It's not John, it's Jack," she repeated as I was loading everyone back into the car. And then I left truth in the ditch, because it would know how to find us again, and drove off.

When we arrived at the cottage, I sent Anita to bed, because I was tired and I was expecting Winslow to show up. Given that everything else was going badly, it was obvious the halfwit was going to appear and, sure enough, half an hour later he left his cottage and got into his boat with Bill. If we'd been in a movie, we'd hear the same background music playing in my head each time I saw Winslow heading for the north shore—the chords accompanying the shark's arrival in Spielberg's famous movie, to be specific—but we weren't in a movie, we weren't in anything, we were in life, where the predictable spooling of scenes doesn't trigger a soundtrack. So, to make up for the deficiencies of real life, I started humming the famous refrain, *DA-dum DA-dum*, and then the *DA-dum* became a sort of cosmic mantra and I lost touch with reality. I was propelled into an astral voyage smelling of patchouli, while Winslow's boat turned into an enormous shark fin, around which formed a vaporous, reddish cloud, before the stroke of a paddle made the whole scene disappear and brought me back to earth.

A few minutes later, Jaws arrived on the bank asking me what was wrong.

"Everything," I replied. "The whole nauseating predictability of life," I said, and then I told him to whisper, because someone whose identity he didn't need to know was sleeping inside, after which I tiptoed back into the cottage to make us a couple of Pink Flamingo Sperms, which we drank while admiring the sunset, despite the mixture with which we were trying to quench our thirst being frankly disgusting. Still, after the third glass we began to forget the taste and started seeing life through rose-coloured glasses, which was no small thing. I picked Piaf's song back up where I'd dropped it that morning, a sign that the links in a chain always end up being attached, and that a smile in the morning is no friend to distress. And then, since Winslow didn't know the words of the song very well, but was being joyously transported amid the flotsam of the sunset, he invented a game in which we had to list everything pink in life, from babies' skin to women's vulvas, and then anything with *rose* or *pink* in the name, from Rrose Sélavy to Rose Ouellette, a.k.a. La Poune, whom I felt obliged to describe to Winslow and did this so effectively that he fell in love with her on the spot. The gradual effect of our whimsical game was for us to discover that pink was everywhere in the universe, starting right at the bottom with coral reefs, climbing up dunes of fine sand, then moving into the trees and sky, from where it went back down again into the depths of the oceans.

"Fuck, Robert, we're surrounded by pink," Winslow said, somewhat prosaically, even though it was blue and green which actually dominated at Mirror Lake. But we didn't care, we were in a Rose Period just like Picasso's, and we drew delicate lines of magenta, fuchsia, raspberry, on everything we could. I even told Winslow about Rosie Bolduc, and he promptly fell in love with her too, which didn't bother me, because clearly he was having a tender moment and swooning at the slightest reference to feminine graces. Pink Flamingo Sperm might have tasted disgusting, but it had advantages, and we were just discussing Peter Sellers in *The Pink Panther* when Anita appeared.

"Pardon me, gentlemen," we heard her say, "but I must get ready for my scene. Tell Mr. DeMille I'll be on the set at once," and we turned around to see a larger-than-life Anita coming down the porch steps draped in the quilt that usually lay on my bed. It wasn't exactly the ideal staircase for Gloria Swanson's final scene in *Sunset Boulevard*, but Anita was credible in the role of a fallen and utterly lost star, what with her big, wide eyes, her long bare arms and commanding voice, gravelly from all the shit she took in every day: slaps, alcohol, and other junk hardly as smooth and creamy as our Pink Flamingo Sperm.

This was a wonderful present Anita was giving me, because I'd told her how much that scene moved me, the one where Gloria Swanson totally loses her marbles. Out of all the movie scenes I remember, out of all the ones that make you swallow noisily as your eyes, confronted with the tragic beauty of madness, fill with tears, this is one of the most upsetting. Swanson inhabits the role with such talent you really believe what you're seeing is true; you think she must have lost her mind during filming and hidden in a corner of the stairwell where the camera flashes of newspaper gossip pages bore down on her collapse in real time, so they could serve their readers bloody images of the dark side of fame and fortune. In truth, I've always thought gossip rags have more or less the same function as priests, their job being to keep the little people down and have them believe greed leads to death, as if poor people all die saints.

All this to say that Anita's performance was credible in the semi-darkness, what with the shadows roughly drawn on her face by the forty-watt bulb hanging at the top of the stairs. I told Winslow to shut up and, putting myself in Erich von Stroheim's shoes, went to film Anita Gloria in all her splendour. I shone the beam of my pocket flashlight on her, which only made her face more tragic, and shouted "*Cameras! Action!*" Anita gratified me with a wild-eyed look, lifted her chin, and pronounced in her smoothest voice, "Okay, Mr. DeMille, I'm ready for my close-up." I shoved the flashlight between my teeth and, holding my hands in the shape of a viewfinder, moved slowly toward her as Franz Waxman's music enveloped Anita's face and she became, through the magic of cinema, Gloria Salome, Anita Salome, and finally Salome Salome, her big octopus arms dancing and driving corrupt Herod Antipas crazy.

We did three retakes without any kind of plan, so much were we in our characters. When we were done, Winslow didn't know whether he should cry or clap, and Bill and Jeff hesitated between barking and howling, before, in an enthusiastic show of admiration, they were doing all four — crying, barking, howling, clapping, as Anita and I savoured the brief fruits of our glory and fell into one another's arms like two exhausted ageing stars.

"Bob Winslow, Anita Swanson," I said, by way of introduction, realizing that I didn't know Anita's last name. Then we continued our evening around a campfire, Anita and I wrapped up in my multipurpose quilt. Winslow, curious to know who this Anita was who'd fallen from the munificent sky, was for his part bombarding us with questions about how we got together, and discreetly avoiding any mention of Anita's mauve and green eye, about which she informed him anyway. It wasn't Robert or John, it was Jack, she said, which then demanded some further explication I chose not to be involved in.

We made a nice trio, we did, gathered in the warmth of our muted voices under an August sky parading the history of the universe in our faces with its displays of white dwarfs, red giants, the Milky Way, and other galaxies. We seemed to be part of a symbiosis in which you could hazard our well-being from the tranquility of our expressions. As for the dogs, they were resting peacefully at our feet, not even bothered by the crackling of the fire over which we toasted bread rolls that our memories would assign, in time, to the category of unsurpassable things, along with our mothers' cakes and pies — sugar pie for me, apple pie for Winslow, and sweet potato pie for Anita.

I was closer to my kind than I'd ever been before, and this intimacy simultaneously intoxicated and terrified me. I was well aware that the company of men — and women — would bring me no good in the long term, and, as I have repeated so often, this was why I had fled them. And now the place to which I'd fled had become a meeting place for lost souls eager to forget all pain — past, present, and future — by gorging on bread rolls and beer, Pink Flamingo Sperm having been excluded from the evening's cocktail menu. I wasn't about to wreck the moment. No, I wasn't going to tell them that life was shit, they knew that already, and life, whatever that is, would soon do that for me. I behaved instead as if the planet wasn't hurtling toward catastrophe; as if Winslow, Anita, Bill, and Jeff were not going to die. I ate my toasted buns and we carried on the game we'd named Pink Lady — in Anita's honour, and to keep it related to cocktails. But I did suggest we abandon pink in favour of yellow, since Winslow and I had pretty much done pink.

"Fire!" Anita exclaimed first, stirring the glowing embers.

"Blazes," Winslow said next, putting the word in the plural to include the dozens of little flames dancing in front of our eyes.

"Stars," I added, so as not to break the thread we were weaving that stretched from the glowing centre of the earth to the cold light of the stars. We remained as we were until the early hours, until, apotheosis of a Pink Lady in yellow, the sun appeared from behind the mountains, inspiring Winslow and Bill to get into their boat, delicate silhouettes against the yellow aureole of the sunrise — yellow, the colour of madness! — and glide over the water toward sleep.

Anita and I sat by the dying fire, waiting for Bill and Bob to reach dry land safely. There's no way we would have allowed any mishap and its resulting misery to alter the perfection of the yellow dawn. Then we waved at the two ghostly figures, who faded away with a noise of wood scraping over sand, and, the obvious culmination of our companionable night, went inside to make love, this time without greenbacks or a tiny imitation-leopard-skin bag, after which Anita introduced me to Bambi and Bamboo, two furry leopards whose scruffy little heads were poking out of the top of her travel bag. That's when she told me the zoo story, and then about the collection of Bambis and Bamboos in her bedroom, insisting that there were only four genuine Bambis and Bamboos in the entire world, the two who were waiting for her and her father in the Mozambique brush, and the ones her father, the bastard, bought her on that starry day in July 1980, and which she took everywhere with her like relics of lost innocence.

Just as she finished her tale, rain started falling gently on the metal roof, accompanying the wan sadness of a child turned lady of the night, and in a sudden burst of affection she grabbed my semi-hard cock. Then I closed my eyes, listened to the rain, and thought of those lines by E. E. Cummings, "nobody, not even the rain, has such small hands." I thought about Cummings's rain's small hands as I savoured the delicate touch of Anita's fingers on my cock—though her hands weren't particularly small—convinced I finally understood how this image came to Cummings and how people write unforgettable lines. A little later, after a sleep interrupted by dreams, Anita took me once again, but the rain had stopped, the spell was broken, and I wondered where the idea of *taking* someone came from, conflating the totality of a being with a chunk of erect flesh. A deep self-loathing made me grab Anita's hands, the rain's hands, and force them to move faster. I wanted to put an end to the lies; I wanted the only truth worth sustaining between two people connected by alcohol and sex to burst out in my orgasmic cry. But I didn't come. Three times in as many hours is beyond the capability of a man who's still drunk—a drunk man my age with a slightly enfeebled prostate.

Afterwards Anita yelled at me. Not because I didn't come, she didn't care about that, but because I'd rushed her.

"I'm not a whor—" she started, but stopped after the first four letters, aware that the denial, in her mouth, was not entirely plausible. She was right, though. Outside her hours of work, she wasn't a whore. Some people's work lives do spill over into their private lives, they carry on evaluating increases in mortgage rates while they're watching TV, or trying to find a solution to a plumbing problem or to a grammar puzzle even after turning the lights off, bringing their preoccupations into their dreams, cereal bowls, or the shower, but I could see Anita wasn't like that. As soon as she closed shop, so to speak, she was a woman, plain and simple, no more or less annoying than any other, if a little less content, and after closing time she was free to behave like women in more ordinary walks of life, as was her wont. But her job still coursed through the heads of men writing dirty scripts, even in the shower, which was effectively useless because it didn't erase the words.

I was a complete idiot and didn't have the right to make Anita uncomfortable, not here, not now — never, really, whore or not — and it took me a little while to be forgiven, but I managed to get there a little duplicitously by using Bambi and Bamboo, asking which was which, because nothing looks more like a Bambi than a Bamboo, and seeming interested in their story. "What part of Mozambique did you say, again?" And when I asked her about their names, she opened her eyes wide and looked at me, as if to say, *Bambi and Bamboo, you dunce*, so I specified, "Their surname, Anita, I'd really like to know their surname, and your real first name too, if possible."

A little signal flashing *Danger! Danger! Danger!* started blinking in her suddenly less-open eyes, the tension of the swollen eyelid signalling fear, the fear of getting too involved, of entering too deeply into the deadly territory of intimacy. She was ready to offer up her body and a piece of her past in the guise of Bambi and Bamboo, but showing me the ordinary girl, the Rose Bolduc or Ginette Rousseau hiding behind her pseudonym, was more difficult, more compromising, so I left her in peace.

A half-hour or so later, as she mechanically twirled

a lock of hair around her index finger, she murmured "Jeanne" in her thick Maine accent. "Jeanne Picard."

I was thinking of other things at the time, about the solitude of big spaces, maybe, about herds of caribou grazing in the Labrador tundra, about polar bears sunning themselves on ice floes while they can because the ice floes are melting as we watch, hurricanes rage out of control, and the ozone layer has decided to mosey off somewhere else altogether. I did actually envy those bears. I'd have liked to be one, terrifying people in order to be left in peace—*let me eat my damn fish without telling me about the levels of mercury or any other nasty things working their way up the food chain to poison our existence!* But that worried Anita, and I heard "Jeanne," a quiet, softly spoken little "Jeanne," as I was watching a polar bear travelling, its flesh swaying in the dull silence of a whiteness we used to think was eternal.

"Jeanne Picard," she carried on, and the polar bear disappeared into a gap in the Arctic ice. "Jeanne Picard, it's a shitty name, no one pronounces it right." It was because of her mother, or really her grandmother who left Quebec when she was four, when her father, the grandmother's father that is, thumped the table and announced they were moving to the States, where he thought hell would be less forbidding.

"A shitty name," she repeated, staring at her big toe. Which I was also staring at, thinking that big toes and small toes are the weirdest part of women's bodies. Hers reminded me of my third sister Viv's big toe. According to

Lou, my second sister in descending chronological order, Viv's big toe looked like Céline Dion. She'd noticed the resemblance shortly before I left Quebec, and ever since I had been unable to contemplate Céline without seeing a big toe, which I found depressing, just like her songs, because to my mind she has a big toe for a head. But what was worrying me most under the Mirror Lake skies was the accumulation of coincidences I'd been puzzling over and failing to explain. It was definitely strange that Anita had the same surname as Jack Picard, the protagonist in Morgan's novel, *The Maine Attraction*, a detail I'd almost forgotten. Maybe he was a great-uncle or a distant cousin, I thought, before deciding I was being stupid. How could Jeanne have any relationship whatsoever with a character from a novel? Be that as it may, I didn't like coincidences of that kind, not here at Mirror Lake. "Jeanne Picard," I repeated, looking her straight in the eyes, even if I had trouble seeing anything but the swelling around one of them, less mauve and more green than the day before, and she nodded, adding quietly that she would prefer it if I carried on calling her Anita, Anita Swanson, which henceforth would be Bambi and Bamboo's surname too: Bambi and Bamboo Swanson.

That worked out well. I had nothing against the Picards generally speaking, but Swanson seemed more attractive to me, more poetic, and I liked the relationship the name established between all the Swansons of the world and the oversized white birds singing of death on misty ponds. "Anita Swanson," I murmured, imagining the heavy rustling of the wings of a cygnet taking off from the twilit waters, and then I went out for a walk, followed by the echo of all the real and imaginary names proliferating on Mirror Lake's overpopulated shores: Jeanne, John, Bob, Bill, Jeff, Jack; Jeanne, John, Bob, Bill, Bobby, Jeff, Jack...

It took Winslow's arrival, as he cheerfully rowed himself over in his green boat, for me to decide Picard must be a more popular name than I'd imagined south of the 49th parallel. There could be no other explanation. The coincidence was due to either immigration or blind chance. I preferred immigration because chance, when it occurs too often, usually means the devil, and I didn't want the devil to be behind all this, absolutely not. I didn't want to talk to Lucifer, Beelzebub, or any one of their descendants. I would much rather talk to Bob Winslow, who was hauling his fat carcass out of his boat and asking me, with a wink, if I'd had a good night.

"It wasn't a night," I replied dryly. "It was a day, we went to bed at dawn and it was fucking good, thank you."

Then I noticed that another night was about to fall, that another sky speckled with the unknown was going to overwhelm us and we couldn't do anything about it, we couldn't do anything about anything, Winslow then proving this to the power of ten by announcing that he'd discovered the missing man's identity in a newspaper, "the man from the photos, you know." It turned out he was a prison escapee named Jack Picard, explained Winslow as he waved the newspaper article at me.

I don't know why, but the news barely surprised me. I could see it without reading the article, Jack Picard's name in capital letters, his jovial killer's mug with his prisoner number underneath, and all of it seemed normal, in the regular order of things. What disconcerted me was the fact that Winslow wasn't incredibly surprised.

"Don't you realize this man, this missing person, this Jack Picard, has the same fucking name as one of Morgan's characters?" I pointed out.

"Yes," answered the moron moronically.

"Don't you realize either," I said, more emphatically, "that this man is also a fucking inmate, Bob, a fucking criminal, like Morgan's Jack Picard?"

"Yes, but so what?" he replied, with stunning naivety. "Coincidence. Such is life."

"Coincidence?" I said, and my voice must have gone up at least sixteen octaves.

"Yes." The moron shrugged, as if he thought it totally normal that the bloodthirsty mother-killer Jack Picard had come out of Morgan's novel to take a trip to Mirror Lake.

"Coincidence, you said?" And this time I was screaming. "Don't answer again, it's not a question, *post hoc ergo propter hoc.*" I must admit I was starting to get annoyed, and when I'm annoyed, I don't know why — maybe teenage trauma — the rudiments of Latin I learned from the Brothers of the Sacred Heart have a tendency to surface. Unlike normal people, I don't lose my Latin, I find it, but all scrambled and disordered, without any respect for syntax, punctuation, or the logic of the words, and I say any old thing. "*Sapiens nihil affirmat quod non probet*," I threw out at Winslow, challenging him to prove to me what he was saying, then "*Quis, quid, ubi, quomodo, quando*, eh?" which shut him up as I carried on with a sincere "*Audi alteram partem*," and then Winslow replied that I could yell all I wanted in a dead language, he was sure he'd seen this man before.

"But you can't have seen this man, Bob! Jack Picard is a character from a novel, and a character from a novel has no face, no substance, like a ghost."

"How would you know?" he demanded.

"How would I know? How would I know? I've never written a novel, but I've read enough of them to know that a formulaic phrase like 'the deep black of his slanted eyes in the oval of his youthful face' is no indication the author used a living model. How would I know that you've never seen this man before, Bob? There are no pictures in a novel, Bob, not a damn one!"

And to this, the idiot answered, "So what?" and proceeded to give me a treatise on metaphors. According to him, Morgan was a fucking good writer, good enough to evoke faces, landscapes, atmospheres, stratospheres, rivers, oceans, volcanic eruptions, earth tremors, love troubles, and other states of mind in the attentive reader simply by using words. And as this was the case, Morgan would certainly have been able to paint a portrait that looked very much like Picard. "Isn't that what literature's all about?" he concluded definitively, scrutinizing me like a little lawyer.

"Stop, Bob," I said. "Whoa, *on arrête* right there." The entire ridiculous conversation was resting on a flawed argument, I said, trying hard to prove it to him. "Victor Morgan died more than fifty years ago, Bob, he can't possibly have known the Jack Picard in the photographs. And characters from books stay in them, they don't leave. They can go in but can't come out, *baptême*!"

I must have shouted a bit too loudly, that or offended her beliefs, because Anita came out onto the porch just then, with Bambi in one arm and Bamboo in the other, or maybe it was the other way around, to see what was going on. We quickly brought her up to speed, Winslow with his frankness, me with my recent headache, and explained we were talking about a man who'd gone missing in the area, a prisoner on the run. Someone who might be distantly related to her, I said, but she stopped us with a little wave, which was one of her habits, held Bambi and Bamboo up to her left breast, and told us she knew all about it, her boyfriend was a cop and sometimes let her in on a few details about current inquiries.

A cop?!... I widened my eyes and turned to Winslow, hoping to convey to him that I needed the crutch of a log or a rock, quick, that I wasn't sure I'd be able to stay standing, and he led me to the four-hundred-million-year-old rock, with which I was immediately going to make up, hoping its Devonian wisdom would allow me to keep my calm. "So," I said slowly, after reassuring myself that the rock was up to the task and swallowing the little bit of saliva left in my mouth, tucked in that little pocket between gum and cheek, "your boyfriend is a cop?"

"Yes," she said. "So what?"

There wasn't actually any problem, no big deal and nothing to quibble over, though I was sure to chew in half with my very own teeth the next person who said "So what?" to me. Be that as it may, I was becoming irritable for no reason, everyone knows dirty cops always have a whore within reach so they can be paid in kind for all the petty law-breaking they overlook. And everyone knows cops, and especially dirty cops, learn to hit without leaving any marks. It's not John, it's Jack, everyone knows it, everyone knows the archetype, why was I even irritated by it?

At this point in my deep reflections, I still had no idea if Anita's boyfriend was a cop in Arkansas or whether he was Robbins or the priceless Indiana Jones. If I'd had a choice, I'd have preferred to keep on being in the dark, but I didn't have a choice: I had to find out.

"Don't tell me your boyfriend is Tim Robbins," I muttered between a pair of deep breaths, and the suggestion made Anita burst out laughing because she too thought her boyfriend resembled Tim Robbins a bit. So there we go, that made three of us who thought so. What a marvellous litany of unexpectedly interwoven connections. All of which confirmed either that John Paquette, since that was his real name, really did look like Tim Robbins, or that the latter was just a really good actor, which I couldn't give a flying fuck about, even though I didn't know what a flying fuck was and didn't want to.

I went to bed to sleep on it, accompanied by my headache really making itself at home, and by Jeff, who hadn't
said a word all day. I left Winslow and Anita's shadows to
disappear into the night, along with that of Jack Picard,
who was prowling around the woods of Mirror Lake, and
John Doe, who might well be called Jack Picard and was
no longer prowling. Fuckety fuck and *turlututu*.

The difference between dream and nightmare, between nightmare and reality, between reality and fiction, is sometimes small—as thin as a piece of translucent paper, darkened by printed characters or not. It's so small we no longer know what to call that space-time in which we strut and fret while the great cosmic machine continues to breathe to the rhythm of the expansions and contractions of the universe, *big-bang*, *bang-big*, and all this without ever being concerned in the slightest with our questions. Because the universe has no concerns, doesn't ask itself questions, is happy just *being*—like rocks, clouds, rain— all the things that, fortunately, don't think, because if they did we might have a little problem.

What would come to pass if, one day, the rocks decided they'd had enough and inflicted the same mistreatments on us that we've been subjecting them to for millennia— like in those movies where Mother Nature decides she's had a gutful, and a hurricane, an ant colony, or a reptile armada, to give just a few examples, destroys everything in its path with the exception of the heroes. The pure people, in other words. The people who don't drink, don't smoke, don't take drugs, aren't gay, don't cheat on their wife, and don't succumb to all those little pleasures of this short life. The rocks movie could be called *The Great Stoning* or *Revenge of the Rocks*. If I was given a part in it, I'd be one of the first to die, beaten at full force by a swarm of insanely angry crushed stones. Maybe the four-hundred-million-year-old rock would try to protect me, because the two of us had become friends once we'd got past the initial misunderstandings of any normal relationship, but still I would die pretty early on. I'd be one of those characters who have to be sacrificed so that credibility and morality can stay intact.

But, after all, I wasn't in a movie, I was in real life, in a void which was weirdly starting to look like a horror story or science fiction, proof there's no difference, really, that reality and fiction are the same and that everything is connected, intermingled, mutually destructive, and in a big shapeless jumble. Besides, ever since Jack Picard had emerged from the pages of Victor Morgan's novel to come prance around the Mirror Lake woods, I'd banished the words *reality* and *fiction* from my vocabulary and ceased wondering if what was happening to me was real, or if it all belonged in an endless nightmare. Maybe one spring morning, lying at the edge of the lake amid the heartbreaking lament of the loons and the soft jangling of Winslow's chimes, I would extricate my stiffened limbs from this nightmare. I wouldn't even have made Winslow's acquaintance yet, apart from maybe noticing or inventing him in my dreams, from which he'd rise up with unrelenting joviality and the nightmare would start over and the spiral of time would keep biting its tail, all the while gorging on our shitty little existences and spitting us out into the void before we could even ask what reality is, which is, when all's said and done, a totally pointless question, given that reality doesn't exist any more than fiction does. Period. Nothing exists but a muddle of chances, a tangle of probable and improbable causes, and all you can do is work out how to make yourself a life with that.

In the meantime, I had a few problems to solve, starting with Anita.

When, the day after the evening when I'd deduced we were all swimming in the same libidinous ocean, I opened my eyes, the first thing I saw was Bambi, or was it Bamboo, resting next to Anita on my pillow. Then I discerned one big black eye and a smaller tricoloured one watching me tenderly—another case for nightmare and reality being one and the same, because if there's something I hate above all else, it's waking up next to a person staring at me with limpid eyes and appearing, in the silence, to be quietly considering a host of things about the man who, just a few moments before, was hiding behind his shut eyelids and drooling on the pillow.

A wave of morning exasperation rose inside me, which I managed to hold back by biting my cheeks. What should have been a night of restorative sleep had not relieved my headache at all, and there is nothing worse for an incipient headache than morning irritation. And I was also aware of Anita's hypersensitivity, highly likely to increase headaches. So I dug my molars deep into the skin inside my cheeks and, trying to approximate a smile, gently placed Bambi or Bamboo above Anita's head. And given that a genuine smile is impossible when you're chewing your own flesh, I tried to conceive of a way of getting out of bed without needing to touch her.

Now I knew she was sleeping with Robbins, I had somewhat less desire to rub up against her. To be honest, I had absolutely no desire whatsoever to do so. But as I was not the sharpest knife in the block after a night's sleep that should have been restorative but wasn't, I experienced a moment of distraction during which Anita caught me unawares and moved her lush lips toward my frightened ones. I had no choice, and pushed her away just as her tongue was trying to find a route between my sealed lips, and I got up claiming to have dog breath, wondering as I did so where Jeff had gone now that he'd been expelled from the bed by Bambi and Bamboo, which would not be happening again. The news of Anita and Robbins's lovemaking was still fresh, I couldn't see myself kissing Anita as if nothing was up. It would have been the same as kissing Robbins, as a lot of his mouth bacteria must still have been in Anita's mouth. Those little beasties live longer than rocks, cockroaches, prejudices, popes, and other indestructible creatures, and it was out of the question that I would eat that asshole's microbial flora, even if unconsciously I had already done so more than once. The prospect was every bit as horrifying as the bloodiest scenes of my worst nightmares, and sent me rushing to the bathroom to glug down half a bottle of minty-fresh Scope.

Then I took a super-long shower for the same reasons that had me stripping off the lining of the inside of my mouth.

When, eventually, I resurfaced from the bathroom there was a nice smell of fresh coffee in the air, and I noticed that Anita had used whatever she could find to make the kind of breakfast you'd only put together if you're feeling particularly good, as all around you the opening notes of classic songs about a love you'd like to be equally lasting hang in the air. This state of affairs told me things were bad, very bad: I would have to take action before finding myself permanently stuck with not only a woman in the house but a host of elated Bambis and Bamboos too — and, who knows, a couple of ragamuffin kids I would have to properly educate as Anita washed the diapers and Winslow bounced the smaller of the two brats on his knees and tried to teach it the words to "Yankee Doodle."

As this further vision of horror was appearing on the green and beige walls of the cottage, whose hideousness I hadn't noticed before, Anita was humming "La vie en rose," humming most of it and just a word or two popping up here and there, since nobody had taken the trouble to sit Anita on their lap and teach her the words. I wasn't about to do so either, since there was nothing dolorous about her lack of knowledge. I even went the other way and started to belt out, *"Bleu, bleu, l'amour est bleu,"* just to annoy her; *"Bleu comme le ciel qui joue dans tes yeux,"* which was completely stupid, because I hate that song as much as I do the Trenet ditty where the sun meets the moon, alongside all the other drivel oozing out of a miserable genre that could actually lead Anita to believe that love had bored a hole in my stony heart, though I don't understand at all how you can hope to convince someone that you love them while reeling off such meaningless nonsense. Why not "Blue like the sea lapping at your feet," while you're at it, or "like the swallow enfolding you in its wings," and other stylistic phrases so depressing that you wonder what it would take for the person who wrote them to finally decide to kill themselves.

This particular song did, however, have the benefit of putting me in a foul mood — in other words, into a suitable frame of mind to tell Anita what I had to communicate to her. "Anita," I began, biting into a piece of toast lovingly spread with jam and immediately dropping it onto my plate because the smile Anita wore as she watched me bite into the lovingly jam-spread toast lodged in my throat. But I wasn't going to be intimidated or let myself be distracted by a sentimentalism that had no place in my life, I wasn't about to sacrifice my emancipation from a love that wasn't mutual, nor lasso the rope around my own neck simply to stop Anita from hanging herself with it. At the end of the day, there are limits beyond which I am not prepared to go.

"Anita," I said again, "don't you think, since you have a boyfriend, that it might be better to stop seeing each other?"

I'd chosen the right angle, because exactly the same thing had occurred to Anita, who didn't think it at all moral to have two boyfriends, suggesting I was one of them.

"Aren't you?" she added, half questioningly, half coyly, looking at me out of the corner of her colourful eye, a half-question that I didn't answer, her faux smile still lodged deep in my throat. Whatever the truth of it, in order to solve her moral dilemma, she'd decided to leave Robbins, and to tell him as much as soon as she saw him. I hadn't chosen the right angle after all.

And the skies must have heard, or figured that her desire to renounce her adulterous ways could use a little aid, because this was the moment Robbins's 4×4 chose to careen out of the verdant pines at full pelt, and now the vehicle was framed in the kitchen window in a cloud of dust as menacing as it was imbued with purpose. "Fuck," we stammered in unison, gripping the table. "Fucking shit," was our reprise, as Anita gathered up Bambi, Bamboo, her purse, the underwear that had been lying on the leatherette couch for two days, an orphaned shoe, and a tube of L'Oréal Cheetah lipstick. I have no idea how, with my jangling nerves, I clocked it all. Then she rushed into the bedroom while I cleared up her plate, her cup, her lovingly jam-spread toast, and chucked it all in the garbage, hang the expense, and attempted to appear impassive.

The two of us made a handsome couple working in perfect synchrony, I thought, as I moved around trying not to look as if I was in a hurry. I needed at all costs to prevent Robbins from setting foot in the cottage, filled as it was with Anita's womanly scents, and now the time had come, because Robbins was approaching the bottom

129

of the steps to the porch and clicking his spurred boots as he did so, like Clint Eastwood about to pepper someone with holes in a Sergio Leone movie.

"What's going on?" I said, both to say something and to appear at ease, as I leaned in a relaxed pose on the porch railing.

Before answering, Robbins looked me straight in the eyes, or at least I assumed he did, because he was still wearing those damn Ray-Bans, and twirled the toothpick around in his mouth seven times. I envisaged the thousands of identical bacteria from his mouth that Anita had cloned and which had then immediately descended into the petri dish of my throat, where all the stomach-turning organisms were dying and multiplying, and where Anita's smile was still lodged. Then he hitched his pants up so I could see he had balls and where they were.

It was going badly, very badly, but I tried not to show it. I leaned over the railing and nonchalantly spat on the four-hundred-million-year-old rock, to which I mentally apologized, explaining that the circumstances required some sort of manly gesture from me. After clearing his throat, which added to the nausea I was having trouble suppressing, Robbins opened his mouth full of little creatures racing around in all directions to tell me someone else had gone missing in the area and that the disappearance might have something to do with the drowned man or the dead man, depending on whether you subscribed to the thesis of one or two John Does. The second option no longer held up, given that Winslow had told me the possible second John Doe was named Jack Picard, but Robbins, unaware of my being up to speed, was nurturing what he figured was my innocence by playing up the possibility of two. Regardless, if there really was another missing man, then we were dealing with two John Does and one Jack Picard, and it all seemed a bit much. There must be some kind of rift around Mirror Lake, some kind of spatio-temporal vortex or nebulous zone, a twilight zone, and it was causing so many people to go missing that even Robbins was tempted to call it an epidemic; I could see it in the nervous way he was wiggling the toothpick.

If Winslow had been around, I'd have asked him to help me over to my rock, because I was already imagining what my nights would be like now that there was potentially one dead man and two prowlers around the lake. Or one dead man and two other dead men, since missing people have a statistically high chance of becoming dead people. Or maybe we were dealing with one living John Doe, one dead John Doe, and one Jack Picard at large, a man capable in his ferocious dysfunction of making the Mirror Lake mortality rate shoot straight up like an arrow. But Winslow was never there when I needed him, so I gripped the handrail more tightly and asked what the police were playing at, for fuck's sake, along with a few other clarifications. At which point Robbins revealed that the second missing person was actually a woman, a woman in her early thirties who looked like Anita Ekberg and was called Jeanne Picard...

"Picard...what a nice name...Picard. Hmmm, I don't know her," I replied, filing down the end of a fingernail on one of the porch posts. Then, prompted by nerves, I embroidered my lips with an idiotic smile, with the sole aim of keeping down the little tremors of hysterical laughter convulsing my stomach, jerky spasms like tickling. The top-left corner of my right eyelid started twitching and I covered it up by putting a hand over my face, in the pose of a guy determined not to laugh, but when hysteria comes on, you can't control it and I was wondering how I was going to get out of the situation when young Indiana Jones ambled over and came to my rescue.

"Found nothin', boss," he said to Robbins nasally, and I realized Robbins had been keeping me talking as Indiana walked around the cottage in the hope of gathering clues proving Anita had passed through, but he hadn't found anything. For once I was relieved to see him, and incredibly relieved that Robbins had been stupid enough to leave the task of searching the place to his deputy, because there were no doubt dozens of traces of Anita around the extinguished campfire alone, but Jones had espied nothing, which showed that imbecility hadn't been invented for no reason, the planet needing its fair share of cretins to ensure social balance and the survival of the fittest.

In the moment, however, I was focusing not on Jones's stupidity but the bag of chips he was holding, a blue and yellow bag, the Humpty Dumpty brand, that had caught my eye. It occurred to me that it had been a while since Humpty had shown up, and I realized I'd never made the link between the nursery rhyme character and the one whose smiling face, day after day for at least fifty years, had adorned thousands upon thousands of chip bags travelling across Canada and the United States of America, the moronic face penetrating the collective subconscious and insidiously invading the territory. But what shook me the most, infuriated me, was that what was taking place here was a usurpation, an appropriation of identity, a false representation, because the idiot face in question was not a potato but, as my mother said often enough, an egg, a rotten fucking egg, and yet, without anyone objecting, here he was playing the mascot of tens of thousands of pounds of sliced potatoes that every year fed the obesity of who knows how many unfortunates glued to their television screens.

As I was unable to drag my eyes away from the half-wit's mug crumpled up on the bag of chips, Jones must have thought I was hungry. He held the bag out to me, but Robbins grabbed it on its way past, which didn't surprise me, because Robbins would have sold his mother for the pleasure of annoying me, though it didn't bother me because the fact of the matter is I wasn't hungry. I was merely shaken by Humpty Dumpty's omnipresence, which would no doubt extend into my next nightmare—unless I was already in it, what with there being no difference between nightmare and reality. But at least I wasn't trembling any longer, which was something, so much so that I was able to answer Robbins's bygone question: "No," I said, "never saw this woman around here." Robbins took a photo of Anita out of his wallet anyway, a pretty photo in which she was smiling and projecting that air of lightness I'd witnessed just a few minutes earlier, the lightness of love, so full of promise and which causes a person to see everything through a slight mist, and from this I concluded the photo was old, though this didn't stop Anita's contagious smile imprinting itself on my own face. "Nope, never saw her," I repeated, Robbins wondering why I was smiling like a lunatic. "'Cause she's pretty," I said, forcing my smile and Anita's down my throat, where they could stay warm, and waiting for Robbins to beat it.

Then I was the target of barely veiled threats, in the vein of "If you touch this girl, I'll murder you," which might have led to two dead and one missing person by the lake, or one dead and two missing, since Anita had to be removed from the list. But by this point I was only listening with one ear, because as he was promising me a terrible end, Robbins was brandishing another threat — Humpty Dumpty's squashed, smiling face — at me, and it was clear he and I weren't done yet. "I'll be back," he hollered, confirming my fears and making my nausea rise up again, because there were three or four soggy chip crumbs on his tongue, over which the innumerable tiny starving creatures living in his mouth were undoubtedly scampering back and forth, and then he left, followed by young Jones, without noticing Anita's other orphaned shoe, camouflaged like a Maine leopard in a patch of ferns.

I waited until the 4×4 disappeared behind the greenery of the pines, muttered "Oof," and then "Humpty Dumpty is not a fucking potato, he's an egg," letting all the nervous impulses racing through my body have free rein. When, finally, I was calm again, my stomach hurting from having laughed a laugh that wasn't a laugh, I thought of Winslow, because Robbins and Jones were almost certainly going to drop by his place to show him the photo of Anita, and I shouted at her not to leave the bedroom because danger was still surrounding us. I really needed to stop Winslow from opening his great trap, but had no idea how to accomplish this. I couldn't jump in my boat and head over to warn him, because Robbins would immediately see what I was up to. I could have tried signalling with my arms, or drums, or smoke, but given that I didn't have a drum to hand and knew nothing about signalling, that wasn't a great idea. Which was when the phone rang.

"Oh, the telephone!" as the cuckold in a Broadway farce would have said, but as I wasn't the cuckold and was, for the first time, hearing the impassable mountains of Mirror Lake echo a ringing sound that belonged to another stage of my life, I thought maybe I was dreaming, because dream and reality... But the ringing was insistent and amplified by the mountains' barrier, and I needed to come to: *the phone, fuck*! There were only three real possibilities: either it was a pollster wanting to speak to the housekeeper, i.e. the person who washes the floors and buys all the products necessary to do a bang-up job of polluting the environment, or somebody wanting to offer me a credit card that would make me rich and happy, or it was Fate calling to give me bad news. I ran inside, grabbed Anita's hand before she could pick up the receiver, which I then picked up and put back down. If it was Fate, she'd call back. If it was everyday life at its worst—*Congratulations, you've won a million dollars!*—they would also call back, though in a few hours, which would give me time to change the number or come up with a counterstrategy.

It was Fate, because the insistent *brrrring-brrrring* had started again and was even louder.

"You're not answering?" Anita asked.

"It's Fate," I replied. "Destiny. I have to prepare myself." I took a deep breath, closed my eyes, picked up the receiver and said hello in French, because if it was the Fate I suspected, she would be calling direct from Quebec, her voice jerky with sobs, announcing the death of someone close to me. I'd heard Fate's sad voice before, and from its opening sigh it numbs you from your feet to your head. I knew I would hear from Fate again, it was inevitable, really, unless I died before everyone else—make that immediately, so as not to take any chances—but I didn't want to hear it that morning, and as I was saying *"allo"* I think I was praying. Actually, I don't *think*, I know. Behind my deferentially shut eyes, I said, "I beg you God," this with genuine sincerity, which is what agnostics like me do when they were brought up Christian, a yearning for God returning any time they are made to feel infinitesimally small.

"Fuck, Robert," I heard on the other end of the line. "Don't you answer your phone?" and God, his angels, Fate, and Misery all disappeared under the spell of Winslow's voice. When I look back on it today, I still think it was Fate calling, but that Winslow was the voice of my destiny, the body Fate had decided to work through. But at the time it didn't occur to me. Relief was foremost in my mind, followed immediately by amazement: I didn't know Winslow had a phone, so I hadn't given him my number, which I kept for emergencies. And even if I had known he owned a phone, I still wouldn't have given him my number. But right then I was extremely happy he had it, as it meant that Fate's despairing voice wouldn't have to travel optical fibres from Mirror Lake to Quebec, dematerializing and rematerializing its pain and announcing to my loved ones that I'd taken the inevitable road to the void before them, sent there by an angry cop.

By this point I was pretty well dead to my loved ones anyway, since I'd taken off without a word, like a fucking asshole, leaving behind me the impression of a man incapable of facing reality, because when I allude to the agony of life, it's because I believe in it; reality is far too painful not to be real. All this is to say they wouldn't find the news at all surprising, and it would do no more than allow them to begin the mourning process with a body to huddle over, let their tears flow over, a bier to lower into the earth and an epitaph to write. But I could no longer really figure out what they would be able to write about me. "Robert Moreau, 1951–2004, died in a novel," perhaps, since that's where they always saw me fleeing love or stupidity, taking shelter in a novel, in a movie — in fiction, which they believed was different from reality, which in that instant was being channelled through Winslow's voice bellowing into my ear, and I hadn't even had a chance to express my surprise because Bobby was all shaken up.

To cut to the chase, Winslow had seen Tim Robbins making his way over to see me, and had deduced he'd be on his way to his place next—in fact, he was already there, which I could see for myself just by going over to my window, through which I could see Winslow's cottage disappearing in a great cloud of dust—and Winslow wanted to know if Ray-Bans's visit had anything to do with Anita.

"Yes," I said, as on edge as Winslow was. "Keep your mouth shut, you've never seen her, you've never seen a woman your entire fucking life," I went on, and then I hung up and gave him time to arrange his face and to wipe away the excitement-induced sweat no doubt dripping down his forehead. As for how he'd got hold of my number, we'd sort that out later.

We'd had a lucky escape, and as I sat down in my chair to watch the scene on the other side of the lake unfolding, I thought of the old ad for a phone or telegraph company heralding the advantages of the technology by comparing it to smoke signals. The memory was so distant I couldn't figure out if I'd seen the ad in a movie, in a magazine, on TV, or just made it up. Given that it was so well conceived, and told the truth, I decided I must have made it up. Without a phone I'd have been done for, it would be my spit-roasted carcass that Tim Robbins would be using to make smoke signals, and I spared a thought for Alexander Graham Bell, who'd just saved my life. I might have spared a thought for

God, whom I'd mixed up in the whole imbroglio by sending a sincere prayer up to him just a few moments before, but it's well known that agnostics like me forget about God as soon as they don't need him anymore. If I had believed in God, I might have been afraid that he would take revenge, which he sometimes does. But as I didn't really believe in him, and my relationship with him was on a purely as-needed basis, I chose the option which suited me best, stating that if he existed, then in his merciful goodness he would remember the sincerity of my prayer and gloss over my ingratitude. During this time, Winslow was on the far side of the lake and swearing to a skeptical Robbins that he'd never seen a woman in his life, and Jones was chewing slices of salted Humpty Dumpty as he did the tour of Winslow's cottage before walking over to Robbins to tell him he hadn't found anything, which was to be expected as there was nothing to be found on that side of the lake. Then both of them got back into Robbins's 4×4 in the cloak of a silence that promised they'd be back.

Winslow started to guffaw in a silly, uncontrollable manner — nerves — and I was able to breathe again at last, which gave me a moment to consider just how pleasant the day might have been had I been alone and not sucked into a time-hole into which all the lost souls of the region had also been sucked. I shouted to Anita that I was going on a reconnaissance trip and advised her to stay put until I was back, then I called Jeff, who was sulking in the corner, his big head pressing heavily on the floor, because I hadn't yet made any space for him that day.

"Come on, Jeff," I said cheerfully, "we're going out," magic words instantly erasing the sadness from his big wet eyes and starting up the emotional mechanism that regulated his wagging tail, its metronomic beating displaying to me once more the meaning of pure joy.

It was exactly the kind of August day I like, dominated by the yellow grass shimmering around the lake; a calm day, not the slightest hint of wind, and the clouds in the sky doubled in Mirror Lake, its still waters moving only when water striders skimmed over them or a trout rose to the surface with a lazy plop to catch a narcissistic fly daring to hang out on the surface. I took a deep breath and closed my eyes, full of this beauty that had put an end to my pain the day I convinced myself that trying to understand it was useless, that you just had to take life as it was without trying to understand its mysteries at all. When I opened my eyes again, I saw a moose, an old buck with fraying fur, coming out of the wood a mere fifty feet away from us. I grabbed Jeff's collar — which meant *don't move, don't bark, don't even think about growling* — and we watched the moose gulp back some water, then enter the lake and, spirit proud, set off swimming toward the east bank, the bank of the rising sun. The moose and the setting were in perfect harmony, and neither Winslow nor Anita nor I had a right to appear in it, because the scene belonged to the moose, to coyotes, to foxes — to all the animals on whose territory we encroach, too foolish to stop reproducing and contributing as we do to the demographic curve's exponential rise, too stupid even to be able to conceive of saving all this beauty.

By the time the moose had reached the other bank, my cheeks were wet and my lips salty and my eyes brimming with some of the beautiful clean water I held in diminishing reserve. I watched as the moose briefly turned around and looked at me and Jeff to let us know he'd spotted us long before we'd spotted him, and that sometimes a man, a dog, and a moose together in the same scene can be beautiful—a moment of perfect silence on a clear August day, the yellow grass dozing. Set before this ancestral wisdom, of which I would never have even a tiny fraction, I snivelled some more. The moose disappeared into the pines and I mumbled a prayer, another one, so that no one would shoot this animal when hunting season came around and the smell of gunpowder and blood spread surreptitiously across Maine from east to west.

After this heart-rendingly bucolic scene, I wanted for nothing, though I would have liked Anita to leave, and for Winslow's cottage to disappear along with Winslow, so that all that was left at the perimeter of the lake was Jeff and me, a dog and his man sitting in the dusty summer light watching the deer quietly passing through. This desire being too simple for the people involved to help me achieve, I kicked out into the void, let go of Jeff's collar, causing him to bark like a lunatic and run from left to right with the crazily frenetic movements you sometimes see in happy dogs. And that's what I wanted too, to be happy, as if the word could have meaning in a man's mouth, and for people to leave me in peace free to watch moose, build animals out of sand or maybe a castle to shelter in, with a moat and a drawbridge, just like in novels, just like the one my old toes were building now and the water was seeping into. I could fill it with crocodiles, sharks, and other wild animals to repel invaders—one promptly turning up in the shape of Anita, unable to let me be in my castle for two fucking minutes. No doubt she wanted to be princess of my castle, and were I to give her three days in the dungeon they'd hear her screaming at the other end of Maine and Tim Robbins would come to rescue her, destroying my brattice, my merlons, my arrow slits, and my bartizan with his clod's 4×4.

"Watch out," I warned as she came closer, "there's a crocodile about to eat your big toe." And just as I was saying so, Céline Dion, still looking like a big toe, appeared in the dungeon singing "My Heart Will Go On" as Leonardo DiCaprio and Kate Winslet sank with the *Titanic* and James Cameron proclaimed "I'm the king of the world!" and the world in question caved in like a sandcastle on the borders of a lake that didn't give a damn about keeping promises. "I asked you to stay hidden," I said in reproach without averting my eyes from the collapsed world, and she said she was fed up, that it was too nice to be shut inside, too nice to be alone, disingenuously emphasizing the word *alone*. I agreed with her first assertion, but not the last, which was too final for my liking, like a finale with violins, when two heroes are reunited forever, together forever, never again alone. At the very idea, a big shiver ran through my body, from the occipital to the astralagus, although right then it didn't occur to me that the French for "astralagus" is *astragale*. Had I thought of it, Albertine Sarrazin's novel of the same name would definitely have come to mind and I'd have been delighted, but that didn't happen, I didn't think of *astragale* any more than I thought of *occipital*. Philosophically, I told myself that solitude is something that needs to be earned the hard way, that to obtain it you need to accept the stormy upheavals of the flesh, to which I added: "But what...but seriously, what am I going to do with Anita?"

A big cloud passed over at that moment. The lake darkened, and I turned the page of a novel I would really have liked to read, not even thinking of asking Anita if she had a cousin, an uncle, or a brother called Jack.

The night after Robbins's third visit, I had an HD dream, just as I'd expected — *HD* standing for Humpty Dumpty but also for hard drugs, high definition, and high density. I woke up in a terrible state, in the middle of a scene where Humpty Dumpty, who had taken on the double appearance of an egg and a potato, was both on top of and at the foot of his wall. When the banging on the door made its way into my dream, unless that was what started the dream in the first place, the Humpty Dumpty at the bottom — and with whom I identified, I hadn't crammed Freud for nothing — was hitting the wall with hammer blows, while the Humpty Dumpty on top of it was waving his little potato arms in all directions and shrieking insults like *boar, oaf, lout,* the numbskull. Unmoved, I continued to linger by the wall, the collapse of which would only provide me a semi-release — a supervised release, you could say, since you can't escape your nemeses any more than you can yourself.

In brief, my impatience went unrewarded, because I was pulled out of this dream by an insistent banging coming from the next room, where somebody was obviously trying to break down the door. I immediately thought of Tim

Robbins, who must have discovered that Anita was staying with me and had come to kill us both, and then of Anita, who evidently had raced to hide as soon as she heard the angry *bang-bang*, because she was nowhere to be found, and neither were Bambi, Bamboo, her stiletto heels, bags, anti-wrinkle sunscreen, or her Shania perfume, named after Shania Twain, "Shania by Stetson," which was going to haunt me one day — the perfume, that is, not the singer. Anita must have hidden in the closet, I couldn't see any other way out. I pulled on a pair of pants and yelled that there was no fire and, before opening the door to the bedroom, I whispered in the direction of the closet that I'd take care of everything. Then I went out, donning the appearance of an angry guy not the tiniest bit intimidated, but all for nothing as it was the moron Winslow attacking my door.

"*Baptême*, Winslow, where are your manners?" I shouted as I opened the door, which wasn't even locked, a detail I pointed out to him as I pulled up a chair for him to perch his fat ass on since it was clear he had no immediate plans to leave, and asked him to wait a couple of minutes before he revealed whatever catastrophe he'd come to announce, because it was clear to me that another earthquake was about to disturb the serenity of Mirror Lake's environs. So he sat at the kitchen table while I made coffee and filled Jeff's bowl with kibble. Jeff hadn't even barked when Winslow started beating the door down. The dog was getting soft, I'd have to have a word with him — explain to him that enemies weren't always strangers and that, Winslow or no Winslow, we had a right to privacy. It wouldn't be easy. Jeff liked everybody. Except that ugly Robbins, although Jeff hadn't barked at him the day before either, I was realizing now as I looked back on it. There was a hole in my story there, unless Jeff had some kind of issue with his vocal cords.

To reassure myself about his health, I did something that always makes him go absolutely beside himself: I rolled up on the floor in a ball and sighed, which immediately started him barking, as well as Bill, who was with Winslow and always repeated everything Jeff said. Winslow leapt to his feet to tell me I shouldn't take it so hard. "It's not a disaster," he said, "Robert, you'll find another one."

Another what, I had no clue. What I did know, or what I'd guessed, was that some new disaster had occurred despite Winslow's denials, and once more I told him to keep quiet until I'd finished my first coffee. "You shut your mouth till I drink this coffee, Bob, is that clear?"

The problem was that Winslow was unfailingly obedient, so he sat in silence watching me drink my coffee with his big blue eyes, something I hate as much as waking up to find a pair of big black eyes staring at me from the pillow next to mine, but I didn't give in and drank my coffee right down to the last drop. I listened to the flies buzzing around the table, to the sounds of Jeff's tongue darting about trying to catch the flies, and to the sounds of Bill's tongue as he caught and ate them, adding ambient noise to the slightly uncomfortable atmosphere of the room. To dissipate the discomfort, I poured myself another coffee, offered Winslow one to keep him busy, gave the dogs water to help the flies down and then said "Go for it," words that had the effect of trumpets sounding the kill on a fox hunt, because Winslow immediately launched into a breathtaking tale of which I barely understood a thing, but in which Anita's name appeared a little too often.

After a third coffee, I finally understood Winslow thought he'd seen Anita in town a few hours earlier, and with Robbins, who wasn't looking happy at all. This made Winslow nervous for Anita's other eye.

"It wasn't John, it was Jack," I said, to calm him down, adding that in any case he must have been mistaken because Anita was in the bedroom closet. "Don't panic, Bob, you hallucinated," I said, "Anita is in the closet," which alarmed him in a different way.

"Since when do we shut women in closets, dammit?" said Winslow. "We're not in the Middle Ages here!" I pointed out that there were no closets in the Middle Ages and went to find Anita, whose turn it now was to provide some explanations.

As I went into the bedroom I shouted to Anita that she could come out, that there was no danger, that it was just fearless Winslow come to warn me that he'd seen her in town. When I received no reply, I shouted a little louder, "You can come out, Anita, it's just Winslow."

Faced with the imperturbable silence of the closet, I went crazy, remembering all those stories of asphyxiated children found among the smelly shoes, all the horror stories our mothers told to stop us from hiding in the dark where sins abounded, and I yanked the door to the closet open only to find that Anita wasn't in it. Nor was she among the shoes: the closet was empty of Anitas, there was no Anita behind the curtains, nor under the bed, nor in the drawers, nor in the enormous cedar chest smelling of mothballs, as if the cedar actually needed naphthalene to repel the creepy-crawlies. I've never understood the stubbornness of people who use both cedar and naphthalene — behaviour as bizarre to me as criminals choosing to finish guys off with a bullet when they've already stabbed them twenty times. I'd seen that in a movie, you see everything in movies, and in books too — but the problem was there was no Anita anywhere. Afraid that she might have disappeared or been abducted, I rushed into the kitchen, grabbed Winslow by his checked shirt and asked him to kindly tell me the story again.

I ought to have been happy the whole Anita business had been settled, but in my irritation I wasn't happy at all and didn't notice the small perfumed note Winslow was holding in his right hand. When, after he'd threatened to be as mute as a fish (and here I didn't mention the silent cries of fish), I finally let him go, he brandished the Shania-scented missive under my nose and, jolted by the familiar, invigorating scent, I recovered at least a little of my composure.

"Where did you find that, Winslow?" I asked him suspiciously.

"On top of Victor Morgan's book," he answered — the book sitting meanwhile on the low table in the corner of the living room, eyeing me up. Discovering that Anita had chosen this place among thousands to leave me a message was just too much, because maybe there was a subtext here relating to the links between her and a certain Jack Picard, which I would spend days trying to figure out without ever receiving confirmation that I'd hit the bull's eye. At the time, I was thinking about giving the cursed book back to Winslow, but I changed my mind as there were still a few things about Picard I wanted to check out, as well as a potential message to decode. So I sat down at the kitchen table under Winslow's avid gaze. His big blue eyes, dripping with the slimy lust of creatures feeding off the misfortunes and defeats of others, were once again about to witness a scene that I'd rather have happened in private. Delicately, I unfolded the small scrap of blue paper while the blaring voice of Vicky Leandros, whom I'd always confused with Mireille Mathieu, filled the cottage and told me that "*Bleu, bleu, l'amour est bleu.*" I made no effort to push her away, it would have been pointless, and instead let Anita's heartbreakingly naive words mingle with the song.

Essentially, Anita was telling me she'd left me for my own protection. She'd thought long and hard, and come to the conclusion that for as long as Robbins was alive, she'd be a danger to me, so she preferred to move on. *If that's not love, then what is?* I thought, leaving Winslow to stew in his curiosity as I did so. For a minute I thought about killing Robbins and proving my love to Anita in turn, but the impulse wasn't genuine and would have left me in a pretty fix, because I wasn't in love, even if I was presenting some of the symptoms associated with that state, though these were atypical and had resulted simply from contact with the infected person. It might appear that love is contagious, especially when the other person is insistent, but it's not. The seeming contagion is no more than a form of tenderness, sympathy, or compassion due to the exquisite suffering of the person who's fallen head over heels for you. I was familiar with the phenomenon, because most of the time I am the person who is head over heels, and here I was still uncertain which of the two roles I preferred. The knowledge that someone catches a glimpse of you in their soup bowl and sees you appear on every street corner, or that you are the sole and vapid topic of conversation of someone you otherwise respect, isn't always gratifying, especially when you're made to feel, at least in part, responsible.

All things considered, it made sense to give up on the idea of an assassination. And because Winslow was increasingly annoyed, I told him he was right, that Anita had hit the road. "She's gone," I said, amazed I didn't feel like partying as a consequence. I tucked the piece of blue paper into my back pocket, which would then reek of Shania, the thought only half pleasing to me because, to be honest, I hated that perfume. But I owed it to Anita.

"So, what are we going to do now?" I asked Winslow, who jumped to his feet like a gallant knight and declared that we would go find her and rescue her from the macho Robbins's clutches.

"Are you crazy?" I said, also leaping to my feet. "Are you crazy, Winslow?" (After which I admonished myself: *Stop repeating yourself!*) "Robbins is a cop, we're not. Robbins has a gun, we don't. Robbins is crazy, really crazy, I'm not. And, last but not least, Robbins has Ray-Bans and we don't!"

I think I was a disappointment to him, because he'd thought me braver than that and more in love.

"You already have all the symptoms," he said, trying to convince me I was in love, but what led him to whine the most were Robbins's Ray-Bans. "How exactly do they give him an advantage over us?" So I was obliged to explain at length how it was that Robbins's Ray-Bans rendered him invulnerable. Had this twit never noticed that Ray-Bans made Robbins impossible to pin down, as impossible to pin down as a nest of snakes, protecting him from predators and serving the dual function of camouflage and armour? "He's kind of like Marcel," I added, and since Winslow had no idea who Marcel was I gave him a quick tutorial on the plays of Michel Tremblay and the character of Marcel, who was invisible to everyone if he put his black glasses on. To prove the point, I asked Winslow if he knew what colour Robbins's eyes were. No, Winslow didn't know the colour of Robbins's eyes, nobody did, not even Anita, because — and I was so sure of it I'd have put my hand in the fire and sworn as much — that woodlouse even fucked with his sunglasses on. "So you see, that's what gives him an advantage over us, Winslow."

To which the latter replied, "We just need to buy ourselves some Ray-Bans too."

I gave up, told Winslow to let it drop and went outside with Jeff, followed by Bill, for a walk by the lake.

It was another magnificent August day, just the way I like them, with that slight sensation of heaviness that makes you feel summer's fullness right in the pit of your stomach, and again I wondered why we couldn't just be happy with that, why we always need something else when nothing can equal the beauty of an August sky, the beauty of a storm, the beauty of a star, of a squall, of a moose crossing a lake, a dog running after another dog, a maple tree turning red, a monarch fluttering from flowers to branches. *Because we're fools*, I repeated to myself again; it's the universal answer, because happiness resides in coming to terms with our stillness. And as happiness brazenly strode past, I turned up the bottoms of my pant legs, sat down on the dock, and soaked my feet in the cold water, remembering the time Anita and I had splashed around in the filthy pool at our motel.

She and I had already shared memories and places that belonged to us, like ordinary couples, and a little pain stabbed my heart at the thought that we'd probably not see each other again, that our story was one of those stories with no resolution because they stem from the abnormality of the two protagonists. Sure, I'd always tried to stay off the beaten track, had never wanted to blend into the crowd—wearing red when black was in fashion, eating meat when an entire generation was grazing on alfalfa, smoking when the tobacco police started attacking smokers to ease SUV drivers' consciences. But now I was forced to concede that a modicum of normality wouldn't hurt, to admit that it is easier to climb up facing forwards rather than backwards, and to walk back down again looking backwards rather than forwards, especially when you fall in love, in other words, on your head.

That's it, I've said it, my concession surely the effect of the magnificent August day. I wasn't in love, I was sticking to my story, but despite my eloquent words I was beginning to fall in love, and silently I thanked Anita for her magnanimity, which was breaking my fall right in the middle. I didn't want to fall in love, didn't want to be part of a couple, which would have been the fatal consequence had Anita not come up with the benevolent idea of protecting me. From now on, I would take no more risks, there would only be Jeff and me, the moose and me, the lake and me, the four-hundred-million-year-old rock and me, though I would leave a little space for Winslow, because trying to dispatch Winslow was like trying to get rid of a wart or stop a rabbit from procreating. To mark my resolve with a symbolic gesture, I took Anita's letter out of my pocket and ripped it into a thousand pieces — approximately — and sent them dancing out over the lake, where they fell softly, like a gentle blue rain, in no hurry at all. Some of the drops, no doubt eager to keep feeling the August sun, stayed on the surface, where the letters they contained — *Ti* for Tim, *ov* for love, *miss* for I'll miss you — gradually faded. And then *Tim* and *love* and *missing* sank morosely into the waters of Mirror Lake, waters nothing can resist; a shadow came over me, a friend's shadow, a hand clasped my shoulder, a friend's hand, and Winslow lowered his enormous carcass down next to mine, said "hmm-hmm," and offered me the bag of balsamic vinegar Humpty Dumpty chips he was holding.

In a CinemaScope movie the scene could have been touching. Initially, the camera would have framed two men sitting side by side on a wooden dock in a gorgeous setting that some would have identified as Quebec, others Vermont, and would have captured, in the background, a big yellow dog and a medium-sized yellow dog (Bill had grown) chasing each other, and then, a little further away, in the shade of a tree, a cottage that all lovers of solitude would envy. "Peter," some girl in the back row of the movie theatre would whisper to the guy next to her stuffing himself with popcorn, "that's the kind of cottage I want," without suspecting, poor thing, that the deed of sale would include clauses written in microscopic letters. Then the camera would slowly pan back to the centre of the lake as it moved gently upwards, a movement requiring a crane to be installed in Mirror Lake's unfathomable depths, and the setting sun would skim the two men's balding pates, light up the two dogs' silky coats, and draw starry reflections in the cottage windows. And all the viewers, especially the girl in the last row, her eyes brimming with genuinely felt tears, would be thinking about the happiness that arises naturally from a combination of elements as mundane as a lake, two dogs, a cluster of spruce trees, sunshine, and, finally, friendship, visible in the silent harmony of the two men.

But the viewer would not have known that the first man's silence was due to the fact that he was petrified, and the second man's to the fact that he had nothing to say. What the viewer would not have seen, the close-up not long enough, was the pallor of the first man, and what the viewer would not have heard, what with the sound of Barbra Streisand singing "People" and taking over the movie theatre in full Dolby Surround, was the first man asking the other in a strangled voice, "Where did you find those fucking potato chips, Bob?" and the other one answering, "In your fucking camp, Bob!"

But we weren't in a movie, just in a fucking nightmare, I summarily decided, reintegrating the word into my vocabulary, even as Winslow ostentatiously held up the bag of chips in exactly the spot on which the camera's lens would have focused had there been one, a bit of product placement as you'd find in the barely disguised advertisements designed to bring a little money into the coffers of a movie production, art ready to sleep with the devil so it won't be reduced to the silence to which it will be limited by the devil anyway.

"Impossible," I said. "I don't eat them."

But Winslow insisted, saying that they'd been lying on the low table in the living room and it must have been Anita who left them there. Maybe they were a gift, the asshole suggested in a semi-skeptical, semi-romantic tone. And suddenly I saw Jones innocently appear, emerging from around the corner of the cottage and holding another of the blue and yellow chip bags out in front of him,

Robbins's sly grin preventing me from grabbing the bag Jones was waggling in front of my face, undigested crumbs sticking to his disgusting tongue. The conspiracy jumped out at me in all its nakedness, because it was obvious there had been a conspiracy, a collusion, a scheme, and that they were all in league against me—Robbins, Anita, Jones, even that cretin Winslow—to make Humpty Dumpty travel from my night terrors into my nightmarish life. How had they known? I was clueless. How had news of my obsession reached their ears? I'd suspected it might happen, I'd always talked in my sleep, which more than once put me into rather awkward situations with people ordering me to explain the fantasies my subconscious could no longer recall. As if I were responsible for the salacious shouts one part of me—a part that had never bothered to address me directly—let out!

Anyway, clearly I'd been the victim of an enormous machination in which Anita played the lead and me the silly goose, the Good Samaritan rescuing the woman in distress who just happens to be wandering along the path he's taking with a black eye. What a deception! Anita didn't have a black eye any more than I had a third one, which is why she needed to spend hours in the bathroom dolling herself up, putting on makeup, spraying herself with Shania, not to *hide* her shameful eye, no sirree, but to dress it perfectly! And come to think about it, I had noticed that it didn't look quite right, that it didn't have the natural look of a true black eye, but was a little too plaintive for my taste, a bit too lachrymose, not like a genuine black eye that looks at you with hostility and contempt, as if it would jump right out and mash up your own ugly mug if you so much as dared to say the words *eye*, *pain*, *peroxide*, or *soft green*. *Treacherous* was the only possible adjective to express the underlying nature of the woman suddenly apparent to me. The lowlife had sucked me right in, I'd been stupid enough to think she was in love, and had even sensed something in myself that was on its way to becoming a feeling, I who...

I thought I'd been sorting all this out inside my head, but apparently I'd been yelling everything out loud for a while, because Winslow grabbed my arm and said, "Whoa, Bobby, stop, that's enough, you stop," holding out an almost-overflowing glass of the whiskey that had appeared during the brief ellipsis in time that had eluded me. I must have seemed pretty crazy. The two dogs were watching me from a respectful distance, wondering what was going on, especially Bill, who wasn't used to hanging out with me in day-to-day life and seemed to be feeling sorry for Jeff.

"Jeff's a happy dog," I said to Winslow, because I'd had enough of everyone being on my back, and I took the opportunity to tell him he could drop his posturing, I knew full well he'd participated in fomenting the whole scheme against me, and I wasn't going to drink his poisonous whiskey. He told me I was out of my mind, of course. "You're completely crazy, Robert," he said, and other things in the same vein. I could work him over and end up getting a confession out of him, no question, I would just need to resort to torture.

"How do you know about Humpty Dumpty?" I asked, trying to remain calm and reflecting on how tone of voice often conveys the precise opposite of what you're feeling. But the only answer he gave me was an innocent look—innocent in the sense of "I don't know what you're talking about," but also *maudit innocent*, that semantic pearl in the repertoire of Quebec insults, inferring blessedness, beatitude, and not the state of being "not guilty." So, in order that my tone of voice aspiring to be calm continued to be so, I reformulated the question and took a sip of the whiskey, and because this whiskey, just like any other self-respecting whiskey, was well and truly a poison, with one swallow leading to another, the first glass would be the trigger of what would become the second-most memorable bender in the history of Mirror Lake.

Let me tell you the whole story. After an hour of intense—that's to say macho, tough, inquisitorial—interrogation, I hadn't managed to drag a thing out of Winslow, still claiming he didn't understand an iota of my crazy story and becoming aggressive. So I went to fill my glass and bring him one, along with the bottle, which would allow us to avoid unnecessary comings and goings and might soften Winslow. Now it was his turn to be watched from a respectful distance by the dogs, who weren't very pleased to see that the day, which could have been beautiful—which actually *was* beautiful, if you removed Winslow and me from the scene—was getting worse. After the first glass, Winslow did indeed seem a bit better, this reassuring the dogs, and I took advantage of the lapse to start up the interrogation again, but, as I myself was at the end of a second glass, my questions were a bit fuzzy. My vagueness allowed Winslow to bring the conversation around to what seemed to him to be the central and neglected element of the day: Anita's hasty departure. The suddenness of her departure intrigued him, though I suggested it made perfect sense given the logic of the conspiracy, crafted to have you believe the suddenness of her flight had meaning. In fact, it had no purpose other than to draw attention away from the departure itself and focus it instead on questions concerning the origin, nature, finality, and the why of the hastiness that so unexpectedly changed the course of events.

"Are you following me, Winslow?" I asked, after apprising him of my theory of their treachery. No, he was not following me, said his big innocent eyes—innocent, that is, in the conventional sense. When, with the insistence of someone who's drunk a little too much, I tried to refine my explanation, Winslow steered our arguments in the direction his obstinacy was heading, Winslow himself along for the ride, saying I was too stubborn to concede that I was displaying all the symptoms of a fella trying to extricate himself from love's snares—those were his actual words, "love's snares"—whereas, he said, he was courageous enough to admit that he would miss Anita. For a few sweet but also bitter seconds, I saw again the tiny blue scraps of Anita's traitorous letter floating on the equally blue surface of Mirror Lake, and especially the fragment on which the verb *to miss* was dissolving, conjugated in the future, which really is the only tense that suits when a person is preparing to suffer, though it was missing the *will* pointing to the future, which left *miss*, a.k.a. young girl. *I'll miss you, miss*...It didn't take much for Anita's image to superimpose itself on the little blue scraps where her left hand, wearing a ring with a cabochon, had drifted, and for the tune of "La dame en bleu," performed with forceful tremolos by one Michel Louvain endeavouring to eternally imprint himself on doleful memories, to cancel out Mireille Mathieu's attempts to sing louder than Vicky Leandros in the process.

Evidently it is no longer possible to have tender thoughts without the ambient kitsch of the late twentieth century sticking to the skin like an old piece of gum to the sole of a shoe, I whined. To snap out of my lament, I begged Winslow to talk to me about blue, any blue at all and the beauty of it, needing to be reconciled with this colour aspiring to nothing more than regaining its original purity. This led us to play the Pink Lady game but this time with the colour blue, saving her from the terrible end of the *dame en bleu* by imagining her seated in bushes overflowing with blueberries, little bluebirds perched on her shoulders, or, like Snow White or Sleeping Beauty, swallows, neither Winslow nor I able to remember which of the two was depicted like this, with birds braiding her long, silky hair. Then Winslow declared it wasn't either of them, but the Holy Virgin, which I declared impossible—I pronounced it *ampossybeul*—because the Holy Virgin didn't have loose hair but wore a veil, a big veil made of stars that lifted our eyes to the heavens. The Virgin Mary did not appear, we weren't drunk enough for that, but a minute star, just one, did appear in the early evening sky—it felt like the night would be a chilly one—suggesting that we'd been the victims of another ellipsis in time, this one not worrying us. We might not have been drunk enough to start having visions, but we were sufficiently smashed not to be anxious about a few short hours disappearing, insignificant in the light of the eternity unfolding above our heads.

No, we carried on with our game, changed it up a bit, because of the French word for chilly, which I'd told Winslow was *frisquette*, which made him laugh, just like all words ending in *-ette*. Like the Arquette sisters, Patricia and Rosanna, he said. He could never see their name in film credits without smiling, but before I let him carry on I wanted to know how he knew they were sisters, something I'd always wondered about. He didn't know, he said, it just seemed obvious to him that with a name like that, which he pronounced *Arkwett*, the simpleton, they had to be sisters. Okay. Then we started listing off all the movies they'd been in, only to realize with amazement that Rosanna was part of the cast of Luc Besson's *Le Grand Bleu*, and that in fact life was an endless series of astonishments, a web of inexplicable interactions in which each atom inscribed itself in the logic of the Big Everything. The only connection we could establish between Patricia and blue, apart from it being the colour of her eyes, was David Lynch's

Blue Velvet, in which Patricia didn't have a role, sure, but that doesn't matter because she did act in another movie of his, *Lost Highway*, of which Winslow hadn't understood a thing but must have had some blue in it. I did not dare admit that I had failed to grasp all the movie's subtleties too, I can be really annoying on the subject, so we put *Lost Highway* to one side and focused on *Blue Velvet* and Isabella Rossellini, especially the scene where she yells as she disrobes beneath the stars. Alcohol was screwing with our memories, neither of us able to remember what the title referred to. "Maybe Isabella's dress was made of blue velvet," I suggested, but Winslow told me I was confusing everything, that not hers but the Holy Virgin's robe was made of blue velvet, night blue, sky blue, night-sky blue, and together we raised our eyes to the starry heavens where we nearly did see Mary, having finished the bottle of whiskey and seizing on that as a reason to go back into the cottage. To which Winslow added, with a guffaw, that it was starting to get "friskwette." *Friskwette*, fucking French people!

And the night carried on like that, careening between whiskey, Isabella Rossellini, and the Virgin Mary. We also discussed Anita, it goes without saying, the wound still too raw for the alcohol to be able to mitigate its burning pain. Our inebriation was such that Winslow was almost able to convince me there hadn't been a conspiracy at all, and that if there had been a conspiracy, neither he nor Anita were mixed up in it. "It's no longer a conspiracy," I said, "if half the people are not involved." Winslow took advantage of my proposition to inform me he was right, that there hadn't been any scheming, "No fucking plot, Robert." I think they call this kind of reasoning a *petition principii*, but I was too tipsy to start analyzing what he was saying. Instead, I tried to explain to Winslow that the omnipresence of Humpty Dumpty in my life was something we could no longer ignore. "Coincidence," he said, "pure coincidence. Don't let a fucking potato ruin your life," and those were his last words, as soon as he'd finished he started snoring, comfortably ensconced in his chair. I managed to say, "Humpty Dumpty is not a fucking potato, Bob, he's an egg," and then I too fell asleep.

I was dragged out of my slumber in the early hours by a knocking at the door, still in the same position I'd been in an hour or two earlier, sitting squarely on my chair, head down and my chin touching my chest. In my dream it was Winslow, disguised as Humpty Dumpty, who was knocking on the door, but when I opened my eyes there he was snoring in front of me, chin on his chest and a thread of drool hanging down, so it couldn't have been him outside playing the fool or pretending to be a monster. A great shiver ran through me when I realized Humpty Dumpty himself might be waiting on the other side of the black glass, but I pulled myself together and called myself every name under the sun, from *drunkard* to *idiot*, because I was ashamed that I'd knocked back too much and that my fear was irrational, if I have to spell it out. It could only be one of two people: Anita or Robbins. I kicked Winslow, who fell out of his chair whining, "No!

No! Humpty Dumpty is not a potato, he's an egg," words that made me tremble again, dreading that my particular anxieties had penetrated Winslow's dreamscape. But, not having the time to dwell on it, I gave the fool's flabby flesh another kick and told him we had company. Mired in his sleepy fog, he initially begged me not to open the door, saying it was Humpty Dumpty, but then, following the same reasoning I myself had pressed into service, he smoothed his meagre hair against his head and sheepishly agreed it could only be Anita or Robbins. Nevertheless, I was a little nervous as I staggered to the door, you never know what life has in store — and I was right, I was right a hundred times over, for life is a fabric of disturbing and macabre surprises.

It was Jack Picard.

N o need for me to identify him. Right off the bat, grinning, he introduced himself. "Jack Picard," he said in a hoarse, sonorous murderer's voice forged deep in the mysterious, hazy reaches of the underworld—such as you'd imagine, and correctly, a murderer's voice to sound like. Civility demanded that I introduce myself in turn, though right then it seemed a little too much to ask. I stood there petrified, as had been happening a lot over the past week or two, and during the time I stood there petrified, a few questions—highly pertinent in the circumstances—crossed my mind.

Am I still asleep or am I having a major episode of delirium tremens? That was the first, the question of course launching me into a dizzying reflection on the nature of true and false, of the plausible and the burlesque, dreams and nightmares, antimatter and bosons, all concepts I'd studied. And as I couldn't answer the first question, which contained innumerable and prickly sub-questions, my mind, in a state of high alert, bifurcated and started to consider the murderer's manners. Since when do murderers knock before coming in, or to put it another way, since when do murderers knock on the door before knocking you off, behaviour not exactly helping their cause, because if you announce you've come to knock someone off by knocking at the door, the would-be knocked-off person has time to respond and surreptitiously knock off the first, so from this I deduced that Jack Picard had no intention of doing us in, or at least not immediately, because otherwise he wouldn't have knocked before he knocked us off, or he would have knocked us off without knocking, which is basically the same thing.

It's ridiculous, the things that run through your head when you're terrified. While Picard stood waiting on the threshold, I wracked my brain contemplating the possibility of an immaterial being migrating from one dimension to another, or, to put it simply, about the chances of an abstraction materializing. But since when do characters from the pages of a novel leave them and move out into the tainted, volatile air of a reality whose existence nothing authenticates, thus hazarding their disappearance forever? From the time I'd entered into Mirror Lake's gravitational field, I could see no other explanation, which brought me back to the first question and its corollaries but also to one of my recent conversations with Winslow. "What am I doing in this mess?" I sighed, and then, "Am I still asleep, am I drunk, or maybe both: am I sleeping *while* drunk?"

It was only when the spiral started eating its tail, and my questions started tripping each other up, that I came out of my ossified mineral state and rejoined the land of the living, the latter really no more than a figure of speech, because the more you advance in age and wisdom, the less you have any idea what wisdom means. The only person in the room who seemed to be genuinely alive was Picard. As for Winslow, he had the same expression as the four-hundred-million-year-old rock, which led my mind down another question-track. I started to wonder if this rock, and therefore any rock, had feelings, if the universe's fate worried it, and if it was tempted to bang its head on something soft when things were going badly, me basing this postulation on the fact that rocks, not in the least frightened by hardness, must feel some kind of revulsion toward soft things. Which answered my earlier question: yes, rocks also suffer angst.

During this time, Picard was waiting, the fact of which prompted me to observe my own position in the light of our frequent propensity to assume that murderers are impatient. Actually, as far as murderers go, Picard seemed quite high up the pecking order of values regulating social relations, so I invited him to come in—as if I had a choice—and this led to Winslow opening his eyes wide in surprise, his face still petrified in the inorganic magma of the four-hundred-million-year-old rock his features had taken on.

What followed was kind of confusing, because I still hadn't yet absorbed the fallout of the second-most memorable bender in the history of Mirror Lake. When Picard showed up, I was floundering in the muddy waters of one of those moments in which your environs alert you to their disequilibrium, in which the sight of the tiniest bread-crumb, jam stain, or morsel of potato left on a plastic tablecloth by a carelessly handled tea towel makes you resolve never to eat again. In short, I wasn't feeling too good and, to be frank, needed a drink, which, it seemed from the evidence, was also the case for both Winslow, whose stare seemed to be fossilizing, and Picard, who was a little pale.

I found a clean glass for Picard, sat Winslow back down on his chair, signalled to Picard to have a seat, and waited stoically for him to get out his gun and tell us that we were now hostages. But he didn't have a gun, and he wasn't thirsty, although he was definitely hungry, hence his looking a little pale, so I told him to help himself, but that I wasn't his maid—crazy how bold nausea can make you. If I were a hero, I'd have attacked him from behind while he was rummaging in the fridge, then tied him to his chair and phoned Robbins. Which reminded me that I hadn't yet asked Winslow how he'd got a hold of my phone number. There'd been too much happening, I hadn't had time to concentrate on the basics. But I wasn't a hero, and I didn't want to make Robbins happy—and, more germane, had no idea how to lock him in a camel clutch, bear hug, or any other fighting technique that allows you to overpower an opponent.

When I was young, around nine or ten, I'd been a pretty big wrestling fan. And then I'd grown old, but that's another story. Every Sunday after mass, good weather or bad, I'd sit in front of the television with my brother and watch *All-Star Wrestling*, featuring the Rougeau brothers, Little Beaver, Tarzan "The Boot" Tyler, Édouard

Carpentier, Sky Low Low, the entire gang of cheerful lunatics knocking chairs on each other's heads while the audience yelled for the referee to crack down on moves that threatened to ruin the show. I can still hear the shouting as the commentator started speaking. "Ladies and gentlemen, in the right corner, *Jaaaaacques Rrrrrougeau!*" And the crowd would go wild, my brother and I whistling and yelling, "This is awesome!" or "Ho-ly shit!"—indifferent to the anxious sighs of our mother making dinner in the next room. After the show, we started wrestling each other, which our mother didn't like either, even if it was a ritual without which the harmony of our Sunday mornings would have been disrupted. Since I was already too stupid to stand up for myself, it was always my brother who acted the part of the good guy, and three times out of four he got to be Jacques Rougeau, nicknamed Jack, which sounded more manly, like in a Western where the real men are all identified by short, sharp monikers: Bill, Bob, Will, Jeff, Jack, Joe.

My friends and I, we were cowboys too. Real ones, right out of Hollywood studios, which was why we gave ourselves dude names that rolled off the tongue more naturally if we were brandishing our plastic revolvers or playing war—which was allowed in the old days, our parents unconsciously recognizing the value of catharsis. My name was Bob, obviously; Raynald Bolduc—Rosie's cousin—was Ron, preferring that to Ray; Denis Bélanger was Bill, because of his father's suspect admiration for Billy the Kid; and Yvan Lapierre was Jim, in honour of Jim

Bradley, alias Jungle Jim, Yvan being his biggest fan after Ginette Rousseau, who liked to imagine herself Goddess of the Lions. I forget who the others were, but one thing is certain: we'd already been influenced by American culture. Otherwise we'd have been called Ti-Bob, Ti-Ron, Ti-Bill, Ti-Jim, according to the traditional Quebec habit of diminutives. A government proud of its linguistic heritage might have commissioned a study on the subject, but it must have been done already, everything's been done, including the atomic bomb and Phentex slippers. We were still got called Ti- anyway, my friends and I, especially once we'd taken off our gangster costumes, our Heroes of the Wild West disguises, and returned to being friends — proof that, despite the influence of American cinema, we'd been formed in Quebec from scrap pieces of a quilted bedspread made to the sound of fiddle tunes.

All this to say that after mass and the Sunday wrestling, I fought my brother in an unfair fight in which I was invariably a bad guy like Abdullah the Butcher, Killer Khan, and others. Of course, my brother won, because he was the good guy and I was bigger and for that reason alone needed to let myself be slaughtered — this is what is known as justice — and because I really sucked at games where you let yourself be punched in the mouth without protest. And as I never gave a toss about learning how to trip somebody up, I wasn't all that keen on the idea of attacking Jack Picard this morning. All I wanted was to find out Picard's story so I could resolve some of the paradoxes in the questions puzzling me.

So let's get back to Picard, who'd sat down on the other side of the table and was eating the leftover roast chicken he'd found in the fridge while I was emerging from the past. When I saw it, I quickly turned away, not wanting to suffer through the spectacle of any food being eaten — especially disgusting to someone who's abused a liquid diet the previous night. And I noticed that Winslow had a hand in front of his mouth and was also trying to find some clean surface to look at, a sign that he was de-fossilizing but not feeling well. The problem, though, is that the human being, as is true of pretty much every other animal on the planet, has five senses, and not looking at Picard was fairly pointless as we could still hear him. Besides, the penetrating odour of cold chicken must have spread as far as Bangor, Maine, and it took all my strength to hold back the surge of bile burning my esophagus.

The most important thing to do in such circumstances is to think about something else and stay calm and still, particularly to be still. I quickly tried to find a topic to reflect on, but in vain. Usually all I need is something tiny, a little flower looking sad, a spot on the carpet, a word that sounds nostalgic, and I'm off, propelled miles away from the scene taking place in front of me. It's a mechanism of self-defence of a kind, though it only works reflexively, thanks to an automatic internal trigger system. Try to activate it yourself and it just doesn't work. So, given the dearth of something to think about, I diminished my expectations and reflected on precisely that — about the fact that you can think in order to *avoid* thinking, just as you can talk without saying anything, and do this with the nuance that thought without a subject can attribute to something that deserves to be articulated on the occasions when you actually want to speak, and if a non-thought does not become thought each time you want to express it. But nine times out of ten, the person thinking about nothing would prefer to keep quiet and focus on the void out of which he is trying to make some sort of *cogitatum* arise. It's very Zen.

And Zen, that's something to reflect on too; I might have dawdled there for a while had Winslow not fallen off his chair again when he tried to get up to go to the bathroom. Winslow didn't have the resources I had, and evidently was unable to think about thinking nothing. I helped him stagger to the bathroom before he soiled the floor, and that's when Jeff and Bill showed up, attracted by the smell of cold chicken, because dogs have five senses too, and I'd actually add a sixth: the good sense not to get hammered. What with everything so topsy-turvy I'd forgotten them, and I deduced from their sudden appearance that only a few tiny seconds had elapsed between the moment the fridge light clicked on and Winslow's toppling over. I also realized that Jeff was getting older and his age was rubbing off on Bill, subsequently suffering from early-onset senility, given that neither of them had barked when Picard came into view, like a killer at dawn, behind the black glass. Looked like I needed to have a little chat with Jeff before something bad happened, and Winslow needed to talk to Bill too, to teach him not just to repeat everything Jeff said, and particularly not to keep quiet about everything Jeff didn't say.

Jeff appeared not to want to chat, and was pretending to Picard that he was a starving dog whose master hadn't fed him. He's incredible in the role of beaten, neglected child. He feigns expressions that would break anyone's heart, even a murderer's, because murderers have hearts too, whatever people say. Otherwise they'd be zombies and incapable of killing people, unless you live in Haiti, where you're better off not hanging out with zombies. The difference between a murderer's and a non-murderer's heart is that the first is a little blacker because it contains more mortal sins than other people's. I have to say I've never understood the notion that all sins merit the same punishment, so that God forgives the murderer and the adulterer equally, this always striking me as particularly hard on the one who's bumped off. As for the cuckold, well, too bad for him, all he has to do is kill his wife's lover and then rise up to heaven to be forgiven.

But maybe God, who's been around for an eternity, no longer takes offence at the infinite difference between good and bad. Perhaps this is where his mercy comes from, from his having seen so much and knowing we are nothing, that we are no more than the minuscule droppings of a chickadee or a sparrow. And one of the six billion bits of bird shit populating the planet was sitting in front of me, at *my* table, feeding *my* dog with *my* chicken, and giving me the stink-eye as though *I* was the asshole. "Jeff is a happy dog," I spat in Picard's face, and a long moan came from the bathroom to confirm it, immediately followed by a sound that was half liquid, half solid, like the sound of vegetable soup being thrown carelessly into a bowl.

You can't spend the whole day staring each other down so, what with Picard being so phlegmatic, I was the one who lashed out.

"What do you want?" I asked.

In reply, he lifted with one hand the chicken bone he'd gnawed clean, which might have meant he'd come to flay us alive or, more simply, to eat. So I attacked from a different angle. "I know who you are," I said, in the tone of a guy who's seen it all before, which made him put on a smile which could have meant two things: that he didn't care, or that my claim amused him, because do we ever really know anyone, including ourselves? If the latter, it also meant that he was something of a philosopher—like the Jack Picard of Morgan's novel.

While I was thinking about this, a third hypothesis snuck into my mind, where, like all sneaky hypotheses, the impression it left was slight but refused to disappear completely. *Could it be*, this hypothesis suggested, *that Jack Picard's tendentious smile means that he takes me for an idiot and isn't Jack Picard at all but, let's say, John Doolittle?*

This possibility made me a little nervous, because I had no way of checking who he really was short of asking to see his photo ID, which is hardly the done thing in these situations. Yet somehow I still dared to say, "Do you have an identity card with your picture on it?" The ferocious glare he gave me could have been interpreted in numerous ways, but I was sick and tired of splitting hairs, and whistled "Ode to Joy" until Picard finally opened his mouth to tell me he needed a weapon.

"I need a gun," he said, throwing it out there as if this was the most natural thing in the world, as if he was telling me how nice the day was or that he liked grapefruit juice. If he'd said "I need a woman," I'd have been annoyed but would have understood. Same thing if he'd said "I need a car," "I need a boat," or "I need a credit card." Really, the only thing that would have disturbed me more than "I need a gun" would have been "I need you." I should have kept to my state of non-thought because, before I was even able to open my mouth, he said it, "I need you . . ." To change the subject, I started to laugh, a nervous little laugh, jerky and nerve-grating, so that I didn't hear the end of Picard's sentence. Trying to control my laughter I blurted out, "Jeff is a happy dog," which had nothing to do with the matter at hand but I needed to say something in order not to look foolish and that's all that came to mind, along with thoughts of grapefruit juice I had no idea how to shoehorn in.

Picard was giving me the same look that Robbins, Jones, and Winslow had when I said "aleatory," a day not so long ago but that seemed to belong to the last century. It was the same way Bill and Jeff had glanced at me the night before—in other words, as if I was crazy. After which, Picard repeated his sentence in its entirety, but this time without the disingenuous pause between "I need you" and the rest. "I need you to get that gun," he said calmly, and, unable to control a fresh burst of laughter adding itself to the first, I answered like a madman, "What, so you can pepper our old hides with gunshots? No way." "No way" was the only part I said in English, but nevertheless he understood the gist of my answer and, giving as good as he got, picked up the knife lying on the counter (proof that you should never leave a knife lying around) and then grabbed Jeff and held it to the poor animal's throat—and Jeff, thinking this was all part of a game, actually carried on wagging his tail!

But Picard wasn't playing, I watched as his murderous nature raced to the surface and furrowed his face with deep, worrying grooves. I swear, there's no better remedy for uncontrollable laughter than seeing someone you love being threatened by a bloodthirsty brute. And there's no better way of sobering up than to feel your own suppressed killer instincts brewing. "You touch this dog, you're dead," I said authoritatively in a voice I didn't recognize, hoarse, hard, risen from the misty depths of archaic worlds imprinted on our genes.

I could see from his Cossack's expression that he knew I wasn't joking, though he also knew he'd guessed right by going for Jeff. I'd have done anything for my dog, and the shit knew it, he'd guessed it the minute he'd set foot in the cottage. I thought, *Well played, Picard.* If this were a movie, I'd have been Humphrey Bogart. And how would Bogie have reacted in such a situation? He'd have lit a cigarette and muttered, "Don't worry, doll"—because Jeff would have been a girl—and then Bogie would have laid his cards down and won with a straight flush. And that's exactly what I was going to do, out of love for Jeff.

"Okay," I said at last, lighting an imaginary cigarette and repeating that if he touched a hair on this dog or any other he was dead. Satisfied with my answer, he asked for a pencil and a piece of paper, on which he wrote down the address of a bar in Bangor. That's where I was supposed to head, where I'd ask for Jack and say Jack had sent me. I also had to bring him some dough—some green, some dosh, some moolah, he added—cognizant, as Roger Waters had sung to the world, that money is a crime.

I was getting ready to leave when the noise of a toilet flushing caught our attention: Winslow, we'd forgotten him. Had he been John Wayne or Bruce Willis, I could have expected some help from that corner, but I'd filed him more under the category of Bozo the Clown, just bigger, so I didn't waste any time on that score. Picard had also understood he had nothing to fear from Winslow, and ordered, "That other bozo, tie him up real tight before you leave." The way he said "that other bozo," as if there was more than one bozo in the room and the other one wasn't him, might have shocked me, but I didn't rise to it, the hour was approaching when I would lay out my straight flush in front of his stunned mug, and then we'd see who the other bozo was. When Winslow came out of the bathroom I was waiting for him with a rope, and he had the surprise of his life when he realized what was happening. "What the fuck," he started, seeing the knife being held to Jeff's throat, and then another "what the fuck" when I sat him back down on his chair and tied his hands behind his back and his feet to the legs. "You're crazy," he panted, his breath stinking of vomit. "You're not leaving me alone with this insane man?"

At the time, I'd forgotten that, unlike me, Winslow had read Morgan's novel all the way through, and that he knew what he was talking about. I had to make do with whispering to him that I wasn't crazy, I was Humphrey Bogart and would get us both out of this jam if he just stayed calm. I could see he had his doubts, but right then only one thing mattered to me: saving Jeff. So I picked up my car keys and, before I left, repeated to Picard that if any of the characters shut up in this room — including Bozo the Clown — were injured or worse when I got back, I'd give him the same treatment as the chicken he'd just stuffed himself with. I told Winslow to shut his trap, "Shut up, Bozo!" and then said "Don't worry, doll" to nobody in particular, just as another voice, come from my distant childhood, echoed between the walls of my skull: *I'll save ya, Olive!*

The bar I had to go to, the name of which I won't reveal so as not to harm tourism, might have been a nice place to hang if you'd switched out the barman for a barmaid and the five or six drunks lurking in the darkness thick with remorse with customers able to stand upright. Its status would also have improved if they'd washed the floor, changed the furniture, replaced the carpet, polished the counter, added a couple of decent lamps, and given the tables a once-over with a damp cloth. From the minute I walked in, I felt as if I'd entered a world that long ago became impervious to the call of the swift outside. I'd have to be tough.

"Double bourbon," I grunted to the guy standing behind the bar before I'd even sat down, but apparently that wasn't the way they did things there. He let me sit and stew for several minutes before he deigned to look in my direction, pretending to read the previous day's newspaper that had been crumpled by the five or six drunks behind me fermenting in their shitty lives, as flies did what flies do and deadened the atmosphere with their buzzing.

"I've come to see Jack," I said in my new hoarse voice and, noticing a slight lift of his left eyebrow, I felt something had shifted in the brain of a guy who'd initially decided I wasn't worth wasting any time on.

"Which Jack?" he asked, still staring fixedly at the filthy newspaper—a response, I'll admit, that I wasn't expecting. Which Jack, which Jack indeed, how should I know? Jack Jack, LE Jack, ZEE Jack, whichever Jack might get me out of this fix and allow me to return to my peaceful existence, to be back with my dog, my lake, my moose, my rock, and my Winslow, for fuck's sake.

"Jack Jack," I said with a hint of annoyance. "I have to talk to him."

"And what do you want with him?" the guy shot back.

"It's private, I'll only speak to Jack," I continued, wanting him to see I wasn't the kind of guy to be impressed by any old Jack. "I'll only talk to Jack."

"Which Jack?" the knucklehead repeated.

Before the most high-performing of my nerve cells decided to either self-destruct or mutually slit each other's throats, which would require a certain amount of skill, I said, "Jack Rabbit, for fuck's sake," because I have a tendency to say stupid things when the complexity of everyday life annoys me. Evidently this wasn't the right answer and, as I could immediately see in the eyes of the knucklehead walking confidently toward me, wasn't even a good joke. I had just a few seconds to redeem myself, because otherwise this affable bruiser would throw me out like a piece of trash, Jeff would die, so would Bill, so would Winslow, as would I, Picard having no intention of leaving a witness to his carnage, and when Robbins pulled up in a squeal of tires, it would be too late: the blood would have dried on the kitchen floor where hundreds of flies would be busy doing what flies do.

"If you throw me out, my dog will die," I shouted before he grabbed my shirt collar, which made the drunks startle before immediately slumping back over their respective tables. But my instinct had aimed true: Artie liked dogs. As I would learn later, he was called Artie—at least one woman had been a little more original in the choice of her godson's name—and he'd had a dog when he was a child, a little fox terrier called Bing who'd been the only light in his existence, just like Bambi and Bamboo had been for Anita, a dog two street kids named Jack Ryan and Jack Bryan had unfortunately chosen to attack, the first Jack consequently having his balls cut off and then the second one losing his too. Artie didn't mess around when it came to dogs, you could tell that right away. So my revealing the threat hanging over Jeff allayed his fears somewhat, but it wasn't enough, he had his orders, I needed to be more precise about which Jack I wanted to talk to. In the stress of the situation it didn't occur to me to say that another Jack, Jack Picard, had sent me, which would have solved the problem immediately. Instead I asked if I could make a call, and Artie pointed at the grimy telephone hanging at the end of the bar.

As I dialled the number, I prayed like never before for Picard to answer, despite believing even less in God than I did the last time I'd invoked his name. I was even so fervent as to promise to the Almighty—that's what I called him, hoping to flatter—that I would commit to a novena if Picard would just answer the fucking telephone. But God, no fool, didn't appreciate the word *fucking*, didn't believe me about the novena, so didn't grant my prayer. After twenty rings I hung up, redialled, tried the thing with God again, flattering him though promising nothing, but God wasn't stupid, and it didn't work. The third time, I didn't even bring God into it—pointedly ignored him—and focused really hard on Picard, calling him every name under the sun, and on the thirty-second ring, Winslow answered.

For a moment I thought I'd been too quick to judge Winslow, believing that he'd somehow managed to free himself and knock Picard out and tie him up in turn, but I was overestimating Winslow's capabilities, God not having answered his call either, even if the jerk had been praying for three hours straight in the hope that the hostage situation was all just a bad dream. "Thank God," he sighed, hearing my voice and unaware of the indifference of his God who had nothing to do with Picard, at the end of his tether, finally pushing Winslow's chair over to the ringing phone and advising him to keep totally still—if he misspoke a single word, Picard muttered, he would sink the sparkling kitchen knife longing to be used on fresh flesh into his big paunch. After a brief exchange I realized Winslow was no Bruce Willis, that I had to accept him as he was, and told him it was urgent, he needed to put Picard on the line.

"Picard, it's Moreau," I started.

"I know," he said. He was furious.

"There are three Jacks in this fucking bar," I said, imitating his tone, this to let him know he wasn't intimidating me, though I didn't yet know if there actually were three Jacks in the fucking bar. I chose the number randomly to make him take me seriously. "Which Jack is the right one?"

Silence.

"Which Jack, Picard?" I repeated, omitting to ask him for a physical description of the guy in question, which might have helped me.

"Which Jack? Which Jack? Jack Jack," he said, concluding with: "My Jack, THE Jack!"

Circumstances had changed while Picard had been enjoying his stay in the slammer, and clearly he was unaware that the Jacks had multiplied in the meantime. As for his Jack, he was simply Jack, Jack Jack, that was all I needed to say—and that Jack Picard had sent me. Had I at least mentioned that Jack Picard sent me?

Silence at the end of the Bangor line I was holding in my sweaty hands. "Of course," I exploded, breaking the silence. "What do you take me for?"

Then I hung up, after pleading with him to stay calm, that I had an idea and would quickly sort this out. To be honest, I was a little shame-faced when I turned back to Artie, to whom I explained that I'd been sent by Jack Picard—who only knew one Jack, ZEE Jack, the first Jack.

"Who are you?" Artie muttered, put on his guard by the mention of Picard's name, and The Who's hit song "Who Are You?" started playing in my head at the same time as the credits for *CSI: Las Vegas* started rolling, though it wasn't really the right moment, even if I did want to watch an episode and settle warmly into my armchair, with Jeff at my feet lying on my slippers, the comfort of which I was sadly missing. Seeing that I was slow to react, Artie came closer and, casting his enormous shadow over where I was sitting in the single patch of light in the bar, again asked, "Who are you?"

Who are you? Who are you? Like it's even possible to answer that question without getting bogged down in metaphysics. Who are you? Nobody, some dumbass, an idiot who fled to the woods trying to get away from it all, thinking he might be able to disappear into nature, be like a mole or a shrew, for God's sake. Who are you? What a question! Was I asking who he was? Then, noticing that Artie was showing signs of impatience, I ended up blowing off the metaphysics and saying "Robert Moreau," though I could as easily have said Denis Labranche and it wouldn't have made a difference as he had no idea who I was and, besides, a name has never defined the fundamentals of anyone's identity, as his answer proved: "Robert Moreau... never heard that name."

"I'm a friend of Jack's," I said, which was a barefaced lie, but who cares.

"Which Jack?" the idiot said.

"Picard!" I yelled, which made the half-dozen drunks jump; Number Five even knocked his drink over.

No need to be upset, said his eyes stretched wide, and then he disappeared behind a moth-eaten curtain, exactly

184

like in Bogart movies, which I'd forgotten during the journey from Mirror Lake to Bangor.

To kill time as I waited for him to come back, I stole
his newspaper, which was full of blood, dreadful crimes,
exploding bombs, ripped-apart bodies, run-over dogs.
Which made me think of Jeff, who must by now have
realized things were going badly, even though he didn't
read the paper. This gave my courage a boost and I put
the newspaper back in its place and started reading the
labels on the bottles arranged in front of me, a little less
depressing than the rag Artie was clearly enjoying. I'd
reached the end of the first row of bottles when he came
back to tell me that Jack wouldn't be long. I nearly said
"which Jack?" to be funny, but kept quiet, laughed a little
to myself, scratched my nose, my forehead, my ear, tilt-
ing my head to one side, my eyes half closed, because a
hysterical laugh was bubbling up inside me. And then I
ended up pinching my thigh: this had to stop.

The atmosphere immediately lightened after Artie
went behind the dirty curtain and then appeared in front
of it. I was even granted my shot of bourbon — on the
house — and a grunt that could have passed for a degree
of politeness. I picked up the glass, and while I waited for
Jack to arrive — the Jack I hoped would be the right Jack,
ZEE Jack — I carried on reading, very slowly, so I didn't
miss any bottles. My mind started losing itself amid the
different lettering and gilding decorating the labels and
I became nothing more than a decoding machine that
understood zilch about what it was decoding, as is true of

all machines, no matter what we say about their intelligence, so much so that I didn't notice Jack arriving. He sat down next to me, in the shadow, waiting for me to react, which I wasn't about to do since I was in machine mode. It was Artie who pulled me out of the coma I was in by entering my field of vision to pick up the Smirnoff vodka, the name of which I was spelling in my head. I blinked and the first thing I saw was Jack and, colouring his entire left arm, a tattoo of some kind of Shiva whose own multiple arms were unfolding around his twitching biceps. I also noticed that he was quite small for a Jack, though not for a moment did I believe this to be a measure of his ferocity. Generally, in movies, the smallest guys are the meanest, and I decided to believe in the plausibility of fiction.

"Are you Jack?" I asked, as a way into the subject, which wasn't very subtle, but I wasn't used to this kind of situation and had to start somewhere. As the other man didn't seem to think my question was very appropriate — Shiva's frenzied squirming was a sign he was about to get mad — I quickly added "Jack Jack, are you Jack Jack, THE Jack, ZEE Jack?" After a couple of seconds, Jack Jack nodded his head, Shiva calmed down, one of the drunks burped, and we were ready to talk about serious things.

So I told Jack Jack why I was there, all the while staring Shiva straight in the eyes, Jack Jack keeping his profile to me, and when I'd finished he asked why he should believe me, since there was nothing to prove it was really the freak Picard who'd sent me. He had a point there, although it was really only half a point, because how would I even know he existed if Picard hadn't told me about him? I thought I was being pretty intelligent when I put that out there, but Jack Jack didn't exactly share that opinion — he wanted tangible proof. Running out of arguments, I told Jack Jack I'd just been on the phone with Picard, which seemed to be tangible enough proof for him, because immediately he shouted for Artie (which is how I found out his name) to go and look for Jack. Right then, I thought, as any sensible person would, that there were only two Jacks, otherwise Artie would have asked "which Jack?" But no, I have to think they knew instinctively which Jack they were discussing, that they would recognize one or the other by their tone of voice, or that there was a certain Jack hierarchy according to which they always appeared in the same order.

Ten minutes or so later — during which time, following Jack Jack's example, I hadn't opened my mouth except to put the edge of my bourbon glass to it, Artie, who had reappeared, refilling it every time it threatened to be empty — I was flanked by two Jacks, a Little Jack, and a Big Jack, the second surely pushing six foot six. There we sat, arranged in order of size, with Big Jack on my right, me in the middle, and Little Jack on my left, like the Dalton brothers minus one. Little Jack's mean expression immediately led me to think of him as Joe Dalton, and of the big one, who looked stupid, as Averell. As for me, to avoid any confusion I decided to be William. It was right at that moment that a kind of kaleidoscopic stripe lit up the mental space I was moving in, and Joe Dassin, wearing a ridiculous white suit, appeared in front of the Smirnoff bottle. I realized immediately what was about to happen, but before I was able to repel the singer's image, he was humming "*Tagada, tagada, voilà les Dalton, tagada, tagada, voilà les Dalton,*" and I knew I was in for it: for the next few hours I would be saddled with the most desolate song in my endless repertoire. I downed my freshly filled glass in one go, hoping the alcohol would erase Dassin and shut him up, but the results were diametrically opposed to what I'd counted on. The unexpected powers of memory, which I sometimes marvel at, sought out the rest of the lyrics in some deep fold of my brain, and they flowed out onto the bar like a thread of foam and bile, just as the two Jacks were talking with their heads down, drawing abstract shapes with their fingertips in the sticky ring-marks left by their drinks and around which the thread of foam and bile was spreading.

While my eyes followed the image Jack Jack's fingers were creating, of an octopus or a Vitruvian Man, I was following, over Joe Dassin's ditty, the conversation he was having with the other Jack, Big Jack. Essentially, Big Jack needed to find a weapon, ammunition, and some dough for Picard, who was in a fix. I was the one in the fix, in case they hadn't noticed, but I kept my mouth shut, all the more so because Little Jack became enraged, just like Joe Dalton, when Big Jack wanted to know if there was any tangible proof that Picard had sent me. When he saw the colour Little Jack turned—a bright crimson, suggesting the risk of an internal hemorrhage—Big Jack saw it was pointless to insist. He slipped behind the filthy curtain and immediately returned with a third man, the third Jack, the Middle-Sized Jack, who sat down next to me as Averell shuffled to the end of the line. Seated in this order, the third Jack became William and me Jack, resulting in four Jacks sitting at the bar, talking about a fifth Jack.

The parade of Jacks was a little mind-boggling, so I ordered a coffee from Artie and he asked me if I'd like an ice cream cone with it. Which meant he didn't have any coffee. And then, somehow, I found myself with a Magnum, a box of ammunition, and a wallet of bills in front of me. To be certain I wasn't tricking them, the Dalton brothers decided that Artie would accompany me, this not pleasing me too much, but as I was a little drunk and clearly had no choice, the idea of a second driver was welcome. Except that Artie refused to drive. "What, so you can point the gun at my head? Do you think I'm an idiot or something?"

"What if I give you the gun?"

No way. Artie didn't want to take the wheel because in movies it's always the driver who's in a weak position and gets trapped. Amazing! Artie didn't only like dogs, he also liked cinema. That would give us something to discuss on the journey, which could well be a long one.

I waited for Artie to close up his till, went to take a piss, he went to take a piss, and then we left the three Jacks behind us in the darkness of the bar, unaware that, outside, the swift was still animating fecund nature with his melodious song. After we passed the first intersection I started breathing a little again and suggested to Artie that we might turn on the radio, so that once and for all I could bury Dassin, who was finishing his refrain in the glovebox, indifferent to the compassion he inspired in me. Artie's answer was no, he didn't like music. Okay, that was a good thing, otherwise we wouldn't have discovered the onion.

I should explain what I mean by that. As Artie and I were leaving Bangor we heard an odd screeching noise in the car. At first we thought a small animal must have found its way into the vehicle, maybe a squirrel or a field mouse. I stopped driving with the intention of letting the animal out, but all we found was an onion rattling under Artie's seat. I wanted to let it out anyway, just as I'd have done with an animal, but Artie said, "No, let's keep it," putting the thing in the middle of the back seat to keep an eye on it. Artie explained that he had a certain fondness for objects, that when he was little a potato became his confidant for a few weeks after Bing died. At that point, of course, I didn't yet know who Bing was, so he told me the story, highlighting his emasculation of Jack Ryan and Jack Bryan, two who wouldn't bother another dog for the rest of their fucking lives. As stories go, it was pretty bloody, but somehow touching. And then the potato showed up, Artie said, and he called it Bing, in memory of Bing. It was a New Brunswick potato, the sweetest type, with little eyes and everything, Artie added, and then he went quiet, moved by the memory. If I hadn't been slightly drunk, I'd have thought Artie had a couple of screws knocked loose just before or after he was born. I was drunk, though, and intoxication renders people sentimental, so piously I joined him in silence, then broke it by telling Artie he could keep the onion, that I'd give it to him. But he didn't want it. "Your car, your onion," he said.

To pass the time, we tried to come up with a name for the onion. At first, Artie wanted to call it Bing, but in my opinion, I said, all these Bings and Jacks were starting to be silly, and I asked him how back in Bangor they managed to figure out which Jack they were talking about. "It's all in where you put the stress," Artie said. "For Little Jack, you put the accent on the first letter, for Middle-Sized Jack you put it on the second letter, and for the tall one, on the third and fourth, which sound identical — [k], [k]," Artie said, using the phonetic pronunciation and sputtering slightly because of the weighty velar occlusive. Conclusion: you can only effectively identify three Jacks despite there being four letters in the name. Beyond that, things would start to be confusing. "Ha, clearly I should have known," I said. Returning to the subject of the onion, we reached a compromise and called it Ping, Ping the Onion. Artie was pleased, one thing led to another, night fell, because it had to fall, and then we arrived at Mirror Lake without having had the chance to chat about film.

I was a little nervous as I stepped out of the car, because I wasn't sure what we'd find inside the cottage. With a guy like Picard, ready to do anything to avoid the darkness, you never know what might happen — hence the double-speed hammering of my heart, which Artie couldn't hear. As I started up the porch stairs, he put his big hand on my shoulder and said, "Ping, did you forget him?" Ping…I'd left him in the car and, to stay in Artie's good graces, went back to get him. "Come on, Ping," I said, loud enough for Artie to hear, "I'm going to show you your new house."

I could tell from the way Artie smiled that he was satisfied, it didn't take much to make the asshole happy. I walked back to the steps, saluting the four-hundred-million-year-old rock on my way past—I, too, was something of an animist—and we went inside.

I was wrong to worry. Everyone was asleep: Picard on the couch, Jeff on the carpet, Bill on the carpet, Winslow too, on the spot where his chair had tipped over. Artie found the scene touching and wished he had his camera with him, but I was irritated more than anything. Neither Jeff nor Bill had so much as batted an eyelid when we arrived, which wasn't normal, and a thought raced into my head that filled me with panic: if neither dog had reacted, they must be dead. I raced over to Jeff, just as Winslow woke up with a start, yelling "NO! NO! Humpty Dumpty is not a potato!" and Picard leapt off the couch and grabbed Jeff and the knife before I could. Jeff started to bark, Bill too, and Artie pinned Picard down in a bear hug. Even Ping joined in, rolling along the carpet in sync with the hustle and bustle of the moment and emitting noises of frying and excitability.

Frankly, the scene was ridiculous, and frankly I was sick of our behaving like idiots, so I stood in the middle of the chaos and shouted, "Whoa, stop," but nobody was listening to me except Ping, who took a hit and, out of breath, rolled to a silent stop in a corner of the room. Around me, the swearing, the gasping and delirium, Humpty Dumpty, Humpty Dumpty, the barking, the biting, the tripping and vicious uppercuts continued. Total chaos, which I stopped by cocking the Magnum and firing a shot at the ceiling, prompting a chandelier to fall and land on Artie, who fainted, whereupon Picard grabbed Jeff and the knife again.

We were back at square one, but at least I could avail myself of a little silence—if I ignored the ambient noise of people catching their breath. Now it was a revolver versus a knife, but Picard had an advantage in the form of Jeff.

"Okay," I conceded. "You give me Jeff, I give you the gun, but you give me Jeff first."

I suppose Picard didn't trust me, because he wanted me to hand over the gun first. But given that I didn't trust him either, we were at an impasse. Whatever, if I wanted Jeff back, I'd have to let go of the Magnum, but what evidence did I have that Picard wouldn't just shoot the whole lot of us, including Jeff, as soon as he had it?

"You have my word," Picard said, but what was a crook's word worth?

I was considering this when Winslow, who'd read Morgan's novel, butted in to say I should give Picard the damn Magnum, he would keep his word, because that's what happened in the damn novel.

"What the hell are you talking about?" I muttered in Winslow's direction, whispering not because I wanted to confide in him, but because an invisible hand was squeezing my vocal cords.

"I'm telling the truth," Winslow shot back. Then he told me that, in the novel, Picard takes hostages in a scene very similar to the one in which we were currently starring, and that he didn't kill anyone when the fool who'd driven a couple of hundred miles to find him a weapon finally gave it to him. Absurd, really, the whole situation was utterly absurd; had we been in a novel, or some classic stage play, someone might have used our example to demonstrate Aristotle's theory of verisimilitude and its opposite.

"So?" said Picard and Winslow in unison, and I lowered my arms, because I was surely in a dream, and you don't die in dreams. You might be beaten up a little, but that's where a dream ends. I handed Picard the gun, Picard released Jeff and the knife, and Jeff jumped into my arms. Bill didn't know where to go because Winslow was still tied up, and Artie peered our way, stunned by the tableau Jeff and I formed. "I'm in a dream," the jerk snivelled, and Winslow asked politely if someone wouldn't mind untying him.

Ten minutes later we were all sitting around the table with the cold chicken, and Winslow, who thought I seemed a bit depressed, kept telling me you couldn't rewrite history, that when it's written, it's written; when it's done, it's done. I told him my view of dream and reality, one that Picard, who was something of a philosopher, didn't entirely share. As for Artie, he was eating with Ping sitting in front of him.

"What is this onion?" Winslow finally asked.

"It's Ping," I said. "A magical onion. Nobody can touch it."

Picard thought I was a nutter but, at that point, someone else's opinion of me mattered as much to me as what they thought of Father Christmas, whom I have no time for. Then Picard told us the story of his escape, which happened during a meal with six other prisoners. Just like in the novel, Winslow remarked, not in the least bothered by the situation that was making me, on the other hand, rethink my entire conception of the world.

"Life is a storybook," Winslow said to boost my morale, though Picard was the one who cheered me up by talking about one of the prisoners, a man called Bob, who was completely obsessed with Humpty Dumpty, and he asked Winslow if he suffered from the same fixation. "Are you obsessed with this potato?" he asked.

I should have got the hell out of there — it was the ideal moment — but I was too afraid of ending up in a different novel. So I started laughing, what else could I do, and asked Picard what the other prisoners' names were, but I already knew the answer: Bill, Jeff, Artie and Robert, who didn't like being called Bob.

"Just one missing," I said to Picard. "With you, that makes seven." I was afraid he would tell me the seventh one was called Ping, but it was worse, his name was Tim.

When he said the name, Winslow and I looked at each other in the manner of two guys who know each other well enough to be able to communicate without speaking, and we shouted, "Everybody move, the cops are coming!" The others didn't understand right away, but when they heard tires squealing outside, they thought it was best to believe us—even Picard, who knew that this particular scene wasn't in Morgan's novel. Time was pressing, so I took charge of operations. I dispatched Winslow outside to delay Robbins for as long as possible and, with memories of Anita, sent Picard into the closet in the bedroom, and told Artie not to move, that if anyone asked him any questions, he should just say he was my cousin.

"What's my name, then?" he asked.

"Artie, your name's Artie," I said a little dryly.

"You have a cousin named Artie? That's funny..."

I didn't respond, the fella was clearly even more stupid than I'd thought. I barely had time to notice the Magnum and sit down on it before Robbins entered, unleashing a volley of barking from Jeff that was immediately imitated by Bill and made me rejoice inside. "Good dog," I should have said to him but, given the circumstances, I ordered him and Bill to be quiet. Jeff seemed a little frustrated, and Bill disappointed, but there was no way I could make every Joe and his neighbour happy.

"Having a little cocktail party, are we?" scoffed Robbins with a hammerhead-shark smile, as he noticed the chaos in the cottage that we'd not tidied after the brawl I'd started.

"Yup," I answered, more laconically than ever.

"What brings you here?" chimed in Winslow, conscious of the deliberate pithiness of my reply. It was obvious, really: there'd been a report of a Picard sighting in the area and Robbins was doing a tour of the cottages just in case someone was in a sticky situation.

Winslow assured Robbins everything was fine, that we'd just arranged a little party, we were having fun, we hadn't seen anyone, we were just having a laugh, we'd phone him if we spotted any shifty guys through the window. Either Robbins was bored, wanted to introduce a little levity, or didn't believe us, but he decided to sit down at the table and start making conversation with Artie. This was the moment of danger: if Artie opened his trap, we were done for. Hastily I abandoned my silence to answer Robbins's questions in his place. Robbins was annoyed and wanted to know if Artie was mute. "Yes, he's mute, completely mute," I confirmed, looking Artie straight in the eyes to be sure he understood. And he did, the idiot. If we'd been alone I'd have given him a kiss, but that could wait until later.

Seeing that he wasn't about to get anything out of Artie, Robbins turned to Ping and asked, "What's with the onion?"

Why they were all so interested in Ping, I have no idea, but it was starting to get on my nerves. "It's Ping, a magic singing onion, so don't touch." If I was to appear a lunatic, I might as well go all in.

Disconcerted, Robbins glanced skeptically at Ping, stepped up, and declared that he was going to have a look around the cottage. Believing he meant the outside of the house, I didn't react, but when I noticed he was heading for the bedroom, I stood and shouted "NO!" revealing the Magnum, which Artie noticed and promptly sat down on. I was so impressed I decided I would owe him two kisses when Robbins made himself scarce. "Do you have a mandate?" I asked, but Robbins was baffled. "A mandate," I repeated, "a piece of paper, an authorization."

"Oh!" he exclaimed, bowing to my lack of vocabulary. "You mean a *w-a-r-r-a-n-t*."

"Yes, a warrant, letters rogatory, whatever you want to call it, you dickhead, do you have one?" No, he didn't, I was correct, though all he had to do was come back with one.

After our little exchange — which showed, as Bob Winslow and Ludwig Wittgenstein also believed, that using the right words facilitates conversation and can even save lives — Robbins knew something was up. "What's going on in here and what are you hiding in that fucking room?" he said threateningly.

"Nothing, my privacy, get a warrant and I'll give it up."

Robbins stared at me straight in the eyes, we were doing a lot of looking people straight in the eyes that night, and in the reflection of his Ray-Bans I saw the whole story of Little Red Riding Hood flow past. *What big eyes you have, grandmother, what big teeth you have!* The lie was written all over my face, but what could I do about it — I *was* lying. If there hadn't been any witnesses I'm certain Robbins would have ignored my request for a warrant and kicked the bedroom door down with his spurred boots, but as we weren't alone he had to yield.

I wasn't sure the verb *obtemperate* was appropriate, but

I wanted to use this word rather than *obey*, so I said it: "Obtemperate, Robbins." And then I let him have a turn at stewing in his own ignorance. A few seconds passed, a long enough pause that someone outside the scene might have thought we were bored or had forgotten our lines, after which Robbins headed to the door with an "I'll be back," an assertion which was becoming tedious and didn't tell us anything we didn't already know. As the oaf exited, he tried to catch Artie out by clapping his hands and shouting "*Boo!*" which naturally made him—and everyone else in the room except Ping—jump.

"Ha!" said Robbins triumphantly. "I knew he was a fake."

I reminded him that Artie was neither deaf nor a fake, but mute. If Robbins had eyes, I'm sure we'd have seen how uncomfortable he was feeling, but the Ray-Bans hid that sort of thing.

As Robbins left, I could see that he was still questioning himself and wondering where he'd gone wrong.

"What a bloody fool," Artie whispered once the door was closed.

Robbins immediately reopened it and barked, "Who said that?" And despite being a little slow, Winslow had his antennae tuned in, and he immediately sacrificed himself by saying, "Me." Robbins didn't believe him, but without a lie detector he didn't have many options, so he left again.

As for the rest of us, we stayed fixed to the spot, as though we were on a postage stamp—or, more accurately, in a film still—and we waited for the 4×4's roaring to die away before we moved. It was actually Picard who started the movie rolling again by coming out of the bedroom with Anita's orphaned shoe, the other one still waiting for its parent or Prince Charming in the ferny copse near the cottage. Picard wanted to know where the woman whose perfume permeated the closet was hiding because, he said, he needed a woman.

"I need a woman," he groaned lustily, words I'd have made him take back had Anita been there, but she wasn't any longer, which I told him. She was gone forever, I said, looking down upon the miserable memories stirred in me by the abandoned shoe, no doubt deliberately forgotten due to some sort of Freudian slip.

When I was lifted out of my reverie, I heard Winslow, the traitor, murmuring, "...in love with her," while Artie's eyes got damp. I protested, saying I was no more in love with Anita than with Artie, walking over to plant the two kisses I owed him on his cheeks. My deed contradicted my words, but in truth I wasn't contradicting myself, which everyone understood, including Artie.

"What's going on now?" someone said. "I'm getting out of here," answered Picard, gathering up his things and my car keys, which I tried to get back despite the Magnum's sinister maw pointing at me. "I need a car," he declared, in a voice that brooked no refusal.

I refused anyway, telling him Robbins would catch him before he'd even buckled his seatbelt. "Robbins suspects something, and he's keeping an eye on us." No doubt Robbins was lying in wait at the top of the road for Picard to show. "And what about Artie," I added. "How am I going to take him back to the three Jacks if I don't have a car?" I was pretty sure they'd not be pleased seeing him arrive on foot three days later.

"I can stay," said Artie quickly. He would have liked to change his life and move to the lake with dogs, friends, and birds, but was unaware just how wild nature was, how deceptive her gentleness.

All of which had no effect on Picard and the plan he had in mind: Artie would drive, and he'd hide in the trunk. It was yet another crazy scheme bound to fail, but I stayed mum, as doing otherwise would have been a waste of saliva. Artie said his goodbyes to Ping and told him to behave, patted Jeff's big head, Bill's middle-sized head, and then left with his shoulders bowed, haunted by the images of a dream snatched away as soon as he'd sketched it.

"And don't forget, you're mute," I reminded him, in case they met Robbins, as they most certainly would, and to show me that he'd understood — I could see as much in the subtle smile playing in the corners of his chestnut eyes — he didn't answer. I have to confess, I would miss Artie. I didn't recognize myself anymore. Even though I had, since time immemorial, resolved to hate the entire world, it had only taken a few hours for me to grow attached to a brute with the blood of two kids on his hands, and whose feet were no doubt soaked in the brains of a few other strangers. I was getting soft, just like Jeff, and needed to have a serious word with myself.

After they'd left, the cottage seemed empty and

sad—like after a party, when all that's left in a messy house is women's fickle perfume and the memory of laughter, of a congenial voice and the clinking of glasses. So I offered Winslow one last drink, because he was a little gloomy as well and needed a pick-me-up. Whatever guilt I may have been feeling about my mild alcoholism would abate by morning. We sat back down at the table with Ping and the cold chicken, Bill and Jeff at our feet, and threw them a few scraps of the brown meat because Picard had eaten all the white, and took stock of the never-ending day.

"In Morgan's novel, what happened next?" I asked Winslow. Nothing. He didn't know, he said. The first part finished like that, with Picard's departure, and he couldn't remember what happened next because he'd read it one morning after a night before and needed to reread it when he was sober. For a moment I was afraid this would be the end for us too, that nothing lay ahead of us, the lights were going out, the cottage was disappearing, the lake emptying, and the mountains flattening out and transforming the landscape into a long, arid purgatory. But we weren't in a novel, we were in a nightmare, as I kept repeating to myself.

Winslow was irritated. "Stop asking me about the novel, Robert, we're not in a fucking novel."

The dawn rose on his wise words, because it was time, and, because it has to rise at some time or other, a cuckoo woke up, and a loon started its lament as beautiful as the beginning of the world, as desirable as the end of time.

II.

SECOND BEGINNING

During the days that followed Picard's tempestuous irruption, Jeff was able to enjoy a degree of peace, though I was not. I spent much of my time scrutinizing the lake, the gravel road, the endless trees in the forest, certain that at any moment I would see Jack Picard's hirsute head behind a yellow birch I'd been watching suspiciously, Artie's bulging eyes in the trembling shadows, John Doe's eroded features in the vaporous cloud of mist that rose each morning from Mirror Lake, and then Anita's black eye in the foliage of a bush just a little more disturbed than you would expect it to be. Basically, if it hadn't already happened, I went crazy.

I strode around the lake muttering old-fashioned words like *turbulence*, *turpitude*, and *tribulation* that I'd found in some small compartment of memory where I store things that might be useful during a disaster. These three words epitomized, to my depressed mind, the collapse of the pitiful Eden that my propensity to dream had led me to imagine inhabited the shores of this heaven-cursed lake. If I'd lived in an earlier century, I'd have written tearful letters deploring the torments brought about by prideful man's foolish desire to return to some kind of original purity he does not merit. It would have been a relief to lament in a style that wasn't my own, knowing that someone, across the seas or over a border, was waiting for the faded envelope in which my pain burned. But I was born in the wrong epoch, in the era of messages that are coded, laconic, efficient, and stuffed full of mistakes, and which travel at the speed of lightning, without leaving any time to be tempted to mope. So I walked up and down the beach muttering, and wrote words in the sand that nobody— including me—used or understood anymore, if only to alter my thoughts and put out of mind that life was nothing but tribulation.

"Turpitude," Winslow said in his Maine accent the first time he came to read my beach. And then, to rattle me a little, he said, "Tut-tut, Robert." He could see I wasn't doing well, because you don't write words like *turpitude* when your head's in the right place. But I needed more than a morale-boosting *tut-tut* to regain control of my chaotic life, and this was obvious to Winslow, so he tried suggesting a range of activities from *pétanque* to Monopoly via Ping-Pong and water polo. But the whole affair was pointless. Even the Pink Lady game got no reaction from me. Winslow tried with red, mauve, and green, which contained infinite possibilities, but the mechanism had broken after the encounter with the Daltons and Picard. "Green as Graham," he chortled, proud of his subtlety, in front of his chilly audience. "Green as the magnificent mountains," he bellowed at the top of his voice, while I sank down into my turpitude in the sand. *Tains, tains,*

tains, responded the green mountains, lending him a hand. But in vain. It didn't work. I was depressed. On the lookout and depressed.

If I'd been at all sensible, I'd have made the most of this restful period and nursed myself back to health. I'd have played in the woods with Jeff, raced to the lake for no reason except that the lake was there, the water beautiful, and the summer splendid. Strictly from the viewpoint of temperature, you could say the summer was outdoing itself, proving itself worthy of all the hopes I'd bestowed on it while I'd been shivering through the last months of winter, my nose glued to a window behind which all of Quebec waited, year in and year out, to see if perhaps this time there'd actually be a thaw before the snow returned. I can even recall standing behind a window like this and blowing on my reddened fingers and shamefully rejoicing at the prospect of global warming. I know climate change is not a good thing, and of course I don't want to deliberately contribute to glaciers melting or the triggering of hurricanes and tsunamis but, as some of this has already happened, I'd thought, why not enjoy it a bit before we die? Feeling guilty about a situation whose consequences I couldn't reverse seemed as futile as refusing to eat Winslow's fish once it was on my plate. You have to act in advance. When it's dead, it's dead. You might as well eat.

All this to say that since summer was here in all its splendour, I could have made a little effort to behave normally and consume the meal before me while it was still hot. But no: experience and my natural mistrust convinced me the situation was too good to last. Undoubtedly I wasn't catching the rumbling beneath the blissful silence that had finally fallen over Mirror Lake, its shimmering blue water a screen that was blinding me. I would pay dearly for any lapse in vigilance.

So I kept watch, I was apprehensive, I anticipated the unknown as Jeff chased squirrels, and Winslow, who'd given up on the reappearance of a smile on my face that only blossomed when I was annoyed, tanned his flabby body as he let his fishing rod dangle gently over the edge of his boat, just in case. As for the fish, whose mute cries accompanied my complaints, now would have been the time to act; I could have dismantled his fishing rod, tangled his line up around a branch, and stolen his hooks, but I was too beleaguered about the state of my own pathetic existence to worry over the destiny of other creatures. That's how catastrophes happen. One minute you're gazing at your navel and then... *boom*! You're coshed in the back of the head. By the time you come to, the floor of the oceans has been scraped clean and the Gulf Stream has decided to see what it's like somewhere else. Too bad for us, and all the worse for the generations who will or will not come after.

In sum, instead of getting on with things, I waited for the threatening clouds gathering on the horizon of my near future to fall on me with an infernal roar or, more likely, in the form of a disagreeable endless drizzle, the parade of crazies treading the soil around Mirror Lake having given me a taste of this apocalyptic vision. If I'd been clever, for want of being wise—though I do think the two qualities go together—I'd have read Morgan's novel to see what happened in it. But I was too afraid of discovering I wasn't who I thought I was, and that I had, in a parallel life, committed some crime I'd completely forgotten. I did try several times to open the wretched book, but every time I came across the words *Humpty Dumpty* or *Robert* I closed it again, as if shutting a door to keep hordes of vermin out, and ran to jump in the lake, though without reaping any of the benefits of a healthy swim.

After having demonstrated all the symptoms of a man in love, now I was presenting those of someone suffering from a raging depression, and who knows what depths I might have sunk to had the future not been hastened by an incidental event. Essentially, I was doing so badly at that time that on the day I heard Robbins's 4×4 sending the gravel flying on the road I actually felt an enormous sense of relief: the dreaded calamity was finally here, my wait hadn't been in vain, I could let the tension dissipate.

I was in the cottage making myself a sandwich and telling Ping the story of Cinderella, into which I'd introduced a few variations by switching the pumpkin for a squash, the stepmother for a food processor, Cinderella for a carrot, and Prince Charming for you-know-who, this after wondering, quite legitimately, whether there were male and female onions. Since I'd not been able to come up with an answer to the question, I resorted to my gastronomic knowledge and decided that any marriage between a carrot and an onion would, by and large, have a good result. I wouldn't have bet my shirt on the healthy issue of such a union, but I could alter the outcome of the story; two heroes don't have to procreate in order for us to believe in their happiness. All this deployment of a mad imagination just to try to cheer up Ping, who was looking worryingly pale! He was wasting away day by day — softening, in fact, transforming into something alarmingly limp. I'd even noticed that a tiny green mark had appeared on his golden pelt, near his little onion bum. I didn't make a fuss, Ping was just an onion after all, and I wasn't *that* crazy, but he'd kept me company in my misery and I was attached to him in the way anyone would become attached to a plant that offers its sleepy leaves up to the sun and says hello to you every morning. And, if it made me feel better, why shouldn't I talk to my onion? Ping did indeed make me feel better. There was something peaceful about him, something marvellously uncomplicated, not to mention that Ping was a wonderful listener who never complained.

So there I was, telling him the story of Cinderella and not sure if I should hand the role of fairy godmother to a tomato or an asparagus stalk, which would lead, on the one hand, to a chubby, snickering fairy, and on the other to a skinny but rather juicy one. I was vacillating between tomato fairy and asparagus fairy when I heard the squealing of tires I'd have recognized anywhere. Leaving Ping contemplating, in a blissful state, the beauty of a Cinderella that would truly blossom only after a good wash, I went to the window to make sure that my desire for the tragedy to unfold wasn't playing tricks on me. It wasn't. The 4×4 was indeed there, its angular form taking shape in the August sun as the cloud of dust it had raised started to settle.

"We have company," I whispered in Ping's direction, but Jeff was the one who reacted, delighted that something was happening at last. He rushed to the door, barking rabidly. "Good dog," I said in appreciation, opening the door in the hope that he would rush over and assault the intruder. It was a lot to ask, but fine, at least he'd barked, and that was something.

"Hi," I said to Robbins, almost gaily. "Who disappeared today?"

Hypnotized by something at the centre of the thicket on which his Ray-Bans were trained, Robbins behaved as if I didn't exist, poked up a little pile of black earth with the toe of his boot, and dove behind the clump of trees. Irritated that Robbins was ignoring me, but curious to learn what had caught his attention, I called out a bit more loudly, "Hi! What brings you here on such a wonderful day?"

Mucor ramosissimus, answered the thicket. At first I figured it was the name of the new missing person—a Greek or Slavic name, the sound of it implied, which suggested a change from the roll call of what had been, until now, local missing persons. At least we'd not have a second John Doe who would turn out, later on, not to be an authentic John Doe. But it did occur to me that if Mucor Ramossisimus had died in the thicket, then he must have been a very diminutive Greek, because otherwise his feet would have been visible to one side or the other. I was right on that point — Mucor Ramosissimus was small, but he wasn't Greek, or so I concluded when Robbins started to brandish a mushroom at me from behind the thicket. I was an idiot, I decided — this preferable to letting Robbins take on the job. I told myself my Latin was a little rusty, as was everything else I'd conceded to whatever fate the passage of time and the seasons had in store for me.

Which is all it took for an inexpressible sadness to insinuate itself into the blue of the sky, and for the shushing of the little waves lapping at the shore to be tainted with the melancholy of too-clear days when nothing evades the lucid scrutiny of a soul perceiving the vanity — but also fragility — of everything. "The price of depression," I said, "even if I can't afford it," the whole universe then deciding to join in. The little waves were obviously demoralized, the birds seemed as if they had only learned to sing to express the depth of my dejection, and the wind, carrying the plaintive moan of a harmonica afflicted with despair, was clearly in need of something fortifying.

As for Robbins, he was chomping away on his mushroom with the superior attitude of someone with nothing else to do, and I secretly but violently wished that he would start to convulse and spit up green foam as he succumbed to a terrible suffering. But no, it seemed *Mucor ramosissimus* wasn't poisonous and that Robbins knew what he was doing — or he didn't know what he was doing at all and had got his mushrooms mixed up. While he was excavating his molars with a toothpick — the man could really be gross—I asked him again what had brought him to my place. If nobody had died, then the tragedy I'd been anticipating had changed and taken on an unfamiliar form.

"Anita," he said, as he speared a piece of mushroom with the tip of his toothpick—super gross—"Anita, which is to say Jeanne." He must have learned from Jeanne that she'd swapped her name for Anita. The day already seemed sad enough without bringing women into it, but apparently I wasn't the one who got to decide. In principle, and if I'd been smart, I would have told him I didn't know an Anita and asked, "Anita who? Anita what? Which Anita?" But because I was depressed I burst into tears and whined like a fool that I missed her. By way of consoling me, Robbins grabbed me by the collar and spat in my face, saying that if I ever went within ten feet of her again, he'd kill me. Then he raised his arm in the direction of his 4×4 and Anita, who must have been lying on the back seat, or was maybe hiding behind some sort of scrim that had taken on the colours of its surroundings, got out of the patrol car with her head down, mumbling that she'd just come to pick up a few things she'd left at my place.

Seeing her, I should have flown into a rage—this woman had betrayed me, for God's sake. But I was depressed, as I've said. I gulped down a last sob and told her to take whatever she wanted except for Ping, the rotting onion sitting on the kitchen counter next to the half-eaten cheese sandwich which would end its days in Jeff's welcoming stomach or the garbage. Then I went down to sit by the lake, where a boat was gently gliding in our direction, laden with one Winslow, happy as a lark and whistling something like *sassessissou, sassessissam, sassili.* He'd seen I'd had a visitor and, knowing my mental state was teetering on the edge of suicidal, had decided to come over and keep an eye on me in case I opted to hang out with John Doe at the bottom of the lake once Robbins left with Anita, whom Winslow had somehow spotted behind the scrim where she'd been hiding just two minutes earlier.

"Hello, stranger," he called out cheerfully as he climbed out of the boat. "Wanna fish with me?"

If there's one thing that enrages me more than anything, it's naturally jovial people who think that just by casting some of their natural joviality your way, they'll make you want to dance a jig. I stood up, walked over to his boat, snapped his fishing rod in two, and said, "No, I don't wanna fish with you." And then I marched back to the cottage as Anita was leaving, clutching a brown paper bag whose contents I asked to inspect, because Winslow had managed to ignite a healthy dose of the anger my depressed state had suppressed.

I also took the opportunity to tell Anita what I thought of her. But when I gave back her bag, my heart twinged as I noticed her forlorn expression, behind which were silently sheltering the words *you haven't understood anything, you stupid idiot.* But I didn't see these words, I only noticed them afterwards, when it was too late, which is always what happens in tragic love stories. One person hears nothing of what the other person is striving to explain, or misunderstands, interpreting what is said in their own fashion and the situation sours and becomes dramatic. It's what happened to Romeo and Juliet, and it was happening to Anita and me, too. We were victims of the irrevocable constraints of tragedy, and trying to escape them was as pointless as endeavouring to bring Shakespeare back to life so that he might rewrite the end of his story of mad love.

When, at the top of the gravel road, Anita's shadow disappeared along with that of Robbins's dusty 4×4, leaving in its wake faint traces of unleaded gas and Shania perfume, I must confess I was a little shaken, which did not stop me from telling Winslow to take his whistling self back to the south shore and stay there. I hurt him deeply at that moment, just as every fool does who pushes away helping hands reaching out over the precipice. But, nonetheless, he behaved like a proper gentleman and pulled out the blue letter that Anita had slipped into my pocket, before — without whistling — he returned to the shore to which I'd banished him.

Women are perfectly capable of being laconic when they so desire. I had an aunt like that, Hortèse, who would have been Hortense had the priest who baptized her not been half deaf. She usually expressed herself by means of proverbs, or onomatopoeia, a sort of modern-day Sibyl whom people would consult to find out about their near future or to be advised on what attitude to adopt should they suffer a reversal of fortune. "*Bof,*" she would answer most of the time, meaning there was nothing to be done or that it was pointless to worry, and you'd go back home and let the situation deteriorate or sort itself out.

"What did Hortèse say to you?"

"Bof."

"*Bof?*"

"Bof."

Ah, well, there must be a reason, we'd think as we dropped our heads and gazed at our feet shuffling through the mud, or slush, depending on the season.

Sometimes she was a little chattier, but no less enigmatic. When my uncle Jules went to tell her that my aunt Lourette—who had been christened by the same priest—was cheating on him, she replied, "Like father, like son," so that everyone believed Rosanna, Uncle Jules's mother, was also cheating on Uncle Jules's father, Rosaire, making him a cuckold just like his son. Yes, *like father, like son*.

Some in the family interpreted it differently. For this more feminist faction of my ancestry, Hortèse's ambiguous maxim indicated that in reality it was Uncle Jules who was cheating on Aunt Lourette, just as his father Rosaire had cheated on Jules's mother — Rosaire's wife Rosanna, to be more precise. *Like son, like father*: turn it around and, hey presto, everyone's a scoundrel! It's incredible what ensued: two divorces, one abortion, and a poisoning attempt, but things settled down when Aunt Lourette, who'd become manic depressive in the meantime, confessed. She was so unhinged that people were hesitant to believe her, but as my uncle Jules was so profoundly hurt, my aunt Hortèse concluded that only the truth hurts, the trapper had been caught in her own trap, and everyone took to their beds. Those who sleep forget they're hungry, she would have said. Everything would be better the next day.

I don't know why I'm telling you this, because Hortèse's ramblings have absolutely nothing to do with my story. Still, that's what I was thinking about when I read the contents of Anita's delicately perfumed letter, blue as the sea and the sky. Anita had started with a drawing of a heart, then of a heart breaking, and then an arrow, under which she had written page 216, nothing more. I'd examined the sheet of paper from all angles, trying to figure out if Anita might have written in invisible ink, and went to look around the cottage to see if perhaps a part of the letter had been lost on the way. Nothing. Clearly Anita had just one thing to say to me: page 216. Once I'd settled on this explanation, it wasn't hard for me to work out that the reference was to Morgan's novel. What other book could Anita possibly have been alluding to in such an allusive manner and still expect me to understand? The mere sight of Morgan's novel making me want to leap into Mirror Lake's inestimable depths, I had no choice, it was a matter of survival, so instead I entered a phase of denial, checking page 216 in every other book longer than 216 pages that I'd brought with me to this den of iniquitous murderers.

It's incredible, the number of messages you spot when you're looking, and after a few hours of uninterrupted reading, I had a multitude of options before me, each one more terrifying than the last and all of them meaningless. I had to confront the facts: whatever it was that Anita had to say to me was spelled out clearly in Morgan's novel, which I didn't have the courage to open. But finally I picked up *The Maine Attraction*, trampled my pride underfoot and set off in my boat with Jeff to ask Winslow if he would read to me a little. When I reached the middle of the lake, my loon let out its plaintive cry, a clear sign that it was early morning, that I hadn't slept the night before, that time's course had once again got away from me. I paused, wanting to abandon everything, wanting to throw the damn book into the water and copy John Doe, wanting to capsize and let myself sink, but I could hardly do that to Jeff, who had nobody but me in this dreadful world and loved me unconditionally.

"Okay," I said to the big head whose eyes were flooding me with love. "We won't capsize today, but as for tomorrow, I'm not making any promises." "Sufficient unto the day is the evil thereof," I added, thinking of Hortèse, who probably would have said, "Who moves his feet, loses his seat," an expression whose meaning I cogitated on for a while and decided meant nothing, because you don't even have to move your feet to lose your seat and, even when you do, most of the time you'll return to find the seat is still yours, short of being cuckolds like Jules or Rosaire. Hortèse was out to lunch and, to be frank, I'd had enough. I started rowing again, but hesitantly, because I was no more in a hurry to go and humiliate myself in front of Winslow than I was to discover that the course of my life had been determined by Victor Morgan.

As I was docking, I noticed Winslow was awake, which would save me having to get him out of bed. A lamp was shining in his kitchen, and I could see Winslow's heavy silhouette in front of it. He was assiduously making breakfast, the way men do who have quietly resigned themselves to the absence of a woman to scramble their eggs, and who subsequently sit down and indulge themselves in a silence penetrated only by the wind—when it's windy—or by their dog's panting if they have a dog, cheerful birdsong when it's not raining, or the sound of the rain and less perky birds when it is, and then the glug of the coffee maker, the thunk of the toaster, and occasionally the knock-knock of a hungry friend, because the fact is I was starving when I knocked on Winslow's door, *knock-knock*, and so starving I was ready to concede that this big heap of harmlessness was actually my friend. *Knock-knock*, I rapped at the door again, Winslow evidently deep in thought. If I'd been a little more perspicacious, I'd have noticed Winslow was sulking, not daydreaming, because I'd been rude to him the day before. After waiting a minute or two, I noticed that every ten seconds or so he would cast a furtive glance in my direction, to make sure I could see he was pretending not to see me, that he was ignoring me the way you do someone who has hurt you.

Winslow was in the right, I hadn't been very nice to him at all. If he wanted an apology he would have it, the truth of it being that I needed him, but also because he looked quite affecting in his blue and yellow apron, the colours of Provence, and no doubt an item that was the inheritance from a lover from the distant past, whom he pined after so much that in the serene silence of solitary dawns he'd chosen to surround himself with memories of her. Be that as it may, I was dreading the scene to come, which would probably be like making up after a domestic, me taking the part of the lout who never takes into account the pride, dignity, and feelings of their partner. I'd play the clueless jerk who's too wrapped up in his own little miseries to notice those around him are bleeding.

But all is fair in love and war and I wasn't intending to spend the day in his doorway. I knocked again, for form's sake, and then in I went because doors at Mirror Lake are never locked, which at least means they won't end up being kicked in by some crook or wandering John Doe. I'd noticed that Winslow often accentuated his discomfort by saying "hmm-hmm," which must have a particular meaning for him, so thought I'd start with a "hmm-hmm" right off the bat to let him know I was feeling guilty, and then I mumbled, "I'm sorry, Bob."

This sequence obviously pleased him, because I heard him swallow something down the wrong way, like someone who is moved but wouldn't admit it for anything. And yes, I was right, we were making up after a lovers' tiff. All I needed was to execute the steps in the right order, as I'd learned to do over my long career as a sonofabitch, and Winslow would break down and snivel.

"I'm sorry I'm such a bastard," I added, adhering perfectly to the second step of the reconciliation process, which consists of painting yourself in the worst-possible light after you've grovelled and apologized. It was working, because Winslow was now looking unabashedly my way, but it wasn't enough, it was incumbent upon me to curse myself even more, to humiliate myself, to confess out loud to my callous nature and kneel down and promise I'd change. "Okay, Bob, not only am I a sonofabitch, I'm a fucking bastard, I understand *nuttin'*, I never listen to you, I'm a monster, a Nazi, a worm, and I have no idea what a nice person like you is doing with a piece of trash like me, and—"

Which is when Winslow waved a hand to signal that I needn't go on. "I mean," he said, "I'm not your wife, Robert, and I won't be fucking you tonight, so get a grip."

Fine, my little game had been rumbled, but it had worked. Winslow had spoken to me.

"Have a seat," he said grouchily as he rose from his seat and went to make me some eggs. Eggs! If I was to be granted eggs then Winslow must have really forgiven me. Feeling as light as the breeze, I headed to the table after whispering in Jeff's ear that he could follow me, that Uncle Bobby wasn't mad anymore. Uncle Bobby! We can be so maudlin when we're happy! I sat down as Winslow took the eggs out of the fridge and pondered the semiotics of the process of morning reconciliation. As I did so, I spotted on the packaging an image of a little egg with two legs, rubbing its stomach and smiling toothlessly at whoever was about to eat him. In less time than it takes a virus to latch on to innocent prey, my prevailing thoughts, inevitably governed by the symbolic—which, as it happened, had appeared that morning in the shape of eggs rich in fertility and sexual references—grabbed me by the throat and none other than Humpty Dumpty took the place of the little egg with legs. Was Winslow doing this on purpose or what?

For a moment, the full impact of the plot and its immeasurable extent weighed down on my bowed spine and I regretted everything I'd just said to this oaf who, not wanting to appear too cheery, was whistling through one tooth as he stood at the frying pan. I took a deep breath and rebuked myself for thinking that Winslow was about to banish eggs from his menu simply because I'd been traumatized as a child by a particularly irritating specimen that consumer society's ignorance had turned into a potato, which made me feel a little better but didn't stop me from wondering if Humpty Dumpty's mother was a chicken or some other egg-laying bird, you know, the existence of which Lewis Carroll's storytelling had not revealed.

When Winslow served me my two eggs, he of course noticed that I was preoccupied — this despite my efforts to smile at him nicely, the way you would after an abscess has been lanced, heavy clouds blocking the sky have drifted away, or floodwaters receded. "What's going on?" he said in a worried way.

"Humpty Dumpty," I said. "I was wondering if he had a mother and, if he did, whether she laid him, in which case some charitable soul should have had the goodness to eat him before he became what he did."

Ever since Winslow had also started having dreams about Humpty Dumpty, he'd been more attuned to questions about the character's life, and we both started conjecturing about Humpty Dumpty's origins. We wondered if his mother had been disappointed when she saw his big smooth face after a labour that must have unfolded with intense suffering; if they had lived in a nest, she and he, and if the father was still in the picture or had abandoned the mother and his grotesque offspring — which could explain Humpty Dumpty's dreadful personality. There was a long biography to be written, and we started laying the foundations for it in order to distract ourselves and not veer too close to the heart of the matter that had brought me to Winslow's table.

After cooking up a few different hypotheses, we stuck to that of the mother hen and the ugly child. Which was this, more or less: that Humpty Dumpty's mother was a kind though not very smart little hen that a shameless cock had knocked up after an ignoble courtship. As soon as the relationship was consummated, the cock disappeared without caring about what became of the little hen, who had decided nonetheless to take the pregnancy to term, incubating Humpty Dumpty with all her mother-hen love. But this turned out to be a pointless endeavour, because her son was tarnished from birth and, aged fourteen months, left the nest and told his tearful mother to take a hike, her ever-weaker clucking marring the dawns, days, and dusks of Humpty Dumpty's native village of Saint-Zurin until the enfeebled hen expired one spring morning without ever having seen her ungrateful son again.

"The fucking bastard," exclaimed Winslow at that point in our tale, and if Artie had been there, it would have been worse.

For his entire life, Humpty Dumpty tried to deny his country origins, to mask the henhouse scent that clung to his shell, the result being that people started mistaking him for a potato, a quintessential symbol of the bucolic life and testament to the impossibility of concealing the truth of your rustic nature without consequences.

"The biter bit," Winslow gloated, and he hadn't even known Hortèse. We changed the subject before we threw up our eggs because, were that to happen, other mothers less hennish than Humpty Dumpty's would send their little degenerates to market before they irreversibly ruined the entire species' reputation.

"You can't make an omelette without breaking an egg," Winslow went on. "We can't put all our eggs in one basket, goddammit," and I wondered whether or not I was involuntarily transmitting my thoughts and if Winslow, as a consequence, had captured the family memories resurfacing to my mind as I started to mull over Anita's confusing letter.

I was telling myself I'd have to check it out again later when Winslow asked what had so upset me about Anita's letter that I'd decided to swallow my pride and come talk to him. When I heard him say that, I think I was afraid — no, I don't *think*, I know I was afraid — that I really was transmitting my thoughts to Winslow, he was reading me like an open book. That or we'd been turned into conjoined brothers whose brains were able to communicate internally due to such a shocking mistake of nature. Winslow must have seen how seriously scared I was, because the imbecile made everything worse by confessing he could read me like an open book and, hard to overlook, that I'd been crumpling Anita's letter between my damp palms for the last ten minutes. He didn't need to be Einstein to figure out what was bugging me. I ground my teeth, then smiled, which I hadn't done for some time, before offering Winslow the damp, crumpled scrap of paper tarabusting me. "*Qui me tarabustait*, you know, that was bothering me," quickly translating the word so he wouldn't have to look in the dictionary.

After Winslow opened up the letter, he groaned, which was a bad sign, then frowned, and, as I had done, turned the page backwards and forwards looking for a code underneath the message. He held the missive under a lamp, threw flour on it—for fingerprints, he said—and handed it back to me. "You broke her heart," he said. I still needed Winslow, so kept my mouth shut and breathed deeply, because a person who doesn't breathe will die of asphyxiation, after which I placed the letter beside Winslow's dirty plate and put my damp index finger on the words *page 216* before quickly removing it, so that Winslow could read what his eyes had so carelessly overlooked. As a result of the pressure, the number 216 was printed on my fingertip, another sign that fate was desperately trying to mark me with its seal, so I put the fingertip in my mouth to make the ink disappear, which meant, symbolically, that I was striving to eliminate all traces of page 216 by swallowing the integers that represented it. And then I waited for Winslow to figure it out.

"Undoubtedly a reference to Morgan's book," he finally spat out, and I hastily put the book under his nose, open at page 216, so we'd be done with it. Without my needing to explain what I was expecting of him—Winslow knew me like the back of his hand—he started the fateful reading of page 216, then closed the book and, to augment the suspense and annoy me, scraped his plate clean with his knife, scratched his forehead diagonally, and then told me to go away, he wanted to be alone, which wasn't at all like him and was a sure sign that page 216 was pretty horrific.

"Why?" I remember shouting, turning pale as I did so and wondering where the blood goes once you've taken on the pallor that comes to anyone when the body has been emptied of the liquid circulating in your veins since birth; it's unbelievable when you think about it, all this old blood continuing to make its way through our bodies' arterial networks for decades without ever letting up.

"Why?" I repeated.

"Because you're dangerous," Winslow answered slowly, as his blood flowed back to that undetermined part of the human anatomy where anxiety holds it until things settle.

"Hang on, Bob, you can't throw me out like an old shoe just because Anita's been deranged by this Victor Morgan stuff. Morgan wasn't even dead when I was born — no, I mean he was dead when I wasn't born or, if you prefer, he died before I was even born, which is to say he was absolutely dead, right, so couldn't have possibly known that I'd be born, unless he knew my mother when she was at school and learned from her that she'd become pregnant with me. Are you *crazy*, Bob?!"

"Writers are visionaries," he replied gravely, unaware that he was passing the time by contradicting himself vis-à-vis the power of fiction and the relative freedom of those who create it. "Read it for yourself," he added, holding the book out to me. At first I refused to look at a single page of that garbage, promising myself that as soon as this was all over, I'd round up all existing copies of the novel, copies of a book that was sick and deserved to be destroyed, and make an enormous bonfire out of them — a howling pyre, an auto-da-fé of all the demons, like in *Fahrenheit 451*, the difference being that I would be justified in reducing to ashes such a heap of deceitful flights of fancy generating dissension, tit-for-tat misunderstandings, and putting outrageous ideas into the heads of reasonably normal people.

"I said you were dangerous," Winslow repeated, having read my thoughts again. The blood that had taken refuge in a clandestine pocket of my circulatory system rose up to my face like a tide that could no longer be contained, and I turned as red as a peony. I know I did: red as a hot peony, a stewed tomato, a brand-new Christmas stocking. I'd let myself get carried away, Winslow was right. But be that as it may, I too was right, because if my brain really was coming up with dangerous ideas, then wasn't this the fault of Morgan's novel? *No*, my brain answered, *you haven't even read the damn book. It's simply ambient madness sending you off the rails: calm down, control yourself.* So I did, I controlled myself like a defeated poker player gathering up sticky cards on a dirty, grimy table and opened the novel, first of all to page 94, to prepare myself, then to page 122, and then to page 205, so I could take a breath before diving in. But I cracked, I wasn't brave enough, and asked Winslow to tell me what happened on page 216.

"It's simple, Robert, you will kill me," he said, no more animatedly then if he were letting me know it was about to rain. "You'll kill me tomorrow," he added. "It's written, it's my destiny."

So, according to Morgan I would at last decide to murder Winslow on the following day. A good idea—and a crime Anita had apparently wanted to warn me of so that I might rethink this good idea. How absurd! Anita and Winslow were hardly stupid enough to believe that a novel—one written before I was even conceived, or even thought about, let alone born, not even at the planning stage—could presage my future. So, fundamentally, I was being asked to believe that when I was no more than a vague hope, when my mother didn't even know what my name was going to be, or even if I was going to be called anything one day, that a novel could describe my future. "It's my destiny," Winslow repeated wearily, while in the background Darth Vader appeared in all his diabolical majesty, spitting under his iron or tungsten mask, whatever, then raising his fake black-gloved hand and proclaiming, "*It is your destiny, hrchch, khhhchrch.*"

The situation was grave and I needed to do something, provide proof of my own self-determination, for instance. I grabbed the novel out of Winslow's hands, opened it again to page 205, to give myself a few stretching exercises, and then took the plunge. When, on page 217, I closed it again—because you need to read a little further than page 216 to understand it—I'd turned white again. I knew it, I felt like a sock that had been soaked in bleach and abandoned in the snow, and wanted to get the fuck out of Winslow's house.

In summary, page 216 explains to the reader why the character called Robert had been imprisoned, and how his fate is intertwined with that of his victim. Robert, whose last name we don't find out in the novel, is an ordinary guy like you or me—well, more like me, to be honest—who, weary of life's depravity, abandons everything to hide out deep in the woods, or more precisely by the edge of a lake, hoping to enjoy the seclusion he has anticipated in peace. Until this point, everything is fine, as was I. But it all becomes a little more complicated when, one fine August 17, when the birds are singing, the sun shining, and the lake reflecting, Robert loses his mind and murders his neighbour under the pretext of his being part of a conspiracy designed to drive him crazy. The neighbourhood cop, accompanied by a young woman with whom Robert is secretly in love, discovers the two of them after the carnage, the neighbour impaled on a fence picket and Robert lying prostrate on the ground nearby with a huge bump on his skull, a result of the fight he and the neighbour have had. That was the end of our story, the one frightening Winslow so, and I tried to soothe him by explaining that I understood his fears, given the bizarre events we'd all been experiencing, but, at the risk of repeating myself, *The Maine Attraction* was a fucking novel. "It's fucking made up, Bob." Besides which, there weren't any picket fences nearby, and even if there had been there's no way I was strong enough to skewer him with a picket.

Evidently my argument didn't suffice, because Winslow, staring into the distance, kept muttering incoherently about his fate, about the mistakes we make in our interpersonal relationships, and the trust we often confer on strangers too hastily. As he provided a litany of all the things that should have alerted him to the danger of me, I was thinking how correct he was to have declared my arguments unconvincing: I didn't even believe them myself. The novel had already shown us what it was capable of, and I needed to find some other way of reassuring the two of us, so I thought of Bill and Jeff, who were lying in the lower-left corner of my field of vision, the best corner, and sleeping side by side like a couple of well-behaved children not for a moment deserving the outpouring of violence Morgan had conceived. But I was well aware that violence is not distributed according to whether or not it is deserved, and that pure souls aren't immune to its devastation. And I knew, too, that I would never engage in any activity that would see two innocent, inoffensive animals suffer. I loved Jeff too much for that. I loved him unconditionally. Which prompted me to ask Winslow what would become of Bill, what would become of Jeff, were he to die and me end up in the slammer.

I cannot say my query left him indifferent, but certainly Winslow was hoping for something else, maybe for me to suggest that Morgan had made a mistake. So I dug a little deeper in my brain, to the place where it starts to become a big hole, picked the novel back up, leafed through it, read a few short passages, and finally shouted, "Eureka! Bob, Robert kills his neighbour Bob on August 17 — and the 17th isn't tomorrow, it's today. So it's impossible for me to kill you tomorrow, no?"

Aside from my reasoning not being at all reassuring, I'll admit that it was also wrong. I suspected Winslow had detected the flaw in my logic, because he looked my way as though he was the one about to kill me, telling me that Morgan's novel had been written in a leap year, you stupid fool, which is how he'd worked out that August 17, this year, would fall on the next day. The man knew how to count, it has to be said. I'd been anticipating a more robust refutation, but his held: the danger that I would kill him tomorrow was still there. Taking the floor again, he decided to ask me where I stood.

"What's your position, Robert?" he asked.

My position... my position... well, it was pretty complex. I couldn't just define it off the cuff, my position on a chessboard with a few pieces missing and in a match where the dice were loaded.

"What do you mean by 'position,' Bob?" I replied. Was he referring to my opinion concerning the interaction of reality, nightmare, and science fiction, which I'd already shared, or asking what I thought of the motives for the murder Morgan described? Was he referring to the entirely hypothetical situation of his imminent death, or what?

"That's exactly what, Robert," he shouted. "Have you ever considered killing me?"

Had I ever thought about killing him? The question demanded a moment's reflection, and above all a few lies. Of course I'd wanted to kill the jerk, and more than once, he must have known that by now, but between the idea and reality falls the shadow—there's a gap, a step I would never have taken, not even in my most incendiary rages. But, if it is, as Hortèse would have said, the intention that counts, then I had already bumped Winslow off several times and was likely to assassinate him again in the nearish future. And that was when my umpteenth genius idea of the morning came to me. That was when I realized that we didn't have to follow Morgan's novel to the letter, i.e. literally, but could read it as allegory, as a metaphor for the murderous intentions punctuating our dark days. And if Winslow did die tomorrow it would only be figuratively, I quickly explained to him, leaving out a few of the lesser details about my intentions — things were bad enough as it was — and guaranteeing him that he would live to see the end of August and maybe even the late passing of one or two of the Perseids.

Ah, the Perseids... just the sound of the word gave me a sharp pain in my sternum, as if the narrow blade of a scalpel had cut into the tender flesh covering the muscle that allows our heart to beat until its exhaustion. I looked up to the sky, which was giving nothing away, since we were still in Winslow's kitchen, although the minuscule fly droppings constellating the ceiling did satisfy my nostalgia for happier days, and prompted my imagination to transform the stains into the dozens of starry bodies in which, in the past, I used to lose myself, when I was still able to gaze at the night sky without being afraid that a meteorite would follow a trajectory aimed directly at me. Perhaps Mirror Lake itself was the result of a meteorite falling, the effects of it still being felt thousands of years later by the people who'd had the audacity to settle on the edges of its crater.

Too bad: I was one of them and I was staying. I told Winslow not to worry, that we would sit together on the beach this evening and the next, the two of us fully alive. We'd silently gaze at the sky, on the watch for the ephemeral lights coming straight at us from the distant Perseus constellation. If we needed to, we'd invent other families of shooting stars, other constellations — the Winslow Curve or the Moreau Square — simply for the pleasure of thinking only about what doesn't exist and therefore cannot hurt us.

I'd moved him, Winslow pleased to see me once more becoming the person he liked, but he was still waiting for an answer to his question. "That's all well and good," he said, "but you haven't answered my question, Robert."

So I lied, pushed by a fraternal affection born of the sight of constellations of fly shit. I answered that not the faintest idea of strangling him, impaling him, making him keel over, had ever entered my mind, and certainly none of these things would happen tomorrow. Any more and I'd have said, "I love you, Bob," but instead I concluded with "I like you," this due to the invisible stars' influence, the worst thing being that I meant it. "I like you too," the big ugly mug said, and, like true friends, we jumped into each other's arms, slapped each other on the back and called ourselves idiots, all this to Bill and Jeff's great delight, as they'd been starting to find us dull, but were now able to be lively and participate in our joy.

And then, to show we were sincere, we took Morgan's novel down, like true jackasses, to say his story was full of holes, of the unsaid, of contradictions, and whatever tenuous links could be made between his dubious story and our own lives were pure coincidence, as we'd already said many times. If we had to class every novel that bore a passing resemblance to our own lived experience as prescient, then writers would do better to become fortune tellers, which would pay better. But they wouldn't do so because writers love living in penury, it's good for inspiration.

We laughed a lot, collecting all the tiny details of Morgan's novel that had supposedly become real at Mirror Lake and arranging them in a little heap on the table, next to our plates on which the egg yolk had dried, creating random patterns like a Jasper Johns painting. Jack Picard? Coincidence! Picard's escape? Coincidence! Anita's pregnancy? Such is life!

I was in the middle of blowing my nose on Winslow's tablecloth when he came up with that. "Anita's pregnancy, Anita's pregnancy," I kept repeating like a damn parrot, slapping my thighs and smoothing down the tablecloth. Then, for a second, the image of Winslow bouncing a little rugrat on his knees and trying to teach him the words to "Yankee Doodle" was reflected in the cafetière in which I could see myself straightening my quiff.

I stopped. "Whoa, Bob," I said, "where did you get that from?"

"Page 221," he guffawed before using the tablecloth himself.

"Does Morgan say who the father is?" I asked with the seeming cheeriness of a swaggerer. "Seeming" because, performed without conviction, my swagger was tepid, without the brass, the big drum, and all the hoo-hah.

"You," Winslow said in reply, thus destroying all the efforts we'd made to ridicule Morgan's novel and cease identifying with the characters.

"You mean *Robert*," I corrected him.

"You, Robert, same thing," he hiccuped, wiping away the tears his hilarity had elicited. A little more, and he'd be rolling on the floor, which was, would you believe, clean — if you didn't count the bit of dust from the morning, that is, Winslow being the tidy sort. As for me, everything was suddenly less funny.

I don't know why, but I tend to believe more in bad news than good, probably because there's more of it, and it is usually more credible. I shouldn't have been anxious, because we had just decreed, by who knows what authority, that *The Maine Attraction* was nothing but a web of lies, but recent experience had taught me the distinction between true and false is not always as unequivocal as you might like; that transparency is sometimes made of shady elements, and that delusion or illusion may be founded on verifiable and verified facts. And then, wasn't it Anita who had directed our attention to these pages? Perhaps all she wanted to let me know is that latex isn't a failproof material.

As the possibility of having been screwed by a manufacturer of condoms was not cheering, I asked Winslow if there was also any good news in the chapter Anita had flagged for us, any positive aspects or some such. He must have thought I was kidding around, because he was seized by another bout of demented laughter, and it threw him to the floor this time, where he rolled around like Ping on the night of the big fight with Picard, and I let him make a fool of himself all alone. I told him I was going out for some air, accompanied by Jeff and leaving Bill to roll around in our breakfast crumbs with Bob.

As soon as I set foot outside, I was surrounded by a heady smell of apples. There wasn't an apple tree nearby, it was just my early years asserting themselves before I was too old or senile to admit that childhood, if you are lucky enough to have had one, is the most beautiful thing that can happen to a person. "An appley day," I murmured, inhaling the redolent air and thanking the heavens that our brains are endowed with this thingamajig that uses ambient odour to invoke the other, more distant, smells with which we have always associated them. In my case, it is the damp August scent that, every time the temperature is perfect, arouses the intoxicating scent of the apples we were planning to steal from Goodwife Cadotte as we walked across fields scattered with dried-out cow pies and yellowed hay.

"It's an appley day, Jeff, we mustn't dishonour it," I said, and Jeff understood. Jeff always understands when the thing to be understood is too simple for most people to comprehend. Down he went with me to the lake, breathing in the balmy air with his big nose, and we gathered stones to skim across the surface of the water displaying the exquisite clearness that had inspired its name, and we didn't stop until we'd beaten our record. "Fourteen!" I shouted when the stone finally stopped, and Jeff jumped up on me, barking elatedly. Then we sat down and listened.

Somewhere, a woodpecker was pecking for its dinner, a blue jay was squawking at the top of its voice, because who cares if you don't know how to sing, that's no reason to be quiet on such an exquisite day; a group of mosquitoes was forming a perfect cloud above an area of the lake that they'd chosen for reasons unknown, and in the distance, near my dock, a dark mass was taking shape.

I was in a good mood, my head still in the apple clouds, so to speak, so immediately I thought it was the moose, my good-luck moose come to confirm the beauty of the day. With a tremble in my voice, I whispered, "Look, Jeff, it's our lucky moose," but Jeff's indifference made me realize the moose in question had no antlers, and if this dark shape really was a moose, then it would have to be a female. I squinted to get a better look, but all I managed to do was distort my vision — I don't really know why we stupidly screw up our eyes instead of opening them wide when we want to focus on something, which is surely more logical. Probably it has to do with being myopic, or not actually wanting to see what you would if your eyes were wide open. Obviously short-sighted people are that way because they would rather not have too clear a vision of the world. Short-sighted people are cowards.

Anyway, after pointlessly accelerating the ageing of the skin around my eyes, I returned to the cottage to look for a pair of binoculars.

"Why?" Winslow wanted to know as he put away a dishcloth, annoyed that I'd made him do the dishes all by himself.

"Because there's something close to my dock, some dark shape, Winslow, a dark figure I can't quite make out."

On top of the irritation he was feeling, he didn't like me saying "dark shape, Winslow, a dark figure," and I put my hand over his mouth before he could say the words I dreaded hearing every bit as much as I was afraid of seeing what his unuttered words would have designated.

"Where are your binoculars?" I said again, and off he went to find them before heading with me and Bill to the spot on the beach where Jeff was waiting for us. I let him look first, and after I did we looked at each other, taking it in turns to mumble, "John Doe, *baptême*, it's John Doe, dammit."

Never believe the dead won't come back and visit you one day.

"What should we do?" one of us said.

"Let's haul him in before the lake swallows him up again," said the other.

Two minutes later, we were rowing like mad toward the north shore, busting a gut and screeching out "Po' Lazarus" — I'd taught Winslow the lyrics I don't even know when — horror-struck at the thought that Mirror Lake could play such a dirty trick on us. Galvanized by our excitement, the dogs were barking at both ends of the boat, Bill in the direction of his shore and Jeff toward ours, prow figures eagerly protecting us from evil spirits and danger.

At the dock, we all rose to get out at the same time and the boat tipped over, Winslow and I landing flat on our bellies in the water the corpse had occupied. We dragged ourselves to the bank, and quickly turned when we saw the state of the dark mass. Bill and Jeff, who reveled in stinky things, tried to get closer, but Winslow and I forbade them in perfect synchrony, *pas touche, Jeff, don't touch, Bill*, which, uttered together, sounded like *pon't toche, Jilf*, but the dogs understood, especially as the dark shape, which we would need to rename, was not emitting the sort of rotting stink that appeals to dogs.

Winslow was the first to risk a proper look, I guess because he's more humane than me, and told me the corpse was really ugly. "I'll find some branches," he said, scampering off.

"I'll get a couple of scarves," I shouted, running away just as hastily, creating a situation that baffled the dogs completely, but no matter, Winslow and I were on the same thunderous wavelength, and we already knew what to do without needing to articulate our intentions in intelligible words. Four minutes later, once we'd found what we were looking for, we were back at the lake, scarves around our noses, branches in our hands, and screwing up our eyes so as not to see too much as we used the sticks to try to hoist the body out of the water without it breaking apart.

Once this hideous task was done, one of us asked what we should do now that John Doe had been pulled to safety.

"We should phone Robbins," said the other, surely not me. No, I was the one who suggested we call for divers, divers as they're sympathetic, meticulous types and not too chatty, or maybe the CIA, the FBI, or NASA. At any rate, this case stunk too much to leave it all up to a county cop.

But Winslow wasn't listening. He went into the cottage to deal with the matter his way, oblivious to the dangers he might be exposing us to. When he surfaced again, I asked the question that had been burning on my lips for so long. Might as well clear it up while we waited for Robbins and all the hassle he was sure to bring with him.

"Who gave you my phone number, Bob?"

He didn't cotton on, and snapped back, "I wasn't phoning you." His periwinkle eyes added, "You idiot, I was phoning the police."

Then I explained that I'd been fretting for ages over the ruse he'd used to learn my phone number, and I wanted it out in the open, but I might as well have conserved my saliva, he could no longer remember, he said, and didn't see how any of this would help us, suggesting another hole in my story, though it was a benign hole that would close up by itself because, after all, how important was it that Winslow got a hold of my number? Not at all.

"Fine, so what shall we talk about as we wait for Robbins to arrive and destroy what little beauty remains in this prematurely withered day?"

"Do we really have to talk?" Winslow retorted.

No, nothing was forcing us to, but it would have helped calm me down somewhat. So we sat down on the beach, diagonally across from John Doe, and perused the lake and mountains that had suddenly lost their appeal. Even the scent of apples had disappeared, the faculties of memory having their limits. Our silence lasted exactly seven minutes—I counted—before Winslow felt compelled to try and shake off the gloom weighing down on our heads.

"Poor guy," he murmured.

At first I thought it was me he was referring to, and I wanted to thank him for the burst of sympathy, but I quickly figured out he was thinking of John Doe, who would probably remain John Doe until the end of time, because how could anyone identify such a decomposed body? I tried to reassure him by saying that nothing could beat forensics, all that was needed was an impression of his teeth, and then they'd be able to find out who this man was through his dentist's or orthodontist's records.

"What if he doesn't have any teeth?" Winslow said. "What if he has dentures but he lost them in the lake, what will they do then?" And then, to prove the eventuality possible, he removed his own dentures and hurled them into the lake.

Evidently, Winslow was taking all this more to heart than I would have expected, because of his humanity, which I mentioned, though I did also think he was making too big a deal of it. I was just about to tell him so when Robbins squealed up accompanied by a man in coveralls, clearly a forensics guy. This would relieve Winslow's worries, surely.

"Where is he?" Robbins barked before Winslow had the time to retrieve his teeth.

"*On ve beash*," said Winslow.

"On the beach," I shouted, to avoid any misunderstanding, although obviously Robbins wouldn't think we had carried him into the cottage. "And he's not going to escape," I added to myself, even though I was conscious that in this terrible place nothing was impossible.

Robbins headed toward the corpse with the forensic expert I'd decided to call Conan, as we hadn't been introduced. Conan immediately leaned over what remained of the body while Robbins inspected the surroundings. "He doesn't have any teeth," Conan began, at which point Winslow beamed at me with the triumphant expression of his that I truly detested.

"They'll just have to use Carbon-14 to date him," I answered, and then Robbins, who was standing with both feet in the water, called out to Conan that he'd found the dead guy's teeth.

"*Vove are my teef,*" Winslow said quickly, and after a curious exchange in which he came across as a blubbering idiot, he was able to retrieve his possession.

"I wouldn't put those in your mouth before cleaning them," I wanted to warn him, but it was too late. John Doe's purulent microbes, good for him, were already gnawing away at Winslow's gums. And what I learned in that moment was that even though Winslow's house was spotless, his personal hygiene wasn't so impeccable. As for me, it would take floods of rain and more before I would so much as dip a big toe into the lake where the vile thing Conan was working over had been macerating.

"I found his wallet," Conan announced to Robbins. Great, if they had his wallet, and John Doe had plastic, then we'd be able to call him by his name. Robbins picked up the object, crouched on the sand, and started to empty it of its dripping contents as Winslow and I watched him fervently, eyes wide open and impatient to know the identity of the person who'd been haunting us for weeks—whose existence I had doubted, even accusing Winslow of nefarious machinations.

"So?" Winslow yelled impatiently, fed up with Robbins being so terse.

"So, we have a problem," Robbins replied.

What did I say about the mess this guy made?

"Meaning?" Winslow asked.

From what I understood of the conversation that ensued, John Doe was a well-known figure, not a John Doe at all, and the announcement of his death would have serious repercussions, so much so that Robbins refused to reveal his famous identity to Winslow. My eyes had been fixed on the body for some time, and I kept thinking the big mug reminded me of someone. There was no way I was about to wait for the local gossip rag to let me know who was my—and I mean *my*—John Doe, so I took advantage of Winslow and Robbins's yelling match to sneak behind the cop and pick up the wallet, which was still lying on the ground.

But as everything was going badly, Mirror Lake had decided to become a circus, and suddenly we saw a dirty pickup pull up near the cottage, and then a big guy, a medium-sized guy, and a small guy get out, the three of them accompanied by Joe Dassin, who was singing, "*Tagada, tadaga, voilà les Dalton.*" If Artie was also with them, then the only people still missing were Anita, the young Indiana Jones, and Picard, who was surely hiding in some thicket or other, and the whole family would be complete. But Artie wasn't there. It turns out the three Jacks had been searching for him because he hadn't set foot in Bangor since he'd gone off with Picard.

While Joe was recounting all this to me, and Averell was playing with Jeff and Bill, who'd not been barking at all, Robbins had stationed himself behind us, the better to hear what the Mafioso was saying. If Robbins discovered I'd had a hand in Picard's escape, I was cooked, so I tried to communicate to Joe that he needed to be discreet. "The man's a cop," I mouthed to him very clearly, hoping that he knew how to lip-read, but he didn't. So I tried making faces, winking, and drawing a finger across my throat in a knife's horizontal line and gagging like I was dead, and then putting a vertical finger to my closed lips. I pretended to be terrified, drew prison bars, feigned distress, but the only result was Joe thinking I was cracked and becoming increasingly irritated. Throwing in the towel, I lowered my arms. I could hardly have been clearer. Let him deal with whatever was coming down the pipe, I decided, I didn't know where Artie was. I had started walking back to where Winslow was standing on the beach when Joe grabbed me by one arm, Robbins by the other, and the two of them started bawling me out at the same time, one about Artie, and one about Picard and John Doe's wallet, and it took me getting shirty for them to ease up a bit, but only a bit, because at that moment the young Jones bounded out of the scrub to tell Robbins he'd seen me palm the drowned guy's wallet.

What happened next was simultaneously confusing and of a piece, like a ballet danced by a bunch of clods. What I remember most clearly is that Strauss's "The Blue Danube," the waltz Stanley Kubrick used in *2001: A Space Odyssey*, suddenly drowned out the ambient noise, and I started to float on the music, which I was using as some kind of defence mechanism as anarchy settled over Mirror Lake — which had, it goes without saying, seen it all before. Young Jones set everything in motion. If he'd leapt out two minutes earlier or two minutes later, the whole story might have gone a different way, which is what we call fate, but he chose the worst moment and, true to Murphy's law, the resulting chaos was barely conceivable. Startled by Jones's unexpectedly bursting onto the scene, Joe stepped in right away, and Robbins thought he was intending to attack him and drew his gun. Jones, who was aware of the misunderstanding despite his not being very bright, intervened by jumping on Robbins, with the result that all three of them ended up on the ground on top of me. Winslow, William, Averell, Bill, and Jeff didn't like what they saw either and raced to pile themselves on top of us and join the melee. Making the most of a narrow opening between what seemed to me to be Winslow's legs, I managed to drag myself out of the hellish circle with the intention of sneaking into the cottage to investigate the contents of John Doe's wallet. I didn't care at all about what might ensue, I had to know who this guy was before dying.

I had just reached the porch steps when a shot ripped

through the Strauss waltz and everyone, alert to the dramatic interruption, froze in place, except for Conan, who hadn't been part of the brawl and who, a true disciple of Hippocrates, rushed over to see if there were any injured or dead—preferably dead, because that was his specialty. Sadly for Conan, though a relief to the rest of us, the bullet had managed to find a route through the tangle of limbs and sink into what was formerly the stomach of John Doe, who could have done without taking a bullet on top of everything else, barely missing Conan, who almost fainted at the near miss. But in the place of fainting, he yelled at Robbins that we weren't in a cowboy movie, dammit, and if he didn't put his gun away that very second, he'd push the stiff straight back into the water.

"Doc, don't do dat," I said alliteratively from the foot of the porch, in this way reminding Robbins of my existence. He re-holstered his gun with a grumble and started in my direction, triggering "The Blue Danube" once more. Thanks to my small head start, I managed to beat him to the cottage and double-lock the door. Time was short, so I quickly rummaged through Doe's wallet as I saw, through the window, Robbins approaching and Winslow and the two dogs coming to my aid in hot pursuit. Behind them, I could make out Joe, William, and Averell, lined up in order of height on the beach. A little further away stood Conan, extricating Robbins's bullet from John Doe's stomach, the lot of them perfectly silent as they waited for whatever was going to happen next. As for young Jones, he'd returned to his thicket.

I yelled to Winslow and the two dogs that everything was fine, that I only needed another thirty seconds to fish the driver's licence out of the damn wallet, which was resisting me in the way objects do when you're harried, their way of letting on that you're behaving like an imbecile. When, finally, I did manage to cleave the recalcitrant wallet open, take out the card, and read John Doe's true name, the single thought to cross my mind was that I was dead, that I'd committed a dreadful crime; that I was dead and that God, just as I had feared, had sent me to hell. As if to prove me right, Winslow, who'd not been bred to fight, took a spectacular tumble over the porch railing, beneath which I suddenly noticed a single old picket post — it got there I don't know how — and upon which he was going to die just as Morgan had predicted. But thanks to Strauss's "The Blue Danube," everything was happening in slow motion and, heeding only a summons to courage, I opened the door with all my force and, in a state of weightlessness, swan-dived, managing to catch Winslow in flight and to push him off course.

All I remember after that is, despite the slow motion, the four-hundred-million-year-old rock hurtling a little too fast toward my head, Winslow collapsing noisily into a heap of branches, *thwump*, safe and sound, *phew*, and then night, with its thousands of stars, falling on Mirror Lake and gently enveloping it. Was I in heaven? Or hell? I didn't care, I had galaxies of hazy darkness all to myself. Then Winslow crawled over to see if I was still in working order and, given that my condition didn't bode well, he brought a large hairy ear to my mouth and waited for me to confide my last words to him. "John Doe is…is…" I murmured into his hairy ear, but then the ear grew to an enormous size and my mind stepped into his auditory canal, wiped its feet in the hallway, took a long slide down the cochlear, *zoooooom*, before it was finally propelled into the shady depths of the ear's Eustachian tube, so named after Bartolomeo Eustachi, as I pointed out to Winslow, who thought the guy had just the one name, Eustachian. Nobody's called Eustachian.

And after that, the stars went out. I could sleep in peace.

III.

NEW SKIN

Roughly speaking: to say of two *things*
that they are identical is nonsense,
and to say of *one* thing that it is identical with itself
is to say nothing.
—Ludwig Wittgenstein,
Tractatus Logico-Philosophicus, 5.5303

When the stars go out, you're justified in thinking you've reached the end of the world. That's what I thought at first, when I felt the universe dematerialize and darken around me, and I'm not sure I was mistaken. But if I was thinking this, then it means there is life after life, though it's better not to hurry its arrival because it's the same, only uglier, like in one of those warping mirrors you find at a fairground designed to reveal the monstrous potential of things simply by flattening them out or stretching them.

When, after striking the four-hundred-million-year-old rock, I did wake up, these were not the thoughts that came immediately to mind. I didn't think of anything, to be honest, as the part of my being that I'd always referred to as "me" was incarcerated in some as-yet-unactivated zone of my brain. Thus it couldn't have been *me* who saw the immeasurable sweep of white surrounding me, but my body, and yes, my eyes. They were the little windows through which the white entered, subsequently firing up the neurons that transmitted "white," but without recourse to comparisons or metaphors; without the capability of associating the white with trains of thought known to me — "white equals snow," "white like snow," "a dreadful winter pallor," and other formulae derived from nature and defining the essential blankness of white. I was in a realm of non-thought, completely and utterly, where any concept of the self is abolished. I was lost in a kind of comatose nirvana that nothing could penetrate except the white, but a white without links or connotations. A free white. Like a non-white.

This state continued for a period of time I cannot calculate because I wasn't there. But then the thing that had replaced me during my absence perceived two objects rising up before it. Feet, the neurons translated — the *me* in me slowly climbing back to the surface via those two feet, recognizing them as things belonging to it. Finally I was able to recall what the world looked like before the stars went out.

Immediately I thought I was dead and, given this fact, I managed to resolve a couple of metaphysical questions that had troubled me during life; there really is life after life, as I said, and the body doesn't vanish simply as a consequence of being dead, because lo and behold, I had two feet. I hadn't seen the rest of me yet, but divined that if I was able to think then I must have a brain and some kind of container preventing it from spilling out, and thus a head, and there had to be something connecting the head and the feet. That said, I did experience a brief sensation of doubt as pictures of God and Jesus came to mind, hovering above the clouds in smooth cassocks beneath which there was no suggestion of a body at all, as nobody has seen God naked. Perhaps the feet drawn at the bottom of the cassock weren't attached to anything and could decide, at will, to walk to the left as the head moves to the right.

Because it was completely uninterested in spending eternity searching for its feet, my brain promptly ordered whatever was below it to feel me up and down, which allowed me to confirm that I had all my parts—plus one, an enormous bruise swelling up out of the right side of my forehead, and which had started hurting as soon as I recognized it existed. And if I was in pain, then I was either alive or in hell. I opted for alive, and waited for this assertion to be refuted.

And yet, despite being in one piece, I couldn't actually move. I felt as if someone had filled my glass with some paralyzing drug while I wasn't looking. I told myself that I merely needed to wait a little and soon I would have the use of my limbs again, otherwise I didn't see the point of having any. To pass the time, I considered what I might do other than think or pat myself. I could choose between singing, praying, or reciting poems. But before I was able to decide, my speech apparatus launched into the first meaningless thing to cross my mind, namely "La dame en bleu," no doubt because I desired with all my heart and soul to meet the Holy Virgin, whom I'd missed by a nose the last time Winslow and I were drunk together, and no doubt she would be showing up any minute if I really was alive.

So as not to spoil the precious moments of peace, I gagged the stubborn lady in blue with her azure silk scarf and focused on the white around me, miraculously landing back on the ice floe where my polar bears had taken their places again, big balls of lard gambolling under the Arctic sun with the levity of creatures delighting in the simple joy of being alive. Astonished by their suppleness and grace, I started gambolling around with them, because I was alive at least until the contrary could be proven, and glad to be so, because life is beautiful when you manage to forget whatever needs to be forgotten. So I went walkabout with the two bears from floe to floe, until I too became a bear, another big ball of lard roaring in a white desert where I was king. And then, like a real fool, I let myself fall backwards and rolled back and forth on top of the ice to scratch my back, flipped over to scratch my stomach, rolling onto my back again until a low voice coming to me from the borders of the domain in which I was king rattled my good cheer with the question "Are you crazy, Bob?"

"Anita," I said before I opened my eyes. She'd heard the call of "La dame en bleu" and come running, also managing to chase away my bears. To unsettle her, I decided to play dead, but it must not have worked because then she said, "Thank God you're alive." So yes, I was alive, I had the proof I needed—and Anita too. I wasn't nearly as alive as I'd been at the North Pole, where my two bears were disappearing into the blizzard, but more as I was used to being, alive and putting up with all the aggravations that come with it, including Anita.

"Hi Anita," I said, opening one eye. I saw she was weeping tears of joy that she was not even bothering to wipe away, delicately, with the tip of a finger so that she didn't smudge her eyeliner. They were genuine tears, unrestrained, making their way down her face and falling hotly onto my hands, the cold hands of a guy who has returned from a long journey to a place far away, if I were to believe the rambling tale Anita was telling me through her tears and of which I did not understand a word.

"I called the others," she added, after shedding one last tear.

"The others? What others?" I said. I was alarmed, both eyes wide open now, a sign of my increasing anxiety, experience having taught me that, when someone mentions "the others," imminent danger awaits. "Hell," should we need reminding, "is other people." Yes, Sartre wrote the words before me, but I felt as if I had a claim on his famous sentence and that I would have come up with it first had I been born earlier and Sartre not preceded me in the knowledge that ultimately it would be other men who would cause my misery, if not his, because "other people," as I had good reason to know, is Agent Orange knocking at your door with a tank of napalm, nothing less.

I'd narrowly avoided the gates of hell and now Anita was telling me she'd made the necessary arrangements for me to go there.

"What others?" I said again for form's sake, because I certainly knew what she was inferring. They were all going to come, Anita went on, to make me happy. Apparently we didn't exactly have the same idea of joy.

On top of it, they'd arranged a surprise, a tiny surprise,

she simpered coyly, conceding nothing. I'd had enough of surprises these last few weeks, one of them my presence in a white room that, after a cursory examination, turned out to be in a hospital. Besides, my right arm was attached to a drip, which in and of itself was a significant clue. "When will they arrive?" I added uselessly, because no doubt they wouldn't delay, problems always turn up with thunderous speed, especially when there are a lot of them.

"Any minute now," she confirmed, and at that very second the hospital room door slowly opened. I was expecting to see Winslow's big red face framed in the doorway when — surprise! — the sweet smile of my sister Lou appeared, gentle enough to break your heart if you have one and, at the same time, cure you of the most infernal migraine.

So Lou was Anita's surprise, my sister Lou, in her immaculate nurse's uniform, with her beautiful nurse's hands and her gorgeous black hair which the years had accentuated with something that only made her more beautiful — that makes all women more beautiful. Lou, my father's crow, had flown over the Chaudière river and the Appalachians to be at my bedside. "Lou," I choked out, trying to swallow the lump rising in my throat.

"Hello, big brother," she said. The word *brother* made the smile stretched across her face crinkle in the form of the footprints that delicate crows had furrowed at the corners of her eyes. And then I cracked, started crying like a baby — or, as we say in Quebec, like a calf, which made me think of veal and overwhelmed me with compassion for the little calves that never get to grow up, small and alone in their sheds for a single season, and I started wailing even harder in the arms of Lou, who'd come to my side and was pressing my head against her enormous womanly heart — enormous because women don't spend their time hiding, and consequently their hearts don't wither away in the dark.

It occurred to me that if Lou had crossed the U.S. border for my sake, then I must have been in a terrible way. "What on earth are you doing here, Lou?" I snivelled.

"I came to heal you, big brother," she said — and with cause. Already she was curing me. When, despite it all, I died in the next few minutes, I would die feeling altogether better, thanks to Lou. Then, given how discombobulated I was, my feelings all over the place, I called myself every name under the sun for having disappeared like a damn barbarian three months before, abandoning my family and the two or three friends who still deserved to be called that, under the pretext that I needed space. As if there wasn't enough space in Quebec! And all this only to find myself surrounded by a bunch of degenerates and murderers.

"And are the others here, Lou?" I asked. When I said the word *others* it didn't have the same effect as when Anita said it, because the others I had in mind weren't the threatening kind but the category of others you'd happily wish on anyone but your enemies. They were my family, brothers-in-law included, my nephews and nieces and the trail of infant girls and boys who would inherit our stupidity in time.

"They're here," answered Lou, "I'll go get them."

"Okay, Lou. See you in a minute, Lou. I love you, Lou," I whimpered as she was leaving and was too far away to hear the whisperings of my heart having such trouble making their way out of my knotted throat.

Ten minutes later, during which time Anita tried to make me look presentable, a tremendous din filled the corridor and the door opened again, this time revealing Maman, Ode, Lou, Viv, and Jim—my whole immediate family—and then Ben, my uncle Chaise, Big Feuillard, and my peerless brothers-in-law, deep in conversation with Winslow, Robbins, Jones, and the Dalton brothers, who'd brought Bill and Jeff along. There was laughter, backslapping, hugging, barking, licking, the shedding of tears, and more laughing, and I remember thinking, *Damn, family's great*, even going so far as to include the twerp Winslow in the gang.

You'd have thought we were in some dubious Eastern Bloc country, at the betrothal of a Mafia don's daughter or a Greek wedding, it was all so exuberant and chaotic at the same time. I'd not have been at all surprised if Anthony Quinn had shown up dressed as Zorba the Greek to do a little folklore number for us. As we waited for Zorba, Winslow was histrionically waving his arms over his head to explain to Uncle Chaise and Ben a technique of his own invention for casting a line. My condition must have improved, otherwise Winslow wouldn't be making such a racket. Even Maman, who was standing quietly in a corner so as not to disturb the pandemonium, finally gave herself up to the general jubilation, though not before she managed to peer at me with one of those discreet looks only she gives, in order for me to see all the pain I've caused her. *Don't start again*, the look said, and—as if I'd asked to be in a coma, because that's indeed what had happened, I'd lost the plot for an unknown period of time—*I'm warning you, above all, do not die before me.*

How long had I been absent? I tried to put the question to Maman, but the Dalton brothers were dragging her off and, had Viv not intervened, I'm sure they'd have abducted her, the shits, if only to see how it actually feels to have a sweet little Mom, the kind that doesn't push you to delinquency and have you cut the throat of your first victim when you start kindergarten. Enough of that, what were these three idiots doing here?

"They're under arrest," said Robbins. Before I'd even formulated the question there he was. And off he went back to his conversation with Feuillard and Ode, who were calling him Bob, as meanwhile Jim was addressing Winslow as Tim, and Winslow had his arm around Anita's waist, and Maman was calling her Miss Swanson. Total mayhem.

And during all of it, nobody was particularly bothered about me, or only slightly, except for Jeff, who was sitting by the side of the bed and looking at me as if I were Christ come back to life, which I basically was in his devoted dog world. It took Robbins proclaiming my exploits for me to become the centre of attention again. But what was he going on about? He was mixing everything up—and giving himself a starring role. I wanted to correct him on a few details, but gave up, my head hurt too much. Besides, his time would come, I would write this story down, tell it as it really happened, and he would come across as the bastard he was! When he reached the end of his own account, which culminated with a "bang!" there was a long silence that did not strike me as a stunned silence of admiration so much as one of embarrassment, no one having anything to add, and then someone suggested they should all go find something to eat together. I tried to say something because I didn't want them to leave, not right away. We could easily order pizza or souvlaki, I said, and if someone was on a diet we could bring a few trays up from the cafeteria, since I almost certainly hadn't burned through my chicken-broth budget while I was comatose.

"How long was I in a coma?" I asked. Was someone going to tell me? They all started rummaging in their pockets or purses and blushing, this one staring at a crumpled tissue, others at their car keys or their health insurance cards, and one even at an old piece of gum tidily folded back up in its original wrapper. It's incredible how interesting chewed gum can be, the burning question whether you'll discard it or if it's worth putting in your mouth again, if it hasn't yet lost its flavour or textu—

"HOW LONG?" I shouted, which made the gum jump, which meant it would now end up in the garbage. The rummaging in pockets and bags was interrupted, but we didn't get much further than that, the silence was total, except for Winslow's hum-humming as he attempted to take refuge behind Feuillard, who was able to conceal the height but not the breadth of him.

"*HOW LONG?*"

"A year," Anita said under her breath.

A year? No. Impossible, I must have misheard. "Sorry, what was that?"

"About a year," she repeated, the voice strained and breathless. Inadvertently, she'd almost put me right back in a coma.

About a year...about a year...what did that mean, when we take into account the relativity of time? Could she not be more precise?

"Three hundred and forty-two days," I heard, deep in the immeasurable expanse of white where I was headed. But three hundred and forty-two days wasn't a year! As far as I knew, or at least before my coma, there were three hundred and sixty-five days to a year. Had things changed in the interim?

There was silence when I asked this legitimate question.

"Maman, it can't be true," I implored, Maman being the only person in the room who wouldn't joke about something so serious. But Maman, true to her courageous motherly nature, corroborated the information, as did the others, the bunch of cowards, who'd finished emptying their pockets and were starting to dust off the bars of the bed as if nothing was up.

Faced with their unanimous acquiescence, I was tempted to take an overdose of saline solution. I sank, like a ship in distress, into an ocean of depression as dozens of questions flooded my brain. And then the room filled with the usual brouhaha that precedes departures, reaching me through the gurglings of my floundering ship. Everyone was picking something up — bags, jackets, caps — the brothers-in-law came to shake my hand, Robbins put his hand on my shoulder, Bill licked my cheek, the Daltons told me they were still looking for Artie, Winslow hummed "See you later, alligator," and Anita hugged me as, all the while, young Jones played with the piece of gum he'd retrieved from the floor and that perhaps wouldn't come to the end of its life in a hospital garbage can. Then they left in order of height and in single file, briefly leaving me alone with Lou, who tucked me in, wiped my forehead, and pulled Jeff out from beneath the bed, where the good creature had hidden in order to stay with me.

When she closed the door, *bye-bye, big brother*, everything turned white and smooth again, the room tilted sideways with sadness, and I tried to find something to think about so that I wouldn't collapse into the void the abated laughter had left in its wake, not a single trace of it remaining in the infinite white reasserting its rights and smothering the groundswell that had carried me earlier. I whistled to my bears, but they'd gone fishing under the ice cap and I couldn't follow them. I tried to gather up a few affecting memories from childhood, memories of snow or storms, but they were out of view too. One of those insipid January winds even childhood can't make warm started to blow and the only recollections that did manage to surface were full of chilblains, frozen-stiff mittens, and the creaking under my boots.

I was right there in the January cold, in the silence, solitary as a clump of ice in the middle of a field, a northwesterly wind blowing its misery along the ground and building a drift of powdery snow up around it, obscuring and finally burying it in the desert-like expanse of the wintry field. I needed to shake free of it, so I stood up and immediately stumbled to the ground with my drip. After an effort that was as hard to quantify as the white, I managed to rise to my knees and make it as far as the toilet. Which I should not have done. I should have let that July day be winter, because I didn't like what I saw when I hoisted myself up to the mirror, I didn't like it at all, and fainted, dragging down all the equipment that had monitored me during my coma as I fell.

Humpty Dumpty. I saw the vile thing in the mirror at first, hence the fainting, which earned me a new bruise, on the other side of my head this time, to balance things out. Trying to get a laugh, someone looking at me straight on might have said, "*Whoa*, cuckold-horns."

When I glanced up at the nurse on duty who found me on the floor, I thought at first it was Lou, who, knowing the whole sad story, had come back to save me from Humpty Dumpty. So I jumped into her arms, or at least as far as anyone can jump when they're in the state I was in. Better to say that I grabbed hold of the back of her uniform as I begged her to remove the Humpty Dumpty face that someone had drawn on the mirror.

"Stay calm, Bob, stay calm," said the voice of the nurse who wasn't Lou and didn't have her sweet voice, "there's no Humpty Dumpty here," she said, and then she called for an orderly to help get me back to bed. She gave me a shot, despite my screaming and protesting that I didn't want her to give me a shot that would send me back into the void. Because I was screaming, she gave me the shot anyway, it was all so stupid, see where misunderstandings and mistakes get you. My speaking became laboured and I asked to see Lou, "You know, the beautiful nurse, a few moments ago she was here with my family," I said, but the dullard told me I was delirious, that I hadn't had any visitors for days. I wanted to ask how many days, but was entering into a soft cottony space, the vast cumulus where bare-bottomed angels amble whenever they're not sprawling around and playing the lyre. The last words I heard were "Goodnight, Mr. Winslow" — but, she'd told already me, I was delirious.

In the dream that followed, I'm in the clouds, I'm thinking coherently, and surrounded by a bunch of winged, chubby-cheeked little Humpty Dumptys playing François-Adrien Boieldieu's Harp Concerto in C major, and I wasn't screaming anymore, didn't have the strength. I gave in. I don't know how long the dreaming lasted, but it seemed longer than ordinary nightmares, which usually have the decency to end as you reach the limit of what's bearable.

When I woke up, the white was clearer, with a hint of yellow, and I could see through the drawn curtains that the sun was blazing away, a beautiful July sun, as far as I knew, unless I'd slept for another six or seven months. Just the thought made me start shivering, fearful it might be a conniving January sun, and I decided that if I had to stay more than another two hours in the hospital, I'd demand a digital calendar connected to NASA. But as I waited, I had other concerns. I needed to know if I was *compos mentis*, or if the nurse with the syringe was the one losing her mind. And that woman, well, actually she hadn't seemed all that much like a nurse, I mean a real nurse, but

I couldn't quite pin her down, because her face had been lost in the neuroleptic fog she'd propelled me into. That was a bad sign.

To help myself, I put myself back in the scene of my rescue in the washroom, the smell of disinfectant making me woozy, the rubber-soled shoes thudding over the white tiles and making that annoying squeak that is hardly a tonic for sick people with delicate nerves — *squeak-squeak, squeak-squeak*, so horribly high-pitched — my eyes focusing on her legs and, reaching her hips, taking in the nurse's hazy and not at all reassuring expression from a low angle, her face unsettling as it bent slowly toward me.

And then something happened, the kind of thing that happens when you have a surfeit of imagination. My memory, egged on by my anxiety, lost its way and ended up in Sidewinder, Colorado, the godforsaken hole where Paul Sheldon, the hero of *Misery*, falls into the hands of Annie Wilkes, a psychotic nurse who might as well have been trained at Auschwitz. By the time I'd readjusted my focus on the nurse's hazy face, she'd taken on the features of Kathy Bates, alias Wilkes, and an axe had replaced the syringe in her hands, exactly like in *Misery*, goddammit! To perfect the tableau, sinister music permeated the room, screeching violins that evoked both the sucking noise of Annie Wilkes's soles on the floor and the music accompanying the shower scene in *Psycho*, a true horror-movie soundtrack, enough for me to hear blood spurting on the invariably white walls. Then the rubbing sound of a door slowly opening conjoined with the music, and Kathy Bates, who was perhaps related to that other maniac, Norman Bates, entered with a grumble and carrying a tray of pills and a variety of purees. Seeing her, I let out a cry, just a faint one, before quickly smiling so that she wouldn't get the syringe out. I wanted to ask her what day it was, but all I could manage to say was "*ning*," I'm not sure why, which she interpreted as a greeting and replied with "Good mornin'."

So it was morning, and I could breathe a little, having read somewhere that psychopaths are more tranquil before noon — between six in the morning and noon, to be exact, or that's what I'd read. Assuming it was July, then according to the position of the sun it must have been around seven, which gave me five hours to escape. Between then and now, it was in my interests to seem co-operative, so I let Bates feed me without protesting, even though I was perfectly capable of eating by myself. As for the pills, I copied Paul Sheldon and hid them under the mattress while her back was turned, there to drug her with if the situation became critical and I didn't manage to escape. But she must have noticed, because she presented another out of the right pocket above her full bosom and stuffed it in my mouth with a spoonful of puree. After that I fell asleep. What did you want me to do? I was fed up with sleeping all the time, I'd been sleeping for three hundred and forty-three days at least, *for fuck's sake*! I was rested, enough already, but try telling that to someone who's not around anymore, because she wasn't; after forcing me to ingest her sleeping pill, she trotted off on her squeaking soles.

I watched as her skirt swooshed through the doorway, the door closing heavily, and immediately I fell back into a dream in which I was Paul Sheldon, sitting at the table with his old typewriter, trying to resuscitate his novel, *Misery*. I was in the midst of pulling my hair out because the only words I could see printed on the otherwise-blank page belonged to the postmodern novel that Jack Nicholson, a.k.a. Jack Torrance, writes in *The Shining*—"All work and no play makes Jack a dull boy. All work and no play makes Jack a dull boy. All..."—when I heard a whistling in the hallway outside my room, a refrain from one of those childhood songs that you can't mistake, like "Oranges and Lemons." I didn't feel at all wary, or at least not until I became aware of some discordant notes in the melody, a few off-chords at odds with the song's innocent air... "Oh no," I muttered when I recognized the tune being whistled, though, before I was able to react, the door opened on Daryl Hannah, who, in her sexy homicidal nurse's costume, was whistling the theme from *Twisted Nerve*, like I needed that, and heading toward me. Which is when the telephone rang and I woke up, sitting upright in my bed but the wrong way round—I mean facing the wall, not on my head (because were that the case, I'd have said "sitting on my head").

"Hello?" I whispered, grabbing the phone that was ringing so insistently. It was Bill, who wanted to tell me something I did not understand because—proof that dogs, who understand humans nine times out of ten, are more intelligent than we are—I'd never bothered to learn the difference between *woof* and *warf.* "Give the phone to your master, Bill," I commanded, but it was Anita who came on the line.

"Sorry, Bob," she said, "the phone slipped out of my hands."

"No problem, Anita," and before she could say anything more I told her things were going badly, very badly, and pleaded for her to come get me, get me out of this loony hospital. "Hurry up!" I said. And then I hung up and decided to make my way to the washroom and lock myself in it until she did.

I was still not confident about my ability to walk, so I rolled to the edge of the bed and then crawled through the smell of disinfectant, acquiring the perspective of a reptile or some short-legged animal. *Let the Fraggles play, gobo, mokey, weembly,* I counted, as I approached my goal tile by tile, and when finally I reached the momo of the last, I gave the door a firm kick, shutting it with a slam, evidence my leg was in good shape and that I could have used my head to get to the bathroom instead of my elbows. I started to stand, which was painful because I was still wobbly, like the flame of a candle burning in a pool of wax, but I managed. My first instinct was to lock the door, but I couldn't, which made me look very stupid, thank you very much, and my second was to look around for an object or a piece of furniture with which to block it, again unsuccessfully. And then my third was to cast a quick sideways glance into the mirror above the sink in order to be certain that I'd hallucinated the Humpty Dumpty I'd seen in it before.

But I shouldn't have.

I shouldn't have, because what appeared to me in the mirror was far worse than Humpty Dumpty. I saw Winslow, Bob Winslow, the one and only, ugly as life and staring at me with his big periwinkle eyes protruding out of a face emaciated from a year of fasting. Confronted by something so horrible, anyone else would have passed out, and I was about to but managed to fight the fainting off; I needed to stare reality in the face. "Every truth..." Hortèse started, but I told her to shut up and approached the mirror with a hand covering my eyes, then spread out my thumb and index finger, because had I not I wouldn't have seen anything. Closer up, the situation was much improved in one aspect but worse in another. Much improved, because I resembled Winslow less when I assessed myself piece by piece — if I separated the nose from the cheeks and the eyes from the forehead — and worse because, in close-up, neither Winslow nor I were pleasing to behold. Exposing myself to such unforgiving scrutiny was hardly an enjoyable experience, but the situation required that I put my feelings aside.

Then I carried out a more exhaustive examination of the face reflected back at me and, with a degree of bad faith, concluded it was not me. Hadn't Winslow and I always appeared similar, and had he not always irritated me for precisely that reason? I'd never wanted to admit it but, in another life and had he weighed a hundred pounds less, the tub of lard might have passed for my brother.

To put myself even more at ease, I decided to proceed

as a scientist would and examine my teeth: teeth are like fingerprints, they don't lie, only I did so too vigorously, they fell out of my gums, and when I gathered my wits again I had Winslow's dentures between my index and middle fingers. *No big deal*, I thought as I studied Winslow's revolting dentures between my fingers, *don't panic, these aren't your dentures, you must still be asleep*, a possibility Anita contradicted when she half opened the bathroom door to tell me she was there. With a mixture of disgust and discouragement, I lisped that I needed her to give me two minutes, found a small bottle of bleach behind a curtain, sprayed the dentures with it, and left the bathroom with a forced smile.

Anita came to my side and bent over to kiss me, but suddenly veered away: "What the fuck did you eat, Bob?"

"Soap," I said, a twinge of irony in my tone, as I thought of Aurore. "Aurore the Child Martyr, you know, the abused girl from Quebec whose stepmother made her eat soap?" It would seem the reference was not clear, so I mimed a little girl spitting up soap bubbles, but either Anita didn't understand or didn't want to laugh, because my joke fell flat. Didn't really matter. Aurore would not have been upset.

"I told you I was in a bad way," I added, and then, gripping her arm, I asked her to bring me my clothes. The pants she handed me were, like Winslow's, three sizes too large, but I preferred to think the pants belonged to the last patient in a coma and that he'd fled without even putting his clothes on, or that he'd died, leaving the pants behind.

Whatever, I had to hurry, I needed to manage, so I used the lamp cord Anita was holding out to me as a belt and we tiptoed out, *tip-tip, tip-tip*, and we hopped quickly, *hop-hop, hop-hop, hop-hop*, into the elevator where, of course, the nurse who thought she was Kathy Bates was waiting for us. Oh so courageously, I took refuge in Anita's arms and French-kissed her for four floors in order to preserve my anonymity. When, at last, Bates exited the elevator, Anita was on the point of chlorine intoxication. For a moment we considered heading to Emergency, but opted instead for a breath of fresh air — which, first good news of the day, or even the year, did indeed turn out to be July air.

While Anita went to get the car, I sat down on a bench and let the sun warm my face without pausing to reflect on the damage UV rays could do to skin that hadn't seen daylight for months. I tucked my anxieties beneath the bench and, sitting in the July sun and inhaling the smell of the hot asphalt and exhaust, gave myself up to the simple pleasure of simply being. It felt like a very long time since I'd been permitted a minute or two of pure relaxation. My year in a coma seemed to me like the length of one night, and consequently I felt as if recent events on Mirror Lake must have taken place yesterday or the day before, and nobody could pretend my life had been at all tranquil since. I didn't deserve it, but clearly God was not of the same opinion and intended to teach me there was no such thing as peace in this base world.

In my convalescence, I hoped I'd be granted little respite once I arrived at Mirror Lake, that I'd have the chance to start over, to pick things up as I'd left them, which, said the nasty and irrepressible voice in my head—not content to merely annoy me but delighting in destroying my illusions—is to say *in total disorder*. To rub it in, the bundle of anxieties I'd stashed beneath the bench started moving, and out of it arose all the questions I'd not answered: Who am I? Is the person I am sound of mind? What, fifty years ago, did Victor Morgan want with me? Is there a meaning to life that isn't death or a coma?

At any rate, even the questions I had resolved didn't answer anything. For example, vis-à-vis John Doe's identity, what was the point of knowing? John Doe was none other than . . . *Fuck!* I'd forgotten who John Doe was. Ah well, the nasty voice shot back unpleasantly, you just said there wasn't any point in knowing. *I was lying*, I said to the voice. *I was trying to appear Zen when faced with life's setbacks but I'm not Zen!*

"I'm not Zen!" I shouted out to everyone including Anita, who was driving up in my car. (What was she doing with my car, which had disappeared when Artie had been requisitioned by Picard?) "I'm not Zen, Anita, I'm not Zen!"

"No, no, *shh, shhh*, you're not Zen," she confirmed, pushing me and my suitcase full of anxieties and questions into the car. "You're not Zen, Bob, absolutely not."

"So who am I, and who is John Doe, and who is Bob Winslow, and why are you calling me Bob, my name's Robert, dammit!" I was whimpering and snivelling, while Anita wondered if perhaps she should seek out Kathy Bates and her syringe.

I was on the point of easing up when I noticed the mock-leopard cover on the back seat.

"Where did that come from?" I asked.

"Woolworth's, but Robert doesn't like it," she said, providing no further explanation. I was Robert and, true, it didn't appeal to me, but how did she know?

"Robert who?" I mumbled, scratching at a little bit of dirt stuck to Bamboo's fake fur—a spot of ketchup or strawberry jam, maybe. I preferred not to learn the answer to my question, so refrained from asking twice.

For the rest of the journey, I didn't open my mouth except to breathe—and to ask who John Doe was, which was a question that struck me as less compromising.

"John Doe is John Doe," said Anita bluntly. She could be unyielding when she chose, arguing that the very nature of a John Doe is to be a John Doe, you can't escape it, certain truths are immutable. Rumour had it he might have been one Bartolomeo Eustachi, but Robert had refuted it.

Anita refusing to enlighten me, I would ask Winslow if I wasn't Winslow. And if I was Winslow, I would ask myself, because I had to be someone somewhere, dammit!

You're out of your mind, I was thinking concurrently. *You're losing control! Comas don't suit you. If you're thinking like yourself, then you are you. That's all that counts—what's on the inside, the soul, the mind, your intrinsic nature, the truth of the self beyond mere appearances.* If I was Winslow, then I was only Winslow on the surface, nothing more. Which reminded me of what my mother used to say as she pushed me into Ginette Rousseau's tentacular arms, completely cognizant that I'd never throw myself upon her and morality would remain intact: she's not beautiful, but she's a good little girl on the inside. The correlation didn't convince me back then, and I can't say my opinion has changed since, but I could work with it.

When the image of Ginette Rousseau receded, we were leaving the highway for the lesser road to Mirror Lake, and my anxiety increased a notch at the thought of being immersed in all my things once more: my cottage, my bed, my books, my Jeff. I was scared that my universe might have fallen apart in my absence, and that I wouldn't recognize Mirror Lake any more than I would myself in the mirror. Anita turned onto the side road that led to my place, proof that I was me, thank you God, otherwise she'd have carried on to Winslow's turnoff. I closed my eyes because of the emotion, but also the fear, and only opened them again when she stopped the engine. But I didn't see much because, gazing on Mirror Lake's beauty, they immediately filled with tears. But Anita had an answer for everything, handed me a tissue, and we got out of the car.

Outside, everything was chirping, sparkling, blooming, and for a moment I believed I was the luckiest man on the planet. I felt a strong urge to go to the lake and dip my toes in. Anita supported me and I asked her where Jeff was, told her I wanted Jeff, repeated that I needed Jeff at all costs; that I needed to experience this incredible moment with him. She gave me a funny look, women are constantly astonished when they realize men have feelings, but she went to get him from the cottage anyway, where the good animal was waiting silently. When he saw me, he launched himself my way and jumped on me, big happy head first, and knocked me into the water, which I didn't care about at all, because I was thrilled, as Jeff was too, ecstatic that I was home at last. And since I could hardly believe it either, I picked him up bodily and we rolled around on the beach, not caring about the sand clinging to our fur and hair, our clothes, making its way into our ears, too bad, and we promised we'd never leave each other again. "Nevermore," croaked a crow, and I quoted it, telling Jeff it wasn't my fault, that I'd been ill, which he understood. He leaned over me — I was flat on my back — and licked my face so much that I started to cry. Anita, watching, gave me another tissue and we stayed by the lake, where everything was still intact and unchanged, thank God. And then, letting out a big sniffle, I heard what could have been a child crying.

"What's that?" I said to Anita.

"What's what?" she said.

"Somebody's crying," I said.

"Nobody's crying," she answered, giving me another funny look. And she was right, nobody was crying. It might have been a bird, maybe a barred owl, or a northern saw-whet owl disoriented in the full sun, or perhaps even the memory of something else I'd read trying to assert itself through my tears.

"Are you hungry?" Anita asked.

It occurred to me that I was starving, that I was

ravenous—like a raven, as I said to Anita. "Nevermore, nevermore, you know, *caw, caw*," but she didn't get the reference. As well as being so reserved, she could also be a little slow, though you certainly couldn't describe her as stingy. My sweet Anita thought of everything. She'd prepared a few things, she said coquettishly as she stepped in the direction of the cottage, and I followed, making no secret of my emotion, so content was I to be there— and relieved, above all, that any trepidation I was feeling had remained in the car, where I hoped the heat would smother it.

"Close your eyes," she ordered once we were standing on the porch. I guessed that she'd organized some kind of surprise for me, but pretended otherwise so as not to spoil her excitement. Then she opened the door, led me across the threshold, and I held my breath until a blaring, riotous cacophony hit me: "*Surprise!*"

I started to breathe more easily, which is no more than a figure of speech, really, as this sort of welcome made it impossible for me to breathe remotely easily, and those who'd gathered rushed toward me to slap me on the back and welcome me home. There was Robbins and, too, his inseparable sidekick, the young Jones; there was Artie, who'd reappeared I don't know when, nor how, as well as a guy who looked incredibly like me and who was called Robert. And there was a Bill, who'd become a larger dog over the course of the year, as big as Jeff and just like Jeff, so that the only thing differentiating them were the scarves they wore, red for Jeff and green for Bill; and there was a small person too, an extremely small person whom I did not recognize.

"This is Robert," said Anita, blushing as she held out the baby, who started to cry. "Robert Junior."

I said I needed a chair, a log, or a rock, that I wasn't sure I could keep standing up. Four chairs were immediately pushed toward me, but I hadn't asked for that many so I chose to lie down instead of sitting. Five big human heads plus two dog heads simultaneously bent over me, depriving me of what little oxygen there was in the cottage, and suddenly I understood how babies must feel when a whole bunch of cooing ladies stand over their cribs. "Who's Auntie's little babba den?" *Auntie's, obviously, you silly cow, you just said so.* This alone could explain the high rate of criminality in large families. Not that I'd read that anywhere, but I would write it. In the meantime, before I died of asphyxiation, I stood up, with enough of a start that the cuckold-horn bruise on my left side collided with the head of the fella who looked a lot like me and was supposedly called Robert. "Ouch!" we both swore at the same time, staring at the other as if each of us was aware of what the other didn't know. This usurper would stick around a while; first of all, I had to deal with the baby. One problem at a time.

"And whose little Robert is that?" I said, pointing at the chubby baby drooling in Anita's arms.

"Robert's," said Anita, blushing again as she turned to Robert, whose forehead was slowly being decorated with a bruise like the one inflicted on me by the four-hundred-million-year-old rock. I would have liked to ask who Robert, father of Robert, was, but didn't dare—yet again I was too afraid of hearing the answer. In any case, Anita didn't give me a chance. She pushed little Robert into my arms like any proud mama, where he gurgled *babababa, zizizi, goo-goo*, and the party started. Anita had inserted a Roger Whittaker CD into the player while I was away, and Robert half turned around muttering "Whittaker" in recognition, and fuck, I saw me as clearly as if I were looking at a mirror, and that overjoyed me. For the first time since my arrival I was happy not to be Robert, because, apparently, I wasn't.

"*Bababa*," I said to baby Robert before starting to whistle along with Anita and Whittaker to annoy big Robert. It worked, because he glared at me in a way that said a lot about the relative pleasure of his seeing me come back, and it was clear to me that he thought I was Winslow, which was unsurprising, because I wasn't Robert.

For a moment, I'd wanted to keep to myself, but couldn't, because here was Robbins bringing me a glass of alcohol-free punch. Given the circumstances I could have done with a little pick-me-up, but Anita had decided that since there would be both a baby and a convalescent at the party, there would be no alcohol. The new Anita was indeed a new woman, and I'd have bet all my money that nobody was allowed to smoke in the cottage either. Never mind, I wasn't smoking anymore and knew where Robert kept his bourbon stash. Quite the hypocrite, he was heading that way and still casting shifty looks my way. As for me, I was half listening to Robbins describe how I'd fallen into a coma, and how Robert, by making his swan dive—"a fucking swan dive, Bob"—had prevented me from skewering myself on an old fence picket. I'd not impaled myself, but had landed head first on Robert's big rock, which Anita subsequently had moved because it was dangerous for Junior.

"You moved my stone!" I shouted, and everybody seemed surprised that I considered the rock to be mine—except for Artie, well aware that people could grow attached to various objects and who came over to console me, which made me think about Ping, who'd probably ended his life in a quiche. "Poor Ping," I murmured, and Artie answered, "Poor thing," though he was thinking of the rock he would show me in a little while. I changed the subject and asked him how it was that he'd returned to Mirror Lake.

It was a long story, he said. After he'd dropped Picard off at Three Jacks Bar, he'd decided to leave the shady underworld and travel the country. He'd driven across twelve states in my car and—needing to survive, after all—holding up a bank or an embassy here and there. To pass the time, he'd started an onion collection. You wouldn't believe it, but there's actually an incredibly variety of onions. He'd found red ones, yellow ones, white ones, pointy ones, ones that don't make you cry, he'd show me them soon, he said, along with the rock, and then, blinking his eyes, he took a little yellow onion that looked just like Ping out of his pocket. "To welcome you," he said with a squirm, and I wanted to kiss him again, the big idiot. I made do with saying thank you, and telling him that I'd name him Ping Two, in memory of Ping, and asked again why he was at Mirror Lake. It was simple: after a few months he'd had enough of the vagabond life, and he'd wanted to come back to see the only place where people cared about him at all. While I was in the hospital, he'd moved into my cottage, which is to say Winslow's cottage, this with the blessing of Robert, whom he considered to be no less than his adoptive father. But I needn't worry, he said, he was going to move into one of the hunting camps scattered around the mountains as soon as possible, which I guessed meant as soon as he'd murdered its owner.

Things were off to a good start. Artie must have been wanted by the police in at least twelve states and I would have him as a roommate unless I lent him a hand and helped slay the lucky owner of one of the hunting camps, whom I'd have the supreme pleasure of meeting before eliminating him when autumn came. And what about Robbins in all this? Why hadn't Robbins arrested him? That was another long story. Artie had once saved Robbins's life during a bank robbery in which, for once, he'd played no part. He'd been window-shopping on a street in Augusta when a big guy in a mask came tearing out of a bank. Immediately afterwards, Robbins appeared at the corner of the street, the big guy turned around, pulled out his gun, and Artie threw himself upon him just as he pulled the trigger, changing the bullet's trajectory. The result? A pigeon had copped it, the big guy became a little guy, and Robbins was still alive. Artie was sad about the pigeon, but Robbins saw things differently and decided to close his eyes to Artie's little habit of larceny. Which wasn't difficult, Artie chuckled, given that Robbins was as usual wearing dark glasses.

It wasn't the first time this joke had an airing, but still he found it so funny he couldn't stop slapping his thighs, the damn fool, yapping like a happy seal, *zouak, zouak*, and waking up little Robert who'd fallen asleep so as not to have to listen to our nonsense. A self-defence mechanism, I told myself—and no surprise, because the child was probably mine. I was contemplating his chubby little cheeks and giving in to the wave of tenderness washing over me when Anita arrived, whispering "How is he, little Bamboo, how is he, *howdidodido*?" Hearing his better half call their son Bamboo, Robert gritted his teeth and smiled tersely as he crushed an imaginary insect—an ant, I reckon, or maybe a stink bug—with his heel. All credit to him, it was that or be impaled. Strangely, I was starting to feel good in Winslow's skin.

The problem was that there were two of us in that skin and, baggy as it was, I felt a little hemmed in. To be honest, I needed some air, so I said that I was going out, the day was too beautiful to be stuck inside. I'd have liked to be alone with Jeff, to be able to take stock of things, but everyone followed me, bringing along the bowl of revolting punch, the canapés, the dog's frisbee, little Robert's walker, his teddy bear, his Bambi, his Bamboo, his bottle, his diaper bag, his hood, his sunscreen, his swimming pool, his electric train, and I asked Anita why she wasn't bringing his snowsuit too. She didn't appreciate my humour, but nevertheless went off to find a small woollen blanket while Robbins and Robert lit up a smoke. I'd not been mistaken, motherhood had transformed Anita and, my own self-defence mechanism, I started smoking again. I needed to have a word with myself.

As we waited, Artie pulled at my sleeve to show me the hole left by the four-hundred-million-year-old rock, which they'd covered with gravel, but was *this* deep, Artie showed by opening his arms wide. *A fucking big stone.* "I know," I said, showing him the bump on my left side, and it was only at that moment that I realized how dogged the bruise was. Surely after three hundred and forty-two days it should have disappeared?

"Excuse me, Artie, I have to speak to Robert," I said, heading toward him as quickly as my condition allowed, to ask him to explain this phenomenon to me, because I was sure he must have thought about it too. Not complicated, he said, I'd fallen out of bed the first time I'd woken up, a week ago, an incident that had immediately put me back into a coma. It was a little brief as explanations go, but I'd have to make do. "Such is life," Robert added with a supercilious smile, and I understood why Robbins had never liked me. When I put on those superior airs I really wanted to hit myself.

"Such is life," I mumbled and, putting on my sweetest Winslow face, asked Robert if he might like to swap his bourbon-spiked punch with me, which he did, though he grimaced. The first sip went down badly, the second did its best, and the third made sure I thought it was divine. For the couple of minutes of my savouring my elixir, everybody was silent because nobody had any idea what to say. Robert asked what the coma had been like. "Black," I said. "Or white, depending on whether you prefer black or white. If you prefer white, then it was black; if you prefer black, then it was white. Not nice. An absence. A void. I must have been dreaming, I suppose, of being cold, being hungry, and in pain, but I can't remember anything. Nothing, Robert, a black hole, a white abyss, it all depends."

We observed a few more seconds of silence, because what I'd just said was profound, and I followed up by conceding that my last memory, excluding that of the visit of my family the day before, had been of the four-hundred-million-year-old rock.

"You have a family, Bob?" Robert asked, and I could see he was about to deny there ever had been a visit, just as Kathy Bates had done, so I changed topics and pursued the subject of the rock. Unsure of where to move it, they'd taken it to the other side of the lake and put it next to my porch. "A souvenir," Robert said, and I couldn't figure out if he was mocking me or serious. What does it matter, I was too exhausted to dwell on it, everything in its own time. Instead I caught up on Ping's news, better off sorting that out right away. Apparently he hadn't ended up in a quiche as I'd anticipated, but as onion rings. The onion Pings were Anita's idea, and I hoped he'd found it funny. "Poor Ping," I murmured, Artie rushing over to console me just as Anita arrived carrying a cake and singing "*Mon cher Bobby, c'est à ton tour*," Quebec's kitschiest birthday song, and you could see from Robert's eyes that he wished he'd never taught it to her.

I pretended to be pleased and served a slice of cake to whoever wanted one, even though it wasn't my birthday. Afterwards, as people around me started to yawn, I announced I was heading back inside, and faithful Jeff followed me because he was the only one who knew who I was. There was no question of my deceiving him, this dog, because I loved him unconditionally, so I pretended instead that it would make me feel much better if I had two dogs with me on my first night back at Mirror Lake. This was the only way of bringing Jeff along without making a scene, and Robert agreed to it, even though I was positive he knew I was about to swap the dogs' scarves, giving Jeff the green one and Bill the red. But before Artie, Jeff, Bill, and I were able to get into the boat, Anita held out little Robert for me to kiss, and I whispered in his ear that he should not turn out like his father, without knowing if I was alluding to myself or the other guy. No matter, the baby understood. First of all, he burst out laughing, *gagaga*, and then, after examining me assiduously, he started to wail and Anita grabbed him out of my arms. The child was so like me.

Still lost in thought, the notion of what we might have done with the kid brought a tender smile to my lips. Artie gave me a little nudge with his oar, and I got into Winslow's green boat beside him, followed by Bill and Jeff, who were both excited about going out on the water. Artie didn't want me to row, so I sat in the back with Jeff and let my fingers trail in the cool water, trying not to think about what was happening to me, all this stuff that didn't make sense. I focused on the tips of my fingers, on the little wakes they were opening up in the lake and the fish who must see these little bits of pink flesh and wonder if they're edible. And then I told myself that if I were Winslow, then I'd go fishing the next day.

Until then I'd pretty well been on top of things, but this last reflection was triggering. The stream of objections I'd been suppressing rose up inside me in a great wave of nausea and suddenly I stood up and yelled that I wasn't Bob Winslow. *Zlow, zlow, zlow*, answered the mountains, Artie made a hard turn to stop us from tipping, and three pairs of large round eyes, belonging, respectively, to Artie, Bill, and Jeff, turned my way as if I were a raving lunatic. But I wasn't mad; if anyone had lost it in this godforsaken hole it wasn't me. "Do you understand that, Artie? They're a bunch of sickos, a gang of crazy people," and I started in on my stupid theory about nightmare and reality. I explained to Artie that since we were in a nightmare, he wasn't real and shouldn't be afraid of falling into the water. If he drowned, it wouldn't actually be him drowning, only the image I had of him, after which we'd all be teleported into a different nightmare where, with a bit of luck, he'd have turned into Jeff and I'd have become Anita.

I blabbered on till we reached the other side, overwhelming poor Artie with a flood of words as vindictive as they were despairing. But he just kept staring at me with his big mute carp's eyes, behind which I did sometimes see a flame of compassion flickering. Neither did he say anything when we reached land, climbing out of the boat and entering the cottage and leaving me to finish my tantrum on my own. I was so wound up that I must have fulminated for a good half-hour, striding up and down the beach and kicking any of the rocks that had the misfortune to be in my way — until one of them, in its shape, colour, texture, and, let's say, its obdurate appearance, brought the four-hundred-million-year-old rock that had been responsible for what had happened to me to mind. Without taking into account the absurdity of my response, I approached it with the intention of telling it my deepest thoughts, but, when I saw it sleeping so peacefully in the shade of the cottage, I quite literally collapsed. I fell to the ground and cried for a good long time — it settles the mind — and then tried to take a calm, methodical look at the whole situation.

"A man falls into a coma," I said to Jeff and Bill, who had been keeping their distance until then. "A man falls into a coma, and when he wakes up, he's no longer himself. Who am I?"

No reply.

"A man falls into a coma. When he wakes up, he has a son — whose father he isn't. What happened?"

Silence around me.

"A man falls into a coma. When he wakes up, the person he thought he was is sleeping with the mistress of the neighbour of the man he has become. Who is John Doe?"

I carried on like this for a while, and with each question the mystery thickened. Either I had gone mad, or I had always been mad but wasn't any longer, or I was still in a coma, that or I was the victim of a grand and devilish machination, as previously I'd believed during that blessed time in which I'd howl at the slightest peccadillo. But none of these hypotheses moved me a single step forward. In the circumstances I might as well have gone to bed, what with night falling and things always looking better in the morning. At least that's what Hortèse said if a question stumped her. She'd wait for night to fall and send the question to bed with the person who'd asked it.

So downhearted was I that I didn't even want to gaze at the stars, as beautiful as always, not even to lose myself in contemplating Ursa Major and Ursa Minor, constellations I called "the widow" and "the orphan" because you could look for a big bear all you wanted but he wasn't there. But ruminating over the mysteries of the universe when I had no idea who I was didn't appeal to me. I called the dogs, who were chasing a firefly. "Hurry up, guys," I yelled, and went inside.

Before my coma I would have been hung up on the firefly, I would have wondered why the insects' tiny phosphorescent behinds have not been glittering much at all in the undergrowth of the American east these last few years, and would have blamed humans — their pesticides, their baffling desire to light up the night by installing streetlamps and floodlights everywhere, as if light is better than darkness — but I was too tired, too sore, too depressed, so I let the firefly fly away, despite the fact that it might have been the last firefly of all time, the last survivor of a time in which its ancestors gaily frolicked, and I closed the door on the night.

In the cottage, the first thing I noticed was Victor Morgan's novel, which must have been sitting on the coffee table in the living room for a year, waiting to reveal to me what my fate would be. As for Artie, he was in his bedroom, from which I could hear the muffled sound of the television. I opened the door to apologize, I owed him that at least, but he pretended not to hear. He was good at that kind of game. He carried on watching his cartoons without reacting, even though the coyote had just flattened itself at the bottom of the cliff where Road Runner had led it. I knew that normally he would have found that funny, but he was hurt, I could see that, and wasn't laughing. He was stewing in his wounded pride and wanted me to know it. I apologized again, but Artie wasn't in a forgiving mood and so I wished him goodnight and, on the off chance he might react, thanked him for the onion.

Nyet.

I went to sit on the porch with *The Maine Attraction*, which no doubt had a few things to teach me.

But I only managed to read a page or two, hypnotized by the soft, tinkling oriental music of the chimes beside the lantern. I could not have put a title to their refrain, but it evoked junks on the Yangtze and the fluttering of fans in the humidity of the Gulf of Tonkin, places I had never been to and would never visit, which hardly mattered because the music of the chimes led me there anyway, informed as I was by the thousands of images travellers had amassed for me from these distant lands. Over the years I'd constructed my own East by assembling the pieces I had in an order I liked, too bad for geographical or historical reality, and I challenged anyone who wanted to compete with the beauty of my oriental dreams. I stayed there looking at the boats criss-crossing on Mirror Lake, and then, when the last boat had slipped behind the wall of darkness rising up at the edges of the water, I went inside and cloistered myself in Winslow's bedroom with Bill and Jeff, leaving Victor Morgan on the bench on the porch where he could wait for me until the next day. I heard Artie's deep voice behind the wall saying, "Good night, Bobby," and then fell into a deep, dreamless slumber.

"No doubt about it, I'm Winslow," I declared to the mirror, which was making the same movements as me but in opposite, though without it seeming so, and I wondered what would ensue if mirrors reflected not just images but sound, too. Would they talk backwards? Would my mirror have said, *ti tuoba tbuod on, wolsniW m'I*? No, probably not. And besides, why did I care? All that mattered was that I had Winslow's face, that, barring Jeff, the whole world thought I was him, and that a person claiming to be Robert Moreau had taken my place on the other side of the lake. But was this person truly me? Apart from the fact that he had my body, did the man also have my soul, my mind—or was he pretending to be me, just as I was pretending to be Winslow because I had no other choice? Was it possible, by some phenomenon unknown to science, that there had been some kind of substitution or, rather, a transmigration, at the very instant Winslow and I had collided over the picket and the four-hundred-million-year-old rock in a slow motion that had allowed my soul to move into his body and vice versa?

No, no, neither was this possible. I'd never believed in this sort of nonsense and was hardly about to start now, even if everything was telling me that certain wonders defy Cartesian dualism. Winslow was reacting exactly as I was, and therefore he was me. If he'd been Winslow, then he would have been amused or touched to hear Anita calling their son Bamboo, and he'd have nicknamed Anita something like Honeypie, Buttercup, or Petal. And if he'd been Winslow, he'd have been happy, but he wasn't, that was obvious, no less so than I would have been in his place.

This reasoning still posed a couple of disturbing conundrums. If neither Robert Moreau nor I was Winslow, then where had he gone? Was he floating somewhere in the limbo of Mirror Lake, waiting for someone to take a tumble so he might be reincarnated? Had he disappeared from the face of the earth without anyone realizing it? While I was formulating these entirely legitimate questions, I had the feeling Winslow was winking at me in the mirror, so promptly turned off the light. No doubt there was a logical explanation for whatever was going on, and I was going to find it.

As I entered the kitchen, Artie was exiting the bedroom and still in a sulk about me. To lighten the atmosphere I started in on another apology, attributing my bad behaviour to my coma and fatigue. "I was upset, Artie," I said. "Don't forget, I'm a sick man." But it wasn't enough. "You know, I like you very much," I went on, "and I didn't want to hurt you. Tell me, are we still friends?"

When I said the word *friends*, all the sadness pressing down on Artie's enormous shoulders evaporated, and he fell on me, wailing, "You're my friend, Bobby. Of course you're my friend." Then he made me sit down while he made breakfast, "Because you're sick, Bobby," and I had the peculiar impression of having already lived through this scene when the chick on the box of eggs seemed to wink at me too.

Baptême! Was it possible that Artie was Winslow? But, if that were the case, then who was Artie? Far too many questions for a single morning, so I decided to attack head on, I needed to be sure.

"Artie, tell me, are you Winslow?" He widened his bulging eyes, the only response he could manage, and I tried a different tack. First of all, I assured him that he shouldn't be afraid of revealing his fears to me, very strange things had been happening at Mirror Lake for some time. I was a good listener, and if he had a secret, he could share it. Then I waited — ten seconds, twenty seconds, thirty seconds — until Artie went to lock himself inside the bathroom. What new tactlessness was I guilty of to have provoked such a reaction? Whatever. I'd been slapped, apologizing another time was out of the question. So, again, I counted: twenty seconds, thirty seconds, at which point I heard Artie blowing his nose and rummaging around in Winslow's medicine cabinet. Surely the idiot wasn't intent on swallowing a bottle of sleeping pills? But no, he wasn't; a nose-blow or two later, out he came with a bottle of aspirin, which he placed in front of me. "Because you're really sick," he said. Then he served up our cold eggs and I noticed his eyes were red — bulging and red.

"What's up, Artie?"

"Yes, I do have a secret," he murmured, dropping his head. Immediately, I swallowed two aspirin, because I could tell the time had come. Artie was about to admit he was Winslow, I would confess that I was Moreau, and together we'd set off to look for Artie.

"Okay, Artie, I'm listening…"

"I'm in love with Anita," the big fool stammered out, but it was too late to spit out my aspirin. "She's so pretty, so nice, so beautiful," he said. "I love her, Bobby."

All things considered, it was just as well the aspirin had gone down, because I had a big problem on my hands here. Artie in love?

"Don't cry, Artie," I said, "I'm sure she loves you too."

"Really?" he squealed, childish hope lighting up his face.

"I mean I'm sure she loves you like a friend — a great friend, Artie, a very great friend. And aren't you lucky to have a friend like her?"

He didn't seem to agree. So, as the eggs solidified, I did my best to console him until, finally, a tenuous smile came to his face.

"It's Robert," he said, looking over my shoulder, and as I turned around, I saw Moreau coming up in his red boat. Clearly I hadn't understood Artie's complex nature, because he was overjoyed to see his rival appearing. As far as I was concerned, Moreau's arrival was not a smiling matter. One of the advantages of being Winslow was that, from my point of view, I could remain quietly at home safe in the knowledge that I would be unbothered, since traditionally I was the needy one , but here was this other fool stealing my role. What was Moreau playing at?

Upon asking this, I realized I was starting to think of myself as a separate person, that little by little I was thinking of Moreau as Moreau and no longer as me. But in that case, who was I? *Stop*, commanded one of the myriad voices that spend their lives monitoring me, *you're driving yourself crazy*. Still, there was something particularly disturbing about my believing I was two people. It was like suffering from a double personality where the second personality is identical to the first. What use is that? Was it possible, in the end, that Moreau was Winslow? *Shut up!* the voice barked again, and the voice asking the questions piped down. *Okay, okay, I'll stop, but I'm sending that cretin back to the north shore as soon as he docks.*

Which turned out not to be possible. Artie beat me to it, rushing outside ahead of me to welcome Moreau and warn him of my bad mood. "Angry," he whispered, and "sick," and "aspirin." While he was offloading his secrets, I lay down on the bench on the porch and noticed Morgan's novel wasn't there anymore. Strange, I was sure that's where I'd left it. I must have been mistaken.

A few minutes later, I was sitting with Moreau near the four-hundred-million-year-old rock while Artie did the dishes.

"I liked this stone," Moreau said, patting what could pass for the rock's head, and I understood what he meant. I also understood that he didn't agree with Anita's decision to move the rock. "I mean, while we're at it," he added, "why not raze the forest, fill in the lake, or buy rubber furniture and cardboard dishes? Why not stop breathing? Hey, she didn't think of that. If we all stopped breathing we couldn't pass germs on to Junior anymore, right? And maybe we should stop fucking, in case our sighs hinder his emotional development, cause irreparable trauma, mess with his Oedipus complex, or leave him stuck right in the middle of his anal phase?"

And he was off, the floodgates were open. Moreau had been brooding over the tribulations of conjugal life without anyone to confide in for almost a year. He'd endured sleepless nights, dirty diapers, Anita's crises, her whims, her recriminations, and couldn't take it anymore, was going to lose his mind, so he saw my resurrection — that was the word he used — as a sign and gift from heaven, even though he hadn't let it show the day before, in front of Anita. Basically, if I understood him correctly, he was excited by my return because he'd have someone to absorb his bile should things go badly. And me, I'd have to be the mediator between a guy who was secretly in love with Anita and another who regretted ever having been in love with her at all.

"But don't think I don't love her," Moreau clarified, because we were on the same wavelength, he and I, whether we liked it or not. But he preferred loving her from a distance, as he had done before. "Before" meant before her pregnancy, before my coma, before our little Robert. In the good old days. But how could I respond to that? Say that I agreed? That nothing was better than solitude? That

I preferred the time when we guys used to drink ourselves silly and throw up beneath the stars?

What would Winslow have done? He'd have advised Moreau to grin and bear it, helped the other man to see Anita was also at the end of her tether and that he needed to give her time. And then he would have looked for a bottle of gin. But aside from it being a little early to start on the gin, I had no desire to console Moreau. In fact, I felt absolutely no compassion for this guy enduring what I'd have had to endure but for the intervention of the four-hundred-million-year-old rock. The truth of it is that I didn't like myself, something I had always known unconsciously, but it was particularly unpleasant to learn it in such an irrefutable way. Ultimately, if I didn't like myself, it was because I was still myself and had never liked anyone. If I'd been Winslow, then I would have liked myself, just as Winslow did. Because it's true that he was fond of me, right? But where was the old fool when he was needed?

Just as I was processing the thought, the dogs started growling; we heard something stirring in the branches near the cottage and Moreau turned as white as a sheet. If he'd been in my hospital room, he'd have blended right in to the walls. Only his two eyes would have stood out from the infinite expanse of white in the scene of another damn nightmare. But luckily we were outside.

"What's happening?" I whispered, but he couldn't answer, frozen to the spot by whatever was this thing that, according to the direction he was staring in, was behind me. "What do you see?" I said more insistently, and the excessively large pupils of his periwinkle eyes advised me not to move. As for the dogs, they were still growling a little further away. If they'd seen a zombie, they'd have behaved no differently.

And there was my answer! They were watching a zombie. The thing standing behind me, if you could call it a thing, was none other than Winslow, so that the dogs and Moreau were looking at two Winslows, one skinny and one fat, wondering if they were losing their minds or if they were in a remake of *Adaptation* with Nicolas Cage playing both brothers, the slim one and the bigger one, the sexy one and the ugly one, or in *Face/Off*, with Nicolas Cage in the roles of Sean Archer and Castor Troy, the good guy and the bad guy. While they were working through that, I was thinking that I'd been transported into an altered version of *The Family Man*, in which Nicolas Cage plays a man who meets a kind of genie and sees what his life might have been like had he married his former girl-friend and had kids. By the way, examine me closely and you can spot a slight resemblance between me and Cage, something I'd need to think over again.

"Don't panic," I said to Moreau and the dogs, "there's an explanation." Slowly, I turned around, not knowing at all how I was going to react to Winslow, who would be nothing more or less than a second double of myself. If I didn't submit to an identity crisis in the next few minutes, then I'd be fit for the asylum. "Don't panic," I repeated to myself like a mantra. "Don't panic, don't panic, don't panic, don't panic," and then I closed my eyes to soften the shock. When I opened them again, the thing shuffling in front of me did indeed look like Winslow, but smaller. "*Grrr!*" it growled, ferociously enough that I leapt back, stumbled, and fell on something hard, and dozens of stars appeared in the daytime sky.

When I woke up, I was surrounded by an impenetrable expanse of black, which didn't seem like good news, because a coma is all white or all black, depending on your mindset, just as I'd explained to Moreau. I also had a dreadful headache, which at least reassured me I wasn't dead. I opened my eyes a little wider and noticed a shape moving, black on a black background at what seemed to be the edge of the vast black expanse. "Winslow?" I said almost inaudibly, but the shape didn't answer. I felt all around me, knocking a few things over, like dentures, a glass of water, a bottle of aspirin, and an onion, and the shape jumped. "Help!" I yelled, just as a lamp was turned on, a door opened, and two dogs barked: I was back to life.

"How long, how long has it been?" I asked Moreau, whose pale face was framed in the doorway, and Artie, who was shining a flashlight at me.

"A few—" Moreau started before he was interrupted by Jeff bounding in and racing up onto the bed to lick my face.

"A few what, Moreau?"

"A few..." he resumed, and then it was Bill's turn to jump up on the bed because he thought I was Winslow, the poor beast, "...a few hours," he managed to say in the interval before, you never know, a third dog were to arrive, and finally I relaxed.

Ten minutes later, the three of us were sitting around the kitchen table with a bottle of gin and a bowl of chips, the brand of which I preferred not to know, and Artie was telling me that, through the kitchen window, he'd seen the bear sniff me, thump me on the back, and then slowly return to the woods waggling its big behind. Artie insisted it was a nice bear, not a mean bone in its body, but that wasn't the thing preoccupying me. What was the colour of the bear's eyes?

"As-tu vu ses yeux?" I asked Moreau.

Yes, Moreau had seen its eyes.

"What colour were they?" I continued in French.

"Brown, I guess. What other colour would they be? It was a black bear, it had brown eyes."

"You're sure they weren't blue?"

"No, Bob, the bear's eyes were brown," he reiterated. But given that the sight of the bear had terrified him, Moreau wasn't the most reliable witness.

"Artie, did you see the bear's eyes?"

But Artie wasn't listening. His furrowed brow suggested he was trying to solve a particularly difficult problem of logic.

"What's the matter, Artie?" I fretted.

"You speak French perfectly, Bob," he said, staring at me as if I was a freak of nature. But he was right, it was true, I'd spoken to Moreau in impeccable French, another piece of irrefutable proof that I was me. Artie sometimes had unexpected flashes of lucidity and to put him at ease, I explained that I was able to do so because of all the blows I'd taken to the head. Then I closed the discussion before Moreau was able to pitch in, though he seemed to think my bilingualism was completely normal. He knew a thing or two, this guy, that I would have liked to have known myself.

Not sure what else to talk about, I chose a practical subject, the four-hundred-million-year-old rock, which this time had left a dent of a bruise right in the middle of my forehead that resembled the eye of a Cyclops or maybe a third eye, and I said that if it was a third eye, then maybe I'd have the gift of second sight like Johnny Smith does in Stephen King's *The Dead Zone*. I'd said it as a joke, but when I thought it over calmly, I could see there were several similarities between my fate and Johnny Smith's.

I must have lost contact with earth — "Odyssey, this is Houston, do you read me?" — as I was mulling over the troubles Johnny Smith and I had in common, because suddenly I noticed a hand waving in front of my face. I heard, "Bob, Bob, are you here?" but didn't know how to answer because, all things considered, Bob wasn't there, and suddenly I could feel the weight of my immense solitude. I was the bearer of a secret impossible to share, and I had never felt so abandoned, isolated, and misunderstood in my life. Jeff was the only being in the world in whom I was able to confide, and Jeff didn't care one iota whether people thought I was Winslow or not. For him, appearances were totally unimportant, and he was absolutely right. I should have trusted in my own wisdom and remained myself, despite the counsel of the night that, ever since I'd returned to Mirror Lake, had urged me not to make waves and to behave like Winslow, that this was the simplest way forward as I waited for the truth to show its great haggard face.

The night before, after a dreamless sleep, I'd woken up at around three or four in the morning, a little lost in Winslow's bedroom, and heard the night speaking in Hortèse's voice and whispering in my ear that I didn't need to rob Peter to pay Paul. The night's message was, let us say, enigmatic, and I asked the voice to clarify. It added that one picks up where the other leaves off, that half a loaf is better than none, that you need to choose the lesser of two evils, and other such platitudes. Basically the voice was telling me to keep my mouth shut, but before it could come out with "he who laughs last laughs loudest," I ordered it to be quiet, and buried my head underneath the pillow.

I had always believed, trusting a certain mythology, that night had a warm, sensual voice, a voice that slipped lasciviously into your dreams to tickle your fantasies and cover you in a sweat that was blessed because it was a result of sin. How mistaken! Night has a grating voice, identical to Hortèse's, and it feeds nightmares, anguish, and guilt; it prevents you from sleeping and leaves you with bags under your eyes. Certainly, it is nothing like the voluptuous sweet nothings of a lover, nor soft lullabies summoning Morpheus to your side. When night speaks to you, it's neither to comfort nor enlighten you, but to let you know you have problems, big problems, the darkness concealing their true dimension. Because that's what night said to me: *shut up, play dead, things are bad enough already.*

It was pretty depressing, really, and in the tone of a guy who wants to be alone I told Artie and Moreau that I was going out with the dogs. I went down to sit near the lake, in which the light of the moon was softly undulating but the stars not reflected, the stars too far away, too small, and, like vampires, too dead to have a reflection, though in truth the only vampiric thing about them is their attraction so impossible to resist. Whatever. I lay down on my back ready to be vampirized, and gazed at the portion of the universe visible from Mirror Lake, as it sank into interplanetary time. After making their usual reconnaissance, the dogs came and lay down by my side, and when I put my hand on Jeff's head, I could see his future, just as Johnny Smith sees the future of the people he touches. Perhaps it is more accurate to say I saw his dream, saw our dream of future days, drawn inside the same big bubble above our heads.

We were on a beach on a starry July night. An owl was hooting. At our feet, small waves expired, sighing, in the sand and we could hear the wind whispering in the pines. "These are the most beautiful noises in the world, Jeff," I said, these and the sound of rain on a wood-shingle roof, of a loon lost in the mist, all part of an unending dream in which the rain succeeds the owl, the owl the merle, the merle the loon, the fog the rain, as, at long last, the sun the clouds, which were lifting off the surface of the lake with the lightness of being of someone who has slept soundly there, a cheek against the cool water. We were fine, and we were alone.

It's not actually that difficult to make such a dream come true. Everything we needed was within reach. The problem was that other people were close by too, seeking the same paradise as us and driving it further away, always further away. Conclusion: paradise is a con, and that's what God wished to demonstrate by catapulting me into Winslow's skin. Still, maybe he also wanted to prove to me that I was fine as Robert Moreau, that I should have been content with that and not spent my time pitying myself while three-quarters of the planet was starving to death or had bombs dropping on their heads. And since when had God and I made up anyway? Since I'd become Bob Winslow, I figured, or from that moment when only divine intervention could explain what had happened to me.

Speaking of divine interventions, something started moving in the branches next to the cottage, and Bill, Jeff, and I all jumped to our feet, convinced that the bear was coming back for another visit, but it was a raccoon doing his rounds of the garbage cans. Bill and Jeff raced off after him and the little animal's mask disappeared at top speed behind the cottage, and I remembered that my question about the bear had never been answered. Did the bear have Winslow's eyes, as I had thought before I fainted, or did he not, and I'd imagined it? There was only one way to find out: track the bear down, or wait for it to return. If I was allowed a bit of space, I'd attend to it the next day, and maybe I'd take a quick trip into town to fetch a copy of *The Dead Zone* and figure out how it was that Johnny Smith had ended up in my story.

I never was able to find a copy of *The Dead Zone*, which doesn't matter, because not only was I already familiar with Johnny Smith's story, but I knew how a guy like that would feel, I understood the painful loneliness of someone directly connected to the invisible, someone besieged by images mere mortals cannot see — someone paranormal, basically, a circus freak-show people find fascinating and terrifying at the same time. The only difference between Smith and me was that nobody actually knew who I was, including me.

I was still intent on buying the book. Anyway, I was getting ready for the drive into town when I heard Anita shouting on the other side of the lake, shouting unpleasant words like *bastard*, *irresponsible*, *selfish*, and then another *bastard*, all of them aimed at Moreau. It was all a bit much; Moreau could be hard to take, but calling him a bastard was insulting his mother — in other words my mother — which I couldn't accept. We needed to have a talk. Immediately after her barrage, I heard the door slam behind a dejected Moreau. He stood on the porch for a minute examining the tops of his shoes, as if they might somehow encourage him, but the only thing shoes can do, if you help them a little, is walk, squash insects, or kick walls, empty cans, and pebbles, if they don't like pebbles. Moreau's shoes decided to walk, kicking up a few stones in front of them as they went, and then I watched as they—the shoes and Moreau—headed for the red boat tied up at the dock.

Straight away, I turned and told Artie I was driving into town and wouldn't be back before nightfall, perhaps not until next month, but the oaf had heard Anita yelling and was already jumping into Winslow's car, which is to say my car, determined to help her or console her, depending on what was needed, and I stood there, arms dangling, staring first at my shoes, which needed a good cleaning, and then at the car disappearing in the dust. *Fuck.* To let off steam, I kicked a few stones that should never have decided to settle in Maine, and waited for Moreau. I could have run off and hidden in the woods, or underneath the cottage with the raccoon, but Moreau would have found me. It was written, or else it was going to be written. *It's your destiny*, Darth Vader reminded me as he popped up for a moment in my gloomy mind, *and you can't stop fate. Yes, you can always choose to kill yourself, but that's still fate and changes nothing. You might as well put up with whatever is poisoning your life while leaving it to us.* So I decided to sit down on the four-hundred-million-year-old rock, said "Hi rock," and apologized for kicking its little sisters' heads, but either the rock was indifferent, it was sulking, or it had no familial feelings, because it didn't bat an eyelid. I'd hoped it would rise to the occasion and apologize, in turn, for hitting me, but it maintained a stony silence, the verb *apologize* evidently not part of its vocabulary.

Nonetheless I stayed sitting on it and watched Moreau approach. I could also say that I listened to his approach, because he was humming the Soggy Bottom Boys' song "I Am a Man of Constant Sorrow." That's also the tune I would have chosen — because I was Moreau, because I knew the soundtrack to *O Brother, Where Art Thou?* by heart, and because, standing in front of the mountains, I was suddenly filled with an enormous sadness. *Des millénaires de montagnes*, as Élise Turcotte put it so well — the "millennia of mountains" — against which Moreau's defeated voice was echoing, because his heart was not light. Once he reached the shore, I went down to help him pull his boat up on the sand, but as the dispirited fella put a hand on my shoulder so that he'd not lose his balance disembarking, I saw his fate and it was the same as Johnny Smith's. *Fuck!* With his touch, my brain's dead zone was suddenly activated, or so it seemed, I started trembling and seeing flashes, all sorts of strange shapes, and then the image I was seeing settled and I was catapulted onto the north shore of the lake on a beautiful August afternoon, perched over and, together with Winslow, trying to roll a dead body up onto the beach.

At the time I thought I was having a flashback — that I was reliving the day Winslow and I had fished John Doe out of the lake, and would finally find out who the guy was. Which is when Anita arrived and events got more complicated. Winslow and I were harpooning John Doe with our branches when Anita came up to tell us she was taking Junior to her mother's house, because she didn't want him witnessing the scene. I answered that we weren't planning on inviting the dead guy in for a cup of tea, but she told me to take a hike and said the atmosphere was creepy, that the corpse was giving off morbid vibes, and we anxious men giving off a bad smell, all things that might leave indelible yet indecipherable scars in little Robert's brain, which at best would mean we'd be paying for psychoanalysis once he was twelve, or, at worst, that he'd become a serial killer, a fucking sicko who'd plunge his girlfriends' heads in bathwater and capsize his ageing parents' boat in the middle of the lake with a predator's smile on his face. "Is that what you want, Robert?" Regardless, if Junior turned out badly it would be my fault, and so?

"Let her go," advised Winslow. "She's still rather fragile." I let her go.

The rest of the vision pretty much resembled what Winslow and I had been through the year before. Tim Robbins arrived in a squeal of tires with Conan, the forensics guy, who was wiping his glasses on his white hazmat suit. A little later the Daltons showed up, followed soon afterwards by Anita's mother, a kind of ersatz Ma Dalton who glared at me as if I was the one who'd drowned John Doe, and now it was my turn to flash a predaceous smile. It all degenerated into a brawl for the most nebulous reasons, and once again I found myself skewered on the fence picket that had reappeared beneath the porch. That was the end of the vision, and still I didn't know who John Doe was.

My vision had only lasted a few seconds. When I returned to real time, Moreau was just about out of the boat and swearing because he'd put his left Doc Marten in the water. "Are you okay?" he asked, gazing up at me, because I must have looked somewhat startled.

"I'm okay," I replied, wanting to add that he could speak to me in French, which he knew perfectly well, but the detail was irrelevant next to what had just happened to me.

If my vision really had been that, then it meant there was another John Doe in the lake, or that someone else would drown soon. It also indicated Winslow would come back, that or I would put on a hundred pounds and become a bona fide Winslow. It also meant Anita had a mother and that I would die by being impaled. But was it really me who would die? If Winslow resurfaced, would I be reintegrated into my own body? And who was the real Robert Moreau? Was he me, or the guy next to me who was shaking his waterlogged boot and telling me Anita had kicked him out and, if I didn't mind, that he was going to chill at my place for a couple of days just until the storm blew over?

Yes, I did mind, but given that I was not actually me it was incumbent upon me to demonstrate delight. That's how Winslow would have reacted, and he'd have given me a big slap on the back too, which I did a little sheepishly. But upon contact with Moreau, my brain's dead zone joined in the fray before I could file a complaint, say a prayer, or tell God his actions were excessive. This time, at least, I was entitled to a cheerful vision, surely.

Which came to pass that evening. Moreau, Bill, Jeff, and I were sitting around a campfire, just like in the good old days, with a couple of empty bottles beside us. Moreau was cooking sausages and I was saying, "Red, red as red roses," rather poetically.

"A rose is a rose is a rose," Moreau declaimed to make himself look intelligent, and then I carried on with red, red as strawberries, as raspberries, as cranberries, red as cherries, tomatoes and McIntosh apples, Cortland apples, and so on and so on. We went through all the fruits, big and small, edible and not, everything the earth brought forth that was red, including anger and rags to a bull. The Pink Lady was back, to our great pleasure and also that of the dogs missing the felicity of our drunken evenings. When the game ended, we all looked up to the sky, inhaled deeply, smiled, and I saw myself ask Moreau who John Doe was.

"You don't remember?" the imbecile guffawed.

I said no, that I was drawing a blank on the subject. Which didn't go down well because he was too drunk to remember. End of the second vision.

"Are you okay?" Moreau asked again, and I muttered, "No, no, I'm not. Who is John Doe?" Immediately, I knew the question was pointless, because the future had taught me that when night fell on Mirror Lake I would still be clueless about the identity of the man who'd suffered this misfortune. But I hazarded the question anyway, in case my future was less headstrong than my fate. Were that so, it might be possible to alter it. I was playing a dangerous game, I knew, trying to change the course of things is like imagining you're God, or at least one of his subalterns, who don't always do good work. And it's impossible to predict just what series of catastrophes you might set in motion should you involve yourself in matters that don't concern you. Arthur Bolduc, Ti-Ron's father, knew as much. One day, at a bend in the Cordon road, he tossed a hubcap that had been lying in the middle of the asphalt into the ditch so that it wouldn't cause an accident. Just one hour later, Julienne Lessard, blinded by the beam of sunlight bouncing off the hubcap, ploughed into the ditch in her husband Grégoire's brand-new Chrysler. *Requiem in pacem*, Julienne. Filled with pain and remorse, Arthur had gone back to find the cursed hubcap and restored it to the middle of the road. Then, the following day, Damien Jutras smashed his head in after skidding on it with his motorbike. The moral of the story? Everything has a place, and everyone should mind their own business, just as Hortèse and the majority of the villagers had decreed, imploring Arthur not to try to outwit fate again. Mind your own damn business, Arthur!

A cautionary tale, certainly, but my curiosity was too insistent, I was desperate to learn who was hiding behind the cloak of the pseudonym John Doe. "WHO IS JOHN DOE?" I asked Moreau again, and he recoiled from my unexpected tone. "Who is John Doe? Who is John Doe?" But I was the one who should have known who the guy was, I was the one who'd rummaged through his wallet, not Moreau. Except for me, Tim Robbins, and maybe

Conan, nobody knew who John Doe was. As Robbins had said, it was someone very important, someone whose identity could only be revealed once the investigation was over, but the inquiry was certainly dragging its feet.

I didn't believe him. I didn't believe him for the good and simple reason that he would confess to me that very evening that he'd forgotten John Doe's name. Besides, how could you forget something you never knew? Can you explain that to me, Moreau? And, hang on a minute, Winslow wasn't the one who'd gone through the wallet, Moreau had. Could he explain to me, then, why he was lying? No. He couldn't enlighten me on the subject because I was the one who'd filched the damn wallet. We went back and forth like that for ten or twelve minutes, during which time our voices grew louder and louder. It might even have come down to fisticuffs had a grunting noise in the undergrowth not reached our ears. We stopped in our tracks and I said, "The bear, fuck, the bear, the bear"—the bear I needed to stare right in the whites or the blues of its eyes.

Leaving Moreau to himself, I rushed into the under-growth and called in a low, steady voice, "It's okay, Winslow, don't go, I recognize you, don't move, Winslow, stay there, I know you're the bear," but I must have fright-ened it off. All I managed to see was a wide brown rump with a white mark on the left buttock disappearing into the low branches. But, next to the bear's tracks, I did perceive a colourful object on the ground, an object extremely famil-iar to me that I had recently misplaced. Just as I bent down to pick it up, a ferocious growling silenced the birds—I hadn't even noticed how many were chirping—and a deathly silence fell over the forest. Clearly the bear didn't want me to pick up the object, and had this been a scene in a movie, the viewers would have been terrified, the girl sitting in the back row would have dug her nails into the thigh of Peter, her boyfriend, who would have been entirely justified in shouting and knocking over his popcorn, thus sending a wind of panic among the hysterical people scattered through the theatre, among whose number the girl with the sharp nails, Pierrette, must be included. But I didn't let the prospect put me off and bravely grabbed Victor Morgan's book despite its being shredded and covered in slobber, and ran out of the woods. Now I had the evidence I needed: the bear had to be Winslow, not only because he'd attempted to destroy *The Maine Attraction*, but because if he was that afraid, then of course he was Winslow.

"Look what I found near the bear's tracks," I shouted to Moreau, brandishing the object in the air. "This bear is not a normal bear. He wanted this book, Robert, he wanted this fucking book. He stole it from me." Obviously Robert thought I was losing my mind, which is what I too would have thought in his position, which I practically was. He must have been wondering: *Is this man as disturbed as he seems—even if he is only unconsciously showing it—or is he simply mocking me?* Let him wonder, I knew Winslow and the bear were the same. And besides, I was ready to wager it was written in the book—another reason Winslow

316

wanted to rip it into pieces, whether out of a desire for vengeance or because he was hoping in this way to negate the spell the book had over him.

"You should be happy," Moreau said, seeing my vexed expression concerning the state of the book. "First of all, it's a lousy novel. Secondly, all it's brought us is trouble. And really, what use is it to learn your future if only to find out you're going to die? We already know that." I concurred, but only partially, because I wanted to ascertain which path would lead me to the picket post—the latter becoming, in the circumstances, the last picket staking out my existence (my Last Spike, essentially)—just in case it was possible for me to take a detour, and I had it in mind that Victor Morgan might be able to help me in this undertaking.

Without worrying about Moreau, I took the tattered book out to the four-hundred-million-year-old rock, where I tried to fit it back together. Hopeless. It was missing pieces, the ending had disappeared, and there was nothing I could do with the rest. It was wrecked.

"Where's your copy, Robert?"

He no longer had one, he said. He'd burned it on Anita's orders, since she'd decreed the book to be a bad influence on him.

"But you did read it, Robert? You know how it ends?" No, he said. He didn't know the ending. He'd never managed to get past page 94. Every week he'd started reading it again, and every week he'd stopped at page 94. For once Anita had been right, the book was driving him crazy.

"But don't you want to know the ending, Robert?" I asked.

We were going in circles. Moreau had no interest in discovering how the story ended, his final argument being that we would find out soon enough. I didn't agree and decided I would head into town as soon as Artie returned to buy another copy of *The Maine Attraction*—and, while I was at it, *The Dead Zone*, too. Until then, what with having Moreau on my hands, I'd take advantage. We spent the day cleaning the property, picking up branches, clearing the undergrowth, and tossing out a pile of old junk from beneath the porch. We even unearthed an old crib, which Moreau took for Junior.

"Do you have children?" Moreau asked as we excavated the crib, sleeping under a heap of planks. Good question; did Winslow have any children? If I could trust in our conversations then no, he didn't have any—unless he'd quarrelled with them, which wouldn't be like him. Or maybe their mother, a woman of great beauty but incredible coldness, had abducted them years before, breaking the heart of poor Winslow, who'd subsequently attempted to drown his pain in alcohol and food, becoming obese and stupid and keeping quiet about his children's existence despite, deep down inside him, the scar that wouldn't heal.

"Yes, I had a child," I heard myself murmur, lapsing into silence to emphasize the words' dramatic effect. I stroked the wood of the crib. "A little guy named Bobby. Bobby Junior," I added before falling silent again, my evocation of this hypothetical child making me sadder than I could have imagined. And then I told Moreau Bobby's story. By the end of it we were both crying, Moreau because he worried Anita would leave him with little Robert, and me because I had two sons I didn't know, one real and one fake: Robert and Bobby, Junior and Junior. To console ourselves, and to reward ourselves for working so hard, I fetched a couple of beers which we drank to the memory of Bobby Junior who, if he'd turned out well, was no doubt caring for aids victims in Zimbabwe, or defending great causes with Greenpeace and the like. Unless he'd devoted his life to teaching snotty little brats the difference between an auk and a penguin, a thankless task from which he would recover by playing baseball on Sundays with his son — because maybe, just maybe, I was the grandfather of a young Babe Ruth whose little blond head I would never have the pleasure to ruffle. Which was all we needed for a volley of hatred to be levelled at Bobby Junior's mother, the worst damn egotist the world has ever seen, and who'd only married Winslow out of self-interest — though what that self-interest might have been, we deftly ignored — only marrying him once he'd paid for her studies. She didn't have the right to deprive Bobby of a father with so much to impart and she would regret the marriage one day, but too late, well done her, how fucking selfish, though not so well done for Bobby. Poor Bobby.

On the second beer, we changed the subject, it being too painful for me to have to think about my missing son. I was such a good actor I even believed myself, wondering if perhaps Winslow did have a son — and if I was in the process of becoming Winslow through these tender recollections of the boy. I'd have to ask the bear.

Later, we lit a fire with the branches we'd gathered, washed a few potatoes and put them on the embers, they'd go nicely with some sausages, and then, as Mirror Lake was submerged in darkness and the moths came out to feed the bats, we understood that we were friends, Moreau and I, until death do us part. We had no choice. If blood hadn't been so frightening to both of us, we might have nicked our wrists and made a blood pact. Then star time arrived, time of the Pink Lady, now dressed in red, and finally John Doe time. "Who is John Doe?" I asked Moreau, and the oaf guffawed with laughter, exactly as he had done in my vision. Exactly as if I hadn't changed the future. Exactly as if Arthur Bolduc had left the hubcap in the middle of the Cordon road.

It was raining the next day after Artie had returned, a good hot rain drumming down on the metal roof and playing a piece for us no score could ever equal. Artie crept into the house in the middle of the night without making a noise, and went to sleep on the couch while Moreau was snoring away in his bedroom like a sad angel with broken wings descended from the heavens, nostalgic for paradise. An angel not so much fallen, no, as slightly pitiful, lost in the face of the immensity of the firmament and of earthly suffering, the extent of which he could not have imagined. A disappointed angel, let's say.

At seven in the morning, Artie was already banging the saucepans around, a fair indication he wasn't happy. When I arrived in the kitchen with my tousled hair, I saw he'd only set the table for two people. Was I his second guest, or the one he was annoyed with? His smile said no, he wasn't annoyed with me. That was a shame because I wasn't hungry at all, but as I didn't want him to be any more irritated than he was already, I sat down but did specify that I didn't want any sausages this morning, thank you. He threw a sombre look my way, his eyes bulging, and I said, "Okay, Artie, fine, but just a little one." That made him happy.

We ate in silence at first, but I could see something was worrying him, so I asked him if there was anything he wanted to get off his chest, hoping these morning confessionals wouldn't become a habit between us.

"It's Robert," he began.

"Yes, I know, I knew it," I said. "Go on, Artie," and I sat in the pose of an attentive psychiatrist.

"He slept in my bed…"

He slept in my bed…Put it like that and it was true, he slept in my bed, Robert slept in my bed, Bobby stole my bed, it all sounds quite dramatic. Should I have laughed or cried? Neither, Artie's big eyes told me. So I defended Moreau. I mean we were friends, right?

"We thought you were going to sleep on the other side of the lake with Anita, Artie, that's why Moreau took your bed. But we'll change the sheets, don't worry."

I shouldn't have mentioned Anita, he took it badly. He wasn't the kind of guy who'd take advantage of a woman's momentary vulnerability to jump on her, he shot back. He respected women too much to do that, and Anita in particular. "She's so smart, so beautiful, so nice…" If I thought he'd slept with her, he went on, I was a bastard, a fucking bastard, a nothing. In just ten seconds I'd become the villain, my plate had disappeared, its contents ended up in the dog bowl, and I looked like a lunatic. I tried to explain what I'd said, then changed my mind, I had nothing to explain. I pulled on my plaid shirt, my cap, and my running shoes, brushed my dentures, and went out.

The rain was falling in one of those magnificent

summer downpours I like so much. A warm, quiet rain refreshing the atmosphere and washing down the trees, the flowers, the rocks. The whole world was bathing in a shower and smiling, its mouth open wide, even the four-hundred-million-year-old rock offering its big grey head up to the softness of the rain and emitting a light vapour of contentment while drops bounced lazily on the lake. So relaxing was the rain that I didn't conceive of the anonymous raindrop characters as thousands and thousands of John Does; no, instead I thought about thousands and thousands of diminutive and lovely Chinese girls running in the streets of Shanghai or Beijing beneath their parasols or straw hats, what with the music of the chimes still in its oriental phase. Even the mosquitoes seemed pleasant, gathered in a corner of the porch and frolicking as they waited for the rain to stop. No sign of the bear, though, despite my leaving out a sausage and a potato for it. The raccoon must have snatched them, but I didn't begrudge him doing so, the day was too beautiful to be angry and besides, wasn't that one of nature's immutable laws — first come, first served? Winslow should have hustled.

Normally I would have enjoyed such a day. I'd have gone swimming with Jeff — it's so lovely swimming in the rain — or I'd have gone fishing. Winslow liked it and the fish bite more when it's raining, but the times were abnormal, as usual, and I had shopping to do. I whistled for Jeff. Bill arrived, I asked him where Jeff was, he told me he was in the cottage, and I went to find him. I swallowed two aspirin for my headache, didn't say goodbye to

Artie, and the two dogs and I headed to Augusta in the fine drizzle and gloom, humming the blues.

In the first bookstore I visited, the bookseller, a young man, didn't know who Victor Morgan was and didn't have *The Dead Zone* in stock. It was the same thing in the second, they hadn't heard of Victor Morgan either, and oddly enough they'd sold their last copy of King's novel just ten minutes before I showed up. In the third, I asked to see the manager, who I could see assumed I was nuts but he was at least polite. He offered to check and see if the Victor Morgan was still in print, and told me he'd never heard of the author. "Is he American?" he asked, letting the question mark devolve into suspicion, as if casting doubt on my memory. *No, he's Zulu, you jerk*, I thought, deciding in my mind he was a dunce. But I followed him to the computer monitor anyway, and after we'd checked the sites of every possible distributor, publisher, and warehouse, I understood that even the computer had no idea who Victor Morgan was. Nothing. No trace of Victor Morgan. It was as though he'd never existed. And as for *The Dead Zone*, there was just one copy left in the whole of the state of Maine.

By the time I was back outside, the rain had doubled in intensity and naturally I stumbled into an enormous puddle, just like Bill Murray does in *Groundhog Day*, prompting the same hilarious laughter from each of the dogs, their two blond heads framed in the window of the car on the other side of the street. Since the dogs were laughing, I decided to be Zen about it, stepped in another puddle, recited a haiku, and went to phone Stephen King to tell him he ought to check in on his agent. But as neither Stephen nor his wife Tabitha were at home, I left a message and hung up cursing. Then I looked up Victor Morgan in the directory. And it must have been my lucky day: there was one. Someone was going to have to pay for Victor Morgan's disappearance and I didn't give a toss whether or not this particular Morgan was the right one. His mother should have married a Polish guy or called him Gerard. His problem, not mine. So I phoned him and railed and put him in his place like a stinking piece of rotten fish. I'd never seen a fish, rotten or not, be put in its place but was sure the scene would not be a pretty one. I gave him a real piece of my mind, called him every fishy name that popped into my head—fish eyes, fish face, chub, hammerhead, blubber mouth, shark, poor salmon. After I hung up I felt a little better. And on my way back to the car, I carefully walked through the same puddles again to appease the dogs, who, having seen *Groundhog Day*, were expecting as much.

Once I was in the car, I undressed, stripping off everything but my hat, not wanting to get into trouble with any morality police. As I scoured the glove compartment to find something to dry my face with, I came across a Johnny Cash tape, so Bill, Jeff, and I drove home to Mirror Lake listening to classics like "Cry! Cry! Cry!" "Get Rhythm," "I Walk the Line," and "Folsom Prison Blues." I'd discovered Cash quite late, but better late than never, and I wondered how I'd managed not to know about this giant for so long—because Cash truly was a giant, unforgettable, a guy who goes looking for the lonesome cowboy deep inside you and puts the taste of dust and iron in your mouth. Listening to Cash is like listening to the beating heart of the United States of America with its craggy-faced men, their nostalgia for wild spaces, and women chopping wood as they give birth. It smells of animal shit and drought, of desolate plains stretching back as far as memory goes, of tribulations and of love, all these smells receding with the setting sun, when the silhouette of the lonesome cowboy disappears over the horizon or is struck by a Remington bullet just before the credits roll and the final music plays. Listening to Cash makes me feel really good, even if it makes me melancholy, which isn't quite a contradiction, though fortunately the sun pierced through the clouds just as we reached Mirror Lake, because I'd started crying like a baby, a very small baby lost in the wilds where his mother has succumbed to the heat.

"Why are you naked?" asked Moreau when I climbed out of the car. But I ignored him. I headed straight to the lake, dove in, and let the cool water take care of the rest. For a brief moment in time, the absent but obsession-inducing faces of John Doe, Victor Morgan, and Bob Winslow were erased. After a minute's breaststroke, accompanied by Bill and Jeff, I went back inside the cottage, still ignoring Moreau, whom I'd suddenly decided was responsible for my misfortune; and Artie, without allowing me a minute to get dressed, accosted me. He wanted to know where I'd been, if I'd seen Anita, if she was okay, if she'd talked about him at all, and if she'd done so with a tremble in her voice, a subtle one, "she's so nice, so beautiful, so pretty..." No doubt because I was in a foul mood, I told him that Anita had a lover and I'd been playing golf with Stephen King.

He only seemed to absorb the second part of my answer, which meant, from a psychoanalytical point of view, that he'd desexualized Anita's image by rendering their love platonic, with the effect that his eardrums refused to vibrate as soon as someone said anything that might evoke his beloved's genitalia. So he resolutely put any potential lover of Anita out of mind and focused instead on Stephen King.

I told him about our golf game in great detail, and embellished it with everything a fictitious scene can possibly be embellished with. As I was describing King's exceptional swing, I noticed Artie's big round eyes staring at me, his big bulging round eyes with their incredibly dilated pupils marooned in the white of his face, white as the first snow, pale as an early winter, his mouth open to ask a question that had frozen before it could be born on his moist lips, his plump, moist lips.

"What's going on, Artie?" But he stood, petrified, hypnotized by a tiny dot apparently sitting right in the middle of my face, on my nose or just next to my third eye, which wasn't quite in the middle. "What's going on?" I repeated, but his eyes, which had moved away from my face and settled on another vague spot in the corner of the room—a dead fly, a mouse crap, a cookie crumb—did not seem to belong to someone able to speak.

While he thawed, I went to get dressed, thinking that perhaps I'd been a little rough on him, slandering Anita. I may also have made an error in my psycho-analysis, attributing a purity of intention to Artie that isn't available to just anyone. When I returned, Artie's posture confirmed that I'd been perspicacious on the psychoanalytical front, because it appeared that not only had any trace of my comments about Anita been wiped from his brain, but he'd elevated me to his own personal pantheon. I was a god, a god who hung out with other gods, and he wanted to know when I was going to ask Stephen King to dinner. Artie told me dinners were his specialty, and that he already knew what the menu would be. So as not to disappoint him, I said we'd invite him over the following week — which I shouldn't have said, but my intentions were good and the truth of it was that I had other things on my mind. Cornering the bear in which Winslow had been reincarnated, for one. And given that Winslow was the only person on earth who'd read *The Maine Attraction* all the way through to the end, and since he was the living memory of Victor Morgan I needed to find some way of attracting the bear and making him talk.

But, first of all, I had to solve a few logistical problems.

Question one: How do you catch a bear?

Question two: How would I attract Winslow? (With fish, my unwavering common sense opined.)

Question three: Was there any fish in the fridge?

"No," Artie said.

In the freezer?

"No."

Could he maybe go and buy me some little fillets in town?

"But the lake's full of fish," the moronic Artie replied. And it was too late to go into town, the shops would be shut.

Indeed, it was starting to get late. With all the palaver, I hadn't noticed. The lake was taking on the pink hues of a sunset I'd have had the joy of contemplating full on if I'd been at my house on the other shore. Confronted by this deplorable reversal of fate, a new wave of sorrow unfurled inside me, a few tears pearled in my periwinkle eyes, and Artie tried to console me by promising to buy me fresh fish in the morning, first thing, immediately after breakfast. As for tonight, we still had some sausages he would cook on the fire Moreau was in the process of lighting.

Moreau! I had a few things to say to him. I thanked Artie, valiant Artie, and went out to join Moreau with the intention of settling matters with him once and for all. This had gone on long enough: I wasn't Winslow and didn't want to be him. All I wanted was to return to the past, to my cottage, my north shore, my bed, my Jeff, my books, my peace. Moreau knew things, and he would tell me them tonight. Moreau was oblivious, so I decided to go straight in for the kill.

"You know I'm not Winslow," I said immediately, looking him right in the eyes.

He held my gaze and, after a moment's reflection, conceded that I'd not actually seemed myself since I'd come back to Mirror Lake.

"That's not what I mean, Moreau. I'm not Bob Winslow, and you know that."

He thought some more, and then said my private life was none of his business, he didn't care what my real name was and, in any case, knowing it wouldn't change a thing because in his heart I would always be Bob Winslow. Good old Bobby.

At that point I practically started to yell — no, not "practically," I did. I just started yelling. I yelled that my real name was Robert Moreau, for fuck's sake, that his son was mine, that he'd taken the opportunity of my back being turned to transform Winslow into a bear and take my place. Moreau looked at me as if I'd gone mad, genuinely mad, he took fright, he ran away, I caught him, I jumped on him and pushed his face into the sand. Had Artie not intervened, I wouldn't have spared his skin, which was actually mine.

After Artie separated us, we lay on the sand for a few moments, still staring each other in the eyes as we caught our breath, which is when I saw a flash streak across his face, some kind of light, an indication that perhaps he had just started to understand something. He admitted that when he'd found out Anita was pregnant by him he'd dreamed of being in my place, but in fact he preferred his own, given that I was ill — was I ever. Then he added that he was leaving for my north shore right away, which I forbade him to do. We had stuff to sort out and he wasn't going to get out of it that easily. We were about to wrestle again when Artie grabbed a hold of our collars, mine plaid,

Moreau's striped, and dragged us away from the fire, one of us in his left hand and the other in his right. Then he sat down between us and told us to make peace. We each forced a recalcitrant smile and Artie started cooking the sausages and said we weren't very nice.

The Great Bear had time to do a lap around the pole before any of us said anything worthwhile.

"Yes," Moreau said occasionally.

"No," I'd quietly answer every now and then to the questions Artie posed about Stephen King.

Artie hadn't read King's books but had seen *It* and *The Shining* on television and wanted to know everything about him so as not to seem like an ignoramus when he came for dinner. Enthusing about *The Shining*, he stood up and imitated Danny, Nicholson's child, the kid who sees fucking terrifying twin girls everywhere, with big foreheads and abundant wavy hair, just like my sisters' dolls, Vicky and Nicky, who, when I was little, used to monitor my bedroom door with their mean plastic eyes. "Redrum, redrum," he groaned, his expression frozen in some kind of trance, and I asked him to imitate Nicholson instead, or even Donald Duck, as that child gave me shivers up and down my spine. "Redrum, redrum," he continued, walking around the fire and going to look at himself in the lake, "redrum, redrum, redrum."

When finally he came back to the fire, he continued to bombard us with questions as he wrote backwards on the sand. But for his voice, all we could hear was the crackling of the fire, an owl's cry, and, from time to time, the rustling of a moth's wings. The last must have annoyed Moreau, because he caught one mid-flight and crushed it in his hands, sending Artie into a rage, shouting that we had no right to kill innocent creatures without cause. Moreau retorted that Artie ate sausage and that sausage, wasn't it true, was made from innocent creatures. He shouldn't have said that. It was as if he'd stabbed him right in the heart, poor Artie leaving us and repeating "redrum, redrum, redrum," before throwing up behind the cottage.

The rest of the evening unravelled lugubriously. We watched the fire slowly go out and spoke just a few useless words—yes, no, maybe. *Yes*, *no*, and *maybe* are not always useless words, I know, but that particular evening they were of no use whatsoever. We went to bed with our backs slumped, our shoulders hunched, indifferent to the Pink Lady who was waiting at the edge of the forest in a captivating yellow princess dress, or was it a wood fairy's dress, that she'd put on just for us. Before turning out the light, I heard Artie murmur "Goodnight, Bobby, goodnight, Robert," before at last grunting, "Goodnight Tony," like Nicholson's bastard son talking to his finger, and I couldn't fall asleep. I counted cracks in the ceiling until the wee hours wondering how this story would end and if I was ever going to become myself again one day.

In the end, I did sleep that night, though only for a minute or two because I had a hellish nightmare. I know from experience that you don't have to be asleep to hobble along horror's tortuous paths, but for this category of nightmare you do have to be asleep, otherwise everything is meaningless.

I'd become myself again and had struck upon the brilliant idea of holidaying with Winslow in the Rockies, don't ask me why. We'd chosen the Overlook Hotel for its tranquility, the hotel in King's novel where Jack Torrance tries to kill his wife and son. I really do have a knack for unearthing peaceful places. From the moment of our arrival, we'd been pursued by the bloodcurdling screams of Jack Nicholson, priceless in the role of Torrance, so we took refuge in Kubrick's labyrinth, which I have called that because it's not in the novel, endeavouring to cover our tracks by walking backwards in the artificial snow. We covered them so well that we managed to get lost, which led to an epic argument with Winslow shouting *left* while I yelled *right* and vice versa. "We came from the left so we need to leave by going right," Winslow argued, labyrinths invented for him to believe the right path was the wrong one, to which I replied that if we kept turning the same way, going around in a circle, we should, logically speaking, reach the middle, so that all we needed to do was turn in the opposite direction to find the exit. Winslow didn't agree, so I told him to choose whatever route he felt like and I set off on my side. We must have passed each other at least twenty times, casting hate-filled glances at each other, when Nicholson joined us, closely followed by an irate Humpty Dumpty, and I woke up before either of them was able to decapitate me.

Near the cottage, a few birds were chirping, two or three crows were croaking, and one Moreau was whistling an unfamiliar tune, which was impossible, unless he'd learned it during the year I was in a coma. Whatever. I shut myself in the bathroom, dunked my head under the cold water and took two prophylactic aspirin, a precaution against the coming headaches. I entered the kitchen, and Artie had become vegetarian and was trying to come up with a meatless menu for our dinner with Stephen King. He told me he could no longer go into town to buy me fish because it was against his principles from now on.

"What will I give my bear to eat?"

"Blueberries," he said, and that was his last word on the subject.

I could have gone into town myself, but I was too tired. As for fishing: no way. So I furnished myself with a pot and went off to the blueberry bushes, but as the season was not yet at its peak, I had to be content with a quarter-pot of soft raspberries. For small fruit, the beginning of August is the worst time. Strawberries are over, raspberries are dying, and the blueberries are pale. It's very sad.

Back at the cottage, I tipped out the raspberries that had already turned in the heat, trampled them on the four-hundred-million-year-old rock, and went to look for a jar of liquid honey and poured it over the raspberries. Then I hid behind a tree and waited for Winslow. An hour later, the rock was swarming with ants, but still no sign of a bear.

"What are you doing behind that tree?" asked Artie, who'd stepped outside to shake out the tablecloth for lunch.

"Waiting for my bear," I answered, and he rolled his eyes, his way of indicating that I'd be waiting a very long time. He was right. I waited for two weeks. But not behind the tree. Every morning I'd leave him a snack on the rock, near the lake, or in the undergrowth, but it was always the ants and the raccoon enjoying it.

Other than that, life continued on its quiet way. Artie had proved incapable of deciding to murder any of the hunting camp owners, and had instead resolutely ensconced himself in the house, asking me each morning whether or not I'd telephoned Stephen King. Moreau visited us whenever he quarrelled with Anita, which was every other day. Eventually I headed over to see her, since I'd opted to behave like Winslow while I waited for him to show up. I have to admit that I was getting quite attached to little Robert, who could twist my father's heart around his little finger simply by opening his mouth. He just had to gurgle a *gagaga* and I melted. I'd have bought a flight to Greenland if the kid had asked me to. But as I was unable to confess to him that I was his father, and he was too young to be exposed to such trauma, I had to play the jolly uncle spoiling him, indulging all his whims. I even tried to teach him the words to "Yankee Doodle," if only to make Moreau mad. Of course, he couldn't remember all the words, but he did remember *Doodle*, and every time he saw me coming he'd call out "dad-daddu-doodle" as a pretty spit-bubble rose to his baby lips. Anita said he was calling me Uncle Doodle, but I knew he was calling me dad, Daddy Doodle.

My contact with the child softened me a little, but so what? I even became friends with the raccoon, to the great displeasure of the dogs, who had both moved in with Artie and me, which suited Anita. I'd wager that was why Moreau came over to see us so much — to have a chance to visit Jeff, because he loved that dog unconditionally, as I well knew. Back to the raccoon, I'd named him Albert, Albert Raccoon, and every morning he was stationed at the corner of the cottage waiting to see where I put his breakfast. "Hi Albert," I'd say as I went outside, "Hi stone, hi lake," before setting the previous night's leftovers near the lake, in the undergrowth, or on the rock, which was a little tired of the routine, I think. After Albert had eaten, he told me about his night and then he went to bed.

Life was continuing its peaceful course, in other words, without any notable incidents, except that one night Artie accidentally put Ping Two into a vegetable stew. I had trouble consoling him, but in the end I managed to by convincing him Ping Two would continue to live inside us, that there would always be a little piece of Ping Two in both our souls. Once the crisis was over, he wanted to give me a third Ping, but I refused, on the pretext that it would hurt too much when we had to part. We'd had two Pings and that was enough.

Then, one morning, what was supposed to happen happened, the bear revealing itself right after my moose. I was stacking wood under the porch when I saw a shadowy form on the lake. My first thought was of John Doe, and a great shiver ran through me and I wanted to run away. But during this time my brain concluded its character was inoffensive and pleaded with me to calm down. If it wasn't yet another of the innumerable John Does saturating the lake, then it could only be the bear, my bear, Winslow!

"The bear," I whispered to Jeff, before slowly proceeding down to the beach, taking quiet, cautious steps with my trembling legs, only to realize that it wasn't a bear but the moose, our moose at least, "Jeff, look, our moose, shut up, don't bark." I might well have been disappointed, and was a little, but this old buck was such a beautiful sight, looking so regal with its humped back, that I filed the bear away for later. I sat down on the sand, Jeff sat down next to me, Bill joined us, and we admired the enormous beast as it waded majestically through the lake, leaving a massive wake behind it that closed up again almost as soon as it formed, to the extent that within a few seconds there would no longer be any evidence of this animal at all, but for the traces it would leave in the marvelling eyes of those watching it from the beach: Bill, Jeff, me, and the raccoon.

Albert?...What was he doing there? It wasn't his time. He whistled a sentence in raccoon, and if I'd spoken better raccoon then I'd have understood what he was on about. I'd have known he was talking about the bear, who'd installed itself twenty feet behind us, at most, cleverly waiting for us to stop swooning over the moose.

Jeff saw the bear first, or maybe it was Bill, I forget, and the fur rose on his back and he started to growl. Nobody needed to sketch it out for me to see that my patience was finally going to be rewarded. I told the dogs everything was fine, that there was no need to be alarmed, and slowly, very slowly, turned around, half twisting my shoulders, rotating my pelvis, bending my knees, lifting my right foot—I was turning to the right—putting my right foot back down on the ground...

The bear was huge—huge, brown, hairy, and alarming—and beside it was another creature, medium-sized, brown, and hairy, a baby bear, a young bear, a yearling. For a moment I thought the bear standing in front of us wasn't the right bear, but I recognized the little white patch on its left buttock. If I'd been capable of telling the difference between a seal and a sea lion, then I would have already noticed it was a female bear. So, Winslow had been reincarnated as a woman and had had a little Winslow, a Winnie, contributing like Anita to the increase in Mirror Lake's overpopulation.

"Congratulations, Winslow," I exhaled between my teeth, and then I felt my cheeks puff out, a bad sign, and

I was overcome by unstoppable crazy laughter, which is effectively a pleonasm. This was not the moment, I know, but laughter that can't be stopped cannot be controlled, and makes me need to pee on top of everything else. So that none would leak out, I started hopping from one foot to the other and tried to think of something sad, but uselessly, since it was unstoppable, as I said. Mother Winslow, though, had no sense of humour. She stood up on her back legs and pointed at Albert the raccoon. What did she want with the raccoon? At first I was baffled, but then I realized she was annoyed with him, no doubt because he'd been stealing her breakfast for the last two weeks. That's how I interpreted her anger.

One of my guiding principles has always been that friendship is sacred, so here I was confronted with a serious dilemma. If I let a bear take the raccoon, I was abandoning, in very cowardly fashion, a friend in need. Because our lives were intertwined, Albert and mine. On the other hand, when it came down to it, Winslow was also my friend and wouldn't appreciate my betraying him. That said, Winslow's life was not in danger and Albert's was. But if I protected the raccoon, I was offering up my own hide to the bear. Had Winslow become so bearlike that he would rip me apart if I defended Albert? Another dilemma. While I was thinking this over, everyone around me was growling — Winslow, Winnie, Bill, Jeff, and maybe a couple of other stray critters — and I couldn't concentrate. As for Albert, he was doing his best to disappear.

"Silence!" I finally screamed, my shout indeed having

an effect for a second or two, during which we could hear nothing but the waves lapping, since they can't become silent at a moment's notice and without any warning. I barely had enough time to say, "Good, let's not be upset, let's think this through," when the growling and agitation started up again. I was on the verge of pulling Albert into the lake and throwing myself in after him as I whistled for the dogs when Artie opened the door of the cottage and called out in delight, "A baby bear! A baby bear, Bobby! A baby bear!" as if I hadn't seen it myself. Still, the fool did manage to create a diversion for long enough that Albert was able to slip away and I to order the dogs back inside. I had business to sort out with Mama Bear and they were getting in the way.

But I'd been worrying for nothing because Winnie was afraid of Artie and took off into the woods with Winslow in her wake, this is how mothers react.

"Winslow, don't go! We have to talk! Winslow, fuck, stop playing the fool..."

Too late. He'd gone. And worse still, in all the kerfuffle, I hadn't even noticed what colour his damn eyes were. *Wrrrik, wrrrik*, whistled the raccoon, who'd come back to sit at my feet, maybe to say, "Phew, that was a close call," or "Sorry, I don't know," and then he looked up at me with a timid smile. Me, I had absolutely no desire to smile at all. I went for a pee, shut myself in Winslow's bedroom, and ripped apart his cap. That relaxed me a little.

By the time I left the bedroom, the sun had already set. The light had been dim for a while now, not beautiful at all. I decided to go outside and look at the stars, which only shine at night. Albert was waiting for me by the four-hundred-million-year-old rock below the porch.

"What are you doing there, Albert? I don't have anything for you."

He said he didn't want anything, and then he waited for me to notice the object, the dirty white object, that he'd dug up. A piece of Morgan's book! Holy shit! Albert had a few pages of *The Maine Attraction*, almost intact, that had escaped Winslow's destructive urges. I took them and thanked Albert without noticing what was weird about the situation, and quickly returned to the porch to examine the pages by the lantern light. When I realized the pages numbered 216 to 221 were in my hands, a black veil, entirely opaque, fell over my eyes, hiding the starry sky, the light of the moon reflecting on the barely moving surface of the lake, and Artie's big face as he bent over to offer me a cup of tea.

He'd discovered Earl Grey at the same time as vegetarianism and was obsessed.

"No, Artie," I muttered from the depths of my blindness, "I wanna bourbon."

While he went off to fix me a bourbon, I thought back on the contents of pages 216 to 221 and recalled that the action narrated in these pages had taken place on August 17 in a leap year. If I subtracted three hundred and forty-two — the number of days my coma had lasted — from a year, counted backwards to the day I left hospital and, using my fingers, added two for the days I spent in the endless expanse of white, then the date matched exactly, today was August 17, which meant that the events of Morgan's novel would take place the following day.

I could pack my bags and leave Mirror Lake before the sun rose the next day, or, better still, leave immediately, without suitcases or goodbyes; but some sinister, implacable force would have caused me to retrace my steps, because my destiny was here, at Mirror Lake, and fate, like stupidity, cannot be undone.

The mystery-charged atmosphere hanging over Mirror Lake on August 18, which I will call the 17th to prevent any confusion, wasn't simply a product of my imagination. *This looks bad*, I thought as I half opened my bedroom curtains, *we're in for a long day.* Then, to prove myself right, I got dressed, ignoring the darkness and its intimation that I could still shove my head under the pillow for another two or three hours and not feel guilty. I made myself a good strong coffee and went out, leaving Artie to bury his snores in the depths of an innocence he might lose that very day. Unlike me, the sun had not yet risen, and the earliest of the morning birds, some insomniacs no doubt among them, were emitting delicate trills to greet the imminent arrival of the light they could sense by virtue of whatever is their ability to measure time's passage, though of course it could also be that their matinal conversation was nothing more than a way of keeping their insomnia-induced boredom at bay.

But for the anxious chirping of a few neurasthenic sparrows, the silence was almost total, and the layer of fog concealing Mirror Lake was so dense that it was impossible even to know that there was a lake in front of you.

Anyone unaware of Mirror Lake's existence and choosing to go for a walk might have headed directly into the water despite the faint, nervous lapping emanating from it. As for those who did know Mirror Lake, they risked stumbling over who knows what, and, if they were truly unlucky, smashing their heads in. Being familiar with a place is no guarantee of safety. Uninterested in tempting fate, I wiped the bench on the porch with the sleeve of my shirt and sat down as Bill and Jeff, sensing something afoot in the fog, wisely stayed close, their ears pricked and eyes fixed on the impenetrable veil surrounding us.

Anything we could see was grey and wet, washed in gloomy colours heralding bad news. Ed Wood and, closer to us in time, John Carpenter would have found it the ideal setting for a horror movie, the tableau completed by the hooting of a barred owl, *ho ho ha ha ha*, that made all three of us turn, ready to pounce on anyone, man or beast, that might tear through the veil to attack us. Then I told the dogs it would be a very long day and that, whatever came to pass, they mustn't forget I loved them — "yes, Bill, you too" — and would carry on loving them even if I were to disappear into the limbo of Mirror Lake, or the limbo Victor Morgan had created. I'm pretty sure they understood, because their big brown eyes watered up and took on a delicate sheen of sadness, love, hope, and powerlessness.

Meanwhile, more birds had woken up and added their song to the chorus of depressive sparrows. I must have counted about twenty birds dispersed around the cottage and seeming to ask themselves whether or not it was worth waking up or if they were better off, in weather like this, returning to their nests. Then it was the turn of my loon, whom I'd not heard in ages, to add his voice to the hesitant concert. *Hoo, hooo, hoohoohoo, tourloulou, tourloulou,* he cried and trilled, and with such melancholy that the dogs really did start to cry, and I started wondering why sadness was so frequently lovely, why, three times out of four, it was clothed in beauty's apparel. I was drifting on the spleen these reflections had caused when the little voice in my head—which annoys me but, for all that, is still mine—retorted that ugliness isn't especially funny either, referencing Cyrano de Bergerac and Quasimodo. Couldn't disagree. What is more heartbreaking than the pain of an ugly person? No matter how repellent, an ugly person's suffering engenders a certain amount of compassion, whereas the suffering of a beauty—should you be prone to spite and not especially beautiful yourself—prompts you to secretly rejoice. Seen from this perspective, you wonder why it is that ugly people feel so sorry for themselves, but that's forgetting the terrible truth of being hideous: ugliness, if it changes at all, only does so for the worse.

You're starting to sound lugubrious, the little voice added, *get a grip.* But I didn't need to do that. The sun gave me a shake, its first rays beginning to stream delicately through the mist and down onto the lake immediately in front of us, the loon was now calling in a less melancholy fashion. And then, little by little, the haze evaporated and the lake reappeared. The rising heat created images to go with the sound, and the birds chirping their song and travelling from branch to branch were visible once more. The dogs, delighted to forget their dawn shivers, ran out to the water.

I, too, was happy that the sun was finally revealing itself. However much I like rain, I couldn't have coped had it rained that day. I was desperate for light, as much of it as possible, in order to orient myself in the dark labyrinth Moreau and I had entered.

Speaking of Moreau, he was late. If I thought back to August 17 of the previous year, he'd knocked at my door, or, rather, Winslow's door, before sunrise. But I had to take account of the fog, of the fact of his being a father, and of the inconvenient truth that he now had a woman in his bed. Events wouldn't transpire exactly the same way they had the year before, this much was obvious, impossible even, though I was not yet sure this was something I could celebrate.

Anyway, the sun was up and best to take advantage of it while I was still of this world. I went down to join the dogs by the lake, removed my running shoes, and walked along the strip of soft sand where folk who don't wish to leave footprints never venture. Then I rolled up the bottom of my pants and walked toward the cold water. A residue of mist remained at the centre of the lake, stretching languorously toward the patch of fog still obscuring the north shore, while on our side the lake was like a mirror. Never had its name seemed so apt. My legs were reflected in front of me, a little twisted by the diffraction of the light waves my footsteps made. Higher up, the reflection of my checked shirt was also undulating, and then, higher still, was the mirror image of my face swollen from lack of sleep. But something seemed to have changed in this face. Had my third eye disappeared in the night? To know for sure, I crouched down and peered more closely at myself.

That day I was expecting anything to happen, though I certainly wasn't prepared for what I saw. The image the lake was reflecting back to me was no longer Bob Winslow's face but mine, Robert Moreau's! I rushed into the cottage to check the image out in a more dependable mirror, and Artie, who'd not been up long, yelled at me because I was leaving sand and water all over the floor. I left him raging away and double-locked myself in the bathroom. Before I could look truth in the face, I sat down on the edge of the bathtub and felt my pulse, only to notice that I was experiencing serious tachycardia. While I was at it, I also took my blood pressure, and I wasn't doing well. Abjectly refusing to die before learning my identity, I swallowed a couple of aspirin and stood before the mirror.

In conversation, disappointment can manifest itself in different ways. The verb *to disappoint* can be conjugated in every tense or swapped for synonyms — or phrases like *that hurts me*, and others like *darn*, *what a shame* or *shit*, or interjections like *oh darn!* or *shit!* But with faces, the expression is always the same. When disappointment reigns, it falls. As did mine. But not enough for me to fail to recognize myself. My third eye had indeed taken on a certain pallor, but I was undoubtedly Bob Winslow. If I scrutinized myself closely, I could identify resemblances to me, but by and large I was Bob Winslow, and even more Bob Winslow with the weight I'd put on.

"Who am I?" I asked Artie as I left the bathroom. Not used to questions of this nature as soon as he was out of bed, and not very keen on philosophy, Artie let out a great sigh and chose the simplest answer. "Bob Winslow, you're Bob Winslow, Bobby. And your eggs are ready."

"It's important, Artie. Don't you think I look like Robert this morning?"

"No, you don't look like Robert. You look like Bob, and your eggs are getting cold."

Clearly it was impossible to have a serious conversation with Artie, so I went back down to the lake, crouched over the water again, and saw the same thing Mirror Lake had displayed to me a few minutes earlier: me. Then I went to ask the bathroom mirror for a second opinion, returned to the water and then back up, three or four times in a row, before concluding that the lake wasn't seeing the same thing as the mirror was. Which of the two was misguided? A total mystery. If the mirror was in the wrong, that meant Artie was too. If it was the lake, it meant I was myopic or that it didn't know how to reflect properly anymore. I needed a third opinion—which Moreau could provide when he finally arrived.

As I waited for him to get his butt over here, I gathered some rocks and arranged them in order of size and colour, the result telling me what I already knew: pink rocks are the rarest, and white rocks are neither as rare nor as beautiful as you might think. The most beautiful rocks are striped, the ones with a thin pale line through the middle. That's what I think, and anyone who doesn't, I decreed that morning, is an ignoramus, dispersing the third pile of rocks with a kick for it to be understood this wasn't the moment for Neanderthals to contradict me! And then, once I'd had enough of rocks, I played tic-tac-toe on the four-hundred-million-year-old rock, drew a hopscotch grid in the sand, and jumping into the air almost smashed my head in three times. I told Jeff a story, told Bill one, looked at my watch and said, "Whoa, enough! If the hooligan doesn't show, I'll have to go meet him." I yelled to Artie that I was off to find Moreau, that we'd be back soon, then whistled for the dogs and, just as we were getting into the boat, I noticed the raccoon watching us, half hidden behind the pile of logs I hadn't finished stacking beneath the porch. This will make me sound like an idiot, but I had the feeling the racoon was laughing. But I was too busy to bother about him. I'd find out when I got back.

As I paddled over, I thought about the racoon's attitude. What if I'd mixed things up all along? Was it possible...was it possible that *Albert* was Winslow, and the bear simply a bear? What colour were Albert's eyes again? It's stupid, but sometimes there are people I've known for a while and if someone asked me I'd still not be able to say what colour their eyes are. That's how it was with Albert. It was pointless wondering. I'd see when I came back — if I came back, that is. As it was, I couldn't see a thing. We'd moved into the bank of fog covering the north shore, in defiance of all meteorological logic, and I only knew we'd arrived when the boat went *crrshshsh* on the sand and the counter-force pushed me into Bill, grazing my third eye on the edge of the boat on the way past. *Darn!*

To avoid a fourth eye on my forehead, I crawled over to the porch, climbed the steps on all fours, and found myself face to face with Junior. "Doodle!" he cried, after which Anita, who was knitting in the fog, exclaimed, "Bob, what are you doing here?"

So there I had my third and fourth opinions: I was Winslow, alias Doodle, in the entire world's eyes except my own and the lake's.

"Hi Anita," I said. "I have to see Robert, it's urgent."

She pointed to the cottage with her knitting needle and I went inside. When Moreau saw me arrive on all fours, blood on my forehead, he raised his eyebrows, which was the best he could offer in the way of compassion, and waited for me to explain myself. I showed him the pages of Morgan's novel and told him how I'd got hold of them. While he was examining them, I also reminded him that today was August 18 of a non-leap year—in other words, August 17 in a leap year. But saying this was unnecessary, fiddling with the pages I'd held out to him, he was already turning pale.

"What should we do?" he asked.

"Go back to my place, watch for the corpse to appear, cross back over to fish it out, then call Robbins and wait for what happens next."

"Wouldn't it be easier to watch for the drowned guy

from here?" he started. Then he thought some more and added, "Whoa, hang on a minute," this his introduction to making me understand we were panicking uselessly, that we'd fished John Doe out the year before, and that he wasn't going to reappear just because it was August 18 of a non-leap year, for fuck's sake. And what's more, how would we find a drowned man in a fog where you can't even see your own shadow? His last argument didn't stand up, but I raised no objection.

I let him finish, showed him my bleeding third eye, and told him about Johnny Smith and my vision. Then a ray of sun landed at our feet and we heard Anita call out that the fog was lifting. We swallowed hard, looked at each other, and wondered again what we should do. Moreau was of the opinion we should vamoose, take Anita, Junior, the dogs, some food, two or three bottles of bourbon, and hole up in some sordid motel from which we'd be able to phone Robbins and Conan after registering fake names under the receptionist's baleful, lusty eye. I was just about to agree to his plan when Anita raced through the door to tell us there was a dark shape on the lake.

"It looks like a moose," she said, but I heard *mouse*, which led, because of my nerves, to a new burst of hilarity.

"A mouse, for God's sake, a fucking mouse!" I said, and then I played Winslow's part and fell from my chair.

"A *moose*," Anita articulated more clearly, handing me a tissue to wipe the scratch that had appeared near my third eye after my little tumble, which had thrown me near Junior's chrome-plated toy car. I needed this whole story to come to an end, because if it didn't I wouldn't have any forehead left.

I stood up and examined the pattern my blood had left on the tissue—it resembled a Zorro-style *Z*, very stylized but otherwise uninteresting—and followed Anita and Moreau outside as I threw my cape over my shoulders. Yes, there was indeed a dark shape on the lake, a dark figure, but it wasn't a moose, or a bear, or a fucking mouse, a beaver colony, or a shoal of cod. It was a John Doe, there was no doubt on that front, but, unlike the previous year, he was on the far side of the lake. Just like the four-hundred-million-year-old rock, said the disagreeable little voice inside me. We had to go anyway, otherwise Doe would get away from us. Having understood what hung in the balance, Anita picked up Junior and announced that she was going to her mother's. Events were not unspooling as they had in my vision, but close enough that my agitation was on the increase. So I shook hands with Junior and stroked Anita's head and wished the pair of them good luck. Moreau did the same, and as to the rest, there was no need to consult with each other. We jumped in the boat with the dogs, Jeff at the back, Bill at the front, stern and prow, each toward his own shore, and rowed so hard that our biceps felt on the brink of exploding as we belted out "Po' Lazarus" louder than we'd ever belted it out before. It was beautifully done, to be honest. We were perfect. The Cohen brothers couldn't have directed us any better if we'd been in one of their movies. Should I get out of this alive, I thought, I'd give them a call and pitch my services or a screenplay.

When we touched land, Moreau went to look for branches, I went to get scarves and Artie, and then the lot of us returned to the lake in perfect synchrony, the three of us working as one to haul the dead guy out of the water. Before we called Robbins, we poked the corpse with the ends of branches to find his wallet. He didn't have one. But he did have teeth, which was beneficial and meant I wouldn't have to retrieve my dentures from the damn lake. To ease the tension, I tried to pull my dental plate out of my mouth with the intention of throwing it nonchalantly into the undergrowth, but apparently it was soldered to my gums, because I could no longer remove it. I started yanking at it with both hands with my feet pressed against a stump when Winslow asked what I was trying to do. *Winslow?... WINSLOW!*

I quickly stood up and went to pat him down, wanting to know where he'd come from. I was so happy to see the big oaf that I didn't wait for him to answer. I threw my arms around his neck, hugged him, and pulled out his dentures to be sure that I wasn't mistaken. *Jesus, Winslow!* Winslow was back, I couldn't believe my eyes. He was even wearing his cap, the moron. And I'd become myself again, because surely Winslow and Artie would have noticed I wasn't me.

But whoa, there, hang on a moment. How was I to know if I had actually become me again if I had always been myself? How would I know that I wasn't the Moreau who'd always been Moreau, or that there wasn't still a Moreau inside Winslow? How could I be sure I wasn't still, even if only a little bit, Winslow?

Ignoring Bob, Bill, Jeff, and Artie's astounded stares, I pretended I had to do something urgently and went to lock myself into the bathroom, where the mirror, which was starting to get tired of all this, confirmed I was me. It didn't answer all my questions, but that was enough, and I knew not to stay in this diabolical place a moment longer. If everything was about to happen as my vision predicted, then I would knock my head again, and be led into an infernal cycle perpetuating itself from one August 18 to the next, August 18 becoming the 17th every four years, in a terrible loop that would re-loop each year. I would slip on the tail of some fucking snake that ate itself every twelve months, and I didn't want any more of this, never, might as well die. I was preparing to escape through Winslow's bedroom window when Winslow came to tell me that Robbins had arrived with Conan.

"And what exactly are you doing on the window ledge?" he asked.

There are four things a person can do on a window ledge: get ready for their imminent suicide attempt, clean the windows, plan an escape, or play guitar. I told him that I was measuring the length of the curtains and sighed. My fate had a sacred determination, and that being the case, I might as well confront it bravely. I climbed down from the windowsill, dusted it off, and followed Winslow, saying a prayer as I went.

Outside, the first thing I saw was the four-hundred-million-year-old rock, which was waiting for my destiny to be concluded. The first thing I heard was Conan, who was wiping his glasses on his hazmat suit, shout, "I found his wallet." Given that Winslow, Artie, and I had not found the wallet, I thought John Doe must have swallowed it — it does happen. Not often, but it happens. Before things could get worse, I went to stand by the lake, and looking down at my feet I noticed the lake was now reflecting Winslow's image back at me. Can't trust anyone anymore.

Nothing else made much sense, but it suited the drift of the story. Mirror Lake disappeared under a new cloak of impenetrable fog, out of which every now and again appeared a leg, an arm, a fist, a red or white face, depending on the mood and state of its owner. I remember seeing the Daltons show, as well as Anita's mother, whom I'd not yet had the pleasure of meeting, because you can't do everything. It's even possible that Stephen King turned up, apologizing for being late for dinner. What a mess. Then, when Strauss's waltz struck up in the fog, I saw myself in slow motion gliding directly over one of the *X*s I'd drawn on the four-hundred-million-year-old rock in a game of tic-tac-toe; it's ridiculous what goes through your head when you're in slow motion. After impact, I remember opening my mouth to gurgle "John Doe is... is..." and then I was propelled to a place where knowing what your colours are is useless, because there aren't any.

There is only one past. And there is only one present.
On the other hand, there is a multitude of futures.
But only one of them can happen.
—Philippe Geluck, *Le Chat*

When the stars go out, you're justified in thinking it's the end of the world. When they light up again, you have several choices. It really depends where you are. If you open your eyes on the chimerical splendour of Mirror Lake, you can tell yourself you're in a dream or a nightmare and nobody will contradict you. I've been living on Mirror Lake for twenty years and I still haven't managed to figure out if I'm dead, in hell, in paradise, or in some transitional place you could call purgatory.

When I returned from limbo the day after August 18, three hundred and forty-two days that I'd had neither the pleasure nor the misfortune of living had passed, but at least I was Robert Moreau. Little Robert was a year older, Anita had a few more wrinkles at the corners of her eyes, which only made her more beautiful, and Winslow's face was a little crumpled, but he definitely was good old Winslow. I preferred seeing him in front of me rather than in my mirror.

Over the next few weeks, I tried to make him admit he was Albert, the racoon, but the imbecile stuck to his guns. He'd never known a racoon by the name of Albert, he said. So was he the bear, then?

"Answer me, Winslow, for God's sake. If you were not the raccoon it means you were the bear, no?"

But all my queries went unanswered. Winslow categorically denied having been anything other than himself. When I tried to elicit information about Victor Morgan's novel, he claimed there was a gap in his memory concerning the subject. I called him a liar but to no effect. Winslow would clearly be no help, so I researched other avenues in my effort to discover who Morgan was, but apparently the writer had fallen into such total oblivion that all traces of his time on earth had been erased. But I still have pages 216 to 221 of *The Maine Attraction*, which prove beyond a doubt the novel's existence. And if there's a novel, there must be a novelist, there's no getting around it.

As for Anita, she seemed happy to know I was back, and we tried not to yell at each other too much. We picked up the game we'd invented solely for ourselves, and depending on whether the evening was sad or languid, we slipped into the skins of Marlon Brando, Lana Turner, Fred Astaire, or Elizabeth Taylor. Anita was exceptional as Martha, the hysterical woman in *Who's Afraid of Virginia Woolf?*, and one day she also agreed to play Juliette Lewis's Lolita for me. After that, I no longer dreamed about Juliette Lewis. In my darkest, wildest fantasies, it was Anita, the incredible Anita Swanson, who took her place.

Little Robert resembled me more every day. It used to be that looking at him was like standing in front of a mirror, but a mirror that makes you look younger, that allows you to travel through time at the speed of light and confirm that yes, you weren't too ugly a few years ago, and you might have not become so stupid had life not decided to run you over. But that wouldn't happen to little Robert, I would be there to protect him, or like all parents, that's what I claimed, forgetting that he would leave me one day and there would come a moment in which I'd no longer be able to do anything to help. The stubborn will do exactly as they please, period.

And then what had to happen happened. Time's inexorable passing brought us to August 17, John Doe rose up from the abyssal depths of Mirror Lake, I made a swan dive through the air, smashed myself on the forehead, and an attentive ear—Artie's ear, it turned out—leaned over me, and three hundred and forty-two days later I was Artie. This year, come the morning of August 17, I took no chances and told everybody that if by chance Moreau cracked his head on the four-hundred-million-year-old rock, nobody should go near him. I made up some story about the connections between the neurons and synapses when you take a blow to the head, and they swallowed it, unless they simply wanted to make Artie happy. Unfortunately, the racoon missed my explanations and, before Strauss's waltz ended, I felt four little paws gripping my shirt. When I woke up I was Albert.

Being a racoon does have advantages. You're totally chill, breakfast is served every morning, and nobody bothers you, since nobody is interested in wrecking a racoon's placid life. While I was Albert, I really did try to have the four-hundred-million-year-old rock moved, but without success. The rock will likely still be there even after the entire surface of the earth has been destroyed in a nuclear war or a Klingon invasion.

Over the course of two decades, following a cycle I've ceased to try to understand, I've been Winslow, me, Artie, Albert, Jeff, me, Junior, me, Robbins, Bill, each of the Dalton brothers in turn, Conan, Jones, Winslow, and me, etc. The only person I've never been reincarnated as is Anita. Which is a shame, because I really would have liked to inhabit a woman's body once in my life, especially Anita's, so I might have learned what I looked like in her eyes, and how it is that the weight of her breasts, so full of her woman's story, could sometimes be such a burden. Knowing as much might have helped me console her in those moments when I'd see her past blow across her face in the interlude between two sorry smiles seeming to apologize for everything—life, misery, all the horrors we are forced to endure for the sake of a little beauty. Anita might often have been forced to trade her body for a bit of cash, but her soul wasn't so easily ravaged.

That said, I've been all the others—except for John Doe, who rises out of the mist once a year just to taunt me. The worst occasion was when I turned into Robbins. I was obliged to chew a toothpick and see the world in brown for twenty-three days and twenty-three nights because, as I can now confirm, Robbins doesn't take off his sunglasses to go to sleep. They are fixed onto his head. He'll die wearing them. The best time was the few weeks when I was Jeff. I had no other aspirations but to play, rest, eat, be on the lookout for squirrels, and take care of my master—who was me, as it happened. I looked at me and I thought I was good-looking. I looked at me and I thought I was intelligent. I looked at me and loved myself unconditionally. Furthermore, it was the only time in my life when I truly understood the meaning of the word *Zen*, which stood out in capital letters in front of me whenever I got carried away thinking of nothing. The Jeff year was a happy year, a year of grace, affecting not only my ego, but what I shall call my humbling experience of the world—but, like anything of merit, it didn't last long enough.

The truly disastrous aspect of my situation is that I only live for twenty-three days a year. If I was Buddhist, I would claim this was my *samsara* and that I was moving through successive states that would lead me nowhere, for the simple reason that I am too slow or not Buddhist enough to attain enlightenment. Since I have never been reincarnated as a Tibetan monk, and as I prefer not to know how good my karma is, I chalk it down to fate and make the most of those twenty-three days. I spend the rest of the time in total blackness or total whiteness, depending on the year. And as for the people whose identities I borrow, I've still not managed to figure out into what limbo they disappear while I exist in their place. Neither do I have the slightest idea of what happens in my head when I'm not there. When I do become myself once more, all memory of this parallel space-time is erased. Still. I try to see life's positive side. I don't have any choice. And I tell myself that if I do, I'll not age so quickly and will be acquainted with just one season, the most beautiful, the season of summer and the Perseids.

This year I'm me, but I have no idea who I will be the day after August 17. Maybe the four-hundred-million-year-old rock, whose vertiginous knowledge will complement Jeff's teachings and allow me to reach my nirvana. I actually believe that were I to become a rock one day, it would turn out to be the last cycle of my reincarnations so that I'd still be lying there in a few million years, frozen under the crust of an ice age, or serving as a landing rock for extraterrestrial spaceships. I'd also bet that some other guy has been shut up in the rock for four or five centuries with his tomahawk, and he's fed up with being trampled underfoot and is patiently waiting for someone to free him.

If this does happen, it will probably be soon, because the banks of Mirror Lake are less populated now. Jeff died a long time ago, on the saddest sunny day of my life, promising me that he'd wait for me on the other side. On the other side of the lake? The other side of the mirror? I don't know, I will see. We'd just been out walking in the woods—very slowly, because his old bones hurt him—and when we sat down on the beach to rest a little, he put his big head on my thigh and I saw in his moist eyes that he was at the end of his strength, that his dog-love could no longer keep him alive. *Let me go*, his tired eyes were saying. So I replied, "Okay, Jeff, run, go look for a star," and that's where he went, toward the sky constellated with infinite lights. Before leaving, he assured me that when my human solitude was attacking me with a sabre right in my sternum, he would never be far away. Then his eyes drank in Mirror Lake, a place that had become an earthly paradise for him, turned back to me, smiled his painful tired-dog smile, and suddenly he wasn't suffering any longer. He went off, stroking the tears soaking my face as he went, tears mixing with ones I'd previously shed for Alfie, the first dog in my life.

Bill was terribly upset, but he got over it, as did we all, despite the scar. He joined Jeff a few years later, on another indescribably sad day, and Mirror Lake was never the same again. Junior had left for university and only came back to visit Anita and me occasionally. As for that big chump Winslow, he kicked the bucket last year in a tragic kind of way. I was at his bedside as he passed, and his last words were "No! No! Humpty Dumpty is not a potato, he's an egg." Then he let out a big sigh, and was no more. When the worst of the pain had passed, I got myself a dartboard, drew Humpty Dumpty on the target, and emptied out my heart; it hurt too much knowing that stupid potato had haunted Winslow's final moments.

Anita, Artie, Junior, and I gave Winslow a first-class burial. We buried him behind the cottage, with his cap, his plaid shirt, and his fishing rod, beside the dogs as he'd requested, and sometimes I think I catch sight of him roaming by the lake. That's the feeling I had yesterday evening, when the mountains were melting into the darkness. I was convinced he was there, right next to me, with the dogs.

"Yellow as a star," he began, and I carried on with "yellow as the sun, yellow as Jeff, yellow as Bill . . ." and he heard me, I know he heard me, as did Jeff and Bill, their big tails beating against the timber of the dock wood to show how overjoyed they were that we were reunited.

"Look, Jeff," I whispered, "that's where I'll go meet you shortly, you see, up there, in the memory of time," and Jeff licked my hand, my neck, and my face, collecting a few tears as he did so.

I stayed with them until dawn. And then, when one of my loon's progeny started a lament for the new day, I stood, turned my back on the lake, and murmured, "See you soon, racoon."

Montreal, by Baldwin Park,
July 2005 to June 2006

ACKNOWLEDGEMENTS

First and foremost I would like to thank my partner, Pierre, for his presence, his patient reading, his comments and suggestions and, of course, his lake. I would also like to thank my sister Viviane, who inspired the story of Ping, and consequently, Ping Two, as well as my nephew Éric (my favourite hydrogeologist), who provided me with crucial information about the world of rocks generally, and about the four-hundred-million-year-old rock in particular.

A thousand thanks to Guy, my official linguistic repair guy, as well as Bernard, Élise, Jacques, Louise, Sylvain, and, again, Viviane, who wracked their brains to help me choose images evoking Mirror Lake or gave me a hand when it was time to find a title for the novel, which I decided in the end to call *Mirror Lake* because, even though I find the word *mirror* unpronounceable, that's its title and there's no getting away from it.

My thanks also go to Jacques Fortin, president of Éditions Québec Amérique, for his unwavering support; to Normand de Bellefeuille, my editor, to his accomplice,

Isabelle Longpré, and the rest of the team at Éditions Québec Amérique, whose contagious enthusiasm is the best antidote for writer's migraine.

I would also like to express gratitude to House of Anansi Press for the English translation of *Mirror Lake* and its enthusiastic support of French-Canadian literature. And to Noah Richler, the literary director of Arachnide, for his understanding at all times. Thanks to J. C. Sutcliffe for her formidable work — apologies for the headaches Robert Moreau and I must have brought on — and to managing editor Maria Golikova, designer Alysia Shewchuk, copy editor Gemma Wain, proofreader Allegra Robinson, and the rest of the team at Anansi.

I also thank the Conseil des arts et des lettres du Québec, and the jury members who awarded me a grant to write this novel.

NOTE

All of the characters and events in this novel are entirely fictitious. So is Mirror Lake, which is a figment of my imagination, despite there being two lakes in Maine with the name, neither of which I have ever had the pleasure (or misfortune) of visiting.

I would also like to clarify that I have the utmost admiration for the prodigious talent of Tim Robbins, whose name and features I borrowed to create the sheriff character. Nobody could have played this part better than Robbins.

©P.

ANDRÉE A. MICHAUD is one of the most beloved and celebrated writers of Francophonie. She is a two-time winner of both the Governor General's Literary Award and the Arthur Ellis Award for Excellence in Canadian Crime Writing. She has won Le Prix Saint-Pacôme du roman policier, France's Prix SNCF du Polar, and numerous other awards. Her novel *Boundary* was longlisted for the Scotiabank Giller Prize and has been published in seven territories. *Back Roads*, Michaud's eleventh novel, was the third to be published in English, and *Mirror Lake*, which won Le Prix Ringuet, the fourth. She was born in Saint-Sébastien-de-Frontenac and continues to live in the province of Quebec.

J. C. SUTCLIFFE is a translator, writer, and editor. She has written for the *Globe and Mail*, the *Times Literary Supplement*, and the *National Post*, among others. Her translations include *Back Roads* by Andrée A. Michaud, *Mama's Boy* and *Mama's Boy Behind Bars* by David Goudreault, *Document 1* by François Blais, and *Worst Case, We Get Married* by Sophie Bienvenu.